The Garden of Wives: Book Club Edition

A NOVEL

DANIELLE LACARAK

For the women

Contents

Note to the Reader

Trigger Warning: Sensitive and Distressing Content

This novel contains material that may be disturbing or triggering for some readers. Topics addressed include alcoholism, slut-shaming, body-shaming, underage drinking, miscarriage, oppression of women, non-consensual sexual activities involving minors, sexual and familial abuse, torture, coerced abortion, suicide, and BDSM. For those sensitive to animal distress, it also includes the death of a dog.

Reader discretion is advised. If you find these subjects potentially traumatic, please consider your comfort and safety before proceeding.

DANIELLE LACARAK

"Anything may happen when womanhood has ceased to be a protected occupation."
Virginia Woolf

Prologue

ONE YEAR AGO

There's something not right.

The other day, I let go of one of the girls in the deep end of the pool. I was teaching Janey to doggy paddle. She just slipped off my arms. I watched as her tiny body floated down, down, down to the mosaic floor. I counted each bubble as they floated up.

That's when I realized I can make this all stop. If I don't end them now, it will just keep going…

I can end it. Right here. Right now.

I am a good mother.

CHAPTER 1

BLAIR

BLAIR NOVAK SPREADS THE icing thick on the red velvet cake. She's been up since the crack of dawn, her cake rising with the sun. She licks the spatula clean, takes a sip of wine, and rubs her aching eight-month belly. The tickling warmth of alcohol combines with burning sweetness, stretching into her veins, taking root. Giddy, she tosses the utensil into the sink, watching the suds float. She feels a sharp kick deep within her and frowns.

She heaves herself onto a cushioned stool in her expansive kitchen. Hot California sun streams through fluted windows, illuminating creamy white décor and the finest state-of-the-art appliances. Bouquets of fresh eucalyptus and white orchids scent the air-conditioned room. Veined marble cools plump forearms as Blair leans over her creation—a three-layered, red velvet cake with cream cheese frosting. Her grandmother-in-law's recipe and her husband's favorite.

A lock of golden red hair falls onto the finished masterpiece. Blair lifts her head, sucking the sugar from the strand before tucking it behind her ear. She takes another sip from her stainless-steel tumbler, rolling the cool liquid around her mouth. The tangy sweetness sends shivers down her spine.

Pregnancy, for Blair, is a joyful curse. A chance to be herself and think normally again, for a little while anyway. But everything has its season. Once this baby is born, life resets to normal. It's almost too heavy to open the curtains for.

Jessa.

Blair's heart pangs. She shoos the murky memory away, a tragedy that almost destroyed their beloved neighborhood, the Gardens of Orchid Hill. The worst is over. She survived.

So yes, Blair deserves this six-ounce glass of wine concealed in her temperature-controlled travel mug while she suffers the final trimester of her tenth pregnancy. Yes! Ten hormonal pregnancies, including four miscarriages. She's now considered geriatric in the world of motherhood.

Don't get her wrong, Mrs. Novak lives for her children. She eats, breathes, exists solely for them. And when they're not with her, she spirals out of control and into the kitchen, a baking tornado. She started enjoying a glass of wine with lunch after her oldest left for college, and she perfected her macaron recipe a few months later.

Maxwell studies psychology at Cornell, following his father's footsteps. He's quiet, confident, and elusive. His absence is keenly felt by his adoring siblings. Blair wishes she could command the same respect. She finds it impossible to discipline Seth and Brody, her Irish twins, wickedly funny and only nine months apart. Almost grown men with a few semesters left between them. Redheads like their mother with piercing blue eyes and sharp features like their father. Since the moment they came shrieking into this world, they haven't given Blair a second to rest. The problematic pair keeps everyone on edge with their endless pranks. Like the time they cellophaned every toilet seat just for fun. Blair never got over that one. Neither did the housekeeper, who conveniently disappeared that evening, never to return. The younger children enjoy the shenanigans, but it keeps the staff on a revolving door and their poor mother's head in a vice.

The biggest headache of all comes from Blair's only daughter, who insists on being called Kit instead of her birth name, Grace-Katherine. Kit recently started menstruating. Her sulking mood swings and teenage apathy are wearing on her exhausted mother.

Good Lord, how quickly they develop.

Her easiest child, for the moment, is also her youngest, Buster—a name forced upon Blair by family tradition. Newly seven and the sweetest of all, Buster loves hugs and being dirty. He entertains himself for hours scrounging the backyard for bunnies.

Rambunctious but gentle. When it comes to babies and animals, Buster's the first to ask to hold them, cradling what needs to be supported and using gentle hands. A sensitive soul, unlike his older brothers.

Blair Novak is a good mother—too good, in fact, for too long. This morning, she got all four children ready for school—by herself—with trendy bento boxes crammed full of nutritious cookies and homemade goodies cut into tiny masterpieces, each with a matching thermos of hand-pressed organic juice.

Juicing—the latest craze all the school moms won't shut up about. Luna Peaty, a room mother and peacocking neighbor, started the whole thing. "Fresh pressed. Better than Whole Foods," she had gloated last week at the bake sale. "But you must drink it immediately. All the nutrients are lost after the first fifteen minutes. So they say."

Blair secretly suspects Luna covets attention, even from her macarons. Always promoting her little business. It's sad, really—a faded pop star reduced to multi-level marketing. Fame and glory were once air and water to Luna. Now, she's lucky to get her own husband's affection.

It's like she's trying to revive her old career using fresh pressed juice. Anything is possible with Looney Luna.

Blair giggles at her own joke, tucking a disobedient strand of copper hair behind her ear. She gulps down the rest of her wine and refills her tumbler to the tippy top. She only has so much time before she needs to hide the bottle in the bottom of the recycling bin.

After the kids cannonballed out of the house this morning, Blair scavenged their rooms, unearthing dirty laundry from nooks and crannies. Three loads of darks sit neatly folded on the living room sofa. She has two loads of whites left to go and a hamper full of handwashing. Lord, she does miss the help. With all the technology these days, you'd think someone would've invented an automated clothes-folder by now.

It should be a crime to have this much laundry and be this pregnant, a jail sentence straight out of hell. Her husband is certainly taking his sweet time replacing the housekeeper and the nanny. Both left within weeks of each other. Such a nightmare!

Why Bianca left so abruptly is anyone's guess. Blair never had a nanny run out on them in the middle of her shift before. And a decent one at that. Must be a new record. She has a sinking suspicion Seth and Brody have something to do with that too.

Last night, she had mentioned it to her husband. "You know, honey, it would be easier to use one of the online services. There's an app now that makes the whole thing so easy. I could do it all myself, if you're too busy." She had waited patiently as Dr. Daniel Novak bent over his laptop at the kitchen island.

Daniel refused to turn around. He shrugged, mumbling, "It's so hard getting to know someone who'll be in the house. Besides, staff is already pre-vetted through ELITE."

"The tech company? Wouldn't it be better to use an actual service agency this time?"

"They've expanded exponentially within the last decade."

Then why is it taking so long? She wanted to scream at her husband.

Now, in the quiet of her living room, Blair sucks deep breaths. Her thumbs find her temples and rub gentle circles. Halfway through her second mug o' wine, the buzzer goes off in the laundry room.

My life is defined by a series of beeps.

She reaches for the wine bottle, pops open the tumbler, and refills her mug before replacing the top. She puts the plastic cover to her lips and relaxes her throat. Everything negative washes down in a single wave of mindless freedom.

Blair's chest expands with gas, a flash of heartburn fueled by cream cheese icing. She releases an acidic belch without ceremony. No one's home to judge. She rocks herself up and off the stool, steadying herself on tiny feet and petite legs. This pregnancy has been vicious. She feels like Humpty Dumpty or, better, Violet Beauregarde at the chocolate factory right before she gets rolled away for punishment. Good thing wine doesn't turn skin blue. Just the lips.

That's why I stick to white.

With swollen fingers, she swipes the inside of the empty icing bowl, sucking sugar until her teeth hurt. Everyone worries she'll get gestational diabetes, but Blair doesn't care. So *what* if she gained eighty pounds on her five-two frame? So *what* if she gets buzzed when the kids are at school and her husband is working? No Care Blair. She just wants to taste something good. To feel good. She's sick and tired of being so darn good. The sugar will cover up the alcohol. That's all that really matters.

She feels another kick in her belly. Another girl. She is doomed.

CHAPTER 2

AMARA

ACROSS TOWN FROM THE Gardens of Orchid Hill, in an upscale medical building, Amara Sullivan checks her image using her cellphone for the hundredth time that morning. She sits upright and rigid at her fertility doctor's office, waiting to get her blood draw done and over with.

The dreaded pregnancy test.

She stopped checking urine tests at home a while back. It's always better to let the bad news come later in the evening when she's safe with her happy pills and oversized tub. After each negative test, Amara allows herself one double vodka martini, extra dirty, with not one, but three olives—the fancy ones—hand-stuffed with blue cheese.

Martinis are the only dirty things Amara can stand. The rest of her life is pristine, from her starched white West Point education to her coveted marriage to celebrity plastic surgeon Dr. Levi Sullivan, the most sought-after doctor in Orange County. Before falling madly in love with Dr. Sully, Amara served five excitingly grueling years in the army before being unceremoniously discharged. Let's just say, they agreed to disagree.

A small door opens into the serene waiting area full of white orchids and soothing waterfall sounds. A nurse in salmon scrubs appears, holding a clipboard. She smiles, recognizing Amara.

"Mrs. Sullivan, we're ready for you."

The nurse flashes a bleached smile as Amara collects her designer bag and rises from her seat. She towers over the nurse. Almost seven feet tall in six-inch heels, she clicks down the hall as she's led to the phlebotomy room.

Her golden tan and sweeping blonde hair scream California, but her reserved attitude and resting bitch face exude East Coast cool. Amara's mere presence is enough to terrify children. Their smudgy smiles and filthy hugs are met with an aloofness, often confused with malice. She practically repels them.

Amara has never cared for children. In fact, she wasn't entirely sure how she decided to begin this journey in the first place. But once Amara has her mind hooked, there's no stopping her. Every month she comes to the fertility clinic like clockwork, hoping to check this box and move on with the list. Only then will she feel content.

As she settles into the reclining medical chair, Amara crosses her legs, a record-breaking forty inches long. She wears a nautical shift dress, the thick gold zipper cold against her back. A cream leather jacket capes her sharp shoulders.

She places her crocodile satchel on her lap, arms out to the side, palms down. Her hands grip the padded armrests. Her heart quickens. Fear prickles her skin as her mind tries to remember and forget simultaneously. Amara closes her eyes.

"Love your outfit today," the nurse says to distract her. She turns over one of Amara's arms, tying the tourniquet around a bicep to find her vein.

"Thank you." Amara forces a smile. She squirms when she sees the butterfly needle.

"You're our best-dressed patient by far. We love all your outfits. Especially the shoes!" The nurse pauses to ogle Amara's classic peep-toe platforms with the coveted red soles. "We all follow you too, by the way. Wow! Sorry, I must sound like a stalker." She swabs the inside of Amara's elbow with an alcohol pad.

"No, it's fine." Amara smooths her dress and adjusts her jacket using her free hand. Her other hand white-knuckles a foam ball. She softens her face and looks at the nurse. "You can never have too many followers." Amara cringes inside. She hates self-promotion, but it's her job. If you can call it that.

It's the only job Levi allows her to have, especially after his marketing team gushed about increased online presence, burgeoning profits, and free advertising. Yadda yadda. Amara's a walking billboard. The perfect "after" picture. A post-surgery dream. Even though she's never had a stitch done, not even a drop of filler.

The nurse pricks a vein and pops the vacutainer.

As the single vial fills up with thick, dark blood, Amara closes her eyes. She should know the results in a few hours. For dinner, she's preparing poached salmon with salad. She'll only eat the salad, allowing the effects of her one martini to last into the torturous night. Levi will be upset upon learning that, once again, his sperm and money failed to fertilize her eggs. The doctors will push the aging plastic surgeon to try IUI or IVF. It'll be more money, more invasive, but better for the sperm quality. The nurses will remind him—again—he still hasn't done his semen analysis.

To Amara, the cost of it all doesn't sound as bad as the injections. Amara abhors needles. Levi's always trying to get her to try Botox, but Amara insists she doesn't need it quite yet.

"It would relax that grumpy face of yours," he'd said once during their honeymoon.

The look she shot him after that comment could've murdered.

THE SULLIVANS' MODERN MANSION settles in darkness. Each light in the house powers down except one. They're upstairs, in a small room off their bedroom meant to be a nursery. The walls are painted black. Steel hooks dangle from the ceiling. An antique cupboard, intricately carved and made of dark polished wood, stands against the farthest wall. Its cabinet doors carved with various scenes portraying a group of hounds hunting a doe.

Amara lies on her back atop a padded massage table in the center of the room. Naked and still, her hands dangle by her sides, knees bent, slightly parted. A visual gift for her husband. Her golden hair nests around her head as she focuses on the wooden beams supporting the vaulted ceiling. Her breath slows. The effects of her single martini comfort her.

She hears him approach the cabinet and remove the four-millimeter purple parachute cord. Slowly, methodically, and without acknowledging her, he sets to work. Amara understands this is her penance for that haughty look of disrespect on their wedding night—the one Levi's grown to loathe more with each passing year. So, they've concocted a routine. Every evening after dinner, Amara allows Levi to prove who's in control.

Tonight, her husband ties the Shibari ropes extra tight. He starts with her ankles, making firm but beautifully symmetric patterns. Each leg first tied individually, then together. When he completes the knots just right, he fashions a harness around her hips and buttocks. She allows him to assist her into a kneeling pose so he can tie off her breasts and wrists. Her nipples toughen as the chord tightens. She gasps when he fastens his signature knots along her sternum for extra discomfort. It's going to be a long night.

I will be a good wife.

I love my husband.

I love my life.

Amara focuses on rhythmic breathing as her husband pants around her with increasing excitement, gathering the hooks for suspension. She smells the whiskey on his breath as he connects her to cables hanging from a wooden beam. A faint dark halo around his hairline reveals a recent dye job. His handsome face and aging eyes twist into a lustful grin as he struggles with his height. He made the last loop too short. Now, he'll have to stretch. Despite his small stature, Dr. Sully has exceptional strength. Built like a boxer from the waist up, it's his other half he's constantly overcompensating for.

Once the air reeks of his salty sweat, Amara hangs above him, bound in a corset of purple knots. Levi positions himself in the corner of the black room, unbuttoning his damp shirt and discarding his tie. In the beginning, he only used his tie. Now, despite his elaborate setup, Levi is perpetually unsatisfied, increasingly escalating his needs to reach climax. Sometimes dissolving into desperate, flaccid jerking that results in outbursts of anger and heavy drinking. Those are the worst days.

Amara's mind floats as she hangs on display for her husband's pleasure. Her briny breath ventilates in a rhythmic pattern. Levi's eyes never leave her, devouring her flesh. Every pucker of her skin under the tight cord sends his blood south. He slowly unbuttons his slacks, finds himself growing, barely a handful. Pathetic. He'll have to work for it. When finally ready, he empties himself, aiming at his desire—his wife under his complete control—then leaves her suspended and dripping. A wet rag left out to dry.

It wasn't always like this. They used to touch each other. Kiss each other. Tear each other's clothes off. Over time, Levi's game became their regular routine, like loading the dishwasher after dinner.

No verbal communication needed. Amara knows what to do. What he expects. What to give him and what to keep for herself. Sometimes she doesn't mind the complicated lacing choking her nakedness. It helps clear her mind, focus her thoughts on nothingness, like meditation or drills at West Point. She feels numb and whole simultaneously.

He keeps her suspended for hours, sometimes overnight, depending on his mood. But even on the worst nights, Amara understands there are worse fates. For all the wives of Orchid Hill know, anything is better than going through the red door.

CHAPTER 3

CASS

I JOIN THE WOMEN a bit later, but my story begins two years earlier, beside the road, just outside a 7-Eleven. That's when I met Sean. He took me completely by surprise. Shields down. Defenses off. I'd never given much thought to relationships. I'd been on the road for a while searching, or to be honest, escaping. Everyone leaves eventually. Or dies. Either way, they abandon you. It's colossal, the loneliness. Easier to stick to yourself, minimize the hurt, but being a loner is lonely.

Sean Maccabee rescued me from isolation, from myself. He accepted me as I was. Never snooped. Didn't ask imploring questions or judge when I preferred to stay home for a quiet night on my birthday instead of throwing a huge party. He knew I despised crowds. Assumed I wouldn't mind when we eloped a year later.

Thought I would prefer a more intimate event—just the two of us. Alone. Secluded.

That's why I found it baffling when he wanted to move to The Gardens of Orchid Hill. He even signed us up to help with refreshments at a block party, much to my distress.

"I think it's for the golf club or something. To get to know the neighbors," he said at the time. "The green is fantastic!"

We didn't even golf.

The day we had met started out like any other. Thurgy, my mixed-mutt companion, and I cruised north on Pacific Coast Highway, trying to avoid the traffic on the freeway. Thurgy sat copilot on my right, the enormous expanse of Pacific blue on my left. Going on our second year of van life, we had it down pat. I honestly don't know which one of us enjoyed it more.

We had just spent a few weeks down around the Grand Canyon. I could have stayed and watched those sunsets until the end of time, but poor Thurgs was ready to leave. The desert heat was rough, and his eyesight wasn't what it used to be. Any chance he got, he would bolt out of the van and chase whatever he thought he could see. I never saw anything. It was as if he had a death wish.

Life in our little bus was simple enough. Eat. Drink. Chill. Sleep. Every afternoon I'd look for a place to park and light up. I had already scoped out a parking lot in Huntington Beach where we could camp by the waves and walk across the street to get some real food. Alas, the universe had other plans.

That fateful day, we crawled up PCH bumper-to-bumper in the busiest, most beautiful part of Laguna. Still smiling. Thurgy with his cool water in the cup holder and the AC blasting his snout; me with a pre-rolled joint tucked behind my ear and an iced coffee.

Without warning, The Green Fairy—the name we bestowed on our converted VW—shuddered a desperate and disheartening clunk before lurching to a dramatic halt right in front of a bustling 7-Eleven. The cacophony of traffic horns flustered me as I failed to squeeze any power out of the gas pedal. Defeated and shipwrecked, I set it in park, put on the hazards, and called AAA.

Then I did the absolute worst thing.

I opened. The van. Door.

In that flustered moment, my dear Thurgy hurdled past me and into freedom, his newly trimmed nails raking against my thighs. Just like that, he was gone.

I.

Was.

Fucked.

I wish I could say this was the first time or promise it wasn't a regular occurrence. Unfortunately, I can do neither, as this is what happens when humans get a dog and do not take the time to get it adequately trained. By the time I adopted him, he was too far gone. His previous owners never realized that, like humans, dogs need love and care too. And so, after chaining the poor creature up and without him knowing any better, Thurgy, full name Thurgood

Marshall, ran for his life, sometimes straight into traffic, any chance he had. His thirst for freedom unquenchable.

I dashed after him, but it was too late. The sickening screech of brakes and a desperate yelp almost brought me to my knees. Panicked, I rushed to my friend, my sole companion, as he limped to the safety of the grass, panting painfully.

"Here, let me help."

I looked up to thick, dark eyelashes looming over me. Before I consented, he knelt down to assess my whimpering pup, oblivious to the grass staining his linen pants. He wore topsiders without socks. A stereoscope of my family sailing the Atlantic flickered across my mind. He looked expensive, like a shiny watch. He looked corporate. A little too corporate for my Liberal father. A younger version, maybe, of what my older brother, Garth, had aspired to be. The stranger took off his tailored jacket and carefully wrapped Thurgs.

"I think his back leg's broken." His jaw flexed as he spoke.

I forced back tears, crouching down, Thurgy's limp head in my shaking hands.

"I have a friend not too far from here. A vet. He can help." He reached into his back pocket and took out his phone.

"Um, thank you," I said to the stranger, then turned my attention to Thurgood. "Hear that, Thurgy? You're going to be alright, pup." He mewed painfully. Panic pulsed my temples. "But my van? I have Triple-A on the way."

"I'll call my assistant to come wait with it. My office isn't too far from here." He pushed some buttons on his phone, then stuck out his hand. "I'm Sean, by the way, Sean Maccabee."

"Thank you, Sean." I shook his hand. His palms felt silky. "Cass...Crane."

"Cass—that must be short for Cassandra. Lovely to meet you." He looked right into me, dark eyes shining. "Let's get this dog some medical attention." He stood up and placed the necessary calls.

"It's just Cass. And his name is Thurgood, Thurgood Marshall." I scooped him up gently in my arms and followed Sean.

Inside his fancy car, Sean attempted conversation. "So...you named your dog after the first black Supreme Court justice?" he said, looking at the bundle of gray fur and expensive linen in my lap. "Isn't that...I don't know...a little racist?"

My neck almost snapped as I gawked at him. "Are you kidding me? Thurgood Marshall was my mother's favorite human of all time. We also had a cat named Cicero, thank you very much." I looked out the window and rolled my eyes. *Who is this guy?* I remember thinking. *Judging by his shiny black two-seater and gold watch, a man with more money than self-awareness.*

He pushed a button, and we got moving. "Do you come from a family of lawyers or something?"

I shrugged, watching the palm trees pass by, praying Thurgs would pull through. "Maybe I do."

"Really? I'm a lawyer. Assistant D.A."

"Fancy." I was about to tell this kind, handsome man just how little I cared when I heard my mother's yuppie voice as clear as I could see through Sean's windshield. *Don't be rude!*

Sean slowed down at a red light and put his blinker on. "Crane...sounds familiar." He drummed the steering wheel as he thought out loud. "Hey! Are you related to Thomas and Nancy Crane? From Rhode Island?"

"Yeah." I shifted in my seat, uncomfortable with where this conversation was heading. "Um, are we almost there?"

"Yup, it's right up the road here." His thumbs stopped dancing as he signaled the turn. "Wow! So, you're a Crane. How old were you when they worked on the Lincoln case?"

Oh my God. This is not the time. I wanted to beat him over his beautiful head. I managed to remain calm. He was trying to help, after all. "I don't know, probably eleven or so. They didn't discuss it with us much."

"I bet! Tragic what happened to those girls." He resumed drumming. "Hey, how are they doing, your parents, if you don't mind me asking? I haven't heard much about their work in a while. Did they retire early or something?"

I remembered that case. My parents were organizing a takedown of a mega-corporation that had profited by abusing women for decades. "They're dead."

Sean's thumbs halted. "My apologies. I'm so sorry." His lush eyelashes fluttered with embarrassment. *Women would kill for those eyelashes.* He cleared his throat, a poor attempt to clear the air.

I looked at him with globs of threatening tears and a wilted Thurgood in my arms.

"Well, not this little guy, if I have any say in it." The car growled as he pressed the accelerator. "And I always get what I want," Sean added.

After the vet had successfully set Thurgy's leg, we left him overnight for observation. Sean drove me back to the parking lot where my van was towed to, the one I had picked out before all the craziness. The lot was right off PCH with a panoramic view of the ocean. Palm trees lined the grass in between asphalt and sand. It had a snack bar and a bathroom with an outdoor shower. Several other cars and campers had parked for the night. I could tell it was a favorited spot for nomads like me.

Emotionally exhausted and mentally drained, I was ready for a joint and a good night's rest. My hand flew up to the pre-rolled I had tucked behind my ear the whole time. I smiled. Small things.

"That's where you're staying?" Sean pulled me from my thoughts and into the parking lot. The way he looked at my van made it sound like an insult.

I pretended I wasn't offended. "Yup!" I said a little too enthusiastically as I opened the car door. "I'll chill here tonight, then call around tomorrow to find someone to help me fix the bus." I gestured towards my dilapidated vehicle. "Well, Sean, it's been real. Thanks again. You're a lifesaver."

Then came the awkward exchange. As I was about to swing my legs out of his car, Sean leaned in for a goodbye. One I misjudged, horribly. Instead of leaning in for the quick peck on the cheek Sean offered, I turned in for a half-hug, and then, well, he sort of kissed me. Technically, we brushed lips, just barely, a wisp. And all I could think of was— *When's the last time I had a proper shower?* But Sean didn't pull away. Instead, he pulled me towards him. His fingers twirled my mess of unwashed curls. He extended his lips, the slightest tongue. His hand on my chin. This stranger. I pulled away, alarmed, confused, and something else I couldn't quite identify.

"You have the most amazing hair I've ever seen. It's so...bouncy. You must get hit on all the time." He reached out, bunching handfuls of curls like he was making a snowball.

I pulled away. "Uh, yeah, it's all me. I'm sorry. Are you hitting on me when my dog is..." I couldn't finish the sentence. I was madder at myself than the situation.

"So sorry. My apologies. I'd never..." He coughed, gave me his number, and made me promise to call. "So, we can contact my friend, the vet, and follow up on Mr. Thurgood Marshall."

"Sure." I remember trying to sound disinterested, like nothing just happened, but I found myself floating as I walked towards The Green Fairy. I giggled like a schoolgirl. (Like a moron.) Like everything I tried so hard not to be. Sean took me entirely by surprise. It wasn't in my nature to get befuddled around guys. I mostly avoided them—single girl on the road and all. But everything about him was so warm, so charming, from his flashing smile to his deep, charcoal eyes.

So, when he showed up at my van the next day unannounced with coffee and blueberry muffins, I was smitten. Head over Birkenstock heals.

"CASSANDRA, HAVE YOU SEEN my lucky pocketknife? You know, the one my dad gave me." Sean shouts from the bedroom, calling me back to the present.

"For the millionth time, you know I hate it when you call me that! Did you check all your pockets? It's probably in the jeans you wore last." I finish boxing up my books and tape them firmly shut. *PRECIOUS CARGO* labeled on each one. "Do we have to go?" I ask as I find him in our bedroom.

"You know we do, babe." He drops his duffle bag full of law books in the middle of the floor and comes over to kiss my forehead. "Besides," he looks around at the mess of boxes, "we're running out of space." He sits on the stripped bed and pulls me into his lap, my hair a cloud of frizz on this unusually humid day. I sweep it over my shoulder and out of his face, knowing what he'll say next. "And..." he pauses for dramatic effect before whispering, "you know...babies."

"Come on," I moan. "You know how I feel." He knows because I told him the moment he proposed. I need to find some direction first. With Sean so career-focused, it's really put my life in perspective. Like, what am I supposed to do now? No van. No job. What's my purpose? If Sean has his way, I'll become a breeding machine. I'm in no hurry. There's still time. I'm barely thirty. Sort of. Right now, I need a goal, a direction. I won't let myself be derailed. I've postponed my life long enough. "We have plenty of time."

"Maybe we should freeze your eggs? Or make embryos. You know what they say, the older you get..."

"Oh my gahd! You're wicked funny." I push myself off him and walk away from the conversation. "What would you like for dinner?"

He leans back on the bed and flexes, admiring his biceps. "How about the Mediterranean place down the street? But no garlic this time!" He gives me a double wink before resuming his packing.

I roll my eyes teasingly as I unpocket my phone to order dinner.

The last night in our Irvine apartment feels like the end of an era, our beginning, now ending. I'll miss the beige two-bedroom with vaulted ceilings and the never-used-because-it-wastes-so-much-gas fireplace. I could stay in this cozy beige cocoon forever.

Thurgy's last home. Turns out, Sean doesn't always get what he wants.

Sitting cross-legged on the carpet, we crowd around an upside-down box stacked with falafel and shawarma from one of our go-to favorites. We share a bottle of wine and indulge in greasy baklava. Later, we make love for the last time in our apartment, on the duvet, in front of the fireplace we light for the very first time. We savor every moment. Neither of us mentions children for the remainder of the evening. I relax and enjoy my husband, my IUD secretly in place.

SO-CAL NEWS

CASE SOLVED IN MURDER/SUICIDE: MOTHER OF TWO KILLS FAMILY THEN SHOOTS HERSELF

Nearly a year after a tragedy that has since cast a long shadow over the community, the Irvine Police Department has officially concluded the investigation into the deaths of Michael and Jessa Harvey and their two young children. This case has haunted residents of the Gardens of Orchid Hill since last May. Bringing a measure of closure to the harrowing incident, authorities announced that no third party was involved in the fatalities that occurred within the seemingly peaceful family home.

The absence of forced entry or signs of trespassing at the scene initially baffled investigators, but subsequent forensic analysis has now provided grim clarity to the sequence of events. The evidence conclusively determined that the revolver involved, which was registered to Michael Harvey, was in fact discharged by his wife, Jessa Harvey. Jessa, the mother to their two daughters, aged 4 and 7, is believed to have used the firearm late on the night of Sunday, May 13, 2018. Intriguingly, the gun at the center of this tragedy was a wedding gift from Jessa's father, adding a poignant twist to the already devastating circumstances.

When contacted by investigators, Dr. Daniel Novak, the psychiatrist formerly treating Jessa Harvey and resident at the Gardens, confirmed she'd been battling depression but stopped therapy abruptly a few weeks before the tragedy. He declined to comment further.

Local police made an official statement. "We believe Jessa Harvey gave her daughters a bath around 8 p.m. on the evening of May 13, 2018 in their usual fashion. During this time, we believe she submerged each daughter individually, ending their lives consecutively. Evidence suggests there wasn't a struggle because of the lack of bruising on the girls and the slight amount of water found on the bathroom floor; however, this could've been cleaned up afterward," informs Detective Eddie McWilliams. He concludes, "This type of behavior is not uncommon with maternal filicide-suicide cases, however rare these cases are. Most importantly, residents of the Gardens of Orchid Hill can now rest easy, knowing there is no killer on the loose. We want to stress that there is no lingering danger."

Little is known about Jessa Harvey aside from her brief modeling career. At 17, the former model mainly worked in print ads. She hit her big break modeling at the 2008 Paris Fashion Week. Three years later, she met her husband, Michael Harvey, at an annual promotional event sponsored by ELITE, the company he would later join.

Engaged in January 2012 and married by June, Jessa Harvey delivered her first daughter shortly after, ending her runway career as she traded designer purses for diaper bags.

In 2017, the Harvey family relocated to the iconic Gardens of Orchid Hill. Neighbors remember Jessa as quiet but sweet. Some even described her as a little sad.

"She kept to herself mostly. We rarely saw her at the block parties these past few months," said Gardens resident and former pop star Luna Peaty.

"She was an incredible, loving mother, and she was my best friend," added Blair Novak, neighbor and wife of Dr. Novak.

Currently, it remains unclear if Jessa Harvey has any living relatives. No family has come forward to claim the body. Mrs. Harvey's remains have been cremated and stored until someone comes forward. Authorities are asking for anyone who knows the next of kin of Jessa Harvey to contact the South Coast Funeral Home.

CHAPTER 4

BLAIR

"You spoke to the press?" Dr. Daniel Novak jerks the knot loose from his tie as he undresses in his cavernous closet. His draconian jawline pulsates towards his obese wife, blue eyes brooding.

Blair sits at her vanity, rubbing organic belly butter over her swollen abdomen. A few more weeks and this one will be out and into the world. She stopped praying for a boy. She always prays for a boy. She already knows it's a girl. Blair dismisses her gloomy thoughts with a cool, effortless wave, as if fanning flies in church.

"I didn't know she was a reporter." Blair keeps her tone even, unemotional.

She watches as Daniel pinches the bridge of his sharp, hawkish nose, drawing his eyes closer in a look of concentration. Being married to one of Orchid Hill's earliest residents and a doctor held in high esteem by the community, she's familiar with the curiosity their exclusive lifestyle sparks in others. What baffles her is the sight of a reporter slipping through their meticulously guarded gates to probe into their lives. Their home, the grandest within the cul-de-sac, was supposed to be a sanctuary, secured with hefty payments for the privacy that Daniel insisted on. Her husband, always the dedicated physician, prefers the quiet of his subterranean office for seeing patients, a space directly linked to the emergency bunker, a relic left over from the Cold War. Whether lecturing at the university, consulting for ELITE, or immersed in research in his underground lab, Daniel is a man devoted to his work, committed to contributing to humanity's welfare. Blair knows this routine well, supporting him silently from the sidelines.

She really hadn't known that the woman was a reporter. After three tumblers of wine, she wobbled over to the side of the garage, trying to bury the bottle in the recyclables. The reporter had snuck up on her. She was dressed unremarkably, and neither held a recorder nor acknowledged herself as a reporter. How was Blair supposed to know? Instead, she walked right up to Blair, right down the long rosette driveway, like she owned the place, and started asking questions. Blair was so startled by the intrusion and the feeling of being caught, she happily answered any questions that didn't involve a sobriety test, careful not to sound like she had a mouth full of marbles. Blair was grateful when the woman finally left. Honestly, she'd forgotten about the whole thing until she read it online.

"They were just doing an anniversary piece on the tragedy last year. Jessa was my best friend. And a good person. I didn't say anything dishonest."

"You, dishonest?" Her husband huffs. "Like you know anything about honesty. Don't forget where I found you."

He tosses his dress shirt into the dry-cleaning hamper. His firm, smooth chest displays his dedication to wellness. Daniel frequently complains to Blair about some of his colleagues gaining weight, criticizing it as a paradoxical notion, like an unfit mother.

Blair stops rubbing her belly to stare at her perfectly proportioned husband. "What's that supposed to mean?" she asks, eyes red-rimmed and angry.

He slowly changes out of his suit and into his trusty chinos. "I think we should adjust your sessions. You seem...off this pregnancy. I can't put my finger on it." He glares at her, daring her to protest. She turns her back to him but still sees his burning threat through the mirror. "I think it's time to take you to the next level."

Blair drops the jar of belly butter. The contents fade into the cream rug. She clasps her trembling hands together, sits upright and rigid, staring at herself in the mirror. Pupil to pupil. She'll lose everything once this baby has feasted off her.

Dr. Novak walks over, picks up the jar, and places it on Blair's vanity. "Make sure you do your lessons tonight. I added a new one to the app. Just for you. I think you'll enjoy it, Blair."

Blair keeps her ears trained on her husband's voice—her protector, her savior, her master.

"Blair?"

"Yes?"

"Care Blair?"

"Yes?"

"My Care Blair?"

"Yes?"

"Don't forget the lessons."

"Yes, dear. I think I will enjoy them."

"And don't forget to put this in the punch at your party tomorrow." He reaches into the refrigerated cabinet in their closet that houses their colognes and face creams, collecting a tiny vial. "One drop for each should be enough." He sets it down before her, still commanding her gaze through the mirror. "And make sure the new one, Sean's wife, drinks some." He stomps out of the room.

Blair blinks. She stares straight into the mirror, past herself, and picks up her hairbrush. After one hundred strokes, she slips into her nightgown and sits in the reclining rocker in her dressing room. She fishes the earbuds from her robe pocket and inserts each one.

Using her phone, she locates the ELITE app, finds her husband's new lesson—specifically designed for her—and presses play. Her head fills with a soothing electronic melody set at 396 hertz. The tension in Blair's neck and shoulders evaporates. Fear and doubt subside as her cortisol level drops. Her breathing slows as she falls asleep to rhythmic lulling.

Sometime in the middle of the night, Blair's bladder wakes her. Her head fills with her own voice: "I am not weak...I do not need alcohol...I am an obedient wife...I have chosen this life..."

She repeats the mantra continuously while she shuffles off to the toilet to relieve herself. She keeps mumbling her own words as she flushes and makes her way into her empty bed.

Her husband, still not retired for the evening, remains in his lab, making new apps for his wife and her friends.

Chapter 5

AMARA

Amara runs a hot bath with Epsom salt and lavender oil. She sits on the edge of her massive tub, wrapped in a fluffy white robe, examining her raw skin. Her rope burns need soothing. It will be a while before she can show off her bare legs again.

The timing of the situation is unfortunate. She's booked to meet a local shoe designer next week to discuss a series of social media posts using Amara's influencer status. Naturally, her forty-inch legs are the selling point.

In the army, Amara used her stature for practical things—spotting targets, running miles, and climbing over that damned wall. Her height gave her an advantage over other cadets at West Point. Of course, it didn't stop all the Cadet Barbie comments, but by then, Amara had developed diamond skin. Courtesy of years spent at boarding school.

She lightly traces the rope burn patterns on her aching thighs. Dark plum lines weave like patchwork. She'll have to cancel on the shoe designer. For a fleeting second, she considers wearing tights.

At this time of year? I might as well wear fur.

It's unusually scorching this spring. And with water shortages running rampant across California, it's a battle to keep the lawns and foliage alive. Even with the upgraded sprinkler systems, everyone's lawn at the Gardens of Orchid Hill looks extra crunchy these days. All except one.

She balances on the edge of the tub with perfect posture, one of the only things left of her old self. Sometimes it feels like her military education and combat training were a different life altogether. Some days she can't remember anything before she met Levi.

As the bubbles reach the edge of the tub, the doorbell rings.

"Go away!"

The synthesized sound sings again. One of Luna's old hits.

Amara rolls her eyes. She uses her phone to access the doorbell camera and sees her neighbor. "For the love of God." She tightens the sash on her robe, rolls down both sleeves.

The annoying voice bleats for the third time.

She swipes a control on her cell to access the speaker, takes a deep breath, and feigns a smile. "One moment, please."

Sliding on a pair of slippers, Amara marches down the marbled stairs, passing perfectly posed photos of her life with Levi. The picture-perfect Sullivans. She gathers the material of her robe with one hand, closing the gap to hide her discolored skin. Giving her reflection one last review in the foyer mirror, she opens the front door.

"Good morning, Amara!" A very cheerful, very pregnant Blair blinks at her with a basket of homemade macarons.

"Where did you find the time to make those, you petite cow?" Amara swings the door wide to allow Blair entry, avoiding her global belly.

"Bless your underfed heart." Blair pushes past Amara with a tight smile. "When did you find time to become such a capital B? Oh wait, you were born that way." Blair heaves herself down the hall and sits in the modern grayscale living room. "May I have some water? I almost fainted trying to hobble over here in this heat. It must be the Santa Ana winds."

"It's too humid." Amara fills a glass of filtered water from her computerized refrigerator. She sets it on the coffee table for Blair, then sinks into a sofa across from her, carefully covering herself.

"Oh, get me a coaster, will you, hon? I'd hate to ruin your lovely table." Blair lifts the glass off the wood, wiping an invisible water ring with swollen fingers.

"Fuck the table!" Amara snaps. She shoots up to full height—a staggering six feet three inches tall with those legs—and stalks to the wet bar to find a beloved coaster for Blair.

Blair takes a deep drink of water, side-eyeing Amara. "What's gotten your panties all in a bunch this morning?" She arranges her glass and coaster, sits back, pushing wet hair off of her perspiring face, and waits.

Amara offers Blair a guilty look. The rims of her eyes fill with tears.

"Oh, honey!" Blair rocks, attempting to propel herself up off the couch.

Amara rescues her, pulling her inflated friend into her arms for a lopsided hug. She arches over Blair like a weeping willow. The levees break.

"I'm sorry, baby girl." Blair tries comforting Amara. "Your time will come. Just you see! You're still so young."

Amara jerks up at attention. Her default bitch face drains any sign of weakness. At full height, she towers over Blair, even in Blair's never-ending collection of platform heels.

Blair looks up at her regal neighbor. She rubs her belly, stopping with a look of guilt. "So, what does the doctor say?"

"Levi?"

"No, darling, your fertility doctors. What do they say?"

Amara slumps her shoulders and looks into Blair's eyes. Her bottom lip trembles. "What if it's..." Her eyes dart around the room as if someone is listening. "What if it's not...I can't do this!" She breaks into sobs.

"Hush now." Blair gathers the sobbing heron in her arms as best as she can, turning her belly sideways and stretching her arms around her new best friend. She's going through best friends like housekeepers. She steers Amara to the architectural loveseat and helps her lie down, tucking pillows underneath her head and knees.

Amara succumbs. Swaddled in her robe, she stares out the oversized picture window overlooking her sprawling back lawn with drooping palm trees and birds of paradise. The Santa Ana Mountains shimmer in the background.

"Let me make you some tea." Blair hobbles over to the kitchen and starts opening cabinets.

"Vodka would be better," Amara mumbles from the couch.

"I know, dear, but tea will make you strong." A series of clangs ring from the kitchen. The water faucet chirps. "Besides, we still need to go over and meet the new neighbor. And don't forget Luna's thingy this afternoon."

Amara grunts in protest.

The tea kettle whistles.

"I know what'll cheer you up!" Blair sings from the kitchen. "Daniel made new lessons." She carefully pours out two mugs, hands one to Amara. "After this, we'll get you in a bath and go meet the new neighbor." She retrieves Amara's earbuds and sets up the lesson on her phone. She finds a blanket to cover Amara and her poor, wilted, rope-burned body, never mentioning the marks.

CHAPTER 6

KIT

KIT NOVAK DECIDES TO skip school and start the weekend early. Armed with a new graphic novel, she heads to her favorite place, a small dark room featuring a collection of high-end gaming chairs arranged in an outward-facing circle. The chairs are snug and recline all the way. Kit likes to pretend she's in a spaceship, blasting off to an entirely different universe devoid of awkward social situations and teenage consequences. There's even a bunch of weird onesies that look like spacesuits hanging on hooks along the wall. Being in the Doomsday bunker, she's guessing hazmat, although they're unlike anything she's ever seen.

Dim LED lights blink on, recognizing her presence. A faint hum buzzes off the slab floor. If her father ever catches her down here, she'll be grounded for life, or worse. Kit doesn't know what's worse than being stuck in her room without her books or connection to the internet, but she's sure her father has some thoughts. He's full of ideas.

Like how to become the most renowned doctor in Southern California—prioritize work and put family last.

Or the best way to never have a relationship with your daughter—ignore her at all times.

And how to avoid a loving wife and maintain appearances—just keep smiling.

Those blue eyes have everyone fooled.

Kit doesn't understand her father. When she was younger, she idolized him. Her father the doctor. The hero. He was always helping. Someone else. Someone in more need. She wrestled with this as a child, learning to put the necessities of others before her own. She knew not to want anything from him. That way, she can never be disappointed.

At least her mother dotes on her. It helps her feel less sad. Especially when she watches her father scoop up Buster in one arm and muss his hair with the other. She yearns for that familiar routine. That closeness. His acceptance.

Kit found other things to fill the void. At first, it was books. Kit spends endless hours living alternate lives in different worlds. Once she turns that first page, she's fully immersed in its matrix. But the depression of her reality gets heavier once she reaches the back cover.

She's tried other things to improve her reality. So far, Kit's experimented with cigarettes, vape pens, and alcohol. Kit's an intelligent girl. One of the smartest in her class. The only kid in her whole grade who knows how to code. She's fully aware of the damage these substances are doing to her fourteen-year-old body.

I'd rather die young than live miserably.

She pads around the circle of chairs until she finds her favorite seat—the one farthest and most hidden from the door. Judging by the pristine, stiff cushions, it's used less often than the others. She climbs up and reclines all the way until she is practically horizontal. Holding her new book above her, she flips through the pages, images flashing like cards painted in muted greens, blues, and yellows. She settles on a series of illustrations halfway through. "Chapter Ten: Vermin." It's a collage of a young blonde woman trapped in a stark cell with no one to talk to except a rat. Two men guard her cell door, but they won't acknowledge her. The woman looks scared and lonely.

I know the feeling.

Closing the book, she admires the glossy cover. She recognizes the illustration: a close-up of the mask worn by the villain, which has since been turned into a universal symbol of freedom and truth, opposing censorship and control. Kit can relate.

Story of my life.

CHAPTER 7

CASS

ON FRIDAY MORNING, SEAN leaves me with the movers. He won't be home until late. I shouldn't wait up.

"Some neighborhood board meeting with the guys. The road to the White House starts here!" He smacks my ass and skips out the door. "And try to make some friends. We need voters!" he hollers as he spins, grinning dimple to dimple, giving his best Kennedy smile. I can't help but melt.

After the movers unload, I'm tasked with dispatching and organizing our worldly possessions. I'm thankful this place came partially furnished. I don't know how we'd ever fill these rooms. Since I left home, I've only had a few things. Not much room in the van. Unfortunately, the Green Fairy never did recover—like my poor Thurgy. I thought moving from a camper to Sean's apartment was an adjustment. At the time, his modest condo felt like a mansion. This place feels more like the Taj Mahal.

The neighborhood lives up to its name—the Gardens of Orchid Hill. It sounds bougie, like a cheesy romance novel. Apparently, the waiting list to own here moves slower than LA traffic on Friday afternoon. Personally, I've never heard of this place, which is not surprising as I'm an East Coaster who's essentially been living off the grid. Still, it's supposed to be the Neighborhood of the Future, the latest technology. Celebrities and politicians live here. Blah, blah, blah.

That doesn't impress me. What does is the emphasis on privacy and security in the community. Describing it as 'cozy' is an understatement. Behind our guarded gate are fewer than a dozen homes, each generously spaced along a broad street that ends in a cul-de-sac at one end and opens to a park.

Every yard boasts a garden, mostly wilted from the drought—with one exception. Our next-door neighbor. Their home stands out in vibrant comparison. Trees drip with blossoms. Florets cascade over pots. A spectrum of petals pop against a stony facade. The floral celebration showcases an array of orchids. It's a veritable sea of flowers. I doubt they're adhering to water restrictions, but it's not for me to judge, particularly when we have the best view.

My mother would have loved it.

Each house possesses its own character. Some, like the gorgeous villa at the end of the cul-de-sac, exude a Mediterranean vibe with carved doors and stone details. Others, like the angular limestone creation across the street, lean toward a contemporary design with lots of glass and sharp edges. Our home is timeless with a white stucco façade, charcoal tiled roof, and minimal black trimming. Elegant, but modern. Together, these homes create a vibrant tapestry, each showcasing its own charm.

According to the realtor, they all connect. Each house has a door leading to the community's bunker. If the world takes a turn for the worse, we'll be able to shelter indefinitely. Not a lousy amenity to have in California where natural disasters are as common as car crashes.

"Such a great investment!" Sean must have said that a billion times. I've never seen him want something so desperately. Well, besides me. (Insert blush here.) No, really, he's been a true gentleman. When Thurgood passed, Sean was a godsend, accommodating me, putting me at ease. "Can I get you anything? How are you feeling? Did you eat?"

So, of course, I didn't protest the move. Mainly because I see how happy it makes him. I'm going with the flow, taking it day by day, moment by moment. After my family's accident, I stopped thinking too far ahead.

SEAN HAS ALWAYS BEEN the planner. "What's your six-month to five-year plan?" He surprised me on our third date. I think he was trying to distract me because Thurgood had taken a turn for the worse, still at the vet after a month. Because of his age, they wanted me to "do the right thing."

"Um...I don't know. I guess I don't have much of a plan." I remember pushing food around with my fork, avoiding eye contact.

"So, what do you do for money?"

My cheeks grew red. Where I'm from, discussing finances is considered gauche. I'd never given it much thought before; my parents set up trusts for my brother and me, and now that they've all passed...Well, let's just say, it's not on my list of worries.

"I have a travel blog that does okay. I guess I'll need to think of something else, since I'm not, you know, traveling. I don't know. I passed the bar in another life, so I guess I could always return to law, but..." I lifted my head, allowing myself to be distracted by those eyelashes, "...it's not really my passion. You know?"

I waited for Sean to say something, anything, to scold me for wasting my life. But, instead, he stared back at me, kind eyes waiting for me to continue.

In that moment, my world shifted. It was as if everything that had happened, good and bad, led me to him. I felt my brain rebooting. One by one, my muscles relaxed like balloons deflating. I felt safe, secure—a feeling I hadn't felt in a long time. I unraveled before him, unburdening my story.

When I finished wiping snot off my face using a wad of paper napkins from the dispenser at our table, Sean grew quiet. He dipped a fry in aioli, chewing thoughtfully as if he was processing everything I'd just told him.

Blushing, I took a giant bite of my bison burger, muting myself.

"Wow, you've been through a lot," he finally said. "And you still passed the bar? Beauty *and* brains!" He reached over with his napkin, dabbing a stream of grease gliding down my chin. He sat back to admire me while I chewed with chipmunk cheeks. "What? Don't give me that look. You know you're freaking gorgeous, right?"

I broke eye contact and choked down my dinner, conscious of my hair expanding in the evening's summer heat, a massive dandelion of knotted curls desperate for conditioner and a brush. Gorgeous was the last thing I thought when I looked into the mirror, just boring brown eyes and frizz.

"So, what about you?" I asked him later as we walked together back to his car. "What're your goals? What do *you* want to be when you grow up?" I asked playfully.

Sean Maccabee looked at me with those long eyelashes and said, "I want to be the President of the United States of America."

"Shut up!" I nudged him with my shoulder and laughed.

He didn't join me. His eyes were clear. Lips pressed together in a thin line.

"Oh, gawd! You're serious?" I immediately erased the smile from my face.

He was serious.

Sean cleared his throat. Crimson spread across his neck. "I plan on using my time at the DA's office to transition into politics." He opened the car door for me and gently closed it before getting in himself. "You know, do some good for the little people. Like your parents did." He looked at me and grinned with his big politician smile. He definitely had the face for it.

That night, in his bedroom, I unveiled myself to Sean. It wasn't the first time I'd been at his place. He let me shower and cook there while I had the van towed all over town, but I insisted on sleeping in the crummy motel neighboring the vet. That first night we were together, Sean was a complete gentleman. He had no expectations of me. He didn't paw at me hungrily like I was some meal for him to chow through. Nor did he make me feel like I was an instrument for someone else's pleasure. Instead, he made me feel like a goddess. He was gentle and sweet and kind. He kissed and caressed until I became a live wire begging him to ground me. It was a cliché of electricity, like nothing I'd ever experienced.

Sean completely transformed my life. He's my anchor, my home. Without him, I'd be lost in an ocean of self-pity. Orphaned without a direction to sail.

Now, it's his turn. Living in this posh neighborhood is a stepping stone for his political career. He wouldn't have been taken seriously in that bachelor pad.

There's nothing shabby about this sprawling beauty with a three-car garage and wood-burning fireplaces we'll most certainly use. The natural hardwood floors are one of my favorite features. They complement the beams that highlight the Venetian-plastered ceilings. I love the carefully curated and bespoke pieces that came with the home. The plush furniture and natural wood make the house feel cozy yet contemporary.

The kitchen is stunning. Hunter green cabinetry and white marble disguise futuristic appliances. It's a balance of science and style. The refrigerator and other gadgets include artificial intelligence. I never have to worry about leaving wet clothes in the washer or if I shut off the oven. The level of technology leaps beyond my imagination. I control everything from my phone: floor temperature, humidity, ultraviolet saturation. I can even customize the doorbell to play any song I want. I'm still working on that.

The best part of our new home is the sliding glass wall in our kitchen. It extends our exterior living space into the backyard. There's another dining area outside next to a mosaic-tiled pool. A seating area offers a stunning view of the mountains, serenaded by a serene waterfall fountain. It's very Zen. I've already lounged there twice today amidst unpacking to toke.

Another secret I've been keeping from my overachieving husband. My beloved President-in-the-making suddenly can't be married to a pothead. He used to find it endearing. He even laughed about the time I had a joint behind my ear when we checked Thurgood into the vet. Apparently, it's not so funny anymore.

"We need you to quit before the media picks up on your little habit. It's fodder for a smear campaign," he'd said as if he already knew all his dreams would come true.

I tense up when he begins sentences with "we." Sometimes, I question the reality of it all, still anticipating the punchline—balloons, confetti, a 'just kidding!' to reveal the joke.

Mr. and Mrs. Sean Maccabee. The President and First Lady of the United States of America. My parents would've loved to see the day. Garth would've been so happy for me, maybe even a bit jealous.

Due for a break, I collapse into my new favorite chair by the waterfall, stinking and exhausted. Just as I'm about to fish the joint out of my pocket, the doorbell rings.

"Fuck."

I listen to the generic, electrical ding-dong sound I haven't figured out how to change yet, hoping it'll disappear. Centipedes race down my spine. My heart quickens. I take a longing look at my pre-rolled joint (Trippy Lemon Indica, my favorite) and debate answering the door. I slip the joint back into the front pocket of my faded overalls. They belonged to my mother. She gardened in them in her rare moments of free time, staining the knees beyond repair. They're wicked comfy and still smell like her. I pretend, anyway.

Not expecting company, I'm a tangle of curls and braless and, apparently, unable to work the doorbell camera from my phone. I begrudgingly abandon my new favorite spot and tiptoe to our front entrance, hoping for a fleeting delivery guy, not a group of adolescent Jehovah's witnesses. Cautiously, I crack open the door and poke my head out. "Yes?"

Definitely not your typical solicitors. Standing on my doorstep, I encounter the oddest duo. Two women, opposite in every way. One toweringly tall, the other petite. One exaggeratedly pregnant, the other rail thin.

"May I help you ladies?" I eyeball them. They're too well dressed. I shorten the door gap, suspicious of what they're selling.

"Good morning!" says the small, round one, a faint southern accent peeking through. She has the barely creased skin of someone in her early thirties. She's tiny and about to pop a human out at any moment. Enormous breasts struggle inside the ruffles of her dress. I squint at the large diamond on her finger. She thrusts a basket of—*oh-my-God-are-these macarons?*—in my face. I smile. She smiles back.

I swing the door open wide enough to accept the basket. Never one to turn down a gift or homemade goodies.

The tall one looks pissed, poised like a proud empress. She manages a polite smile and extends a hand for a too-firm shake. She has an equally dazzling rock. I twirl my modest gold band with my thumb, a nervous habit. My brilliant cut carat sits in the safe beside our passports and other valuables. Sean hates that I never wear it. I hate that he cares so much.

"Nice to meet you. I'm Amara...Sullivan." She stands with her hip jutted out, somehow elongating her statuesque frame. She wears skinny jeans with peep-toe boots and a long-sleeved shirt looped over her thumbs. I look past them at the sweltering sun and wonder if the weather will change.

"And I'm Blair Novak. I live up the street with my husband, Dr. Daniel Novak. Maybe you've heard of him? He lectures at the university."

"Hi...yes...hello!" I shift the fancy wicker basket with carefully arranged treats to my hip and stick out a hand for a proper greeting. "I'm Cass. We moved in this morning. My husband's Sean..."

They smile and blink, waiting for me to go on.

"...Maccabee. Sorry, I'd invite you in, but..." My voice breaks off as my arm gestures to the mess of boxes behind me.

"Of course, dear." Blair pushes a lock of hair from her sweaty face. She looks exhausted. I instantly regret my rudeness. I look at her shoes–four-inch espadrilles! Her swollen feet spill over the cloth straps like canned dough bursting from a cardboard tube.

"We wanted to welcome you and invite you over to my home later this afternoon, around one, for a late lunch and a girl get-together, if you will."

"It's a sex toy party." Amara adjusts her weight from one hip to the other, her face unchanged.

I admire her bluntness. I can't see her eyes through her over-sized sunglasses, but judging by the distinct scowl on her face and constant sniffling, I'd venture she spent the morning in tears. Or snorting drugs. Cocaine? Meth? I hear Heroin's making a come-back these days.

"Amara!" Blair looks horrified.

Amara shrugs it off. "She may as well know now instead of being blindsided in front of everyone." Her voice is monotone. I wonder if she's always like this or just having a bad day?

"Uh, thank you?" I pipe in. "That's...uh...kind of you." *Hell to the no! Sounds worse than getting a bikini wax from a serial killer.*

As if she can read my mind, Blair grabs my wrist. "You absolutely must come. It'll be at my house right over there." She points at the Italian villa I'd been admiring at the end of the cul-de-sac—a sprawling terra cotta chateau fenced in cypress trees. It could've been plucked from Tuscany. "You must accept. Just bring yourself, and we'll see you at one. Come thirsty!" she winks. Teetering on heels, she sways down the stairs, her belly rocking as she grips the railing.

"Nice to meet you." Amara gives me her crushing hand again. "I'm glad someone finally moved in. This house was like a graveyard for months. We didn't think anyone was brave enough to buy it after what happened."

"Amara! Let's go!" The urgency in Blair's voice alarms me. Or maybe I'm still high from my midmorning break?

Amara drops my hand and turns to leave. As they walk down my cobblestone driveway, I can hear Amara, "What? She's going to find out anyway."

Blair shushes her and grabs her arm for balance as they meander their way down the street towards the cul-de-sac.

Back outside in my new favorite spot, I pull out my spliff and finally light it. It's only half past eleven. Plenty of time to get a decent amount of unpacking done and a shower before I—what am I thinking? I don't want to meet those ladies. They're the exact opposite of my kind of people. I saw the way they eyeballed me.

My blood pressure still hasn't recovered from the entire experience. I take a hit and stuff a pale green macaron into my mouth. Pistachio! I moan with pleasure. My stomach snarls. Lunch does sound pretty good. And like Sean said, it wouldn't hurt to make some friends. Also, I'm curious to find out what the hell Amara meant. Besides, I'm a grown-ass woman. I can handle anything. I take another hit for good measure. Then swallow another macaron. I swoon—salted caramel!

Before heading inside, I scour the backyard, looking for a place to hide my stash. It bums me out how Sean did a one-eighty. I mean, of course he isn't keen on the idea of an ADA's wife smoking weed. But it's legal now. Medicinal. I've explained this profusely, along with the various benefits to my mental health. It's easier to just hide it from him at this point. It's not exactly lying. Right? Out of sight, out of mind. That's why finding a hiding spot outside is ideal.

At the bottom of the waterfall fountain, I notice a brick that looks like it'll come loose if I jiggle it. The grout has worn. I find a stick and work it out. It's a lot easier than I expected. The hole is long and deeper than I initially thought. I can easily store something safe and dry back there where Sean will never find it. I reach my arm to clear out the hole, bracing myself for decaying leaves, some cobwebs maybe, but what I find is more disturbing. It's the hard binding of a book, worn brown leather with a red strap. The lined pages are filled with shaky writing.

It's a journal.

CHAPTER 8

JESSA

THURSDAY, MAY 11, 2017

My previous therapist suggested keeping a journal to help me process my feelings and monitor my mood during this transition to our new home. She warned me to prepare for significant changes in my daily routine. So far, I've been enjoying it here.

Our neighborhood, The Gardens of Orchid Hill, is one long street with a cul-de-sac on one end and a private park on the other. We live behind a guarded gate, although it doesn't seem necessary in this area. The realtor bragged this is one of the safest neighborhoods in America. And one of the most beautiful!

Southern California is everything you'd expect it to be and more, so different from our home in Arizona. It's more exciting and expensive, but Michael's new job at ELITE comes with a nice raise and lots of benefits. We even got a deal on this house, which comes with a golf club membership. Michael's thrilled to finally learn how to golf. He's already made friends with one of our neighbors, Sonja, who promised to show him the ropes. Or is it holes?

I was nervous when Michael mentioned the new job and the move out of state. It was hard to leave the only home the girls knew. The drive over wasn't as bad as I thought. Luckily, the girls slept most of the way. They've always loved the motion of the car. It used to be the only way I could get Rayne to sleep.

Looking back on that first year of motherhood when it was only the three of us—those were the days! Two children are triple as bad. I don't think I've had a decent night of sleep since. It's been hard to bounce back. Michael makes comments about the permanent bags under my eyes. He says I slouch too much. It makes me look like a humpback whale.

I pretend not to notice when my husband comments negatively about my size. I still haven't lost the baby weight, even after four years! It's pathetic. I'm pathetic. It's amazing how Michael still finds me attractive when I can hardly look at myself in the mirror. Getting dressed has become depressing. Utilitarian. Not a pleasure like it used to be. A pleasure I was once paid handsomely for, back when I had cheekbones and a thigh gap. Not that anyone cares about my modeling days anymore.

Michael hopes this will be a fresh start for us, especially for me, once we settle and make friends. His boss, Jeff Peaty, lives down the street, which I find unnerving. Michael said there are a lot of people from his company that live nearby. The Gardens of Orchid Hill is the first of many ELITE neighborhoods in this area. There's going to be a block party barbecue next Saturday, so we can meet everyone. I'm supposed to help with the refreshments. I'm so nervous to meet the other wives. I know how women can be. Plus, I'm a real hot mess these days. These women look flawless. I saw a few of them out walking, exercising I suppose.

It all looks so...exclusive. Oh, there I go, judging before I've even met any of them. They're probably all wonderful. I mean, they all look cheerful and happy. They smile a lot around here.

CHAPTER 9

BLAIR

BLAIR FLUTTERS AND BOBS, a bulbous honeybee arranging glasses, plates, and napkins on her massive kitchen island—the makeshift buffet station for the party later. "I wish you hadn't said anything to Cass about Jessa." She shoots Amara a look as she takes the decorative ice cubes out of the freezer and starts snapping them into the punch. "We don't want to scare her off."

Amara poses on the edge of a cushioned stool in Blair's kitchen. Hands clamped tightly around her phone. Jaw muscles flexing. Thumbs typing rapidly.

"Technically, I didn't. I just mentioned the house." She looks up to watch her only friend buoy around the elegant arrangement. "I'm surprised she didn't already know. I mean, it's been all over the news for months. What? Did she crawl out from under a rock?"

"Hush, now." Blair sets a champagne glass full of spiked punch in front of Amara. "Here, have a drink." She watches the blueberry artisanal ice cubes bob in bubbly magenta fizz while she waits for Amara to get off her phone. It's Blair's signature party drink whenever the ladies come over: pomegranate juice, pear nectar, and Grand Marnier topped with a bottle of champagne and the contents of the vials Daniel gives her.

"This is lovely." Amara stops texting to snap a picture. "You truly are the Martha Stewart of Orchid Hill." She positions her glass under the lighting and shoots a series at different angles. "Mind if I post this later?"

"Not at all." Blair winks, a feeble attempt to cheer her friend up. She's about to move a sizable wooden charcuterie board from the kitchen counter to the dining table when Amara springs off her stool.

"Let me help you with that." Amara extends long sculpted arms, shifting the board's burden onto herself. Once it's settled on the table, she returns to her phone.

Blair can't help but observe Amara's tense body posture and furious fingers. "Who in the world are you texting? The ladies will be here any minute."

A long awkward pause impregnates the air.

Two swift knocks on the door and a single ring of the doorbell break the silence. The suctioning sound of the heavy door opening reaches them before Blair can say, "Come in."

"Ciao! Ciao! It's me, Luna!" A voice carries from the foyer and into the living room. "I brought goodie bags!" She waves her arms, shaking a dozen shiny packages over her glamorous head. The gift bags rustle like dead leaves.

Amara exhales, then rolls her eyes.

Chapter 10

LUNA

Luna Peaty arrives at Blair's sprawling home ten minutes earlier than expected—as usual. This is her party, and she plans to execute it with style and flair. Tonight, she shimmers in a long-sleeve dress, plunging neckline, and a slit up to heaven. Short platinum hair flaunts beachy waves and stylish black roots. She completes the look with mink lashes and her signature pout.

Jeff Peaty's second wife is three years older than Blair, but she'd rather eat carbs than ever admit it. She sweet-talks Dr. Sully into giving her more fillers, more Botox, more silicone—more, more, more! It's never enough for Luna. And the googly-eyed, star-struck doctor indulges her, still a stellar fan after her career imploded decades ago.

Luna is a Hollywood cliché, a classic example of a bright, shiny pop star who burned out too soon. Discovered as a minor with an angelic voice in a Serbian choir, she was enticed by music executives to come to America, where she exploded into an international sensation before puberty. After an—unsurprising—meltdown in front of paparazzi and an unspeakable tragedy involving a minor, she completely disappeared. Until she mysteriously resurfaced several years later.

Build them up to tear them down. It's like an Olympic sport for tabloids.

Luna's voice still rivals legends and can bring hard men to tears. Dr. Levi Sullivan worships Luna. Her mere presence evokes tongue ties and fervent blushing. He has no control over his body when she is near. Luna relishes in it.

"Ciao! Ciao! It's me, Luna!" Inside the Novak home, Luna's sharp perfume precedes her. "I brought goodie bags!" She air-kisses Blair and Amara from across the kitchen, three kisses for each face.

Luna steps into the room, her presence immediately drawing attention.

"You look...ah-MAY-zing, Luna! Where are the kids?" Blair rocks on her tiptoes to look over the kitchen island, clearly scanning for signs of Luna's usually inseparable trio and their bulky stroller.

Luna can't help but notice the underlying tension in Blair's voice, the thinly veiled concern that her little ones might crash this strictly adult-only affair, as specified in the invitation. *What, does she think I can't read?* It's almost amusing how Blair frets over the possibility of children sneaking a sip of the punch when Blair's the one who's been sneaking sips.

"*Au bre!* Those mongoloids? They're with the nanny—the new one. I miss the old one. I forgot her name."

"Bianca," says Blair.

"Yes, that one. Whatever happened to her? She knew how to entertain children. I never had to look at those tragic faces. My poor babies, so ugly." She turns to Amara. "I keep begging your husband to do something already, but he keeps putting me off." She scrunches her nose and shakes her head. Slender ropes of diamonds swing above her tanned shoulders. "Hideous genes! Just like their *baba*."

"Luna!" Blair gasps. "That's awful. A mother should never speak of her children..."

"Or her husband," Amara chimes in obediently, raising her glass to her lips.

"...in a negative way," Blair finishes.

"Not papa, *baba*. It means grandmother in my language. Apologies. Of course I'm devoted to my husband and all three of my unsightly babies." Luna sets down the gift bags on the ottoman in the living room, the same place she put them last year and the year before. "I'm just being honest." Luna's voice purrs, slowly enunciating every word. "Honesty is a respectable quality for a lady of Orchid Hill."

Amara rolls her eyes again.

Luna senses her critical gaze on her, the silent judgment passed on her choice of outfit. She's well aware of the unspoken rift, Amara's inability to grasp the friendship between her husband and Luna, viewing Luna as a faded star, too bright and overwhelming in her uniqueness. Yet, Luna stands unfazed, her confidence untouched by the veiled critiques, ready to lend a hand for the party setup, her usual vibrant self amidst the swirling undercurrents of suburban politics.

Blair hands Luna a fizzing flute. "Here. Drink up."

"Don't mind if I do." Luna finishes the drink in one smooth motion. "Delicious!" She walks over to the punch bowl to help herself for seconds. "Cheers, ladies! Now, come. We have work to do."

Chapter 11

BLAIR

At quarter to one, everything is ready. There are bowls of hummus with crudités, an expertly arranged charcuterie board full of salami rosettes and various cheeses, some of Blair's coveted macarons, and her signature cocktail fizzy and sizzling in the center of it all. The glasses and cloth napkins rest neatly in wicker baskets. Fresh flowers and fruit weave through the island buffet, a feast for the eyes right out of *Town & Country*.

The women of Orchid Hill start arriving and are welcomed into Blair's home—a haven of warm tones and plush furnishings that exude cozy luxury. Fragrances of eucalyptus and white orchids mingle in the air, marrying modern French elegance with Blair's unique southern charm.

Sonja Huang arrives first. As one of the original residents of the Gardens of Orchid Hill, she knows everyone. Her husband, retired mathematics professor, Mr. Huang, spends most of his time organizing his classical music collection. Sonja, on the other hand, prefers to spend her time intimidating the other residents on the golf course. She has a never-ending supply of custom golf gear and an envious two-iron swing. Rumor is she was about to go pro but met her one and only. Their two sons, now grown with families of their own, visit for two weeks every winter to celebrate the Lunar New Year.

"Welcome, Sonja." Blair ushers her in with a wave.

"Good afternoon, Blair." Sonja removes her Coke bottle sunglasses and shearling sandals. Her dark eyes scan the width of Blair's spring dress. "My, you are looking...healthy."

"Bless your heart, Sonja." Blair smiles through clenched teeth. "Please grab a cocktail and make yourself comfortable."

"Don't mind if I do." Sonja shuffles off in stocking feet.

After Sonja, the rest of the neighboring women arrive, primarily stay-at-home moms, apart from the occasional artist or multi-level marketer. There are so many ways to make money on the internet these days. One wife, for instance, makes a small fortune by taking commercial videos of her kids with her phone and posting them online. Another was selling baby moccasins made of vegan leather—until her orders became too much to handle and her husband advised her to quit. Too much stress isn't healthy.

Lilith Cruz, one of the more recent and spirited residents of the Gardens, arrives alone. She stands out, dressed like a spiritual guru with her hand-dyed crop top and patchwork skirt. Tattoos decorate her skin, with full sleeves on each arm. Intricate drawings, beautiful and spiritual, inked in delicate blacks and grays, display flowers, faces, and Mayan symbols. A totem eagle centers on her throat, wings spread wide around her neck. Three stars glint under her right eye. She's swept up her black hair into two messy buns. Dyed green ends stick out. Blair was taken aback by her appearance when they first met, but Lilith's genuine kindness won her over.

"Thank you so much for having me, Blair. This should be fun!"

"I'm so glad you made it, Lilith. Please, come in and grab a drink."

Cass arrives last, ten minutes late. Her brown eyes flicker behind a cloud of dark curls. She looks flushed as if she sprinted over. Relief floods Blair as she welcomes the newbie and points her to the punch bowl. Blair appreciates the effort her guest made to wear a bra, despite not changing out of her overalls and seemingly skipping a shower.

As Blair's gaze lingers on Cass, she can't help but notice the young woman's underlying nervousness. She watches her new neighbor find a secluded corner, as if to compose herself. Luna joins her, stopping at the mirror above the fireplace to check her signature red lips. Blair silently follows the interaction.

In between nervous sips, Cass steals furtive glances at the effortlessly sexy woman. Luna, who reminds Blair of a blonde Jessica Rabbit, seems more suited for a glamorous premiere than a neighborhood party. Blair notices how Cass reacts by adjusting her overalls and fluffing her hair. A mix of empathy and amusement sweeps through her as she catches Cass's wince at her reflection in the mirror, quickly finishing her drink.

With everyone in attendance, Blair heads to the center of the grand room and into a sea of designer handbags and tailored dresses.

"That one's going to need extra help."

"Can someone get the poor girl a flat iron?"

"She reminds me of a young Susan."

"The one who spends all her time in her garden?"

"When she's not drinking, she's tending her precious orchids."

"Because she has no friends."

"Hey, not like we didn't try."

"I've nicknamed her COL. Crazy Old Lady."

"You're so bad, Sonja!"

"Too scared to leave her house."

"Agoraphobic or just antisocial?"

"Neither! She's absolutely brimming with conspiracy theories!"

Blair smiles and clears her throat, prompting the women to disperse in search of seats. Cass observes while nervously picking at her cuticles and scanning the room, clearly unsure of where to sit. Her gaze settles on the vacant loveseat near the window. She heads straight for it, meticulously dusting off her bottom before sitting on the immaculate white upholstery. Blair senses Cass's discomfort. *She's probably debating whether she should have attended or, at the very least, applied some makeup before arriving.*

Luna finishes her drink and claps three times. "Alright, then. Let's get this party started!"

The women settle, the long-standing residents batting their eyes at Cass, Lilith, and Luna.

Amara perches stoically off to the side, ignoring her glass as her thumbs jackhammer her phone.

Lilith finds her way over to Cass. "Hi, I'm Lilith. May I join?" She squeezes in before Cass can open her mouth.

"By all means." Cass sighs. Her shoulders relax as Lilith eases her body beside hers.

Luna stands with her shoulders back and walks to the center of the room. She runs her tongue along a row of perfect white teeth and waits for her cue.

Blair clinks her glass with a spoon. "I'd like everyone to welcome our newest neighbor, Cassandra Maccabee, and re-welcome Lilith Cruz." Light clapping. "Some of you may know Lilith and her husband, Angel, the very successful tattoo artist in LA everyone's raving about. Maybe you've seen his show?" A ripple of chitchat floats through the room.

"Hello!" Lilith stands and waves her ornate arms to the group. The women nod polite smiles.

"Cassandra's a writer, and her husband, Sean, is the assistant DA—the one interested in politics, as I've mentioned before."

The women respond to this last part with claps and cheers.

A nervous voice cuts the room. "It's just Cass."

The applause dwindles. The silence is thundering. As if re-hearsed, the women, in unison, turn to stare at Cass.

Everyone except Lilith. She tilts her head, squinting as if per-plexed by the synchronicity of the silent, wide-eyed group.

"And I'm not really a writer. I used to have this little blog," Cass croaks.

"Oh, dear," says Blair. "My apologies. That's how your husband introduced you. Your birth name *is* Cassandra, is it not?"

"Yes, but I prefer Cass." Her face flushes. She swallows more punch and bumbles on. "No worries...Cass...Cassandra...jus t don't call me Sandra!"

Only Lilith responds with a big snorting laugh. Her dark eyes relax and twinkle.

The rest stare and blink mechanically.

Cass clears her throat and swallows.

Blair can see that she already needs another refill. *She's fidgeting worse than a squirrel caught in a room full of cats.*

"Wait, when did you meet Sean?" asks Cass.

"Why, just this morning. My husband and I bumped into him while he was setting off to work. Either way, it's lovely to welcome you." Blair holds up her flute of sparkling water. "To Cassssss and Lilith. Cheers!" Everyone clinks and murmurs welcome. "One thing you ladies should know about our lovely little 'hood here at the Gardens is that we strive for excellence, not just in our community, but in our personal lives. Each woman here at Orchid Hill is part of a unit—a family of networks, if you will—that lift each other, better one another, not just for us, but for our spouses and their careers."

"Wow, all that is included in our Home Owners Association fee?" Lilith snorts. When no one laughs, she shoots Cass a comical look.

Cass's eyebrows float to the ceiling as she shrugs and shakes her head.

Blair clears her throat and pushes on. "As members of The Gardens of Orchid Hill, y'all have exclusive access to our ELITE Women's Group and phone app. This groundbreaking program tailors to us specifically, led by my husband—world-renowned professor and psychologist—Dr. Daniel Novak. He'll meet with each of you individually, if he hasn't already, and customize a strategy to help accentuate your positive qualities and assist in alleviating any negative traits or habits. Don't worry! Your husbands have pre-approved."

"What the fuck?" Cass mumbles to Lilith.

"Don't worry. I'll fill you in after," Lilith whispers back, tilting her head back to drain her flute. "We're gonna need more punch."

"Oh, and one more thing..." Blair pushes a slick strand out of her eyes and waddles over to the coffee table to pick up a stack of pamphlets. She hands them to Sonja, who takes one and passes them on. "This updated Welcome Letter explains it all: rules, regulations, HOA tips. Plus, everything you need to know about the new Smart home upgrade. Please share with your husbands. Find me if you have any questions." She finds an empty chair and plops down, eyeing Amara, who hasn't stopped texting. "Okay, Luna. They're all yours."

"Enough about our boring husbands." Luna claps loudly to refocus attention on her. "Let's talk about sex!"

THE GARDENS OF ORCHID HILL WELCOMES YOU

AN ELITE REAL ESTATE NEIGHBORHOOD

WELCOME TO THE EXCLUSIVE COMMUNITY OF THE GARDENS OF ORCHID HILL—A FLAGSHIP WITHIN OUR MORE EXTENSIVE NETWORK OF NEIGHBORHOODS. YOU AND YOUR SPOUSE HAVE BEEN CHOSEN TO LIVE AMONG THE ELITE. CONGRATULATIONS ON BEING SELECTED! COUNTLESS PEOPLE APPLIED, BUT ONLY A FEW WERE ACCEPTED. WE'RE THRILLED TO PROVIDE YOU WITH A SENSE OF PEACE AND SERENITY. OUR LUXURY GOLF CLUB AND EXCLUSIVE ACTIVITIES, SUCH AS THE WELCOME BLOCK PARTY COMMITTEE AND THE ELITE CHARITY FOUNDATION, PROMISE ENRICHING EXPERIENCES FOR FAMILY LIFE, NETWORKING, AND SOCIALIZING IN AN IDYLLIC SETTING.

To maintain the pristine beauty of our neighborhood, we kindly request that you abide by the following rules:

1. Please keep your homes and landscaping neat. ELITE will provide a list of certified and vetted gardeners and house staff.

2. Vehicles must be parked in driveways or inside garages. Street parking is reserved for guests only, and overnight parking requires a permit.

3. Please clean up after your pets. Sanitation Stations are located throughout the neighborhood for your convenience. All pets must submit a DNA sample, and you will be notified if your pet's DNA has disturbed the community. Residents with more than two notifications must vacate or re-home their pets.

4. Enjoy our updated recycling system. Please sort your waste bins and have them ready for collection by 8am each Wednesday. Return them to storage by 11am that same day. Garbage attendants provided by ELITE can be added to your services weekly or when out of

TOWN.

5. HOLIDAY DECORATIONS ARE ALLOWED FOR DES-
IGNATED HOLIDAYS STARTING THE FIRST OF THE
MONTH, EXCEPT FOR CHRISTMAS DECORATIONS,
WHICH MAY BE DISPLAYED THE DAY AFTER THANKS-
GIVING. DÉCOR MUST BE REMOVED BY THE THIRD OF
THE FOLLOWING MONTH AFTER SAID HOLIDAY HAS
PASSED.

6. NOISE IS RESTRICTED AFTER 10PM. THIS INCLUDES
ALL NEIGHBORHOOD PARTIES AND GATHERINGS. (WE
DO NOT NEED A REPEAT OF LAST YEAR!)

7. BE KIND TO YOUR NEIGHBORS AND MIND
YOUR P'S AND Q'S. THIS MEANS LENDING A HELP-
ING HAND WHEN NEEDED AND KNOWING WHEN YOUR
NEIGHBOR NEEDS SPACE. NO ONE LIKES A NOSY
NEIGHBOR OR A GOSSIP. WE ENCOURAGE PRIVACY,
PEACE AND QUIET, AND A PRISTINE WAY OF LIVING
FOR ALL OUR RESIDENTS.

8. **DON'T FORGET TO DOWNLOAD THE APP!!**
TO STAY CONNECTED, ALL RESIDENTS MUST DOWN-
LOAD THE APPLICATION AND REGISTER WITHIN 48
HOURS OF RESIDENCY. THIS WILL GIVE YOU ACCESS
TO THE CLUB, SMART HOME UPGRADE (SEE BELOW),

AND DR. NOVAK'S WELLNESS PROGRAM. YOU'LL ALSO HAVE ACCESS TO THE COMMUNITY BULLETIN BOARD AND CALENDAR.

AT THE GARDENS OF ORCHID HILL, WE TAKE PRIDE IN CARING FOR EACH OTHER AND THE ENVIRONMENT. BUILT IN HISTORIC IRVINE, ONE OF THE FIRST PLANNED CITIES OF THE UNITED STATES, THE GARDENS SETS AN ELITE EXAMPLE OF EXCELLENCE AND INNOVATION. OUR COMMUNITY IS DE-SIGNED TO HELP YOU LIVE YOUR BEST LIFE, FREE FROM THE STRESS AND ANXIETY OF EVERYDAY LIVING.

TO ACHIEVE THIS, WE RELY ON CUTTING-EDGE TECHNOLO-GY. WE'RE EXCITED TO ANNOUNCE WE ARE THE FIRST NEIGH-BORHOOD IN ORANGE COUNTY TO GO SMART. WITH THE SMART HOME UPGRADE, YOU CAN ACCESS THE LATEST AND GREATEST IN HOME AUTOMATION, ENERGY EFFICIENCY, AND SUSTAINABLE LIVING. THE PROGRAM INCLUDES:

- A HOME SECURITY AND AUTOMATION SYSTEM THAT LETS YOU MONITOR AND CONTROL LIGHTING, CLI-MATE, ENTERTAINMENT, AND APPLIANCES TAILORED TO YOUR PREFERENCES.

- A CLEAN ENERGY SYSTEM THAT POWERS THE NEIGH-

BORHOOD AND OUR UNDERGROUND EMERGENCY
BUNKER USING SOLAR ROOF PANELS AND GAS MADE
FROM COMPOSTED WASTE.

- ELECTRIC CHARGING STATIONS IN EVERY GARAGE.

- WATER MINIMIZATION TECHNIQUES THAT HELP US
  CONSERVE WATER, INCLUDING RAINWATER COLLEC-
  TION DEVICES, EFFICIENT WATER TAPS, AND TREATED
  AND RECYCLED WATER.

- ENERGY-SAVING, LIGHT-SENSITIVE WINDOWS THAT
  ADJUST TO THE AMOUNT OF SUNLIGHT IN YOUR
  HOME.

- SMART HOME APPLIANCES THAT ARE ENERGY-EFFI-
  CIENT, SELF-CLEANING, AND EQUIPPED WITH AUTO-
  MATED COMPUTER COMMUNICATION SYSTEMS.

- A STATE-OF-THE-ART INDOOR/OUTDOOR SOUND SYS-
  TEM THAT CONNECTS WITH THE NEIGHBORHOOD
  PARK.

THE SMART HOME UPGRADE HAS BEEN APPLIED TO OUR
UNDERGROUND EMERGENCY BUNKER WITH ENORMOUS SUC-
CESS. IT'S NOW A FULLY CHARGED, SUSTAINABLE MINI-CITY
WITH A NET-ZERO ENERGY DESIGN—THE FIRST IN THE NA-

TION OFFERED TO CIVILIANS. EACH HOME HAS ACCESS TO THE BUNKER IN CASE OF EMERGENCIES. <u>PLEASE REMEMBER TO SET UP YOUR PASSWORD USING THE ELITE APPLICATION.</u>

REMEMBER, WE'RE ALL IN THIS TOGETHER. THANK YOU FOR CHOOSING THE GARDENS OF ORCHID HILL AS YOUR NEW HOME. IF YOU HAVE ANY QUESTIONS OR CONCERNS, PLEASE DO NOT HESITATE TO CONTACT US.

WE LOOK FORWARD TO GETTING TO KNOW YOU AND YOUR FAMILY BETTER.

BEST REGARDS,
THE ELITE MANAGEMENT TEAM

Chapter 12

LILITH

After three glasses of dangerously potent punch and one order of strawberry-flavored body oil, Lilith Cruz and her new friend say goodbye to their neighbors and walk back to her place to relax.

"My three-year-old is with his *Lola* for the day, so we have some time to unwind without any distractions before the husbands come home."

"*Lola?*"

"My mother-in-law. She's Filipino." Lilith waves the glossy pamphlet in front of her as she maneuvers down the stone driveway. The heavy shading on her arms accentuates her tan. "Have you read this shit?"

"I'm at a loss." Cass flips through the Welcome Letter. "This all sounds a bit...archaic." She hiccups. "Did we move to Stepford?"

"It's more like Scientology. Leveling up to your best self and all that bull. Everyone's so fake. Everything is so *Ah-MAY-zing*. Wait 'til you check out the app. You're going to freak!"

"What did Sean drag me into?"

"It's worse than you think." Lilith's eyebrows arch. It's been so long since she had a friend to gab to. She didn't realize how much she missed this.

"What do you mean?" Cass pauses to look at Lilith.

"You, my friend, moved into the Murder House."

"Murder House? Oh my gahd, what're you talking about?" Cass shields her eyes from the overwhelming sun with her goodie bag. Inside is her copy of the newsletter and her purchase from Luna—*The* Luna!—as Lilith had kindly pointed out.

"How do you not know this already? It's been all over the news since last year—woman goes crazy, drowns her kids, then shoots her husband and herself. Poor thing, probably depressed or post-partum—or worse. Who knows what goes on in anyone's head?" Lilith understands postnatal mood swings better than anyone. If it wasn't for the help of Dr. Novak, who knows where she would be. *Probably locked away in a treatment facility.* A grim thought, but not so far off. No one fully prepares you for the changes that come with motherhood.

"What?" Cass blinks as if in disbelief. Her head wobbles, most likely from shock and alcohol. Her chest heaves as she takes deeper breaths. Lilith watches her inhale. She envisions Cass's lungs expanding toward the late afternoon sky, stretching infinitely. Cass appears so fragile, as if she might burst like a bubble.

"Right in your house!" Lilith points to the classic white and black structure as they near it.

"That must've been what Amara was talking about this morning."

"Wow, the ice queen actually spoke to you?" Lilith leads the way past the row of magnificent homes and up her driveway to her house—a natural stone manor with white trim and arches.

"Yeah, I think she said my house is haunted."

"I'm surprised she talked to you at all. That woman's a see-you-next-Tuesday." Lilith fishes in her purse as they reach the side door. She fumbles with her bag, erupting in giggles before pushing her inked finger into a pad by the door. "I always forget I don't need a key. I think I'm like the only person on the block who locks my doors."

"Me too!" Cass snorts. She appears half lost in thought. "I think I found her journal," she adds abruptly.

"Whose? Amara's?" Lilith pushes open the beeping door and welcomes Cass inside.

"The woman who lived in my house. Did she have a husband named Michael?" Cass steps past the threshold and into Lilith's stainless-steel kitchen.

"Uh, yeah. Holy shit! You found Jessa's diary?" Lilith leads the way, depositing her purse on the counter. "Water? I'm parched as fuck." She grabs two glasses off the drying rack and holds them under the refrigerator's filtered water dispenser. "Any preference on temperature? This thing'll make you whatever you want."

"Uh, whatever you're having." Cass looks around the bright, modern kitchen. A message flashes across the fridge monitor alerting that the milk has spoiled and the Cruzes are out of eggs.

"I prefer room temp. It's better for the body." Lilith fills two glasses, hands one to Cass, and chugs the other.

Cass slurps. Trails of water fall off her chin. "I've never been so thirsty."

Lilith clangs her glass down with more force than she meant to on the sandstone counter. "So, what did it say, this journal? Hold on a sec. I need to change. I hate dressing up for those women." She bends down to slide off her spiked sandals and disappears down the hall. When she reemerges, grey booty shorts and an oversized V-neck show off her tats.

She holds a carved wooden box. "You smoke? I was gonna roll a blunt."

"Yes! Thank gahd someone else around here smokes doob. I thought I was the only one."

Lilith carefully breaks down a cigar and clears the tobacco while Cass explains how she found the journal. "That's wild!" She fills the cigar shell with hybrid kush, licks the edges, and completes the final twist with a handmade filter. "Have you read it?" She lights the end, takes a hit, then passes it to Cass. Lilith holds the smoke in her lungs as she waits for an answer.

"Just the first entry." Cass takes the blunt, holding it between her thumb and middle finger. She puts her lips over the filter and inhales the sweet, pungent smoke.

Lilith exhales smoothly. "What did it say?"

"Nothing much." Cass coughs. "You're probably right, though. It sounds like postpartum depression. She was already in therapy before she moved here."

"Well, keep me posted. I'm dying to know."

"Will do." Cass coughs again. "Wow! This is good shit."

The colors in the room come to life.

"Yeah." Lilith pulls her bare feet up onto the couch. "So, what's your deal? What are you into, *Cass-don't-call-me-Sandra*?"

Cass's cheeks flush. "Did I really say that in front of all those women?" She passes the blunt.

"Yeah, you did! And it was hilarious."

"Gahd, I'm such a dork." She picks at her cuticles as her eyes dart across the room. "Yeah, so, um...my family died...three years ago. I haven't been doing much since...besides traveling. Until I met Sean. Now, I don't do anything. I need to figure something out since my blog's kaput."

"You should write a book. That would be kick-ass. I fucking love art. Creativity is so..." She takes a hit, releases it. "...transcending. I can't paint enough. It's my guilty pleasure. My 'me time.' I have a whole setup in the garage. You should join me sometime."

"Yeah? That would be awesome."

They watch the evening sun dance around the room. The bamboo plants and Buddha statues animate shadows across the earth-toned walls. Clearly at ease, Cass kicks off her Birkenstocks and tucks her toes under her, mirroring Lilith.

"So, how did you meet your husband? I love a good story. Tell me everything! Start from the very beginning. Where're you from, by the way? I'm betting New England with that accent." Lilith hands the blunt off to Cass like a microphone.

Cass settles into the soft sofa and sinks into her high. She runs her fingers along the blue velvet cushions. After another deep hit, she exhales and begins. "Well, actually, you're right on the nose. I'm from Rhode Island—a family of lawyers, wicked brutal. Wicked boring. I begged for adventure, but there was no room to do anything fun. Mom, Dad, even my older brother, Garth, were severe overachievers. Study, study, study. Work, work, work. Continue the family legacy. Blah, blah, blah.

"Our family motto was 'Be the Best, or don't exist at all.' Life was...mundane. Most nights I sulked in my room, looking out at the ocean, wishing for my family to be abducted by aliens so I could spend time doing things I enjoyed, like reading fiction or writing poetry instead of sailing or memorizing Latin.

"Then my whole world sunk. Literally. I was cramming for the bar that summer when it happened. One day they all went off sailing. I wasn't allowed to go, since I was studying. The next day, our broken boat washed up on shore."

Cass pauses to take a hit off the blunt. She passes it back to Lilith, who's been devouring every word, silently nodding, patting Cass's knee in condolence, waiting for the reverie to continue. Cass can't seem to get the words out fast enough. It's as if she's been desperate for someone to unload on. Like the memories have been stored in her head waiting for their chance.

"It's funny the way life works. That moment should've been the worst thing ever, but it was quite the opposite. I feel guilty saying it. I know how it sounds. I love my family. I miss them every day. It's just, for the first time in my life, I had freedom. I didn't have to do what was expected, but what I actually wanted to do. I even enjoyed it. At first, I was afraid to leave. I stayed for a little while in that big empty house. Even passed the bar eventually. But it was too quiet, and the ocean so unforgiving, mocking me. Finally, I couldn't bear it."

"What did you do?" Lilith asks after a pause.

Cass smiles at the memory. "I got a dog. Named him Thurgood Marshall after my mother's favorite person of all time. He was a rescue. I was told he was part Wheaten Terrier, part troublemaker. Anyway, it's not the pedigree that matters. After almost fourteen years, the previous owners brought him in to be put down even though he still had some spunk left. When I heard the story at the adoption center, there was no way I could leave him there. I had to change his name, though. I couldn't call him Turdy in good conscience. So, Thurgood Marshall it was. I called him Thurgy for short."

"Aww," Lilith chimes in, red eyes squinting. "Do you have pics?"

Cass pulls out her phone from her overall pocket and swipes her finger a few times, searching for Thurgood. Her breath catches as she passes the phone to Lilith, who sets down the blunt.

"Aww, he's adorable! Where's he now?"

"Yeah, unfortunately, he didn't make it."

"Oh, Cass, I'm so sorry." Lilith passes the phone back. "That's horrible. After everything you've been through?"

"I took him on a road trip. Bought an old VW van. Had it refurbished and everything. We went everywhere together. But when we got to Cali..." Cass chokes.

"Oh, Cass." Lilith wraps her arms around her neighbor, pulling Cass's head into her bosom in motherly fashion.

Cass accepts the comfort.

"I'm so sorry for your losses," Lilith whispers into the tangle of Cass's hair.

"It was all my fault." Cass sniffles into Lilith's generous chest. "If I never opened that damn door..."

"There, there." Lilith rocks Cass and smooths her wild curls. "Sometimes these things...they just happen...and no one knows why."

"I relive that day over and over and over again, and you know what?"

"What?"

"I can't wish to take it back because I would've never met Sean!" Cass succumbs to sobs. After a few minutes, and a much-needed release, she peals her snot-covered face off of Lilith's breasts. "Oh my gahd, I'm so sorry. I'm such a mess."

"Girl, I got you. Don't even worry about it." Lilith relights the blunt and waits for the tears to pass.

After several minutes, Cass finds her glass of water. She takes a few deep breaths, a big hit of reefer, and continues to regale Lilith with her van adventures, the tragic ending of Thurgood, and the heroic efforts of Sean, her knight in boating armor.

Lilith returns the favor, the weed teasing her into a chatty mood as she entertains Cass with highlights from her former life as an environmental activist. Once a strict vegan and protester for PETA, Lilith now eats meat and rocks leather like a second skin. Although she still creates art, she doesn't paint as much as she used to.

"I met Angel when I got my first tattoo. I picked out a dolphin to go around my ankle. My hair was totally green back then. I think that's why he noticed me. He asked me lots of questions. Like, grilled me on why I was getting *that* tattoo and its meaning. He persuaded—practically conned me—into getting my entire back done." Lilith turns and lifts the back of her shirt. Elaborate images of wildlife hide within a detailed tree. "But it was worth the pain."

"Wow! That must've hurt." Cass traces the intricate design with her fingertips.

"Not as bad as childbirth, but yeah. It took forever. Over eight weeks. That's how we got to know each other. On the last day of shading, he asked for my number. We've been together ever since. I don't miss activism. It wasn't as much fun as I'd hoped. I wanted to be a painter. It would've been wonderful if I could've made a living as an artist, but you know, life has other plans." She pats her belly and gestures a rounding motion. Anyway..." she waves the thought away with inked hands. "After completing my BFA from UCLA, I never got around to getting my master's. My parents are pissed. Anyways, Angel's surprisingly old-fashioned. He prefers I stay home with Bear. He heard about this place from one of his clients—Mr. Huang, Sonja's husband—and had to check it out."

"Sonja?"

"You met her this afternoon. The golfer."

"Oh, yeah, she seems...nice."

"Yeah, about as nice as my own mother!"

"Where are your parents now?"

"We don't talk much anymore. Dad works special effects in LA. Mom's a pro bono lawyer."

"Small world."

"Yeah, right? I don't understand how two former hippies who taught me how to smoke weed on my sixteenth birthday can be so judgmental of my choice of a husband. It's not because of all the tattoos either. They say—and I quote—'It's the controlling vibes we get from him and how much you've changed since you married.'" Lilith rolls her eyes. "They think ever since my first tattoo, little pieces of me have slipped away. They could at least try to be decent grandparents for Bear's sake."

"I wonder, if my parents were still alive, if they'd disapprove of Sean too? Sometimes I feel changed simply by being with him."

They fall into a comfortable silence as they watch shadow puppets cross the ceiling. Day becomes night.

"I know what you should do!" Lilith breaks the quiet. "You should write about the murders in your house!"

"Now *there's* an idea." Cass giggles. She floats above the couch with her new friend, watching the smoke curl paisleys into columns of light. Their thighs snuggle like sisters.

Lilith's parents would be pleased to know she started painting again in fervor. Almost falling into a trance with each brush-stroke. Her subconscious sends reminders—details of a past life. She paints pictures of things she barely remembers anymore: her grandmother's farm, the horse she rode when she was a little girl, camping at the Grand Canyon with her parents. And she always paints a set of haunting blue eyes. Each painting, a gift of a past memory. Except for the eyes. She can't place those blue eyes.

CHAPTER 13

BLAIR

LATER THAT EVENING, AFTER Luna's party and the kids tucked in bed, Dr. Daniel Novak inquires about the event as they perform their nightly ritual. "Did it go alright?" Blair's husband removes his watch, placing it near his phone on the nightstand.

"Yes, dear. Better than expected." Blair sits at her vanity wrapped in silk. Strong underwire supports engorged breasts. Her robe parts so she can rub cream over her stretched belly. Everything swells, even her earlobes. She feels like a pufferfish in an aquarium—petrified and poisonous.

"Good girl!" He sits on the bed, pinching the bridge of his nose. "Did everyone get the full dose?"

"I believe so." Blair rubs the excess lotion on her hands and arms. "I put the whole vial in the punch bowl like you wanted. It was all gone by the end of the night."

"You did *what*?" He cocks his head, blue eyes dissecting her.

Blair recaps her cream and ties her auburn hair away from her makeup-free face. She looks younger than ever. Her face practically wrinkle-free, thanks to Dr. Sully. The extra pregnancy weight fills her cheeks strategically. She looks refreshed but not overdone in that out-of-control-I-can't-stop-what-I'm-doing sort of way. "I said—"

"I know what you said." He growls. "Do I need to remind you of basic arithmetic?" He speaks slowly and deliberately, as if her ears are malfunctioning. He removes his gold cufflinks with fury. "How can you be sure they each took the appropriate dose?"

"Like I said, dear, the punch bowl was empty by the time they left, and I ensured everyone had at least one glass." She gets up and walks across the room to grab a decorative pillow. "Mrs. Maccabee drank more to calm her nerves, and everyone else drank accordingly. Everything went to plan." She returns with the pillow and drops it at Daniel's feet. With great effort, she kneels before him, knees digging into the wood floor beneath the cushion. "Now dear, are you ready for your evening release?"

"That's not necessary. I don't have time tonight." He waves her away. "The deadline to complete the next phase looms. I need to go back down to the office straight away." He stands up and leaves her.

Blair sighs relief, wondering if her husband is coming down with something.

That's the second time this week.

And then:

Now, how am I supposed to get up?

CHAPTER 14

CASS

DAZED AND CONFUSED, I sprawl out on our assembled bed. It took extraordinary effort to attach the sheets and pillowcases. I'm exhausted and nauseous. What was in that punch? The room spins, and I need to take something for my splitting headache.

Lilith's a doll. So nice to finally find a comrade. My fellow stoner. I like her a lot. She smells nice.

All the lights appear extra twinkly. The colors seem too loud. I need water.

Where's Sean? He should be home by now, helping me.

I need help.

The mattress inhales me like a marshmallow. I'm spread-eagle, still in my mother's overalls, concentrating on the carved wooden leaves spinning patterns above me. The ceiling fan feels sensational. There's a pang in my pelvis. I miss my husband.

I miss my family.

I think of my life and Thurgood and how lonely it could've been if I never met Sean that insane day on the side of the road. He could've been a serial killer. But it was Sean. All clean and concerned. And handsome. His face belongs on billboards, in fairytales. The face of a politician.

I try not to wonder about the family who lived here before. What rooms did they die in? Was there a mess? Who cleaned it up? A horrifying chill passes over me like a wave of nausea. These walls have seen death. I sound crazy. I feel crazy.

Unable to sleep or move, I continue lying in my starfish position, awaiting Sean. It's almost one in the morning when he finally cracks open the bedroom door.

"Still awake?" His voice sounds like satin.

"Uh-huh." I move my body for the first time in hours. My joints crack. Blinding light fills the room. "Whoa, easy on the lights." My hands become visors. "Where were you?"

"You're just sitting here in the dark?" He sets his briefcase down on the lounge chair across the room.

We have the smallest house on the block, but I'm still amazed at all the space.

"Why didn't you tell me about the murders?" I squint at him from my pillow.

He bends down to kiss me, stopping halfway, changing his mind. "Murders?" He feigns ignorance.

"Yes." I sit up. A whoosh of blood rushes back to my limbs. "Amara and Lilith told me about the family who died here."

"Oh, that." He walks into our bathroom. "I thought you already knew. It was all over the news. You didn't blink when the realtor mentioned it."

"She said *a* death. Singular. I assumed some elderly person passed away quietly in their sleep. Not a triple-murder-suicide. It's so..." My mind searches for the right word as my tongue hides. I look wildly around the room. "Oh my gahd! Do you think they died in here?" I try swallowing. My throat is cotton. "I don't think I can sleep in this room."

"Calm down, Cassandra. Don't be ridiculous."

My teeth grind.

Sean produces something from his inside jacket pocket. It's a small envelope, tiny enough to fit a single key. Inside are two white pills. "Here," he hands me one, "take one of these."

"What is it?" I roll the tiny pill between my thumb and forefinger. It's unmarked. "Are you trying to roofie me?" I laugh, half-joking. My mood is peculiar. Odd. Everything feels off, like the whole world shifted to the left.

"Dr. Novak gave them to me. He said they'd help you sleep." He leaves to fill a glass of water from our bathroom.

"Huh?" I examine the suspicious tablet. "How did he...When did you..." My brain fizzes over. How much did I drink? I tend to overdo it sometimes when I'm anxious. Another reason I prefer ganja.

"I met him and his lovely wife Blair this morning. He asked about you. I told him about your social anxiety and insomnia. He helps a lot of women around here. There's even an app." He hands me the glass and pats me on the head.

I swallow the pill, slightly annoyed he's airing my dirty laundry to our new neighbors before we even get to know them. "Oh, okay. Yeah, Blair filled me in at the sex toy party today. I downloaded it already. It's...interesting." After meandering through the extensive enrollment process and answering over a hundred invasive questions, I tried to listen to the first lesson, but it was too much.

"Sex toy party?" Sean's dark eyebrows bounce. "Did you get anything special?" He grins at me seductively, a total goof standing there with bare feet and his shirt untucked.

And those dimples. My body blushes. All the resentment and annoyance melt away.

"Actually, yes, I did. And if you're nice, I'll show you...if you ever come to bed." I hop up to finally undress and slip between the cool, clean sheets, waiting for him to join me.

"Yes, ma'am!" He drops his pants and belt to the floor and tosses his shirt across the room.

"Don't call me ma'am," I giggle.

"My apologies, Mrs. Maccabee, the future First Lady of the United States."

I giggle again as his hands glide all over me.

"Oh, I forgot to tell you..." he says as he rolls on top, "the DNC Vice Chair reached out today. I have a meeting with the committee next week. They want to start grooming me as a future candidate immediately."

I gasp as he enters.

WHEN I WAKE, IT's morning. I'm drenched and struggling to scream out of a nightmare.

I dreamt I was cold and wet, covered in dirt, wearing my mother's overalls. It was dark and windy. The air smelled rotten and boggy, like during low tide. I could hear honking, and cackling like women laughing. Women from the neighborhood, from the party. They were cackling like crows. Making fun of me. "Grungy," they cawed. They pulled my hair, snarling wildly. Their melting faces contorted in reverse gravity. Disoriented and half-frozen, I tried to scream, to say something to these awful women. But I didn't. I couldn't scream or shout or say anything to these horrible, plastic people. Something in my mouth prevented it from closing. A crazed man loomed over me, silently working. That's when I woke up with a jolt. My arms and legs stiff. My throat sore and dry.

"Good morning, sleepyhead." Sean hands me a cup of freshly brewed coffee and kisses me on my forehead. "Last night was..." He closes his eyes and purrs, reminiscing.

"Yes," I take a warm, reinvigorating sip, "it was." Honestly, between the booze, the blunt, and that pill, I'm having difficulty remembering. I take a seat at the kitchen table and cross my legs. Judging by the tenderness down there, it must have been a wild night.

"And you! You were amazing. I've never seen you more passionate."

And I've never seen my husband so excited talking about our sex life. I feel ashamed and dirty. I shrug it off, bury it in my garden of secrets. As long as Sean's happy, I am too.

"So, how was yesterday, babe?"

I'm about to answer, but his phone rings. Sean checks to see who's calling, then sends it to voicemail with the push of a button. "How were the women? Did you make friends? I never gave you a chance to tell me last night." He double-winks and smiles like a hormonal teenager.

"Umm...Well..."

"Give them a chance, will you please? I know they're not your cup of tea, but I think we could make a great life here—great friends—find our *tribe*. It would be nice to socialize with people occasionally, right? I mean, once I become a state rep, there'll be a lot of functions. You should get used to it now."

"Yeah. Of course. I've been trying to tell you how nice Blair and Lilith seem..."

"Lilith? Stay away from that one. She looks like trouble."

"Why? Because of the face tattoos? Actually," I gently protest, protective of my new friend, "she's one of—if not *the*—nicest out of the bunch. She's a mom, and her husband owns a successful business. I heard he has his own show, but that's beside the point."

"I heard he owns a sketchy tattoo shop. Wonder how he made it past the background check? Anyway, be careful." He pats my hair and relaxes in the lounge chair. He looks silly wearing my fuzzy purple bathrobe. It's irresistibly soft. The deal is that whoever wakes up first and makes coffee gets to wear it. He does have his own slippers, sensible dark grey slip-ons. His goofy feet would never fit into my torn-up Tasmanian devil heads.

"Hey, did you know we live in the same neighborhood as Luna?"

His dramatic eyelashes flutter over his coffee mug. "*The* Luna? The Sensation from Serbia?"

"Yeah, I met her yesterday. She hosted the gathering over at Blair's. I can't believe she never changed her name after all that stuff happened."

"That's what a life of drugs and desperation will do. Especially when you don't have a man to guide you. Kind of like how I found you."

"What's that supposed to mean?" I set my mug down on the nightstand and sit up in bed.

"Come on, babe. You know."

"No, I don't know. Why don't you tell me?" I cross my arms and glare, daring him to continue.

"You were something of a hot mess when I met you. A woman on the verge of collapse. My damsel in distress, if you want me to be honest."

"Sean, when I met you, I'd just lost my entire family and was literally, *literally* about to lose the only thing left I cared about. *Of course* I was a mess."

"I found you on the side of the road."

"Because my dog got hit by a car and was dying!"

"You were homeless and crying outside of the 7-Eleven."

"Just because my van decided to break down in the middle..." My emotions whirl. *Oh my God! How could I not know my husband was such a snob?* "Why did you even marry me?" The hot air balloon of insecurities I've collected since puberty inflates. I'm blindsided by tears.

"Oh shit, babe. I'm sorry!" Sean rushes to my side. Placing his coffee alongside mine, he wraps his familiar arms around me. He shushes me, burying my head in his chest. He smells of coffee and sandalwood. "That's all in the past now." He smooths my wild hair. "When I met you, I thought—I knew—you were the most beautiful, gentle creature to ever walk this earth. You and your magnificent head of hair belong by my side. Together, we'll conquer the world."

The heaviness of anxiety evaporates. "Do you really mean that?" I whisper into his chest. "Because you've been the only family I've had in a long time, and if I lost you…"

"Yes, my darling girl. My wonderful wife. I love you so, so much." He pulls back and kisses my wet eyelids and then my nose and my mouth. Urgently, silently, we peel each other's clothes off. My anger and insecurity peel off with them.

CHAPTER 15

LUNA

LUNA PEATY SITS ALONE on Friday night, all dressed up with nowhere to go. Light bounces off her glimmering dress and dances around the room. Dildos and dilators clutter the hand-carved mahogany table. She wishes she had her own office.

Cradling her head in her hands, she calls out to the Smart assistant, "Dim the lights in the dining room."

Her migraine eases.

She's still wearing her sequined party dress. Still fuming over what that *ciganka* showed up in. To her event! Luna suspects the poor girl has been wearing those overalls for months, maybe even years. She may not have any alternative. She could be one of those unfortunate souls who lost every thread of decency in the latest wildfire. And those sandals—filthy. *What does she do all day—cas-*

trate goats? Luna takes a deep breath, counts to four, clearing her mind of negativity.

Stay positive.

Be a good neighbor.

A good person.

A good wife.

She should offer the poor thing a makeover. That's what she should do. She taps a reminder into her calendar to find Cassandra—Cass—and offer her services.

Luna loves a good glow-up. She pings a command from her phone sharing her calendar with her husband. Makeovers are Luna's specialty. She's practically done everyone in the neighborhood. Except Susan. That woman's a hermit.

The sound of acrylic nails drumming against solid wood echoes off the dining room walls as Luna tallies her profits. She enjoys watching the numbers rise, knowing she helped a handful of women reach orgasm. She feels useful and intelligent, things she covets more than lip filler and Botox. Luna would rather be a boss bitch than a primadonna. But she keeps that information clipped to her tits.

Her husband, Jeff, is the numbers man. How much is it going to cost? How big are those boobs? How young are you? Mr. Peaty owns ELITE, the most successful and innovative company around. He also owns an F1 racing team for fun, a hobby that seems to consume most of his free time and weekends. And his passion for Luna.

Her side job came as a ploy to entice him back into their marital bed. Revive and recharge their sex life. Rev up their engines, so to speak. Jeff spends most of his time revving up other engines these days. It's painstakingly apparent to Luna it's more than just cars.

There's an endless supply of young, eager girls ready to pounce on wealthy men. All around the world, they lie in wait, like locusts, ready to crawl out of their dirt hole and into her husband's lap. They swarm tech events, yacht clubs, and racetracks, eager to devour, scenting famished egomaniacs like blood in water. The world bleeds foolish, rich men, and Luna knows firsthand—the sharks in California are aggressive.

Luna sighs, slumping. She has a reputation to rebuild. That's why she kept her name. It would've been easier to hide or fake her death. No, Luna could never disappear. She's a fighter, a daughter of war, at war, in a fight to save her name. She needs to prove to the world she's okay. She's right on track. Primarily for herself, but also for her parents back in the village, who are too embarrassed and ashamed to acknowledge her. Appalled by what they saw reported in the news (if you consider gossip news), they refuse to take her calls, believing the headlines written to shock readers and sell papers:

EXPOSED: UNDERAGE LUNA LEAVES ABORTION CLINIC!

LEWD LUNA LEAVES FANS SHOCKED, FALLS OFF BAR, AND OUT OF CLOTHES. PICS!

LIP-SYNCHING LUNA COLLAPSES IN VEGAS AS HER VOICE CARRIES ON

LAZY LUNA STOPS SHOWING UP ON SET, CAREER OVER ALREADY?

SMASHED: LUNA'S CAREER-ENDING DUI—CHILD FATALITY

Once Hollywood's It Girl, Luna had everything and more: a rising career, a handful of number-one singles, three platinum albums, and a string of awards. Then came the gossip columns. It started with a discreet abortion before she could legally consent, followed by a never-ending stream of DUIs. Mug shot after mug shot plastered in every paper and magazine week after week. It was like watching a China doll pass through a woodchipper.

The icing on the cake came in the form of a fatal hit-and-run. A little boy, almost the same age as her son now. A tragedy that spun her right out of Hollywood and behind bars. Devastating, humiliating, and worst of all, career-ending. She spiraled quickly, then disappeared. Some had speculated she joined a religious cult. Others thought she went to rehab. Rumors of a nervous break-down still float in certain circles.

When she reemerged, a new woman, she had a new look and was—surprise!—married to self-made billionaire Jeff Peaty, founder of ELITE. No one knows where she was during her absence. Not even Luna. She refused to comment to reporters or disclose information during the group therapy sessions she popped up in years later. But she was better in a billion (dollar) different ways and ready to reclaim her life as a wife and mother.

Luna totals up her sales and enters them into a spreadsheet on her rhinestoned laptop before calling it a night. If only the paparazzi could see her now, home on a Friday, accounting, and preparing for bed early. She has—how do you say it?—flipped the script, turned the page. Or is it the other cheek?

She owes it all to Dr. Novak, the miracle doctor. His program has done wonders for her. He forced Luna to face her demons and become the best version of herself. She's grateful for meeting her husband, who introduced her to Dr. Novak. The man is a wizard.

It's a shame he couldn't help Jessa. She was so kind, such a positive influence on Luna. They'd bonded over their shared joy for dressing up their daughters. Jessa was a supreme seamstress. She could sew anything, a skill she'd picked up from modeling.

Jessa, ljubavi moja.

Luna's dearest friend made dozens of elaborate, girly headbands and turbans for the girls. For the twins' birthday one year, Jessa made the most adorable unicorn hennins. Luna especially appreciated how the long flowy veils covered the twins' bovine faces.

She blames her mother-in-law. Had Luna known her husband's mother had the face of a hippo, she would've never married him. A secret she'll take to the grave. God forbid anyone says a single word against the original Mrs. Peaty. Ruth Peaty thinks the girls are simply adorable. She loves harassing strangers on the street, asking them who they think the girls look like, greedily waiting for compliments, oblivious to their discomfort.

With all the children tucked in and kissed goodnight, Luna dismisses the nanny. She dines alone before retiring upstairs. She takes a hot shower to cleanse her body and make herself irresistible. Just in case. She removes every strand of hair from her nose down and most of her makeup. Some pigments are tattooed on, giving her a permanent sultry look. She slips into a silk teddy and makes sure the strap-on is ready in case he's had enough control for one day.

Jeff will be excited about all the orders. All the money. All the numbers. She'll listen to her cognitive therapy lessons like a good girl. An obedient girl. A good, obedient wife. She'll be good—for herself, for her family. For all of them. For all the men.

But Mr. Peaty doesn't come home. Instead, Luna spends the evening listening to her lessons repeatedly until her mind drifts off and she slips into a recurring dream.

She's in a room. The quarters seem familiar, yet she can't place it. It's sparse. Elegantly decorated. Cashmere sheets so soft it could be her own skin. She wants to leave the pleasant space, but the door-knob evaporates whenever she tries to twist it. There one moment, gone the next. She's trapped. Alone, in this singular chamber, in a place she doesn't know and doesn't want to be. She feels an enormous sense of defeat so thick it feels like she's drowning in sand. Every once in a while, a faceless man comes in and pinches her. Tiny, shiny objects crowd her, compacting her like trash. She's unable to move, unable to scream.

Luna wakes, breathing heavily. Her silk teddy soaked. Her husband, still absent.

SATURDAY MORNINGS ARE LUNA'S favorite. She sends the kids off with their respective nannies: Jaxson to tee-ball practice, the girls off to baby ballet. Her stepdaughter Amber, old enough to entertain herself, usually bikes a few blocks down to play with the kids from her old neighborhood. With distractions temporarily disposed of, Luna enjoys her morning routine in peace.

She starts with meditation outside in the Zen garden to purge bad energy. Next, she pulls coconut oil to keep her teeth sparkling and reduce inflammation before her favorite—vinyasa yoga. She especially loves the breathing exercises, reminiscent of the warmups she did for the Orthodox choir back in the village. Luna finishes her mindful efforts with a tall glass of fresh celery juice as she sits in her state-of-the-art steam room.

Ninety minutes later, she throws together a glam bag. Her big job for today: surprising Cass with a desperately needed makeover. Luna grabs her trusty flat iron and prepares to leave, but before stepping out, she slips a bottle of unmarked liquid in with her things, a knowing glint in her eye.

CHAPTER 16

BLAIR

"Stop it!"

"Let go of me!"

"That hurts!"

"Give it back!"

"Mom!"

Blair groans awake. It's too early for an uproar. Saturdays are supposed to be quiet, lazy days.

Until you have kids.

She huffs at the thought. Some days, Blair loves motherhood more than others. Right now, in this moment, not so much.

Looking out over the hump of her belly, she contemplates how she'll escape bed. She could call one of the children. They'll probably laugh or make a face. Or worse, act overly concerned about her health, like she's an imbecile and they've already decoded the universe. She could try the rock and roll method. Hopefully, she'll find the floor with her feet before her weight sends her crashing. Of course, then, she may end up calling the children anyway. Her incorrigible children. Bestial noise mammoths. Their voices bellow from three floors down. You'd think with this much space, there'd be some peace. The contractor promised privacy with room to grow. Exhaling, Blair decides to put her money on rock and roll.

"Oh, dear Lord." She uses her whole body as momentum to roll onto her side. Her petite, swollen legs tiptoe out of bed, finding a firm, steady grip on the rug covering the wooden floor. Memories of hippopotamuses dancing in tutus flick through her mind. She grunts in triumph, successfully standing up.

"MOM!"

"*Stop screaming*! Just give me one darn second. For the love of God."

She overslept. How did she oversleep? Blair's felt off this entire pregnancy, the most exhausted she's ever been. The largest, too. *I've never gained this much weight before.* She's never drank so much either, especially when pregnant. Surprisingly, Daniel hasn't mentioned anything. He's usually right on top of her about her appearance, but he's been so busy working on his latest project he hasn't noticed. *Which is nuts since I've tripled in size.* He's barely been to bed. She takes comfort knowing there's a pullout sofa in each of his offices. *His poor back.*

It's not unusual for Blair to wake up alone with a house full of kids. There are no nannies on Saturdays, deemed Family Day by Dr. Novak. Recently, he's too busy to join, leaving Blair stranded and understaffed with four screaming children.

Is this really my life?

Forty-five minutes later, Blair emerges from her bedroom, her face on, hair perfectly coifed. She takes the elevator downstairs in her bathrobe and finds her daughter sulking in the breakfast nook, engrossed in her phone. One strand of strawberry blonde hair winds around her finger in a perpetual loop.

Blair watches her sweet, bookish daughter. Kit has delicate features and stands taller than her mother. Some say they look alike, especially with that hair. Others argue Kit resembles her father, with his stoic nose and genetic blue eyes. Blair envies her fourteen-year-old daughter. A recent growth spurt shot Kit up four inches, and she still has some growing left. Her two best friends recently sprouted breasts. It seems to be all about bras and boys these days.

There was a time when Blair was unable to recall that age. Today, she is gifted with the full grace of retrospection. She smiles with the blooming memory. Blessed with a full chest before she hit her teens, Blair never lacked confidence. *Early Bloomer. Sex Pot. Red Headed Temptress.* Just some of the nicknames she collected back home in the trailer park outside Atlanta. By fourteen, she'd lost her virginity to a college student. "Hanging out on the wrong side of town," her Mamma had said. By fifteen, she'd claimed the virginity of most of the boys (and some of the young men) within a five-block radius. Everyone knew Blair.

Kit, on the other hand, is the complete opposite of her mother—tall, lean, and graceful as a swan. Blair tried to get her into dance, but Kit quit after the second year. She spends more time reading or on her computer than in front of the mirror practicing pliés. Kit's the self-designated weirdo in the family, the black sheep. But Blair loves her all the same. Instead of dance, Kit joined the computer club, learning to code before she knew how to French braid.

She can be the easiest child of all—simply give her a book and stick her in a corner. No prob-lem-o. Kit loves books, real ones she can hold and smell. The Kindle she got for Christmas still sits untouched. Currently, she's reading the graphic novel *V for Vendetta*. A little mature for her age, but Kit's an old soul who's been reading above her grade level for years. Blair cherishes her daughter's wit, stokes it like a fireplace in winter. She promised Kit they could watch the movie adaptation when she finishes the book, which should be any day now. Kit can read a book a day if she wants to.

Blair's only daughter doesn't fit into any mold. Kit's navigating blindly, making her own mistakes. Blair prays Kit will skip the traditional route, forge her own way, set her own rules. She wants to spare her daughter from a lifetime of judgment about her intelligence, integrity, and especially her appearance. Everyone hopes their daughters will turn out beautiful, but no one understands the dangers of beauty. Even the First Lady isn't immune to the scrutiny of having a vagina.

"Good morning, sweetheart." Blair pads into the kitchen in slippers and goes to give her daughter a kiss. Kit tilts her head away, banishing her mother's lips to the side of her face above her sharp cheekbone. Blair's heart pangs. Her daughter's getting to that age where it's gross to kiss your mother—even in the privacy of her own kitchen. It's enough to make Blair cry. *Or maybe it's the hormones?* "Can I make you any breakfast?" She hobbles over to the stove to start a pot of tea.

"No thanks." Kit's eyes never leave her phone. She continuously twirls her hair with one hand, using the other to scroll. "I already ate."

"I found the *V for Vengeance* movie. It's streaming, so we can watch it anytime." Silence. "So, let me know when you finish the book. We can set up the screen room. Make some popcorn. How does that sound?"

"It's *V for Vendetta*."

"Oh, okay. Anyway, just let me know." Blair shuffles, awkwardly trying to make eye contact. "Where's everyone? Did y'all eat?"

"We had cereal." Kit's thumb freezes on a digital image. A sharp squeak escapes her throat. She smacks her phone down on the breakfast table. The plastic cover, shaped like a retro camera, cracks down the middle. Kit moans. It took forever to find the kiosk that sold the exact same one as Amber's.

"Jesus, Kit!" Blair jumps. "Cereal?" She frowns. "I usually make pancakes on Saturday."

"Um, no, it's cool." Kit's eyes dart from her mom to her broken phone case. "The boys went down the trails to look for lizards. They built some sort of trap to catch them."

"Buster too?"

The tea kettle squeals.

"Yeah." Kit's phone buzzes. She picks it up like it's radioactive and reads a message. "Hey, can I go over Francesca's? Her mom's home."

Blair blows steam off her tea. "Yeah, sure, honey." She looks out the kitchen window towards the grey sky. "But take a slicker with you. Just in case."

It dawns on Blair she'll have the whole house to herself. A rare Saturday without a birthday party, soccer game, or coding boot camp. So much for Family Day. With everyone out of the house, Blair can finish planning the cookout for next weekend. A lot of block parties happen at the Gardens. Lots to celebrate. Birthdays. Anniversaries. Bank holidays. Not to mention the Welcome Parties. Blair throws one for each new resident. It's her thing, what she's known for—that and her melt-in-your-mouth macarons. Nobody throws a party like Blair. They all go off without a hitch. *Well, except for the last one...*

Not that she could ever forget. It was the end of last summer. Blair had put together her standard Welcome to The Neighborhood Party, held at the Gardens' private park. Blair had done an exceptional job getting a dance floor and lights. It was perfect, down to the henna tattoo booth, a nod to their newest neighbors, Lilith and Angel Cruz. Everyone was dancing and having a good time, including Daniel, for once. The busy doctor usually never lets his guard down. "Always on duty," as he likes to say. But at this event, he unwound on his third mint julip and was actually dancing (with Luna nonetheless). Blair was so happy watching Daniel that she never noticed the commotion start. Just as she was deciding whether to cut in and steal a dance, a shrieking voice sliced through the crowd.

"I know what you are! I know what you're doing! All of you!"

Mr. Huang lowered the music. Everyone turned to stare where hysterical accusations spewed.

"You're all sheep! All of you!" sobbed Jessa. "I know what you're trying to do!"

"Get her husband."

"She's hysterical."

"I know. I know everything! And I'm going to tell! I—"

Daniel and Jeff responded swiftly. Each took an arm, walking the upset woman out of the park. Jessa screamed the whole way home.

"You can't do this! You can't do this to me! Let me go!"

Well, we won't have to worry about that at the Maccabees' party.

This year, Blair has everything under control, except she isn't sure if she had mentioned the party to Cass last night. *Did I forget to invite the guest of honor? Pregnancy brain.*

Blair finds her phone and texts Luna: `Please remind Cassssss of Welcome party when you see her!`

Luna replies instantly: `On my way over now`

Blair: `Playing fashion godmother again?`

Luna: `Of course! Who else is going to do it?`

Blair thanks Luna, dumps her still-full mug of tea down the drain, and retrieves her stashed bottle. She has at least four hours before her children bug her for something.

With her mug of wine, she curls up in the screen room. The couches are much softer here. She pushes buttons on a remote until she finds something to watch. She settles on a documentary about the six wives of Henry VIII.

Two hours later, Blair wakes to rolling credits. Feeling despondent, she grabs her tumbler and heads out into her garden with a notebook and pen. Their backyard resembles a Grecian hotel decorated with cypress trees and marble fountains. A sleek infinity pool extends towards the view, flanked by two pergolas dripping in white orchids.

She sits at one end of the long, marble table and scribbles furiously. The more she drinks, the more memories bombard her. Just like all the other pregnancies, her flashbacks have returned. The lies. The women. The fear. She should do something and do it fast. Before she forgets again. Before it's too late.

CHAPTER 17

KIT

KIT HURRIES UPSTAIRS TO her room, white-knuckling her phone. Her mind circles the text message that just came through: `Happy Blackmail Day!!` Followed by a snake of money-mouthed emojis.

Strawberry blonde hair curtains her sharp face. Kit's hair has been her shield ever since she grew her bangs out, an invisibility cloak concealing her as she navigates the middle school hallways.

She chews her bottom lip. Bare feet smack the heated floorboards leading to her room. How could she have ever been so stupid? If she acts fast, she could stop it before it gets out. It all started last weekend when she stole a bottle of wine from the cellar to bring to a party.

She told her parents she was visiting Francesca's house, but Kit and Francesca went to Amber's mom's. Amber Peaty is the only good thing that ever came from Jeff's first marriage to Naomi. Amber's *the* most popular girl in school, and until recently, Kit's best friend. Now, they're frenemies at best.

A few weeks ago, Amber discovered a website full of old jokes. Kit almost died of humiliation when Amber led the lunchroom in taunts:

Yo mama's so fat, when she goes camping, the bears hide their food.

Yo mama's so fat, she stepped on a scale, and it said, "To be continued."

Yo mama's so fat, when she wears high heels, she strikes oil.

Yo mama's so fat, when she sits around the house, she sits around the house.

Yo mama's so fat, she was overthrown by a militia group, and now she's known as the Republic of Yo Mama.

"She's pregnant, you assholes!" Kit hollered back at Amber and her gang of giggling goats while Francesca just stood there picking gum off the cafeteria table. Kit's pretty sure Amber doesn't have a clue what that last one means. Amber can be such a stupid shithead. She never even studies. A C student at best. Kit gets straight A's.

She reaches her room and slams the door. "Cunt!" Kit spits the ugly word into the air. It feels good to say aloud, like purging her soul of demons or hocking up a loogie.

Kit makes plans to hang out with her nemesis. Middle School is so like that. One second, your worst friend becomes your best enemy. Hopefully, this will be the end of their feud, and things will go back to how they were. Just the three of them—Kit, Francesca, and Amber—best friends since first grade. Kit aches for normalcy. She still has a picture framed on her desk of the three of them, once an uncompetitive trio in pink tutus, arms linked, all three grinning with missing teeth.

When Amber's breasts made an appearance before anyone else's in their entire grade, suddenly, she was the center of the universe. Amber's already a head-turner with her mother's spiral curls and her father's light green eyes. Now, she's a beacon to any male within a three-mile radius. For them, the competition is on. They fight over who gets to sit by her, offer to help with her locker combination, or teasingly snap her new lacey bras. It's enough to drive Kit insane with jealousy, but mostly, she cries when alone in her room.

Like now.

Kit wipes away tears. She doesn't have time to wallow in misery. Things just need to go back to the way they were. When boys didn't matter, and nobody cared how big anyone's boobs were. But everything's different now. After the boys began heckling her mother, Kit looked to Amber to defend her, like she always has. Amber just laughed. Her pale green eyes glinted as she flipped her mane of ringlets over her shoulder and abandoned her longtime friend. The next day, Amber prepared the list of jokes.

Almost every second of every day, Kit wonders what she did to make Amber hate her so much. How did they go from sharing a bed to *Yo Mamma* jokes? They're next-door neighbors. They're supposed to be BFFs for life. Something changed after Kit quit dance class for computer club. Amber never understood technology. She rolled her eyes when Kit tried to explain JAVA.

"It's like this invisible language. Once you know it, you can do anything you want—build games, make apps. We could even have our own website!" Kit had said, bouncing up and down. Her strawberry ponytail swung wildly. "What would it be about, though? This one girl from Hack-a-Thon has a blog about her fancy pants chickens."

"Ew, Kit! You sound like an insane-o dork right now." Amber simply left Kit's bed and headed to the door without looking back. "I don't even know what you're talking about anymore. I'm going to my dad's."

It wasn't just that one thing. It was a bunch of little things rolled together. Kit had first noticed something off with Amber last summer. They were in Amber's room at her father's house, getting ready for one of the neighborhood barbecues. It was the Fourth of July. Most of the adults were already drunk, and the party hadn't even started yet. Mr. Peaty had bought a new motorcycle and was eager to show it off.

"Girls? Amber? Luna!" Jeff bellowed from the driveway over the deep growls of an engine. His incessant revving finally stopped once all three came outside to bear witness.

"What's that?" Amber ran to her father.

"Is that a motorcycle?" asked Kit.

"It doesn't look like a motorcycle," Luna had said flatly.

Jeff balanced his vast body on the exotic bike. It looked like it came straight out of the Matrix with its wide curves and thick tires. "This here is a Dodge Tomahawk, one of the top five fastest bikes in the world. I shit you not." He gripped the handlebars and the engines roared. A deep smile spread across his pockmarked face. "Wanna go for a ride?"

They all spoke at once.

"I don't think that's such a..." Luna began.

"Yes!" screamed Kit and Amber.

"Come here, sweetheart."

As Amber started towards her father, Jeff leaned over and grabbed Kit's delicate wrist, pulling her onto the back of his new bike. "Hold on!" He tossed her his helmet, and before she could strap it on tight, he peeled out. Shocked and elated, Kit recalls gripping as much of Mr. Peaty as her twiggy arms would allow. Her ponytail whipped wildly behind her. The whoosh of air rushed past her ears, making it impossible to hear anything but wind. Blurry streaks of color rose like walls around her. For a while, there was nothing but blue on one side and green on the other. Kit had felt like she was in a wormhole teleporting across the city.

When Kit got back, she found Amber sulking in her room. Amber didn't speak for a full forty-five minutes. Kit flooded with anxiety. She desperately needed to talk with her friend, to be told she didn't do anything wrong, that it wasn't her fault, but she was met with Amber's cold shoulder and silence. When Francesca's mother dropped her off, they were a trio again—everything returned to normal. For a little while at least.

Kit flings herself down on her canopied bed, blinking away more tears, wracked with overwhelming doom. Her parents are going to murder her. She'll never be able to show her face at school again, let alone get into a decent college. Her life is ruined. How could she have been so stupid?

Kit finally replies to the text: **wdyw?**

She gets a reply back: **u know what I want**

Kit's chest tightens as her fingers fly over her phone: **impossible. anything else? please**

She gets a reply back: **I want a yes by fri or else**

And another: **gb to ur purfect life**

Kit sits up on her bed and looks around her tidy room, hoping to find someone, something to help her. Her mother decorated the corner room long before Kit was even born. The papered walls have thick vertical stripes alternating in satin yellow and eggshell white. Kit added a few touches here and there. A string of fairy lights twines around the canopy bed. A poster of Ada Lovelace with the words *"Mother of Computers"* scrolled across the top and *"Girls Can Code!"* at the bottom hangs above her computer desk. Framed family photos dot along one wall. There's a professional shot of all seven of them on Newport Beach wearing matching blue jeans and white button-ups. There's one of Kit on a horse in Mexico, galloping in the surf. Another of their old dog Caesar, a beautiful Bernese Mountain. Kit named him after learning about the Roman Empire. He died a few years back.

When everything was still normal.

It's the perfect fourteen-year-old's room, or rather, the room of a perfect fourteen-year-old.

Kit goes into her bathroom to wash her face. She scowls. She has her father's pinched nose and pointy chin. Her blue eyes look gray in the mirror. She always thought they were too close together. Her pale red hair hangs frumpy and greased. Will she ever be as gorgeous as her mother? Her mom may be a blimp now, but to Kit, she's the most beautiful person in the whole world. Pregnancy is brutal.

Maybe it's the drinking? Or is that why she started?

Kit longs to be a smaller version of her mom, to be her mini-me, but instead, she's long and gangly like her dad with the same signature eyes and family nose. *And flat as a goddamn board.*

She wonders what her mother looked like at her age. Last year on a rainy day, before her mother was pregnant, Kit scoured the house looking for old family photos but couldn't find a single one. Nothing from before Blair's marriage to her father. Kit had thought that was weird, but her mother waved it off, claiming they were too poor to own a camera.

"Can you tell me any stories? What was your childhood like? What about siblings? Do I have any aunts and uncles?" Kit had cornered her in the kitchen once.

"I don't know, sweetheart. It was a long time ago."

"What about your parents? Can you tell me about my grandmother and grandfather? Where did you grow up? Did you have lots of friends?"

"Huh?" Blair had stopped emptying the dishwasher and looked at her inquisitive child. "What are you babbling on about, Kit?"

She'd felt the sharp sting of her mother's words. "Nothing...I...I just wanted to know what you were like when you were my age, that's all." Kit slumped out of the room, mumbling accusations. "It's weird you don't remember anything. It's like you're a Martian or something."

Avoiding the mirrors in her ensuite bathroom, Kit dries her face and then searches her closet to find a waterproof jacket and her piggy bank. This will take a lot of convincing and all her cash. She figures she only has a few hours. Her mother will be busy secretly drinking for a while. Kit caught her the first time a few months back when she saw Blair bent under the kitchen sink. Kit recognized the bottle from their wine cellar. She silently watched as her mother poured the yellow liquid into her favorite travel tumbler and stashed the bottle in a grocery bag beside the cleaning supplies.

Kit had never seen her mother drink while pregnant before. She did some research and discovered some European women drink during pregnancy. There were even hospitals that once dispensed Guinness in their maternity wards. Kids her age are allowed to drink in Europe too. *So, it can't be that bad. Right?*

She doesn't let her mind wander for long. Right now, Kit has bigger phish to fry and firewalls to extinguish.

CHAPTER 18

CASS

AFTER UNTANGLING OURSELVES FROM the damp bedsheets, Sean hops in the shower before heading back to work. Again. I try to protest.

"Working on our first Saturday in our new home? Aren't you allowed a break?"

His excuse? Some high-profile case...grinding them around the clock...could propel him into democratic legitimacy. Blah, blah, blah. This explains all the late nights he's been putting in.

I don't mind too much. I have work to do, too. Secrets to uncover. With Sean away this gloomy afternoon, I plan on getting high and reading. That journal must've belonged to the woman who lived here before. Jessa. What would push a mother to murder her whole family? The answer must be in there.

But first, coffee. I still have a pile of boxes left to unpack. After a few minutes and a quick toke, I have a perfect cup of java brewed at precisely 170 degrees. Wet earth and nuts trail the air as I unpack in silence.

DING! DONG!

What the eff? I've only been here two days and already had more visitors than the past two years. Wearing sweatpants and a stained tank top, I open the door, barefoot and braless—again. My nipples perk. Rain's coming. It hangs in the air like wet leaves.

"*Ciao!*"

Luna air-kisses my cheeks three times. She waves a flat iron in one hand and tugs a rolling suitcase with the other. Her cream-colored workout set puts my recycled outfit to shame. She oozes sex no matter what she wears. "Hi, there!" she purrs.

"Helloooooo?" I utter, completely starstruck. I rack my brain, wondering if we had made plans. After having too much punch and barely anything to eat last night, my memory is fuzzy. I'm fairly certain I didn't even speak to Luna directly except to order some body oil. But here she is—*The* Luna, No Last Name Needed—with luggage like we planned a sleepover. "Luna! Wow! So nice of you to—"

She pushes past me and rolls into the kitchen.

I smooth my hair and cross my arms over my chest, feeling slightly put out by the unannounced visit.

"Good morning! Cass, is it? Not Sandra." She winks at me. "Ah! Smells delicious."

I cringe, remembering my awkward introduction. I'm never going to live that down. "Er... thank you, Luna. Why don't you come in?" I try to hold back the sarcasm as I shut the door behind me. I want to try, for Sean's sake, to make friends. "Would you like a cup?"

"Sure. Why not? I could use the extra kick." She sits at the counter and unwraps a pink silk scarf from her neck, revealing a lotus flower pattern. The air is fragrant with coconut oil and fresh lemons.

I grab another mug, cream and sugar, and arrange everything on the kitchen island between us. "So. What can I help you with?" *Let's get to the point so I can return to solving a murder mystery.*

"My love, it is not what *you* can do for me, but what *I* can do for you!" She laughs deep and velvety. Hints of Eastern Europe trickle through.

"For me?" My eyebrows arch with curiosity. I finally relax and offer a smile.

"Yes," she begins, clearing her throat. "Now, please, don't take this personally..." Her voice trails off. Either she's trying not to offend or searching for the right words.

"No worries," I reassure her. "Speak freely. You can be open and honest. This is a safe space," I add. *Maybe she's about to tell me something deeply personal. Perhaps she's leaving her husband.*

That would explain the suitcase. Why did she come to me? My mind races with possibilities. What the heck is about to come out of this gorgeous creature's mouth? I mentally brace myself with a swig of caffeine.

"Okay. I think you could use—how do you say—a makeover."

I choke. Coffee shoots through my nasal cavity and into my lungs, burning. My face blazes. That horrible, lurking childhood feeling resurfaces. I make whiny wheezing sounds as I struggle to breathe.

"*Au bre*! Look what I've done!" Luna hands me some paper towels and gets me water. "Are you okay? I'm so sorry. I didn't mean..."

"No, no." I gasp. "It's fine. Wrong pipe!" Out of nowhere, I receive a few surprisingly firm whacks on the back. They sort of help. "Wow! Uh, thanks. This is, um, so kind of you." I look down at her luggage. It looks as though she packed for a weekend getaway at the Golden Globes. *Is she starting a Miss Orchid Hill pageant or something? This can't all be for me.* "Is this all for me?"

"Sure. Sure. Just a few pieces to compliment your skin tone and that fabulous ass you have! I thought you might want a look."

My skin flushes from the compliments. "What's this?" I pull out a robotic skull.

Luna scoffs. "You've never seen an infrared face mask? It reduces inflammation. That is what makes your face so..." She reaches for the word as she twirls her pointed finger around my nose, "poufy!"

I laugh off Luna's comments, but inside, I want to crawl away into the hole where my weed and the journal are hiding.

"Okay. First things first—hair and makeup." In less time than it takes me to roll a joint, Luna has set up a beauty parlor in my bathroom. She places me in front of the wall of mirrors in a chair she stole from my dining room so I can "watch and learn." It takes over an hour to get my curls flat and shiny. Afterward, Luna shows me how to do a perfect cat eye. We skip the fake lashes. "Keep it simple. You already have so much beauty," Luna says. I feel myself warming to her. "We are not trying to hide. Just accentuate." She swipes my cheeks with a brush so soft it must be made of kittens. "Perfect. *Bravo!*" She holds my shoulders back and smiles through the mirror as she watches me fall in love with myself. I admit, she's amazing. "Now, let's do your wardrobe." She spins around and starts flinging garments out of her carry-on and all over the tile floor. Designer dresses float like falling foliage. "There's a welcome party next week. In your honor."

"Who me?" I remember Sean mentioning a barbecue, but I didn't know *we* were the guests of honor.

"Yes, you." She rummages through handfuls of brightly colored fabrics. Satin. Chiffon. Velvet. Organza. I'm surprised by the variety and varying sizes. Luna speaks into the suitcase while squatting on my bathroom tile, "We welcome all new neighbors with a party in the park." She digs deep, looking for something specific. "So, we must find something special for you to wear. Aha!" She hands me a cobalt blue dress made of ace bandages. "Now, this will accentuate that itty-bitty waist of yours."

"What's that?" I look in horror at the garment that's supposed to be a dress. There are so many holes; I'm unsure where my head should go. "There's no way I'll be able to fit my ass into this."

"It stretches," Luna says deadpan.

It's hard to tell if she's sarcastic, joking, or refreshingly honest. The latter is the one I'm leaning toward. Even though she came over (uninvited and critically insulting), there's something warm and genuine that keeps me from telling her off and kicking her opinionated perfect ass out of my house.

That, and she *is* a celebrity. Her mere presence gives me goosebumps.

"Here." She throws me a beige leotard and shakes her head when I look perplexed. "It's an undergarment. To help you..." She makes a sucking sound and squeezes her hands like she's wringing a chicken.

"I see," I say, but I really don't. Luna is mad if she thinks I can fit into this bundle of spandex. I doubt I can get this past my thighs. Didn't she mention my fat ass earlier? "Well, I'll try...for you, Luna." Unable to stop my face from blushing, I step into the walk-in closet for privacy.

Luna, who's been working nonstop since she arrived, collapses onto the chair she dragged upstairs.

It takes a while to figure out how everything goes on, but I manage.

She fills the awkward silence with her silky voice. "Cass...such a beautiful name."

"Thank you," I call out from the closet, half-listening, half-entangled.

"Do you know the story? Of the Greek goddess Cassandra?"

"Huh?" I suck at multitasking.

"Cassandra was a princess of Troy, a Trojan priestess of Apollo. Extremely beautiful and wanted by many men, including Apollo himself. He fell in love with her beauty and promised to grant her the gift of prophecy, but—he wanted something in return, of course."

"What's that?" I huff, heaving myself into a rubber sock.

"What all men want," tuts Luna. "But Cassandra, the slippery minx, decided she could have her cake and eat it too. She thought she could outsmart Apollo and agreed to his proposal. When Apollo bestowed her the gift of prophecy, he expected Cassandra to give her whole self in return, but all Cassandra gave him was a peck on the lips."

I manage to tug on the control undergarment and squeeze into the dress. With one hand behind my back, I inch up the zipper. "So, what did Apollo do?"

"What all men do," Luna says flatly. "He threw a fit and cursed her. Sure, she had the gift of prophecy, but no one ever believed a single word she uttered again. She was doomed, frustrated beyond despair. Imagine trying to warn your loved ones, and they dismiss you like dirt. That's what happens when you betray a man. You become dirt."

"Do you mind helping me with this zipper?" I walk into the bathroom to show Luna her creation. "How's this?" I can barely breathe, but damn, I look hot! Like, really hot. Sean will flip.

"*Au bre*!" Luna jumps up and dances around me, chirping and preening like my fairy godmother. "Stunning. Absolutely stunning!" She admires me from every angle. "You *must* wear this to the party next weekend. Now the shoes. What size are you?"

"Isn't this a little too much for a neighborhood barbeque?" I panic at the thought of a strange crowd staring at me, every curve on display.

"Darling." Luna stops dead and looks at me dramatically. "This is the Gardens of Orchid Hill. You can never be overdressed. Here, try these on." She tosses a pair of strappy sandals at me and insists I wear them too.

I hold the shoes out in front of me. "These are way too high. I'll never be able to walk in them."

"Practice."

Even with the makeup, my face flushes hot. Luna laughs it off and starts to collect her things. Garments and makeup are sprawled out in every direction. She unplugs the flat iron, wraps the cord, and hands it to me like she's passing down a family heirloom.

"Keep this. You need it more than I do." She bends into her bag and pulls out a nondescript bottle of clear liquor. "Now, let's drink!"

"What's that?"

"*Rakija*—the good stuff from my village."

We go downstairs and drink the fruit brandy out of tiny teardrop-shaped glasses Luna stashed in her purse. She shows me how to take little sips while we sit outside by the pool. The air cools in the clouded sky. She tells me all about her home country, once known as Yugoslavia, now Serbia. She experienced war first-hand as a child. Her parents were ecstatic when she was discovered and sent to America to sing. They prayed she would be safe.

As we drink, Luna explains how a child living alone in Los Angeles survives. How fast she had to mature while being forced into the role of money-maker rather than enjoying her youth. A sweet morsel Hollywood swallowed whole as if she were an amuse-bouche. One moment, she was selling out stadiums; the next, she was a meme. A warning tale to the next batch of bright-eyed, bushy-tailed girls.

We exchange stories easily until I mention Jessa. The atmosphere changes quickly. Luna's eyes darken with the sky. She breaks eye contact. Plump lips tremble on her frozen face. "We don't speak of her anymore."

"Why not?" I probe, not to be insensitive, but I need to know what happened in my home.

"We just don't!" Luna snaps at me, standing abruptly. She grabs the tiny glass from my hand, dumps the rest of my *rakija*, and starts back inside.

"Luna..." I go after her, almost tripping in her awkward heels. "I'm...I'm so sorry..."

She stops, her brown eyes wild with such pain and anger I don't know if she's going to cry out or slap me. With her free hand, she snatches my arm. "If you know what's good for you, you won't mention her ever again." Her head turns towards the threatening sky. "I would get inside if I were you. The rain will ruin your hair and all my beautiful work with it."

Luna grabs her things and departs as abruptly as she came, leaving four angry fingerprints on my wrist and more questions unanswered.

CHAPTER 19

AMARA

THE MORNING SKY SAGS with dark clouds. Amara's favorite kind of weather. She used to love running on days like this. She ran five miles every morning up until her wedding day. Poor Levi, such a worrywart, constantly wary of the dangers lurking after his young, majestic wife. Anyone could snatch her right up. She could twist an ankle. Lose cellphone service. Break a nail. The dangers in Orange County are endless.

When she first arrived at the heavily gated Gardens of Orchid Hill, Amara assumed (incorrectly, of course) she'd be allowed to resume jogging, safe behind the gilded gates. She used to sneak out before sunrise to get in a quick run until her husband found out. But Levi refused to budge on the issue. Amara's number one priority is getting pregnant, and as far as Dr. Sully is concerned, the only way that'll happen is if she lives in a bubble.

Or he chains me to the ceiling.

There are so many things she loved to do—marathons, martial arts, sky diving. Amara, an absolute adrenalin junkie, joined the army to jump out of helicopters, for fuck's sake. Now, her only excitement is driving herself to the fertility clinic. She doesn't miss those things much. Perhaps she never liked them in the first place. Sometimes it feels like she's stuck in someone else's routine, living someone else's life.

Instead of going out jogging on this gloriously gloomy Saturday, Amara spends her time kneeling in front of the toilet, heaving heavily. Chunks of salad and this morning's espresso spew out of her mouth, stream out of her nose. Her long blonde hair sits twisted into a tight bun. Loose strands stick to her face.

Levi's out for an afternoon on the green, getting schooled by Mrs. Huang. Amara retches as each wave passes. The empty house echoes, reverberating sickness like a sound bath. If she weren't pregnant, she would think she's hungover. Maybe she is hungover. Or perhaps this is one of those super realistic dreams.

This can't be happening. What will Daniel say?

It's hard to think. Her brain throbs. She's been having trouble recalling things. Old army friends, the ones able to track her down, tell her she's been acting different, strange, more subdued. Someone even asked if she was taking anything.

"What? Like drugs?"

"No, like Lithium."

Amara does feel different. Aside from this momentary fit of nausea, she feels *better* somehow, less stressed, less worried. Lighter. Ever since she began therapy with Dr. Novak, she's been laser-focused on one thing: getting pregnant.

Now that she's finally...

Amara gags again, leaning deeper into the toilet. When nothing else is left, she sits back against the cool tiles, wrapping her arms around her belly. She feels a deep need to protect this information from her husband, something mysterious and maternal.

She wanted to tell Levi the news once she listened to the voicemail a few nights ago after dinner. She wanted her husband to share in her joy, her triumph, but somewhere deep down, an overprotective feral voice begged her not to mention anything to Levi or Blair or anyone else quite yet.

So, when Levi asked about the test results, Amara said it was negative. Her cellphone was on Do Not Disturb when the nurse called with the elevated HCG level. The voicemail is still saved on her phone. She listened to it repeatedly, attempting to make it feel real.

After puking her guts out all morning, she has no doubts left—it's real. Instantly regretting that dirty martini and the spiked punch at Blair's, *And this morning's coffee,* she fights another wave of nausea.

For the first time in—months? years?—Amara thinks of her mother. She misses her and wishes she would swoop in with ginger

144

tea and a damp facecloth. Instead, Amara's only consolation is a cold shower. She drags her limp body over to the wet room and turns it on tepid. She removes her wrinkled pajamas as she crawls across the floor and sits under the cool water, hands covering her chord-marked belly.

CURLED UP IN A fresh bathrobe on her bed, Amara calls her mother. "Hi, Mum!" She smiles into the phone with cautious enthusiasm.

"Amara! It's so nice to hear from you. How are you, dear?"

"I'm...good. I was just thinking about you." Amara pulls her fleece robe around her and tightens the sash.

"Were you now?"

Amara can hear her mother lighting a cigarette.

"How are things? How's Connecticut?"

"Good, good."

"And Michael Edward?" Amara's mother remarried two years after Amara's father passed away. It's a topic of discontent in their relationship. Nothing personal against the new guy. He's a man-sized teddy bear. The total opposite of Amara's father—warm, cuddly, and truly in love with her mother. It's just that no one will ever come close to replacing her father—she's a Daddy's girl through and through. Amara and her mother are slowly working through it by not mentioning it or speaking about it. Ever.

"Oh, he's good." Amara can hear her take a deep drag off her cigarette, triggering a fit of wheezing coughs.

"Good." Amara waits for her mother's sputtering to calm down. Unfortunately, over time, their lack of communication leaves them with little to talk about other than the usual banter and, of course, the weather.

"So, how's the weather in California?"

"Sunny, as usual." Amara looks out the window at the beautiful, threatening sky. If they're lucky, it'll rain. A double-edged sword in California this time of year, if it rains too much now, the grass will grow green and tall, perfect kindling for late summer wildfires. No rain means drought and extra dry brush. The tiniest spark will blaze uncontrollably.

"That's nice, dear. Lovely to hear. Oh, listen to this—I have some news for you!"

Amara cringes at the over-excitement in her mother's voice. She sounds like she's just won a lifetime supply of Dunhill cigarettes.

She sounds manic.

"What's that, Mum?"

Whenever her mother has big news, it usually turns out to be some sort of dig or backhanded compliment. First, it was Amara's decision to apply to the military academy. Then, it was her choice of men, specifically her fast decision to marry a much older man, and (this is where Amara's mother usually breaks down and sobs) move all the way across the country, leaving her alone and grand-childless.

"Remember your best friend from Sacred Heart? Briella?"

"Yes, Mum. Of course, I remember Briella."

Briella Fiore. Amara hasn't thought of her in ages. How could she forget her former partner in crime? Briella was the only person Amara knew who could party every night and still get straight A's. She was on the Dean's List. Every year. In Yale. Amara's awe had dissolved into jealousy, souring their friendship forever. Amara wanted to be happy for Briella, but at that time in her life, her immature ego couldn't get past Briella's privilege and luck. Like how Briella could go weeks without shampooing and never had to wear makeup. And how her dad was still alive and paid for everything. Amara had always felt that if her father were still living, she would've been the one with more friends, fewer pimples, and a line of boyfriends. She could've been the valedictorian with concert tickets to hand out with an unlimited future eagerly awaiting.

Amara had only been able to handle competing against Briella for a year before she'd decided to follow in her father's footsteps and switch to West Point. She needed to feel closer to him, and far-ther away from bad influences like Briella and Two-Dollar Tues-days. She couldn't wait for the "Stone Cold Sober" principles and homogenized cadet uniforms. She didn't care that she was starting over or committing twelve years of her life to push-ups and barked commands, to no makeup and unflattering clothes. At the time, Amara didn't care about any of those things. She was joining the mother fucking army. And she was psyched!

She wasn't as psyched when she had been discharged abruptly halfway through her service, luckily, with her Economics degree still intact. For a moment, the memory sends her stomach a distress signal, and just as fast, it's gone, replaced with nothing. Her mind goes blank. She's unable to recall details. Her mother's voice calls her back to the present.

Amara's mother thinks she and Briella are still besties even though neither went to each other's college graduation parties, let alone weddings. Best friends through four years of high school and one year of college, then done, like a short-term government contract.

"Guess what?" Her mother loves to keep her guessing.

"What, Mother?" Amara begins to wish she never picked up the phone.

"Well, I just heard from Sandy's mom, who just had her hair done with Briella's mom in the city, and she said Briella and Marshall are expecting their first baby together! Isn't that just wonderful?"

"Wow, Mum, that's…great." Amara places a hand over her belly. "Thanks for letting me know. I'll have to send them a gift. Listen, I've got to go. The pool guy is coming, and I must get ready."

"Hey, when are *you* guys going to—"

"Goodbye, Mother!" She hangs up, her mother still asking the question Amara's desperately avoiding.

CHAPTER 20

KIT

KIT PEDALS HER BEACH cruiser west to find her brothers at Bommer Canyon. She follows the bike trails, avoiding main roads. Her face puffs red as she chugs up the steeper hills, her plain white tee damp under her arms. Kit detests deodorant. She read it causes dementia, and she hates the smell. Beads of sweat build on her upper lip. She second-guesses her outfit. Skinny jeans, overkill. The rain slicker tied around her waist, unnecessary. She pedals faster, trying to obliterate her thoughts. She can't think about last Friday without cringing.

Amber's mom was out of town. Again. Naomi's known to jet off on impromptu adventures with eclectic people, leaving Amber home alone. Of course, Mr. Peaty is a phone call away. At sixteen, Naomi conquered LA, making a name for herself. If she survived, surely Amber could too. Naomi uses her Bohemian upbringing to justify everything, not that anyone would dare challenge her.

It was another typical night of no adult supervision, nothing unusual, just the normal amount of drinking and smoking. Spin the Bottle. Truth or Dare? Kit didn't even want to go, especially after the *Yo Mamma* incident, but Francesca had begged her. Things had gotten interesting fast. At first, Amber acted extra sweet, like nothing but good vibes, full of smiles and compliments. Kit relished the attention, relieved to be on Amber's good side for a change, back in her good graces. When Amber smiles at you, the whole world smiles too. But when she stops smiling…

Kit had basked in Amber's glow that night. Amber's glittering eyes and rushed words made Kit wonder if the It Girl was on something. It wouldn't have been the first time. Amber's always the first one to try new things. She never shied away from a dare or shot of whatever. So, when the bottle Amber spun had landed on Kit, she promptly strutted over and gave Kit a big wet kiss, pushing her tongue inside her former best friend's mouth and twirling it around while everyone whooped and hollered.

Kit wasn't sure how to react. She'd never been kissed before. She and Amber practiced sometimes, but they had never used tongues. She didn't know what to do. Or what it meant. She was left with her eyes closed, lips parted. *And wanting more?* A terrifying thought. When Kit opened her eyes, she saw Amber staring at her, a slight smirk on her wobbly face.

"That's gross, Amber!" Kit wiped Amber's spit on the back of her sleeve with exaggerated effort.

"Oh, whatever! Don't pretend you didn't enjoy it!" Amber winked and went to reclaim her throne on the other side of the game room.

So that was that. Kit had kept swigging her wine, pretending to ignore Amber, as Amber sent blow kisses and fluttered her eyelashes at Kit. Everything was hunky-dory until someone dared Kit to give Ethan a blowjob.

At first, Kit had been like, 'Ew no,' but the more Amber glared at her with those menacing eyes, the more Kit realized what she had to prove. She grabbed the wine bottle off the table and chugged. The sweet, tart alcohol had funneled down smoothly. Her eyes closed as the buzz took effect. She waited for the relaxed, bold feeling. All eyes on her, she could feel them, their irises flickering, frolicking over her feverishly. Eager with greed. Hey, they were all friends, right? Just a silly game. No one would get hurt.

"Not like you've never done it before," someone sneered in a friendly way—or was it sinister?

Kit knows more than everyone thinks. She understands people. Adults, friends, even teachers—they all want something from you. Want you to act a certain way. 'Be a good girl.' 'Be amendable.' 'Play nice.' 'Give me a hug.' 'Come sit on my lap.'

It all blurs together.

When Kit opened her eyes, poor Ethan, with his crooked nose and jet-black hair, looked conflicted with nerves and shameful excitement. Ethan, a shy, brainy kid who hates the spotlight, secretly really, really, really wanted a blowjob. I mean, what fourteen-year-old boy wouldn't? A tagalong, he usually wasn't even invited to those things. It was Ethan's lucky day.

Kit couldn't wait to get it over with. To prove Amber wrong. To prove she was capable. She could do anything.

"Just get it out of the way and practice now, or you'll never have a boyfriend," Amber crooned. "You can use my room." She got up from her post at the head of the table and dragged Ethan and Kit by their clammy hands up the stairs and into her bedroom. It looked like Barbie's Dream House had exploded. Everywhere you turned, something was painted pink or covered in rhinestones. Amber led them to her queen-sized bed and pushed them into a seated position. "There you go! Don't come down until you, um, finish." She laughed and shut the door.

Ethan wasted no time pulling down his pants and underwear. He quickly sat on Amber's fuchsia duvet and covered himself with his hand.

Kit could almost hear his heart racing. She noticed sweat gathering around his ears. She'd quickly realized she needed to take control. This would make her cool again. This would give her street cred. This would convince Amber.

She peeled Ethan's warm hand away from his privates and peeked at his floppy pecker. It wasn't what she envisioned. It looked like a mushroom someone stepped on or a flesh-colored snowman. Kit used her hand to prop up Ethan's thingy. When he gasped at her touch, she recoiled.

"Did I hurt you?"

"No, it's...your hands are cold."

"Oh, sorry." Kit huffed on her hands and rubbed them together. She slid off the bed and onto the floor, checking to ensure the door was closed. All was quiet and still, except for the white noise from Amber's computer humming in the corner. Kit cupped Ethan in her warmed hands and bent her face into his lap. He smelled a little like pee and Buster after a long day. When her mouth found his bare flesh, she could feel his torso go rigid. She twirled her tongue the way Amber did when they kissed. Nothing happened. She heard his heavy breathing, a begging whimper, but nothing changed down there. Wasn't something supposed to happen? Was she doing it right? Would he go and tell everyone she sucked at sucking dick and is probably a big fat lesbo? "Um, is everything okay?" She rocked back on her heels, fishing a hair out of her mouth.

"Uh, yeah." Ethan squirmed. "I think...I think I just need a little..." He grabbed a pillow and covered himself. "Actually, do you...do you think we could just...forget it and tell everyone that we um...did it?" Ethan's shoulders curled into his chest. He couldn't meet Kit's eyes.

"Um, yeah. Sure." Relief flooded her.

Ethan's shoulders relaxed. "Thanks," he said, standing to pull up his pants.

And just like that, it was over. Kit and Ethan rejoined the group as special guests and received cheers and high-fives. All was right in the teenage kingdom again.

Until the text messages had started. How was Kit to know Amber had secretly videotaped the entire encounter? That she had her webcam pointed directly at her bed. That she'd been extra nice to Kit in order to lull her into a false sense of security and get her drunk. Rookie mistake. It wasn't until she'd received pictures and a text message from Amber blackmailing her that she finally understood the magnitude of the situation.

The still shots make everything look worse than what actually happened. Kit had done a bad thing. She isn't stupid. She understands whatever leaks on the internet is there for eternity. Background checks for college, jobs, even future love interests will all see what she did and how low she could go. Her entire future dangles by a pubic hair.

I can't believe I was that stupid.

Never should've trusted Amber.

You can't trust anyone.

She wonders if Francesca had known, but she quickly pushes the thought away. If Francesca sides with Amber, Kit will be alone, friendless, in her own pathetic computer club for one. A lame-o. A loser.

Unlike her stupid brothers—the Princes of Popularity. They're her only way out of this mess. Kit needs their halfwit help for the first time ever, well, mostly Seth's. It turns out, Amber has a massive crush on Kit's older brother. If Kit can convince Seth to take Amber to his prom, Amber promises to delete the nasty video. If Seth refuses, Kit will bribe him with all her money. $412.82. If he won't, she's sure Brody will. But he'll expect more than cash. She'll owe him. And it will be big, bigger than the time he made her his personal assistant and had her lug all his hockey equipment for an entire season. Kit remembers the stench vividly, as well as his fury over her finding those bodybuilder magazines stashed in the inside zipper pocket of his hockey bag.

Let's hope it won't come to that.

Halfway through the canyon, she spots them, her three brothers, huddled around the entrance of the old water tower.

The popular trail once belonged to a cattle farmer. Remnants of the old farm lie rotting and rusty. A sad, wheelless tractor sits alone in an empty field. Old wire fencing clings to pioneer posts, sectioning off the dirt trails, acting as guides for hikers and bikes.

She sees Brody crushing his Laker's hat with both hands, a nervous habit. Seth crouches down and looks at something on the ground. He has a stick in one hand. The other hand rests on his bent knee. And Buster...

Is Buster crying?

The stench of vomit blooms as she pedals closer. A puddle of mushed cereal and stomach juices dampen the earth. Kit screeches to a stop, sending a cloud of dust over her brothers.

"Hey! Watch it."

"You'll destroy the evidence."

"I want Mommy!"

"Evidence?" Kit dismounts her bike and flips the kickstand down in one smooth motion. "What're you guys talking about?"

Seth uses his stick to drag items out of a purple leather purse.

"There's something dead in there," Seth and Brody say in unison. They point to the decomposing door of the rusty water silo. Smaller than your typical water tower and not high off the ground, it's about the size of an old Volkswagen bug. The ladder isn't much taller than Seth.

"Dead?" Kit gasps.

"I want to go home!" Buster's whimpering explodes into full-blown wails. Kit has never seen her baby brother this distraught. He's never feared anything—blackouts, lightning, scary movies. He fearlessly catches and releases spiders with his bare hands. Buster's the courageous one. Daddy's favorite.

"What's that smell?" Kit already suspects the answer, staring at the puddle of regurgitated cereal.

"He puked." Seth nudges his chin towards Brody.

"Yeah! After I saw what was in that thing!"

"What?" Kit can smell it before she finishes her sentence. Under the sweet and sour smell of vomit, another deeper, heftier smell lurks, foul like the core of death itself. Worse than the time the Huangs redid their septic system or the time her class went to the water recycling plant.

Seth manages to empty the purse. A compact mirror, a tube of lip gloss, and a wallet lie in the dirt. He uses his stick to flip open the leather wallet. There's a driver's license tucked into the yellowed plastic sleeve. The picture looks eerily familiar.

"Holy shit!"

"It's Bianca!"

"Our nanny?"

"Oh, fuck!"

The sky darkens. Rain clouds move in. Buster wails.

Chapter 21

BLAIR

Blair wakes up outside, damp and shivering. She had the strangest dream, as vivid as a home movie.

She was dancing with a handsome man, older and charming, wearing a fancy watch and shiny shoes. They spun around the dance floor, panting, song after song. He leaned in. For a kiss? No, to whisper something in her ear. To follow him outside and into the night. Sticky and breathless from dancing, the fresh air would do them good. *Would she like a smoke? Sure! That would be lovely.* She flushed with anticipation as he led her outside and into darkness. The alley reeked of garbage. *So, how 'bout that cigarette?* She pouted and leaned in for a kiss. A black SUV screeched forward. Its back door opened. *Smoking is filthy.* Danger filled the handsome man's voice. He grabbed her by the hair and shoved her inside the van, following behind her. Scared and screaming, she swung her arms wildly and thrashed her legs. A rag covered her nose and mouth. Darkness consumed her. When she could open her eyes, she found herself in a gilded cage. There was a mirror, so she could admire the beautiful silk gown she had on. There was a bed with cashmere linens. There was also an old-fashioned basin for washing, and a bucket for—she didn't want to know. Then, she saw the others, all similarly dressed, their hair in curls and rouge on their faces. A collection of women. A loud clang disturbed the silence. The women whimpered. Footsteps clacked closer, echoing from every direction. When she saw a face flash in the night, she cried too, joining the chorus of fear. Those eyes. She'd recognize those blue eyes anywhere.

Blair jolts awake, no stranger to this nightmare. She's had this dream before, but this is the first time she's seen the person's face. Downing the rest of her wine, she buries the betrayal deep in her garden of secrets and goes inside. From the kitchen, Blair hears the children whispering nervously. She follows their voices to see what's wrong. She hears them arguing about if they should tell her.

"Tell me what?" Exasperated, she looks at her children as all four stare at their feet. She's surprised to find the boys back so soon, *and* with Kit, whom she thought was visiting Francesca. Her head pounds. She doesn't have time for this. She fell asleep before she could get anything done. *And that dream.*

"Mommy!" Buster runs and crashes face-first into Blair's legs.

She stoops over to rub his back and smooth his wild hair. "What is it, my sweet boy?"

"We found Bianca's wallet out by the old water tower," says Brody.

"There's a funky smell coming from it, too," says Seth.

"Something's dead inside. We think it may be...her," adds Brody.

"Who? The nanny? I thought you guys scared her off with your last prank. Don't tell me this is another one of your jokes." Blair rolls her eyes at her overdramatic children. *Full of stories, these kids, a bunch of jokesters.* She isn't falling for it this time.

Seth and Brody share guilty looks.

Seth pulls out the worn leather wallet he carefully wrapped in old algebra homework he'd found stuffed in the bottom of his backpack.

Blair smiles momentarily at the bright red *A* bleeding from the raindrops. She loves her math wizard. She's proud of all her over-achieving children. They obviously all get that from their father. That superior Novak bloodline. Blair hesitates to pick it up. She doesn't want to touch it. She sets down a paper towel on the counter before she lays out the dirty thing like an ancient artifact.

"Where did you get this?"

"Bommer's!" they wail in unison.

"Mom, we've been trying to tell you," Kit groans.

"We think we may have found...a body. *Her* body," says Brody, looking a little green.

"What?" Blair feels faint.

None of this makes sense. Bianca? Dead? She thought the nanny had returned to Sweden to be with her boyfriend. That's what Daniel had said. Bianca had enough of the troublesome Novak children and Americans in general.

Cold dread fills her swollen belly. *Bianca.* The sweet girl had an elfish laugh, with eyes the size of silver dollars, and a pageboy bob. She looked like an enchanted amphibian. Blair nagged the striking girl to get into modeling. *She had such a unique look.*

Barely twenty-two.

"I'm calling your father."

"Shouldn't we call the police?" Kit asks.

Brody and Seth exchange looks.

"Listen to Mom," Seth tells his sister as he removes his cell from his back pocket.

Blair looks at her children's frightened faces. Bianca's cherubic face flashes before her eyes. For a second, she doesn't know what to do. Suddenly, it all returns to her like muscle memory.

I am an obedient wife.

I have chosen this life.

"Give me your phone! I'm calling your father."

CHAPTER 22

JESSA

Friday, May 12, 2017

I finally met some of our neighbors at TGOOH (or The Gardens for short). Blair Novak and Amara Sullivan appeared on my doorstep dressed in this year's spring collection. I tried not to be intimidated, still in my ratty bathrobe worn so thin you can see through it. Blair told me she and her husband have lived here for over twenty years. She has five children—God bless her—but you'd never know it looking at her in that skin-tight Pucci. Not one sleepless wrinkle or hair out of place. Amara mentioned her husband is a plastic surgeon. I bet he does all the women around here. Maybe I should look into it? The thought of going under the knife frightens me, but how fun would it be to get some lipo here, a nip tuck there? Voilà—ready for bikini season! The pool in my backyard mocks me this very moment.

Note to self: get a swim in now and then.

On clear days, you can see the Pacific if you hike to the top of Orchid Hill. That's what Amara said. She loves being outdoors and invited me to go hiking with her sometime. I said I'd see. She sneaks out in the morning before her husband gets up for work.

I doubt I could keep up with her and those legs! She must be over six feet tall, very shiny and blonde and bubbly. Like me before kids. I don't hate her. Who could dislike that sweet smile and kind face? Sweet now, but wait until she has some kids of her own. They suck the chipper right out of you.

Blair doesn't look much older than I am. And with so many children? She must've had an early start. She seems like the Queen Bee around here. I bet she has a wicked streak. You know what they say about tiny redheads—they're fiery. I caught a glint of humor when she gifted me a basket of the most beautiful macarons I've ever seen. She made them HERSELF! Seriously, she must be Wonder Woman or Martha freaking Stewart in disguise.

We've been officially invited to the block party, all in our honor! The girls can hopefully make some friends. Blair mentioned she organized an array of activities for the children. And I'll get to meet "the tribe." It seems the women here unite in helping each other. It's like some suburban utopia. I'm excited to go—warts and all.

SATURDAY, MAY 13, 2017

I've never been anywhere so bright and sunny and clean! We live on the most immaculate street with houses dripping with flowers and perfect green lawns. Incredible, considering this area was once a desert region. Our backyard in Bitter Springs was just a bunch of rocks and cacti. Surprisingly, our water bill barely surpasses our old one. Michael says it's the Smart water recycling system. He keeps reassuring me we no longer have to worry about the bills. It's hard for me, especially after all we've been through.

Blair and I have bonded, mother to mother. She lives at the end of the cul-de-sac and is married to the psychologist, the one Michael keeps hounding me about. Apparently, he helps all the women in the neighborhood free of charge. Not sure how a busy doctor can afford the time. I had enough trouble scheduling appointments with my last therapist once a week, and she doesn't have half the accreditations of Dr. Novak.

Michael thinks I haven't been the same since Janey was born. I keep telling him it's the hormones. I promise him I'll be back to normal soon, like with Rayne. It just takes time.

I don't know why he's so impatient. It's not like he's ever home. He's out all the time. We both thought the new job at ELITE would be easier—more money, less stress. But it's not. The hours alone are enough to make anyone mental. Enough to make you want to jump off the Navajo Bridge. We barely see each other anymore. "Ships in the night," Ma would say.

Worst of all, he's stopped confiding in me. He won't even tell me what he's working on, let alone what's on his mind. I didn't know corporate marketing could be so secretive. Whatever it is, it's big. "World-changing," he hinted.

But even with all the late nights, Michael seems happy. He's genuinely excited about something. Stressed, but excited. I haven't seen him like this since I got pregnant with Rayne. I'm just happy he's smiling again.

Must be nice to have a purpose and a life outside these four walls. To be called something other than "mum" or "honey." I miss working. Everyone forgets I used to have a job too—a whole career—before Michael, before the girls. Now I'm defined by the band on my finger and what I grow in my womb. These legs once walked the runways of Paris and Milan. Heck, they even had their own insurance. Now I can grab loose skin on my knees like flesh handles. Oh, dear Lord.

Anyway, this place seems lovely. I'm almost done unpacking. Blair's daughter is coming over later today to watch the girls, so I can go to her home and have a Girls' Night with some of the ladies from the neighborhood.

Looking forward to a night out and some fun!

SUNDAY, MAY 14, 2017

Oh my Lord! I got to meet Luna! THE Luna! She was my favorite singer back in the day, and then she just disappeared after that horrible accident. Dropped off the face of the earth. One minute, she was all over the news, headlines of scandal and criticism. The next thing we knew, she killed a kid and disappeared. POOF. I honestly thought she got plastic surgery and changed her name. Made a new life for herself.

Well, she definitely had something done. I've found out Amara's husband, Dr. Sully, does all the "touch-ups" for the wives of TGOOH and most of Orange County, but he does it on the down low. I also heard someone mention he once had a reality show called The Butterfly or something like that, where he transformed "ugly ducklings" into queens. It's sad to think women dislike themselves so much they'd rather be completely different people. I mean, I wouldn't mind a little nip-tuck myself, but to not even recognize yourself in the mirror—now I don't know if I could live with that.

Not to say that's what Luna did. She looks...youthful. She's still gorgeous, don't get me wrong. She's one of the most stunning women I've ever seen. It's just that...

She looks like she's clinging. It's the lips. Her lips! There, I said it! She looks like she gets daily injections from white-tailed hornets. But once you get past that, you discover this wonderful, strong personality. She's enticing and fearsome all at once. Must be that Balkan blood.

She has a son still in diapers, but you'd never know it. Her breasts are perfect. She came right over to me at Blair's party and introduced herself. She handed me a glass of something fizzy and alcoholic, which I politely declined as I'm still breastfeeding. I usually get a lot of stares, some eye rolls, or at least a few snide comments when people learn I still breastfeed my three-year-old. At Blair's, no one blinked an eye!

Luna generously offered to give me a makeover. At first, I was a little put off. I mean, I just met this woman, and she basically told me I need help. But it was as if she instinctively knew who I was before and wouldn't accept anything less. And she's LUNA! I said sure! Why not? We made plans for tomorrow. She wants to help me find a new look for the block party.

My big debut! she said.

Ugh! I hear Janey crying. Time to milk the cow.

MONDAY, MAY 15, 2017

Luna came over to help me pick an outfit for the cookout this weekend. She brought a rolling suitcase and enough products to open a salon. I had mentioned I still had the girls to care for and no one to watch them, so she brought one of her nannies.

Her nanny reminded me of that annoying saber-toothed squirrel from Ice Age. *(The girls are obsessed with that movie.) The young woman's eyes swallow her whole face. Anyway, she was unusually quiet. I don't think she said one word to me the entire visit. Not even sure she spoke English. Completely awkward. She had an unusual habit of twisting her arms in front of her like she was trying to hide behind them. Very odd. Bianca was her name.*

After Luna introduced me, I pointed Bianca toward the girls' playroom, and she immediately engaged them with a game she'd brought. Luna carried her suitcase up the stairs and right into my bathroom. Then she grabbed a dining room chair and dragged that up too. When I asked if she needed any help, she reminded me she was there to help me. Apparently, she loves exercise. I let her do her thing. She knew her way around easily.

She set up the chair in the middle of the bathroom "to get the best lighting." We started with my face. Luna reminded me of the professional makeup artists I used to work with. Fast. Focused. I completely forgot I was getting my makeup done by a Grammy winner. Just like old times.

We didn't talk about her Hollywood past or quick exit off stage. We talked about our kids mostly and our husbands. Luna's hilarious. The way she talks about her son! Her "little prince." She seems to adore and abhor him all at once. His fat chubby arms. His chunky double chin. The disgusting crumbs she's always finding in his belly button. She especially despises sticky fingers soiling her alabaster living room. I tried explaining how children are notoriously dirty and destroy everything. Anyone with a child under ten should reconsider white furniture. Luna just stared at my reflection in the mirror with a frozen expression. I can never tell if she's mad or if it's the Botox.

It seems her two-year-old hasn't put her off too much. She's expecting twins via surrogate next year. I couldn't help staring enviously at her figure in the mirror. Must be nice.

She worships her husband, Jeff. (Michael's boss, the tech mogul.) Luna mentioned Jeff's racecar team. Apparently, his new hobby consumes all his spare time. She seems proud of him. A little lonely. Maybe that's why she came over. Maybe she needs a friend, too.

Well, she's a keeper in my Friend's Book! I've paid lots of money at salons and never once felt this good! It brings me back to my runway days. Luna put a gentle wave in my flat hair, added cheekbones, and an arched brow. I looked like I stepped out of Marie Claire with a waistline and everything. I can't help but stare at myself in every mirror. I was hiding in there all along.

For the welcome barbecue next weekend, Luna chose a Diane von Furstenberg wrap dress that flatters my postpartum figure. She reminded me I have beautiful breasts and told me to keep the dress. We had such a wonderful time playing dress-up. I recognized all the designer labels. My eyes bulged as I tried to count how much money she casually threw on the floor.

But when she asked about the scars on my back, I froze. As much as I think I know Luna, she's still a stranger I've just met. When I didn't answer, she stood behind me in front of the mirror. I flinched when she put her arms around me. A real hug. I don't remember the last time I hugged anyone besides my girls. She held me close and quietly for what felt like hours. Then, she gently tugged the tie of my new dress open to allow slack in the fabric. The shoulder of the dress slipped down, exposing a series of raised diagonal scars jagging along my spine. They've been a part of me since I was fifteen. A lesson. A reminder.

Looking into Luna's soft eyes, somehow, I knew she understood. The way a lover or a twin just knows. She traced my scars with the tips of her fingers and didn't say a thing. She didn't have to. Like a battle buddy, she already knew. Horrors hide within our lives as women.

"May they all rot in hell," she spat, then added triumphantly, "You are an exquisite enchantress, a warrior of women. Let us toast!"

For a moment, I thought I would unravel right there on the bathroom floor.

It's strange now, looking in the mirror and not seeing a tired old hag looking back at me. Luna worked her magic. And she's a lot funnier than her reputation suggests, even if her eyes never smile. She surprised me with a bottle of hooch when we were done. She set everything up outside on the patio. I swear she's more comfortable in my home than I am.

She called her homemade booze rah-kee-yah. It's from her mother country. Apparently, they have various flavors made from different fruits. She brought over quince flavor and two tiny glasses resembling dollhouse vases. She poured clear liquid to the top of each tiny glass and handed me one. She taught me how to say "cheers" in Serbian: jee-vah-lee.

At first, I wasn't going to drink because of the breastfeeding. But when Luna saw how big Janey was (she'll be four next month), she said it was time to take my tits back. Reclaim my body for myself. And for my husband. So, I'm trying something different and opening myself up to new experiences. Luna stayed for another hour and had Bianca (such a doll) fix us all something to eat.

I'm amazed at how easy it was to confide in Luna. Like I've known her for years. She reminds me of my best friend from high school, Becca. A beautiful soul.

And, wow, that little drink packs a punch! It reminds me of the Moonshine we made back at the farm. I feel bad having to pump and waste so much milk. But Luna said pump-and-dump is a go-to for all mothers, and I should never be ashamed or worried about having to do anything for myself—if my husband is okay with it, she added.

By the time Michael came home, life returned to normal, and my buzz faded away. He even commented on how refreshed and youthful I looked. That night, I didn't hear one fat joke.

SATURDAY, MAY 20, 2017

Saturday was an unforgettable day. Our new neighbors threw us a party down at the neighborhood park. The girls had a blast! They were over the moon, having their very own slice of green heaven right across the street. And what a beautiful space! Taking up two whole acres, it had everything a kid could want: rock-climbing, graffiti wall, community garden, chess tables, amphitheater, clubhouse, water fountains, and a state-of-the-art surround sound system. You name it, they got it. In addition to all that, Blair organized sack racing, bobbing for apples, and a piñata. The kids didn't know where to start.

This was not the typical barbecue we're used to. For starters, none of the neighbors actually cooked. I expected to see husbands crowding around grills, beers in one hand, spatulas in the other. Funny, ridiculous aprons with bad dad jokes on them. Instead, they were gathered in one large group debating global warming. The wives bustled between the men and their children. Nannies hovered on standby, ready to jump in and serve.

There were no silly aprons to be had. The women sparkled head to toe in exquisite spring garden attire. Seriously, if they'd worn hats, it could've been the Queen's annual garden party. The men sported shiny watches and the latest leisurewear.

Everyone loved my outfit! The women swarmed me with compliments. They're all so sweet and kind. I felt like a bride on her wedding day. All thanks to Luna.

Note to self: send Luna a thank you card.

The food was catered by local gourmet restaurants and stationed around the shaded pavilion. Not a burned hotdog or overcooked burger in sight. Servers dressed in white waited politely to plate and clear. Professional pitmasters manned the barbecue. The smell of charred meat reminded me of home and our Arizona friends. In welcome of coastal California, fresh sushi and shellfish covered a Viking ship carved out of ice so big it lasted all afternoon and still didn't melt. For the adults, a fully stocked bar was set up with top-shelf liquor, and a skinny margarita truck (which quickly be-

came a favorite with the moms) pulled up in front. There was even a chimichanga station, a nod to our home state.

Touches of Blair were everywhere. Vibrant balloons and fresh flowers spilled over everything. She went all out. Only the best. I find her so easy to talk to. She's so tiny. I feel like the Hulk whenever I stand next to her. I doubt she weighs a hundred pounds soaking wet.

Finally met her husband—the famous Dr. Novak. What a charmer! So handsome with those blue eyes. I felt drawn to him the moment I entered the park. Couldn't take my eyes off him really. There's something about him that pulls you in. He exudes confidence. You can tell the men are enraptured by him. They shadow him. Michael was no different. He made a beeline to Blair's husband the moment we arrived, dragging me with him.

I was shocked when Dr. Novak stopped mid-sentence to greet me and introduced me to the group as the famous lingerie model. The men whooped and hollered like I was Gisele. Michael stood by, grinning like a proud farmer showing off his prized cow. I was mortified.

When all the flattery was finished, Dr. Novak pulled me aside. He said he heard about my mood swings and offered his assistance and some pills. If I hadn't been so in awe, I would've kicked my husband for talking about my private life with our new neighbors. But the doctor seems genuinely kind-hearted, not arrogant, and aloof like other psychiatrists I've worked with over the years. I didn't expect him to be so soft-spoken. Someone should mic him!

He seemed very in touch with his surroundings. I watched him have a conversation with Dr. Sully by the monkey bars. They were deep in discussion when Blair's youngest son fell from the top of the jungle gym. Dr. Novak caught him. With one arm! Behind his back! Without even turning his head!

I look forward to his help.

Amara was there too, chipper as ever. I must find out what that girl is taking and see if it's the same thing Dr. Novak gave me. And I need to hang with Luna again. She makes me laugh so hard, like I did a thousand crunches.

Overall, we had a fantastic day at the park with our new friends.

Especially me. Must pump-and-dump. Then lie down. Too many margaritas!

THURSDAY, JUNE 1, 2017

Had my first session with Dr. Novak today. His underground office is nicer than any doctor's office I've seen, and it's conveniently located directly across from the bunker. I assumed it would be dark and dingy as we descended the tunnels, but it's designed beautifully and spacious. I was surprised by the luxurious space. Instead of smelling dank as I'd expected, it smelled of leather and lemons. Mahogany walls showcased various achievements and a collection of war relics.

To access the laboratory, you must go through his office. At the far end, there's a door marked by a plaque with golden letters matching the lettering on his office door: LABORATORY.

Dr. Novak sat behind his desk of ridiculous size, large enough to host the last supper. There was an arrangement of books bookended at one end. I recognized Jung, but the rest were a collection of scientists and philosophers I've never heard of.

Behind him hung an American flag encased in glass. On another wall, a large flat screen doubled as a computer monitor. Pictures of him with the last four presidents took precedence over family vacation photos.

One thing stood out. He had this strange lamp at the corner of his desk. It looked vintage, like the lampshade was made of rotting paper. It looked as if it belonged in the Smithsonian, or the dumpster.

Other than that, I felt relaxed and safe. We mostly talked about my past treatments, what worked for me, and what didn't. Turns out he prescribed me the same pills as Amara! (I snuck a peak in her purse at the BBQ. I know! It's bad. But I had to know. Blame it on the margaritas.) I can't wait to be so happy. If I'm even half as happy as she seems, I'll be good to go.

Dr. Novak showed me the app he's working on. ELITE commissioned him to develop it further and help market it to the public next year. And we get first dibs! It's helped all the women in the neighborhood conquer various issues. He didn't go into detail—obviously, doctor-patient confidentiality and all that—but he did say it could help me and my "baby blues," as he likes to call my episodes.

He gave me homework: Download the app and complete the first lesson. I must list all the things I don't like about myself, then formulate positive affirmations to counteract them. For example, if I feel I lack self-confidence in my day-to-day routine, I could say to myself, "I am a confident and strong woman who can tackle the world."

Dr. Novak said I must produce at least five positive affirmations and record them onto the app. Then, I need to play this list on repeat while I sleep. Hopefully, the messages will stick. He called it 'MindWebbing.' The whole thing sounds a little hokey, but if it works for Blair, Luna, and Amara, who am I to argue?

Monday, June 5, 2017

I had the strangest dream, more like a nightmare. I was getting ready for a party. I took my time, doing my very best to copy Luna's work exactly. It took me hours, and I still couldn't get it right. After years of modeling, you'd think I'd be better at it somehow. Not even in my dreams.

Anyway, by the time we arrived at the shindig, I didn't have a stitch of clothing or a speck of makeup on. I was completely naked. Bare as a newborn.

In this bizarre dream, I looked around, exposed and mortified. I ran to my family, who suddenly evaporated into mist. I had no one. No one would step forward to help me. Instead, I was completely snubbed. I looked towards the wives, my new friends, but they turned their backs and faded into darkness.

Everyone except Luna.

My fellow comrade pushed her way through the gawking crowd and welcomed me with open arms. She wore a pink caftan with flowing sleeves, an angel in pastel. Folding me into her, she was the only one not turned off by my nakedness, adorned me in compliments as she held me. She smelled sweet, like apricots and rakija.

Suddenly, we were alone in a garden bursting with orchids.

"Your beauty is the nectar of Gods," she whispered. "You are a natural wonder."

She stepped back to admire my stark nakedness. I blushed, but I didn't hide. She let her caftan slip, revealing moonlike breasts and a perfect waxed triangle. She smiled, taking a step forward. Reaching out her hand, she traced a manicured finger along my wrist and the inside of my arm. She paused for a moment before she cupped my breast. Moving close enough to feel her hot breath on my face, she kissed me. I could feel her warmth wash over me.

Then I woke up. Completely drenched. Had to change my nightgown before I could settle back down.

TUESDAY, JUNE 20, 2017

Dear Lord, my husband's work has consumed so much of his time, leaving me profoundly alone. Grant us both the strength need-

ed—him to continue his momentous task, whatever it may be, and me to endure these next few months in solitude. Amen.

Last night, Michael overindulged in scotch after dinner and was talking nonsense. Usually, his work is Top Secret, but last night he couldn't stop blathering on.

He announced I'd feel better before I knew it. He said he's been working on something that'll not only benefit me and the girls but the rest of the world. He mumbled something about the Bilderberg Group and presidents.

I didn't understand a thing.

"Even the Jews!" he screamed at one point as I tried to get him into bed. "Big in Williamsburg. Going to change everything!"

For the first time in my marriage, I was mortified by my husband's behavior. I've never heard him speak that way, let alone seen him like that. Incoherent. It's borderline bigotry is what it is, and I won't stand for it. Help me, Lord. So many things are changing all at once. It's overwhelming. I'm exhausted. Dr. Novak says the app will help as long as I practice daily. The pills should kick in soon. I keep picturing Amara's bubbly face.

Monday, July 3, 2017

Today was the first day I agreed to let Dr. Novak hypnotize me. He mentions it every session, but Ma always thought that stuff was hokey. Against the good Lord's plan and all. She once watched an Oprah special where they proved you can implant fake memories. I *finally succumbed after intense discussion with Dr. N and some on-line research. I discovered it can be a great way to uncover suppressed feelings that manifest anxiety and depression.*

At this point, I'll do anything to conquer these horrible thoughts. Dr. N recorded the session so I could play it back later, and boy was I surprised (and embarrassed) to hear myself reveal some deep, dark stuff.

Dr. N had me lay on the sofa in his office while he sat in a chair nearby. First, he walked me through a series of breathing techniques. I imagined myself going down a staircase leading into the basement of my mind.

He had me explore a painful early memory, something scarring. He handed me a metaphoric shovel, and I began digging. What I uncovered was shrouded in shame and doused in humility. Dr. Novak encouraged me to keep digging in my garden of secrets. Inside, there was a name.

Becca.

At this point in the recording, tears drown my voice. Becca was my first love. She had gorgeous black hair that ran straight as an arrow down her back. Her eyes were amber like a tigress. Besides being frighteningly beautiful, she was kind and smart. But when my father found out...

That was a whipping I'll never forget. Becca got shipped off to some Christian camp for troubled teens. While I...

I started a career in modeling. My fifteen minutes of freedom.

Before I got married off to Michael.

But that's all in the past. Today's a gift. Tomorrow's the Fourth of July. Must paint on a happy face.

I will be a good wife.

I love my husband.

I love my life.

I am a good mother.

WEDNESDAY, JULY 26, 2017

I feel off. Not like me. More unstable than usual. Dr. N said I would feel strange before I felt better.

I barely eat. I sleep all day. I had to get help with the girls. Luna offered up Bianca. I felt terrible stealing her, but Luna already has an army of nannies. They all speak different languages. (Of course.)

My memory has holes. I'm unable to recall certain things, losing chunks of time. It's alarming. One moment I'm resting in bed, and then a few hours later, I'm in the guest room or on the sofa with no recollection. I'm trying not to panic. Michael says not to worry, but it's easier said than done. I feel like I'm slipping into numbness.

Bianca seems worried too. She doesn't speak much. She stares at me with those sad, doe eyes of hers, like she's holding her breath, waiting for me to keel over. Whenever I try to talk to her, she scurries away, whispering about checking on the kids or dinner or anything to escape my presence. She never answers my questions directly or looks me in the eyes. She just stares at the floor, chewing her cuticles. The whole thing gives me the heebie-jeebies.

Michael seems to be the only one unaware and unaffected. If he's not working, he's drinking, and if he's not drinking, he's pushing me into the bedroom. Honestly, I don't know what's gotten into him. I wouldn't be surprised if he's taking the little blue pill.

Like we need another baby right now.

TUESDAY, AUGUST 15, 2017

Luna threw an adult toy party at Blair's house. It's hard to look at her without blushing after my strange dream. Must be a side effect of the meds. I asked her why it wasn't at her own house. She shrugged and said in that lovely accent of hers, "This is the way it's always been." I was surprised by the turnout. All the ladies from Orchid Hill showed up. On a school night. Everyone except someone named Susan. I guess she's been a recluse ever since her husband passed. Poor thing.

Anyway, I was under the impression that most of these women were prudes or, at the very least, church-going people like me. Women who were taught that our bodies are fundamental procreation vessels. That sexuality is the Devil, and we should hide it at all costs. It wasn't until modeling that I understood a woman's sexuality is her power.

Then I got married and had kids. Sometimes I wonder what my life would've been like...

I try to push those harmful thoughts out of my head and focus on the present and the program. Dr. N has been a godsend. Without him, who knows where my mind would be?

Despite his help, I've been so off-kilter. During Luna's party, things got weird. I'm not sure if it was the booze in that punch or what, but after a single glass, I thought I was hallucinating. I got extremely dizzy and asked to lie down in Blair's spare room. I must've fallen asleep and into a nightmare.

I'm not entirely sure how I got home, but I vividly remember this horrible dream. I found myself in a strange, dark room. It could've been a fuselage. An unfamiliar man started to undress before me. He was covered in tattoos. What kind of person displays the Devil on the side of their face? I watched, terrified, as this naked man put on a spacesuit and strapped himself into the chair beside mine. I was pinned beside him while he grunted and jerked. Even though he was confined in his own chair, I could feel his hands and sweat all over me. He made me...feel things. It's so embarrassing, I can't even write it down. Dear Lord, I know it was just a dream, but it felt so real.

This morning, I awoke in our guest room, covered in bruises. I must have gotten them when the ladies brought me back. That couldn't have been an easy feat. Also, there's something funny going on down there. It hurts when I pee. Must be all those impromptu rendezvous Mike's been initiating.

Note to self: get to the pharmacy.

MONDAY, SEPTEMBER 11, 2017

Got my first Botox injection from Dr. Sully. He came to my session with Dr. N and did it there so I wouldn't have to travel downtown to his office. I asked him to do my forehead since that's where all the years have laid their tracks. But, before administering the beauty shot, Dr. N gave me one in the neck. "To help you relax," he said. I didn't feel much except a pinch, but I did notice the area was a little red afterward.

Note to self: tell Dr. N I may have an allergy to whatever he gave me to relax.

MONDAY, JANUARY 8, 2018

It looks like it has been ages since I've written. Not sure what happened. I've lost months. Dr. N says it's normal, but I can tell he's worried. He and Michael have whispered conversations around me. It's patronizing and demoralizing. It makes me feel helpless. Defeated.

I've been relying too much on Bianca. She's constantly refreshing my tea, making sure I'm comfortable. The way she stares at me creeps me out. Like she's waiting for me to die. Who knows, maybe this has been her plan all along, so she can step in and be the new mother to my girls and a new wife for my husband. I see the way he looks at her. Her short hair bouncing spritely like her perky breasts. I bet she's the reason why our sex life has been in overdrive. I never did find those little blue pills. And I looked everywhere, tore apart the whole house up and down, ready to flush them down the toilet.

Why am I acting this way? This doesn't feel like me. This jealous anti-aphrodisiac.

This is not me.

When I called Luna to vent, she reassured me everything was fine, fine, fine, and just the way it should be. I don't know anymore. It seems like ever since we moved here, nothing has felt the same.

THURSDAY, FEBRUARY 15, 2018

I can't trust my mind. They're experimenting with it. With us! This whole time! It's happening to all of us right now! Through TV and radio. It's been happening to Americans for decades, possibly centuries.

Timothy McVeigh said he had a computer chip in his bum that made him do it. What if that's what they're doing to me? Our whole culture is run by the media. There's no escaping it. Escaping them. There's nowhere to go. Nowhere to hide. I don't know what to do.

I know they will do the same thing to someone else, find some other family to ruin. I need to stop this. Before I get worse.

It's dangerous here.

There's a loose stone in the backyard by the water fountain where I can stash this journal. I don't trust leaving it in the house. Maybe someone will find this and learn the truth if anything happens to me.

SATURDAY, MARCH 3, 2018

Had another horrible dream about the spaceship. Again. Dr N. said it's a recurring nightmare from suppressed trauma. He diagnosed me as bipolar with schizophrenic tendencies. He thinks I'm crazy. He told Michael I don't know reality from delusion. He prescribed more pills and wants to sign me up for some new experimental treatment. I politely declined.

I know this time what is real. The tattooed man is REAL! He smells like cigarettes and sweat. The Grim Reaper guards one side of his face, and the Devil protects his neck.

El Diablo.

"Always wanted to fuck a famous model."

My body breaks out in cold sweats when I think of him. I shake. None of this makes sense. Every time I try to talk to Michael about it, he looks like he's contemplating having me committed. I'm losing my mind. I'm possessed. El Diablo, the demon, has taken over my thoughts.

And my soul.

I need to go back to church. I need a priest.

Or an exorcist.

THURSDAY, MARCH 15, 2018

The tunnels! We always knew they were there. They connect each home through a circular hallway.

I know what is happening, and I'm sick about it. We have a seriously disturbed group of men terrorizing the wives of Orchid Hill. I'm scared to write this down. It's too dangerous. But it may be the only record. Our truth. Michael doesn't believe me. He thinks I'm unstable. Told me to stop with the conspiracy theories.

I'd rather be crazy than possessed.

Before I can alert the authorities, I need evidence. They're drugging us, turning us into live sex dolls. And they're using the tunnels to transport us discreetly. I'm not sure, but I think every wife in this ELITE neighborhood has been subjected to something wicked against her will. Something she probably doesn't even remember.

Has my husband betrayed me too? Is our marriage, our family life, a lie? Did he participate in this violation, these assaults? Who did he pick as his concubine? Amara seems like his type, with her legs for days and that magnetic smile.

I must do something. At my next session, I plan to confront Dr. Novak with my suspicions and see how he reacts. Of course, he won't know I'll be secretly recording him on my phone.

What's the worst that can happen?

CHAPTER 23

CASS

IT ENDS THERE. THE rest of the pages have been torn out.

Luna left hours ago. She stormed home with her bucket of glam gear, leaving me reeling and unexpectedly drunk. Alone in my backyard, I unearthed my stash and the journal from the hiding spot, hoping to sneak a few hits. I sank into the cushioned patio chair and took a deep hit of indica, holding it in until my lungs burned.

That's when Sean opened the sliding door. Home hours early. Just in time to watch me exhale a thick white cloud. He stared at me with judgy eyes, but he didn't speak. He didn't even acknowledge my presence. He simply turned around and slammed the sliding door. A little too aggressively for my taste. Hard enough to knock down the wind chime I had hung off the back porch. He looked wicked pissed. He didn't mention the tattered book in my hand. He didn't even say anything about my made-up face or pin-straight hair. I was invisible.

When it started to rain (as Luna annoyingly predicted), I stubbornly extended the patio umbrella and hunkered down, determined to finish Jessa's journal. Sean was already mad. No point getting into a big fight about it. As I flipped through the handwritten pages, I watched the cursive go from neat and legible to a childlike scribble. Clearly, this woman unraveled after moving here. I started where I'd left off. By the time I finished, it was almost midnight. I read for hours. Getting increasingly uncomfortable as I turned each page. When I got to the last entry, my head was spinning.

What the fuck?

What happened to this poor family? Was Jessa an unbalanced woman who had a manic break? Postpartum like Lilith suggested? One thing's for sure, Jessa struggled. It seems like motherhood is no walk in the park. When I look for the story online, I can only access SO-CAL News. Police are confident there was no foul play. They concluded she had mental issues and didn't get the help she desperately needed.

I understand tragedy. I've lost family too.

I want to tell Sean about my discovery, but when I run to the bedroom to apologize, he isn't there. Instead, there's a note: *WENT BACK TO WORK.*

Really? This late on a Saturday night?

If I didn't know better, I'd think he's having an affair. Always working. Taking secret late-night calls. When we first got together, he revealed things about his parents. How his dad commuted by train from Connecticut to New York City for work. He told me his father kept a spare apartment in case he "worked late" and missed the last train, but really, he was entertaining hookers. Sean's father took him to a brothel once, right after his eighteenth birthday. "A rite of passage," his father had called it. Sean shared his disgust afterward, and how angry he was at his father for disrespecting his mother. He vowed never to dishonor me. And I believe him.

Though his constant absence annoys me, I miss my husband.

Feeling the weight of Jessa's journal in my hands, I can't help but compare the similarities between us. Blair and Amara's first visit. The sex toy party. Luna's makeover. The Welcome Barbeque.

All of which can be explained away with friendly gestures and neighborly traditions. And who is this demon? Jessa's memory had huge gaps. She clearly had dementia or some other brain disorder or, at the very least, a hormonal imbalance. I mean, come on—Amara bubbly and smiling? That's like calling an assassin cute and cuddly.

I send a message to Sean, apologizing, telling him I have important info I want to share whenever he gets home. It's late. My head pulses in tandem with my heart. The buzz from Luna's *rakija* turns into a full-blown hangover.

Still reeling about Sean, Jessa, and the mysterious Dr. Novak, I toss and turn, glancing at the clock for the billionth time. It's well past midnight. I flip on my bedside lamp and see the little envelope from Dr. Novak.

These will help you sleep.

I try not to think of Jessa as I swallow the unmarked pill and close my eyes.

I slip inside the strangest dream. We're aboard our family schooner, *The Mayflower II*. Mom, Dad, and Garth bustle about, preparing to set off on some big heist. They're going to rob the president of the United States, they say, and apparently, I'm essential for the job—to pick the lock on the White House. They're convinced I can do it, calling me the biggest phony. A fake. I tell them I can't. I won't. I'm not what they think. They bellow with horrifying laughter until their guffaws turn to caws. Their mouths curl into beaks. Their rain boots twist into talons. Before I can comprehend what's happening, blue-black feathers sprout from their skin. In a blink, I'm standing, terrified, in front of my family transformed. A family of crows.

CHAPTER 24

KIT

FROM THE BREAKFAST NOOK window, Kit observes the ominous weather. Raindrops spatter in steady rhythm like a lazy sprinkler. Sunshine escapes through cracks in dark clouds. The world outside feels peaceful yet eerie. *The calm before the storm.* Ominously foreboding.

The adults are talking. It's serious. They speak in low voices in the dining room. Kit's mom disappeared upstairs with Buster for his nightly bath. Kit's father holds court with the neighbors.

She waits in the kitchen as her brothers update their father and his friends. Kit recognizes the voices of Mr. Huang and Amber's dad, but she can't make out what they're saying.

So far, no one has called the police.

Kit doesn't want to think about what's rotting in the water tower. If she thinks too much, she may start crying and never stop. Bianca was part of their community. She was like family. She worked for almost every home on the block. Then one night, she simply disappeared—in the middle of her shift. Everyone blamed Kit's brothers, saying she finally must've had enough. She was the only nanny who stuck with the Novak family for more than a few months. The others came and went with the seasons.

Kit can't lose focus. She has her own life at stake. Her whole future balances like a teeter-totter. She has no choice but to give Amber what she wants. She needs to speak with her brothers. Alone. Waiting for them in the dark, she practices asking them for the biggest favor of her life.

She waits over an hour, tinkering with her phone inside its broken case. Once their filial duty is done, Seth and Brody playfight into the kitchen and tackle each other into the refrigerator.

Kit's voice creeps out of the darkness. "I need a favor."

Brody and Seth jump. Seth jerks his body to face Kit as Brody bangs his head as he opens the fridge door.

"What the eff!"

"Holy shit, Squirt!"

"You scared the fuck out of us."

Kit scrutinizes her brothers, trying to understand what Amber sees in them. Tall and boyish with lean muscles, they look goofy in their pastel hoodies and Blair's bright red hair. If Ed Sheeran and Justin Bieber had twins, Kit's pretty sure they'd look exactly like her brothers.

"I'm serious, you guys. It's important."

"What kind of favor?" Brody rubs his forehead.

"I need one of you to take Amber to prom."

"*Our* prom? No freaking way!"

"Please, please, please? I'm begging!" She slides off the breakfast bench and onto her knees, hands clasped together, beseeching her brothers.

"Hell no!" They unite.

"Please? I'll pay you! Four hundred and twelve dollars and eighty-two cents. It's all the cash I have. You can have that plus all my allowance for the next year. Please? It's a matter of life and death." She grabs the wads of bills and coins from her jeans pocket and solicits a response, hoping for a lifeline from a lifetime of shame and embarrassment.

"Next-door-Amber? No freaking way!" Seth shakes his head violently. His hair barely moves. "She's crazy. *You're* crazy!"

"Dude, she's what, fourteen. We're, like, fully grown adults."

"That's gross."

"That's jailbait."

Kit looks at Brody with her puppy dog eyes. Her bottom lip protrudes, blubbery tears stockpiling.

"Nah, don't give me that look. I'm out too."

"But why not? You don't even have dates." She glares at Brody, her last hope thwarted. He never turns down cash. He once ate the eyeballs off a dead fish they found on the beach for fifty bucks.

"Because...none of your damn business, okay? Just can't." He rotates to refocus on the open fridge, grabs an energy drink, tosses it to Seth, grabs another one, opens it, chugs. They ignore her, trampling each other like wild goats as they flee the kitchen and head up to their room.

"We don't need dates. The ladies come to us!" Seth sings, stopping at the top of the stairs to fist-bump his brother.

Unabashed tears steamroll Kit's face. "Please," she gasps between jerking sobs, "I'll never ask either of you for anything ever again." She swipes snot on her sleeve, following them to the second floor.

"Why's this so important anyway?" Seth squints at her. An annoyed look puckers his face.

Kit follows without answering. She tries to compose herself, desperate to think of a new tactic. When they reach the entry to the bedroom, the boys hurdle themselves to see who can get into their gaming chair first. They plow into each other, holding their shiny cans of caffeine above their heads. They share the second largest bedroom. "Better to house our gaming system," Brody had said, but Kit knows he's afraid of the dark and refuses to move into his own room. If Kit was more like Amber, she could use that information to get what she desperately needs, but she's not, so she doesn't give it a second thought.

Kit hangs in the doorway, jaw gaping. No words pass. She's stuck. She can't tell her big brothers the actual reason. That their only sister, who still sleeps with her teddy bear, is (what society will label her as soon as that video goes viral) a stupid slut. That she gave a blow job to look cool. That she's desperately ashamed and painfully shy to the point where she needs alcohol to be herself. And she's conflicted, because parts of her want to experiment and drink up the world, and it seems everyone else wants you to too, because if you don't, you're labeled a prude, but when you do, you're labeled the other way. She's been numbing her mind to maintain sanity.

Yesterday morning, Kit stole a Mason jar full of fizzy punch. Her mother thought she was at school, but Kit ditched to avoid Amber and further humiliation. After hacking Blair's email and sending a message to her teachers, Kit spent the day hidden in the underground bunker finishing her graphic novel. She had hacked the codes from her dad's phone after watching an online tutorial. Kit's getting sneakier every day. When she snuck into the kitchen for a snack, she spied her mom's punch bowl in the fridge covered in an obscene amount of cellophane with the words *ADULTS ONLY* smudged over the top with a permanent marker. She snatched an empty Mason jar and stealthily filled it up. She was saving it for a special occasion or an emergency.

This is most definitely an emergency.

She chews her cuticles, surveying the boys' bedroom. It's long and rectangular with vaulted ceilings and its own bathroom, complete with double urinals. Plenty of room for their queen-sized beds and gaming setup. The wall opposite their sleeping quarters looks like NASA. Flatscreens blanket every spare inch. The theater is the only place in the house with a bigger monitor. Under the display, shelving units attempt to organize copious gaming consoles. Bins of multicolored controllers tangle with a mishmash of cords. A picture window faces the backyard, allowing light to bounce off the navy walls. Brody and Seth recline in their gaming chairs, glued to the glowing monitors.

Teenage debris litters the floor: aluminum cans, cellophane wrappers, dirty socks. To the right, the walk-in closet door hangs open to reveal a jungle of colorful clothing, backpacks for every occasion, and a cardboard box stuffed with fireworks for the upcoming holiday.

On the dresser by the door, Kit spies an open cigar box. Inside, there's a small glass jar stuffed with greenish-purple buds, a pack of orange rolling papers, a Zippo lighter with an *Eisernes Kreuz* embossed on one side, and a fat, pre-rolled joint. Kit looks at her brothers. They have their headsets on, engrossed in their augmented reality game, and have already forgotten her existence. She points to the lighter. "Isn't that from Dad's collection? He'll murder you both if he knows you have it." They ignore her, absorbed in their mission. "Forget it. Never mind." She swipes the joint and the lighter as she leaves. Her brothers are useless. She'll have to come up with a plan on her own.

At the other end of the hall, in her own room, Kit rummages inside the back of her closet. She pulls out a dusty shoebox tucked under a stack of old sweaters, lifts the lid, and places the joint and Zippo inside. She grabs the Mason jar. It's three-quarters full, still pink, but less fizzy. Kit unscrews the cap and takes a swig. It's sweet and fruity. She waits for the burn to reach her veins. But she doesn't feel anything, so she slurps more, but not too much. *I need to keep my mind sharp. I need a plan.* Fuchsia dribbles down her chin. She stops it with the back of her hand. Screwing on the cap to the Mason jar, she ponders the twisted spliff. She picks it up and sniffs it. It smells like Caesar after he was sprayed by a skunk. She puts the joint back in the box and stashes everything in her closet, way in the back, under a pile of wool.

Her phone pings with a message:

AMBER: soooooo? did he say yes?

KIT: working on it...

AMBER: u have til fri better hurry up

KIT: gfy!!!!!!!!!!!!!!

Kit types out the three letters, then deletes them. She's screwed, and she knows it. She needs to think. She stares at the illustrated face of Ada Lovelace hanging above her desk.

What would Ada do?

She flops down on her bed, observing the shimmering canopy. She lies there for hours, watching the fairy lights come off the wall and twirl around her head. A plan forms.

CHAPTER 25

LILITH

It finally stopped raining Sunday morning. The air smells briny. Earthy and delicious. Lilith, a true pluviophile, loves when everything's clean and fresh after a good rain. She can finally breathe. Rousing early, she sneaks into the garage to a lonely corner impersonating a painting studio. Sadly, it's more of a storage facility than an art studio these days.

Morning light barely crests the canyon, leaving the Gardens of Orchid Hill in twilight. Lilith flicks on the overhead bulb. Solar-fed electricity hums awake. The enclosed space can fit a family of Humvees with plenty of room for Lilith to claim a corner for herself. It feels like ages since she's painted. She can't recall the last time she felt the spark of creativity. The urge to create fades within her more each day.

But not this morning. Today, Lilith awoke from a dream she can't seem to remember. The more she tries to recall, the farther the images and emotions slip away. Nevertheless, her hands are itching to paint and express...something. Though not quite sure what she plans to do, she can feel an idea brewing like a wave building out on the ocean. Lilith waits for inspiration, an ever-patient surfer on the artistic horizon.

She brought the baby monitor with her, just in case. Hopefully, at this hour, she can sneak in an uninterrupted session. She readies herself on a wooden stool before the blank canvas. One hand pinches a perfectly rolled joint, the other dangles a paintbrush. She brings the spliff to her lips every few minutes. When she exhales, smoke coils around her, temporarily tattooing the air.

Shiny black hair tipped with green piles high on her head in a messy bun. An old college sweatshirt with the neck cut off hangs off one shoulder. She's barefoot in a pair of stained sweats, leftover clothes belonging to a different life. The tarp feels rough on her purple-painted toes, but Lilith doesn't care. She focuses on the canvas.

Colors call out to her in waves. Cerulean blue. Viridian. Titanium white. Yellow ochre. Lamp black. She squeezes each color onto a wooden pallet, dipping the tips of her fingers into the paint puddles. She swirls, experimenting with combinations until each hue is just right. Titanium white and cerulean blue. Viridian and yellow ochre. Lamp black and titanium white with a touch of yellow ochre. Perfect for the eyes. She watches each color transform, mutate, like gasoline in a puddle. A metamorphosis.

Lilith selects a large flat brush, loading it with color. She inhales the dusty book smell of the blank canvas and positions her arm. She stills her mind, takes a deep breath. Before the paint kisses the cloth, the baby monitor wails.

She curses under her breath.

Without connecting the bristles to the canvas, she plops the ambitious brush into a can of watered-down paint thinner, stubs out the joint, and leaves, wondering if she'll ever return.

CHAPTER 26

CASS

IT'S BEEN DAYS SINCE I read Jessa's notebook. Things are still off with Sean. He's quiet and distracted. I tried to mention the journal the few times I caught him at home, but he blew me off. Apparently, I shouldn't place importance on the words of a suicidal maniac. When he asked where I had found it, I lied and said behind the laundry machine.

We're standing in the kitchen waiting for the coffee to finish percolating when we have our biggest fight ever.

"What were you doing back there anyway?"

"Laundry."

"No, behind the washing machine."

"I dropped a sock."

"Really?"

"Yup, slipped right out of my hand." My chest twinges with the lie. This is not how I envisioned marriage to be.

"You know there's no way to prove the journal is hers or that she actually wrote it, right? You should know better than that, especially as someone who passed the bar."

"What does that have to do with anything? She names this neighborhood. Her husband's and children's names are in it. I double-checked the internet. By the way, I freaking had to go all the way to a coffee shop across town because our internet has been so shitty!"

"Great! That's the last thing I need—my dope fiend wife traipsing all over town spreading crazy conspiracy theories!"

"I'm not crazy!" My voice ricochets off the slabbed walls. I don't care if the neighbors can hear me or not. "And, for your information, *marijuana* is *legal* in California!"

"That's not the point!"

"What's the point? You never cared before!"

"Well, I do now! You know my career..."

"Oh, you and your *fucking* career. Sorry. Excuse me, Mr. President!"

SLAM!

SLAM!

We go to bed angry, something we promised never to do. The gnawing indignation of being doubted by my life partner keeps me up all night. Who is this man I married? I feel like I'm living in a parallel universe. I ache for the simplicity of life on the road. And Thurgood.

I toss and turn, thinking about what Luna said about the curse of Cassandra.

I wake to Sean's kisses. We find each other under the sheets with urgency. We don't talk. We don't kiss. Our bodies move independently, specific with need. A simple cause-and-effect transaction. We grunt and jerk our way through marital crisis. When it's over, we lie pressed together in a tangle of sheets.

"I'm sorry about yesterday." His lips press against my neck.

"Me too." I wrap my arms around him, breathing in his scent.

"You know," he begins, gently breaking away, "maybe it wouldn't be such a bad idea for you to talk to Dr. Novak. I mean, just to speak to him—in a non-professional manner—about the journal. Ask him some questions. See if he can give you any answers on—what's her name—that crazy woman?"

"Jessa." I sigh. "Her name was Jessa."

"Yes, Jessa. He really is a nice guy, you know...the doctor. I bet once you talk to him, you'll feel better. Ease your mind." He kisses me again on my forehead. It feels patriarchal.

"Yeah, okay, maybe."

"Also, I asked around, did some digging into the information you told me. Seriously, there's nothing to worry about. All those accusations, unfounded. I even had someone do a background check on Novak, just in case. He checks out. Clean as a whistle."

He gets up and stands by the mirror, adjusting his tie. "Maybe he can help you. I heard he helped Luna quit smoking cigarettes. Among other things."

"I don't smoke cigarettes. It's nowhere near the same thing."

"Well, smoking pot was cute and all when you were living on the side of the road with your dog, but..."

"But what?" My jaw muscles tighten. *Will this ever end?*

"But we're...He could help you sleep better is all I'm trying to say. It's worth a shot, right? Will you at least try? For me?" He gives me his best smile. The next JFK in the making.

Despite every nerve ending in my body screaming, 'No,' I reluctantly give in. "Yes, dear. Anything for you," I say, only half-joking.

"Thanks, babe!" He grabs his jacket and heads for the door. "I'll introduce you at the barbecue this weekend. See you later. Love you."

"Love you too." I release a frustrated sigh. Once he's gone, I roll a joint and go for a walk to clear my head.

CHAPTER 27

SUSAN

On Wednesday, dark clouds threaten more rain. Kneeling on her favorite gardening pillow, elbow deep in a bush of mixed *Bletilla Striata*, Susan Franco pulls weeds and gambles on the weather. Having lived in the Gardens of Orchid Hill for a third of a century, she's seen it all—neighbors coming and going, babies born and raised, even those dreadful murders. She mostly keeps to herself but attends every block party to meet the newest neighbors, silently assessing how well they'll fare.

Despite being branded the neighborhood pariah, Susan remains steadfast in her refusal to leave. She harbors a deep disdain for persistent realtors who incessantly hound her. "Sell! Sell! Sell!" They push. "It's a seller's market. You'll make a fortune!" But she doesn't. She couldn't. She wouldn't be able to leave this place. Not even if it was on fire. Every memory of her sweet Stanley is

206

wrapped up in this house. She can't bear to leave. Decades of love saturate her walls. She'd rather fall down the stairs and break a hip before leaving this place to move into some pathetic, stench-ridden nursing home. Susan's a registered nurse. She is more than capable of taking care of herself.

"Good morning!"

Susan startles at a chipper voice bouncing up the driveway. She turns. A woman with wild hair and bloodshot eyes walks toward her. A faint, skunky smell precedes her. Susan squints suspiciously under a large sun hat. She can spot a pothead a mile away. "May I help you?"

"I'm Cass." The two women stare at each other for a second longer than comfortable. "We haven't met yet. I'm your new neighbor." Cass gives a quick wave. "May I just say, your garden is beyond breathtaking."

Susan's gaze is drawn to the woman's fingernails, bitten down to nubs, a sign of nervousness or a bad habit. As she methodically peels off her right gardening glove, revealing each finger with deliberate slowness, she takes a moment to assess Cass. With a studied look, she extends her hand for a firm handshake, introducing herself, "Nice to meet you. I'm...Susan."

Dressed in a denim shirt with rolled-up sleeves and a wide-brim gardening hat, Susan carries herself with effortless grace. Her chic salt and pepper bob neatly frames her feline face, underscoring a timeless allure that has not faded over the years. Susan is no stranger to admiration; men have fawned over her for most of her life. Women, on the other hand, have always been difficult.

"I didn't see you at Luna's...gathering."

Susan removes the other glove. "No, you wouldn't have." With one elbow on her bent knee, she grunts to get up.

"Here, let me help." The stranger extends her arms.

Susan ignores the offer. "Oh, enough of that. I'm fine. I can take care of myself, you know. Been doing it for sixty years."

"So, you've been here—in this neighborhood—a while then?"

"Over thirty years." Susan rests her hands on her hips and shifts her weight from one leg to another. Her bones release gentle pops. She clicks her tongue and huffs at Cass, glancing at her watch, then the sky.

"So, you must've met Jessa?" They lock eyes again. "I moved into her house."

Thunder cracks the air, startling both women.

Susan squints at Cass. Her blue eyes assess the windblown woman. The corners of her mouth turn down. "Are you a reporter?"

"No, ma'am. I write a little, but not for the news. Just a concerned neighbor trying to find out what happened in my house, so I can sleep better at night. Could we chat? It would be so nice to get your opinion. Especially since you know this place so well."

Globs of rain fall. One smacks Cass on the forehead, drips in her eye. Susan does just fine under her hat. The silence stretches.

"If not, that's okay too. I just thought..." Cass raises her arms both in defeat and to shield her frizzing hair. She slowly turns back down the driveway.

"Would you like some tea?" Susan surprises herself.

Cass smiles. "That would be lovely."

Susan leads them around her home, a menagerie of orchids honoring the neighborhood's namesake. Moth orchids. Dendrobium. Boat orchids. Vanda. Cattleya orchids. Orchis. As they wind their way through the colorful path, Cass discovers every inch invaded by blossoms.

"Wow, Susan, I've never seen anything like it. How do you keep all your flowers in bloom while the rest of us struggle to keep our grass green?"

"If I told you, I'd have to kill you." Susan chuckles at Cass's startled face. "Just kidding, dear. It's all about the fertilizer. I treat each one like my own child. Each has its own personality and preferences." She unlocks the back door with a key and welcomes her first guest in over a decade.

Inside Susan's home, flowers continue to propagate—in pots and pans, in glass jars suspended from windows, on fabrics and tapestries, and wallpaper that harks back at least a few eras.

Cass notices the Smart system hasn't been installed.

"So, you're a writer, huh? I've dabbled in the art a little myself." Susan moves a stack of dusty clippings from an embroidered chair.

"There you go. Have a seat." She claims the recliner across from Cass.

"Uh, thanks." Cass carefully sits in the antique floral armchair.

"What books have you written?"

"Um, no books. I used to have a blog. You've probably never heard of it."

"Try me."

"It was called Thurgood the Dog's Travel Blog, a collection of van life adventures on the road with my furry companion, Thurgy. It didn't go viral or anything."

"Nope. Never heard of it." Without warning, Susan springs up and goes into the kitchen. "Is ginger tea okay? It's all I have at the moment," she calls to her new neighbor.

"Uh, yeah. That sounds great."

After a series of clanks and a whistle, Susan returns carrying a tray and sets it on the coffee table between them. "Sorry about the mess. I wasn't expecting company."

The room, cluttered and bursting with floral arrangements, radiates the overwhelming scent of blossoms, showcasing Susan's unmistakable love for her flowers. Her passion for reading is equally evident, with stacks of travel magazines and medical journals claiming every spare surface, while books of all ages and sizes crowd the shelves along each wall.

"No worries. You should see my house. I haven't even finished unpacking yet."

Susan pours Cass's tea from a beautiful copper kettle into two chipped mugs.

Cass smiles at the one placed in front of her: *IT'S NOT HOARDING IF IT'S PLANTS.*

"Smells wonderful. Thank you, Susan."

There's a moment of silence as each woman blows steam and sips.

Susan sits back, cupping her mug in both hands. She curls her legs underneath her. "So, what do you want to know?"

Cass places her mug on the coffee table and begins to speak. She expresses her astonishment upon learning about the murders—the tragedy that unfolded in her new home. "Also," she hesitates, a visible eagerness to share her secret compelling her forward, "I found something. Something I believe belonged to Jessa. I think someone may have been trying to harm her. Drive her crazy, maybe? Someone from this neighborhood." Her question is laden with implications, seeking insight or perhaps an ally in this disturbing revelation. "Would you have any idea who that could be?" she asks, her inquiry hanging in the air, casting a shadow of suspicion and curiosity over the quiet room.

Susan's blue eyes flash momentarily. She makes a straight line with her mouth, gets up, and goes back into the kitchen. She returns with a bottle of bourbon. "We're going to need something a little stronger for this conversation." She pours a shot into each mug, takes a swig from the bottle, then begins. "This neighborhood is not what it seems."

Thunder rumbles ominously in the distance.

Chapter 28

CASS

We both jolt, our laughter tinged with nervousness at the sudden fright.

My eyes expand in the darkened room. "What do you mean exactly?"

"Well, my dear, I'm not sure what kind of relationship you have with your husband, and I'm not trying to cause any trouble for you or your marriage…" Susan gulps her spiked tea. "This neighborhood is…unique. Not one-of-a-kind, if you follow my drift. I've discovered many places like The Gardens of Orchid Hill scattered throughout the country." Her hand flutters to the clippings and articles scattered across the room. "And more are popping up each year. Especially around here."

I tilt my head toward the articles and then towards Susan, unsure what to make of this situation.

"Now, before I go into detail, you must know they've been doing this for ages, centuries even. Probably since man could walk upright. Controlling the minds of the population. If you control how people think, you control the world. Many people don't know this, but there are a handful of corporations out there controlling the media. All of it ruled by a few big men with tiny peckers."

I shake my head. A stray curl dips into my mug. "Wait a sec. What are you talking about?" I lean toward Susan, brows furrowing.

"Programming, my dear. Brainwashing. I'm talking about mind control. Why do you think they call it television and radio *programming*? I'll tell you why. It's because they've been messing with our minds since the dawn of time." Susan's hand flies up to her head, her fingers jabbing at her temple.

"Who?" I extract my hair from my cup and take a skeptical sip.

"Men, my dear. They've been brainwashing women, getting us to believe all sorts of bullshit forever. Think about it—the real reason men throughout history opposed science was its potential to prove them all wrong. Consider the lies they spread for hundreds—thousands of years. A woman can only get pregnant if she enjoys it. The world is flat. The earth is the center of the universe. Everything revolves around them!" Susan dispenses more bourbon into our mugs. "It's enough to drive you insane. No wonder women were deemed 'hysterical' all the time. We were mind-fucked into insanity. Excuse my language." She takes another gulp of what I assume is mostly bourbon. "And they're so sly about it too."

"Okay...but how? This all sounds very..."

"What, crazy? Oh honey, it's happening all around you this very moment." Susan fumbles with some articles on a side table and hands me a pile. "According to my research, there are five things needed to brainwash people: isolation, control, uncertainty, repetition, and strong emotions. At Orchid Hill, the wives are isolated behind their gated community and under the control of their husbands and Dr. Novak. The Gardens of Orchid Hill is uniquely designed. Didn't you notice how you cannot access certain television shows or internet websites?"

"Actually, I don't watch much tv, but the internet here does suck," I clarify.

"It's because of the firewall. You can thank the Smart system for that one. It limits the news and information you're receiving."

"Yeah, we can only get NetNews. I couldn't find any other channels, but censorship isn't exactly mind control."

"Oh yeah? Suppose all the information you're receiving pushes the line of decency, and there's no alternative to compare it to. Are you really thinking for yourself, logically? Could you make an unbiased opinion?" Susan's bosom bounces in agitation.

I ponder for a moment, sipping my hot toddy. The warming spirit takes root. "Well, I guess not."

"Of course not! You might as well be living in Plato's cave. If you control the info going into the brain, you control the brain—not only what it does but also what it believes." Susan slurps her mug, voice strengthening. "You can't even tell your brain is being changed. The ideas slide in, take root, and grow faster than a Dendrobium. Just look at what television did to the Democrats. Nixon turned a whole country Republican by pushing family values when feminism was bursting at the seams. He got all the working men—the ones threatened by female success—to vote for him and the good old-fashioned family way. He turned blue states red simply by tapping into people's fears."

"But what does this have to do with Jessa?"

"Well, let me tell you..." Susan pauses for dramatic effect while she drinks, as if gassing up.

I lean in so far, I almost fall off my chair. Her story doesn't disappoint. I listen quietly as Susan recounts her life with Stanley and how they came to live at the Gardens of Orchid Hill.

"We were one of the first couples to move here, right after the Huangs. It was the late eighties. Stanley worked for a big newspaper back then, in New York City. He was part of their finance department. He came from humble beginnings and was a hard worker. But when we first met, I earned more than he did. That was unheard of back then. I'm not ashamed to say it: I was a hired escort, and Stan was my very first client!"

"I was more nervous than he was. I forgot all the rules and told him my real name! He soon became a regular. Every Tuesday at eight. Over time, we developed a friendship, and eventually, fell in love. Just like *Pretty Woman*. He had me quit my job and move away from the city and all my clients. Away from my friends is what it felt like. He'd gotten a job at ELITE and heard about this revolutionary neighborhood in California through coworkers. The company even offered an employee discount on our mortgage, but there was a catch."

"What was that?" I ask, unsure if I want to know.

"We had to enroll in *The Program*. At first, I thought it just included access to the spa and golf course, but it became like homework. I got stuck listening to these cassette tapes at night. Soft sounds at first, mostly designed to lull you into a deep sleep, then came repetitive phrases over and over again. 'The husband is always right. A mother should have as many children as possible. Men know all.' It was insane. When I talked to Stan about it, he shrugged it off and reminded me how fortunate we were to live in such a grand, beautiful home. I should be lucky I didn't have to work on my back anymore. All the teachings fell on me, it felt like. Stan said he did his lessons at the office, which was a fine excuse for all those late nights."

Late nights. Sounds familiar.

"Over time, his personality changed. He became moody, angry. He started complaining about things he never cared about before;

Immigrants and Liberals were all of a sudden running this country into the ground, along with all the money-sucking leeches of the welfare community. I didn't question him at the time. Back in those days, women weren't as tough and fearless as you ladies are now. And because my husband rescued me from my life as a call girl, it always felt like he did this great thing. The least I could do was go along with it."

"I know *that* feeling."

"Honey, all us wives know it. At first, I wanted to get a job—not go back to whoring. I wanted to be a nurse. I saw an ad about classes at the university, but Stan shot it down. 'No wife of mine...' and all that bull. When I didn't get pregnant after years of trying, Stan referred me to Dr. Novak, our new neighbor. He started me on hypnotherapy and pills. The therapies had silly names like Mindweb and Phantom Bliss.

"When I complained I wasn't getting pregnant, he did an exploratory surgery searching for the cause of my infertility. At that point, I'd been praying for a child for almost a decade. All I'd ever wanted was to be a mum. Over time, I stopped thinking about becoming a nurse. My desire for children overtook everything. I kind of zonked out for a while. There are months I have no recollection at all. When I finally became pregnant, he weaned me off the treatments. I still had to listen to the tapes, but I didn't have to take any pills or see Dr. Novak for therapy.

"That's when it all came flooding back—my want for something more, my desire to go to school, the feeling of being trapped. But the pregnancies never lasted. Once the baby got about seven months, I bled. Every time. Nothing worse than enduring the pains of labor only to get a stillborn." Susan stops to drink from her mug. "Never could get one to stick. Just one dead baby after another. Afterward, I'd fall back into my fog."

"I'm so sorry." My heart aches for this woman. I can't even imagine.

"One night," Susan continues stoically, "Stan slipped and broke his hip. I didn't know it at the time, but it was my lucky break too. Stan had changed after decades at the Gardens. I barely recognized him anymore. When he went in for surgery, I decided to treat myself to some TLC and gave myself a facial. I mixed up some honey and coconut oil, massaged my entire face and neck. A trick I learned from the working girls. That's when I found it."

"Found what?" I watch the room spin, dizzy with anticipation. Or maybe it's the bourbon?

"You're not going to believe me." Susan adjusts her legs and sips from her mug.

"Please, go on."

"An implant. I found a damn computer chip embedded behind my ear! I thought it was a bug bite at first or a cyst. But I kept scratching and scratching until I scratched the darn thing out. Of course, they weren't so high-tech back then."

"Shut. The fuck. Up. That's insane." *She's insane.*

"Once I had that sucker in my hand, it was obvious that Dr. Novak and ELITE were in cahoots. I made a plan to save my Stanley. I had to try. He was the only man I ever felt loved by. And there were so many horrible little men in my life. I deleted and blocked all the radical conservative emails he signed up for and subscribed him to some open-minded news instead. I bought a brand-new satellite television. Had it installed without HOA approval because—screw them. And I reprogrammed all of the remotes. When Stan came home after surgery, he didn't know how to use any of them. He watched whatever I watched, which was definitely not NetNews. Slowly, his point of view and ethics changed back."

"So, you 'un-programmed' him?" I don't know whether to be surprised or alarmed.

"You could say that. Over time, we started to enjoy each other's company more. He went from being a cranky fanatic to someone with kindness in his heart again. We started to do everything to-gether. He became my best friend all over again. When the Smart home upgrade came around, I flatly refused, threatening to call the police if they stepped one foot near my orchids. That's when Stan got sick. When we found out he was terminal, he spilled the beans to me about the whole ELITE organization and what it's been up to. He swore. He cried. Said it was the one thing he regretted in life. Messing with my personality like that. And all those miscarriages."

"Oh, Susan, that's...horrible." I extend a tentative hand. *If what she's saying is true, then...*

"Thank you, dear." Susan squeezes my fingers. "He said he'd just wanted us to be happy but finally realized the severity of his actions. I forgave him, of course, and vowed to help the other women. But when I reached out to Blair and Sonja, they told me I was insane. They call me COL. Crazy Old Lady. I've been shunned ever since."

"Are you saying my husband is trying to brainwash me?" I remember how Jessa described Amara as sweet and bubbly. "How many women are...chipped?" My finger finds my neck and gently rubs behind my ears. The skin feels smooth and flat.

"Here, honey, have some more bourbon." Susan reaches over and splashes an inch into my empty mug. "Now, I'm not saying that exactly, yet you *are* here, dear. But you're still fresh. There wouldn't have been time to chip you yet. But you could've moved into any neighborhood. Why here?"

"Sean's father found us this home. He'd heard of it in *Forbes*, I think. He said it would help with Sean's political career."

"There it is."

"There *what* is?" Annoyance strains my voice.

"The reason why he brought you here."

"What are you talking about?" My skin burns.

"I apologize. I'm not trying to upset you, dear." Susan reaches over and pats my knee. "Did you know that in the Elizabethan Era, women were considered actual property? Like chattel. All their wealth and possessions, including their bodies, were owned first by their fathers and then by their husbands. In those days, gender trumped social status. So, if a woman of wealth was wedded to a pauper, her entire fortune—including herself—became his property. He could squander her entire estate, gambling away every last penny, while she stood powerless, stripped of any right to intervene. Queen Elizabeth the First did it right. She knew the moment she married, she'd relinquish it all. Her husband would be crowned king, and she would lose all her power. Women were—and still are in some parts of the world—considered second-class citizens. In certain circles, it was even debated if we had souls. Can you believe that?"

Frizzy curls fling side to side as I shake my head, desperate to unhear everything I've just heard. I can hardly believe anything that's spewing out of this woman's mouth. "I'm sorry, where are you going with this?"

"Have you not been listening? I'm speaking of ELITE, my dear."

"That's the tech company Luna's husband owns, right?"

"It's more than that. ELITE stands for *Exspecto Luxuria In Toto Electus*. Most people think it's just a fancy luxury brand for techies. Did you know they have the highest collection of intellectual data in existence? Aside from technological advances in energy, their business portfolio extends into real estate, global communication, even biomedical research. They have a secret branch devoted to manipulating the mind. They plan on selling it to the government. It's called Project PSS, short for Psycho-Sanctum Services, and it's run by none other than Dr. Novak. The list of services would turn your stomach, from pills to 'unlock hidden desire' to complete memory wipeout. Their main goal is to control the consciousness. They're pushing for everyone, except the top one percent of the one percent, to get indoctrinated."

My eyes grow wide with fear as I contemplate the stranger sitting before me. "But why would they want to do that?"

"Greed. Power. Money. If they succeed, they'll control everything. The human mind is the greatest wonder in the universe. We still don't know its full capabilities. The possibilities are endless."

"That's an interesting theory." I've met a lot of conspiracy theorists during my travels, but Susan takes the cake.

"It's no theory. Right now, they're designing a program for kids—to control their behavior from as early as two years old."

"No more terrible twos." I blurt out without thinking. My smile fades when I see Susan's sour face. "Sorry, bad joke." I help myself and pour us both more liquor from the dwindling bottle. "How do you know all this?"

"Years and years of research and living, my dear. Your mother-in-law is probably one of their success stories if your father-in-law was so keen on shipping you here. You're obviously a beautiful girl. So, tell me, Cass, if you don't mind, and I apologize if I'm getting too personal, but where's your family?"

"They're all dead. Why? Where are you going with this?" I put my mug down and sit back. Arms cross, eyes narrow.

"My apologies. I'm not trying to offend you, dear; I'm just saying..."

"Just saying *what*?" I want to yank the words out of her throat.

"It's quite plausible, particularly if your husband's actively pursuing a career in politics, that he deliberately chose you as his wife and career partner. Here at Orchid Hill, each wife is molded to their husband's specific needs and preferences. Do you understand what I'm saying?"

"This is insane. Sean and I have a great marriage. He would never..."

"Do you have any traits or qualities he seems to dislike? Has he started showing concern for something he previously disregarded before you moved here?"

I recall our last fight. It came out of nowhere. But I won't betray my husband or my marriage to this...recluse. The other women certainly don't pay her much attention.

She's absolutely brimming with conspiracy theories!

"It would be entirely possible to change different aspects of your personality. Mold you into the perfect politician's wife."

"I don't believe Sean would...Is this what you think happened to Jessa?"

"That woman didn't have a bad bone in her body. No way she would've ever drowned those precious girls—even if she had a chip in her head. I would bet my garden the whole thing was an ELITE cover-up. Things are getting worse. Technology's getting better. They're expanding—quicker than I expected."

I can't control my emotions, so I hide my face in my hands.

"Oh honey, I'm not saying your husband doesn't love you. All I'm saying is he chose you because he thought he could change you into what he thinks he needs. He wouldn't be the first future president of the United States to use Project PSS to find a wife."

"What do you mean?" I grip the mug for support.

"Nixon, Clinton, hell, even Schwarzenegger." Susan drains her cup. "How do you think someone like Melania ended up with an Oompa Loompa?"

"I have to go." I jump up. My head spins from too much bourbon and too much Susan.

Susan's blue eyes sparkle with spirits. "You came looking for answers. You know what they say: be careful what you wish for."

CHAPTER 29

KIT

MEANWHILE, KIT'S COOPED UP in her bedroom. It's raining. Again. She's been working nonstop on Operation Lovelace. She's barely slept. If you can call staring at the canopy, crunching numbers, and writing code sleeping. So far, she hasn't been able to get past the firewall and into Amber's hard drive. The fact that Amber's dad is a tech genius who owns an international corporation has not deterred Kit. In fact, she enjoys the challenge. Every few hours, she sips her mother's delicious pink punch. It's flat, but it fuels her. Better than those energy drinks her older brothers are obsessed with. She's careful not to drink too much too fast.

Time to focus.

V for Vendetta loops from a mounted flat screen in the background. Freedom and anarchy propel her. The explosive fireworks scene is her favorite part. She finds Pyotr Ilyich Tchaikovsky invigorating.

Kit stares at her computer with unblinking eyes. A copy of Hadnagy's *Social Engineering* on her lap. Composition books lie scattered across the floor, filled with every note she's ever taken at every hackathon and coding boot camp she's attended. Kit's using everything in her arsenal. She must find a way to access the Peatys' system. She sent Amber a dozen emails with a hidden phishing attack. So far, Amber has deleted or blocked them all. Even the sneaky ones from the fake accounts. She's not the slowest snail on the sidewalk. If only she applied her wit to something more valuable than destroying lives with wrecking ball rumors.

Think. Think. What would Ada do?

She wouldn't give up. That's for sure.

Kit opens the almost empty Mason jar on her desk and takes a small sip. She rolls the syrupy punch around her tongue. Her brain fires on all cylinders. The lights in her room swivel and socialize. They speak to her. She holds her breath to listen.

Mr. Peaty.

She could email Amber's father! He has no reason not to accept an email from Kit. After all, he chose her over his own daughter for that insane motorcycle ride. If Kit words it right, she could traipse right into his castle, past the moat and armed soldiers. She'll get Jeff to lower the drawbridge himself. She giggles at her brilliance. If this works, she'll celebrate with the joint she stole from her useless brothers.

If it doesn't...

Kit won't allow herself to think negatively. This will work. There's just one thing—she doesn't have Mr. Peaty's personal email address.

Fuck my life!

She looks at the clock. It's almost midnight. She's lost track of time. Wednesday. It's definitely Wednesday. She has school tomorrow, French class with Amber and Francesca. Kit's stomach spasms at the thought. Maybe she could play sick? If she pleads with puppy dog eyes to her father, he may just—that's it! Her father! He'll have Mr. Peaty's email. Kit types furiously on her keyboard. Her dad's address book is on a different server than the rest of the family, but Kit knows his password by heart. He's so predictable. It's the year he moved to the Gardens of Orchid Hill. The year his career exploded, and her mother started birthing an assembly line of children.

As Kit drags her mouse, a phantom curser remotely mirrors her movement across her father's desktop and into his address book. She copies Mr. Peaty's personal email. So obvious she could've guessed it.

As she's about to exit, Kit notices a new folder labeled "Project PSS." She clicks on it. Inside is a Word document labeled

"Menu" and another folder labeled "Patients." She double-clicks on "Menu" and is instantly confused.

PSYCHO-SANCTUM SERVICES

PHANTOM BLISS: THERAPEUTIC PILLS SUBTLY ALTER PERCEPTION, HEIGHTENING SENSES AND UNLOCKING HIDDEN DESIRES.

MINDWEB: DELVE INTO THE DEPTHS OF THE SUBCONSCIOUS THROUGH INTRICATE HYPNOTHERAPY SESSIONS, UNEARTHING BURIED SECRETS AND MOLDING THE PSYCHE TO YOUR COMMAND.

SINISTER SEDUCTION: DARK AND FORBIDDEN THERAPIES EXPLORE THE DEPTHS OF HUMAN DESIRE, UNLOCKING PRIMAL INSTINCTS AND INTENSIFYING YOUR CONNECTIONS WITH OTHERS.

REBIRTH PROTOCOL: AN EXPERIMENTAL PROCEDURE INVOLVING CONTROLLED ELECTRICAL STIMULATION, OFFERING A CHANCE TO ERASE PAINFUL MEMORIES.

SOULCRAFT: ADVANCED NEURO-CHIPPING TECHNOLOGY FOR A COMPLETE RECONSTRUCTION OF ONE'S PERSONALITY, ALLOWING YOU TO DESIGN THE PERFECT COMPANION.

ETERNAL ECHO: UPGRADE HER CHIP TO THE NEXT LEVEL, GRANTING UNPRECEDENTED CONTROL AND INFLUENCE OVER THE SUBJECT'S MIND WITHOUT COMPROMISING HER REPRODUCTIVE CAPABILITIES.

OBSIDIAN VEIL: IMMERSIVE VIRTUAL REALITY SIMULATIONS BLUR THE LINE BETWEEN FANTASY AND REALITY, ALLOWING YOU TO LIVE OUT YOUR DARKEST AND MOST FORBIDDEN FANTASIES.

THE VOID PROTOCOL: WHEN SHE BECOMES A LIABILITY, ERASE HER IDENTITY WITH A MEMORY WIPEOUT AND IMPLANT CUSTOM MEMORIES TO SUIT YOUR DESIRES.

PSYCHO-NEXUS: ENTER THE REALM OF PSYCHOLOGICAL EXPERIMENTATION, EXPERIENCE A CHANCE AT IMMORTALITY, TRANSPOSE CONSCIOUSNESS WITH OTHERS, WHERE THE TRUE NATURE OF THE HUMAN MIND IS UNLEASHED.

It's like her brain has stopped working. A cold rush of air passes through her. The hairs on her arms prick. She moves the mouse to the "Patients" folder and double taps. A password protector pops up. Slowly, she enters the four numbers. One. Nine. Nine. Five. A flood of files shuffle forward, each with a woman's name. She clicks on a few she recognizes.

BLAIR NOVAK: PREGNANT – PROGRAM AFFECTED
AGE: 45
HEIGHT: 4'11"
BODY: BORDERLINE OBESE, DEVIATING FROM PREVIOUS PREGNANCIES
INTELLIGENCE: 60%

PREFERENCES: BAKING, THROWING PARTIES, INTERIOR DESIGN

AVERSIONS: UNHAPPY HUSBANDS, NOSY NEIGHBORS, ENEMIES OF ELITE

COPULATION: DECREASED SEXUAL APPETITE TO 20% UNTIL WEIGHT RESTABILIZES

REPRODUCTIVE GOAL: MAXIMIZING THE NUMBER OF CHILDREN BEFORE MENOPAUSE

[NOTES: PATIENT CONTROL IS BECOMING INCREASINGLY CHALLENGING DESPITE THE ETERNAL ECHO UPGRADE. WHILE THE ISSUE OF MAINTAINING PREGNANCY HAS BEEN RESOLVED, IT APPEARS THE PREGNANCY ITSELF HAS THE ABILITY TO OVERRIDE THE PROGRAM. ALARMING LEVELS OF ALCOHOL CONSUMPTION OBSERVED, WHICH ARE INCONSISTENT WITH MATERNAL SETTINGS. THIS MAY BE A MALFUNCTION OR HEREDITARY ADDICTION. CONSIDER PSYCHO-NEXUS.]

CASSANDRA "CASS" MACCABEE: PENDING IMPLANT

AGE: 35

HEIGHT: 5'6"

BODY: CURVY/HOUR-GLASS FIGURE

INTELLIGENCE: HUSBAND REPORTS EXCESSIVELY HIGH INTELLIGENCE AT 80%; RECOMMEND DECREASING TO 50%

PREFERENCES: WRITING, INDEPENDENCE, TRAVELING; INCREASE SOCIAL PROCLIVITY TO 80%, ADD USING FULL NAME

AVERSIONS: SOCIALIZING, USING FULL NAME; ADD SMOKING MARIJUANA AND GARLIC WITH UPGRADE

COPULATION: INCREASE SEXUAL APPETITE TO 95%

REPRODUCTIVE GOAL: IUD, ON HOLD UNTIL AFTER ELECTION PER HUSBAND'S REQUEST, THEN PARENTAL GUIDELINES TOP PRIORITY, PREFERRED # OF KIDS 2

[NOTES: CASSANDRA HAS EXCEEDED ALL EXPECTATIONS AND SERVES AS THE MODEL OF SUCCESS FOR THE VOID PROTOCOL. SHE IS THE IDEAL PROTOTYPE FOR FUTURE MARKETING, PARTICULARLY AFTER FLOTUS STATUS IS FINALIZED.]

GRACE-KATHERINE "KIT" NOVAK: PENDING PROGRAM

AGE: 14

HEIGHT: 5'5"

BODY: PREPUBESCENT, GROWTH IN PROGRESS

INTELLIGENCE: 90%; RECOMMEND DECREASING TO 60%

PREFERENCES: TO BE DETERMINED

AVERSIONS: USING BIRTH NAME

COPULATION: N/A

REPRODUCTIVE GOAL: N/A

[NOTES: PLAN TO COMMENCE MINDWEB AFTER PUBERTY.]

AMARA SULLIVAN: PENDING UPGRADE

AGE: 32

HEIGHT: 6'3"

BODY: SLENDER/SLIM

INTELLIGENCE: DECREASED TO 80%; PER HUSBAND'S RE-QUEST, DECREASE TO 60%

PREFERENCES: SOCIAL MEDIA MARKETING, EROTIC GAMES

AVERSIONS: RUNNING, MATH, COMBAT

COPULATION: SEXUAL APPETITE INCREASED TO 80%; AL-LOCATED TO D.N. AS PER GENTLEMAN'S AGREEMENT WITH L.S.

[NOTES: SINISTER SEDUCTION INDUCES THE PATIENT TO BELIEVE SHE IS EXPERIENCING AN EXTRAMARITAL AFFAIR.]

Kit hastily averts her eyes, utilizing a command to close the windows of her dad's system. She pushes her chair away from her desk and squeezes her eyelids together. She's spinning, unable to comprehend what she just saw. What was with that list? Why is her name in a file? What is her father up to? When Kit opens her eyes, Ada whispers to her.

Stay on task. You're almost there.

Kit drags herself back to her desktop to send the phish to Amber's father. With one click, she dispatches a Trojan horse disguised as a PDF file titled "Amber's Party Pics." Hopefully, Amber will finally be exposed and grounded forever. *Two birds, one stone.* All that's left is to wait for Mr. Peaty to take the bait.

Easy peasy.

Kit's legs bounce. She can't sit still. She's invincible. There's nothing she can't do. Her mind latches onto the files she stumbled upon and won't let go, like Buster when it's time to leave the park. It's late. Way past her bedtime. Her father is typically still up. It's not unusual to find Dr. Novak working away in his lab until the birds start chirping.

I'll just confront him and ask him about it.

Fueled by the confidence of intoxication, she opens her door and listens to the night sounds. The usual humming of the air system permeates the silence. An ancient grandfather clock chimes down the hall, marking a new day. Light flickers under her big brothers' bedroom door. They must still be gaming. Buster's door is ajar. The pale glow of his nightlight allows Kit to see. She creeps into the hallway. The Smart system recognizes her and lights up the heated floorboards in her path. As she tiptoes down the hall to the stairs, a calming blue hue follows. Bare feet slap the tiles of the foyer. She sneaks past the double-wide mahogany doors and the formal sitting room to the single red door that leads down to the basement.

Every home at the Gardens of Orchid Hill has a red door, locked and ready for emergencies. These doors lead to the underground bunker, which safeguards the neighborhood from nuclear attacks or a zombie apocalypse. Only Dr. Novak routinely accesses the underground facility. He often brings patients through the house, down the stairs to his second office, and into his laboratory.

Kit punches the code into the keypad adjacent to the door. One. Nine. Nine. Five. Each number beeps into the night. She makes a mental note to delete the access log when done. The door unseals and pops open with a *swooshing* sound. Kit starts descending the industrial stairs. The air feels sterile and ten degrees cooler, like a hospital. She gets halfway down when she hears familiar voices. She freezes.

"I thought you always said you wanted a big family."

"You're being ridiculous. Get ahold of yourself."

"But what am I supposed to do? He'll kill me."

"Stop it! You don't know what you're saying. Go home."

"But I love you. Didn't you hear me? Ow! Let go!"

"Amara! Stop this. You're hysterical. I'm bringing you home."

The voices fade away down the tunnels in the direction of the Sullivans' stairway entrance.

Kit resumes breathing, her heart ricocheting inside her ribcage. The chime of her phone makes her wrench in surprise; she was sure she had silenced it. Anxiously, she checks to see whether Mr. Peaty has accepted her clickbait.

EMAIL FLAGGED AND DELETED

Fuck. Fuck! FUCK!

She turns and runs back up the stairs and into the boys' room without stopping to knock. Their door slams into the protective stopper, reverberating loudly.

"Jesus Christ, Kit!"

"Dude, what the fuck!"

She bends over, hands on her knees, panting. "You're not...you're not going to believe...what I just heard."

"Seriously, Squirt, get the fuck out."

"Yeah, dude, knock next time."

"Guys, I just heard Dad with Mrs. Sullivan downstairs. I think he's cheating on Mom!"

"Stop being stupid. Dad would never cheat on Mom."

"Yeah, isn't she, like, his client or something. I thought he helped all the desperate housewives around here. She's probably just getting some professional advice."

"Yeah!" Brody makes kissing sounds. "*Professional advice.*"

Seth throws a pillow at Brody's head, knocking off his headset. "Cut it out!"

"Dude, come on, it's, like, Dad. He's, like, the most reliable dude ever."

"You...you don't understand." The words keep floating away before Kit can form them in her mouth. "He has all these files...on his computer...of all of the wives...of me!"

"What the fuck, Kit? You went through Dad's computer?"

"Isn't that, like, against the law or something?"

"Yeah, it's called HIPPA. Now get the eff out before we tell Dad you're spying on him."

"Wait! How can I remove a pic on a computer if I can't hack into it?"

"What the hell are you hacking? Who *are* you? Anonymous?"

"Uh, delete it manually from the cloud, duh."

The answer is so obvious she can't help but giggle. "Duh!" She hiccups. Kit spins on her heels. The world spins with her.

CHAPTER 30

CASS

Since meeting Susan, my thoughts have been trapped in a relentless whirl. It's been days. I still haven't said anything to Sean. Not that I've had many chances to. I need to process.

I'm outside in my favorite spot, rolling a joint as questions roll around in my head.

Could the man who came to my rescue on the side of the road really be this villainous stranger Susan makes him out to be? Some bigoted control freak trying to turn me into a robot? Am I so naive and lonely I'd marry a sociopath?

I've always thought I had a good read on people. Now I don't know what to think.

How could she say those things about my husband? My Sean! The sweetest, kindest, most generous man I know. The man who drove to the pharmacy in the middle of the night to get me a new heating pad when I had the worst cramps of my life. The man who wouldn't let me pay a single vet bill. The man who vowed to love and cherish me for eternity. Shouldn't I give him the benefit of the doubt?

How well do I really know my husband?

More than I know this Susan something or other. My heart aches with doubt. I miss Thurgy. If only I could smell his skunky breath one last time. I miss our cuddles. He was my last real comfort of home. Sean is supposed to be my new home, my future. I was content in my bubble, traveling the country with Thurgood, removed from pain and heartache. I felt protected, hiding behind social media and the avatar I invented, high on life as I cycled through existence. Sean was a stick in my spokes. I never expected to fall head over handlebars for a stranger I met on the side of the road—let alone marry him.

Did I jump into this marriage too fast?

Can any of these ridiculous stories be true? Jessa never writes about a chip. And I never got a chance to ask Susan about the hypnotherapy and other treatments discussed in the journal. Is any of this even real? Sex trafficking? Devil worshiping? Did Jessa make the whole thing up? Just another crazy person believing in lizard people? Or was she a depressed schizophrenic like Dr. Novak diagnosed?

I need Lilith. She must know something or at least have heard something. And I trust that she'll tell me the truth.

I leave Lilith multiple obscure messages to call me back, then roam the house searching for hidden cameras. I can't shake this feeling of paranoia. I never put much thought into all the technical perks or what type of security we have. I'm sure there's more to this Smart system than solar windows and walls that change color. My sweep, however, turns up empty.

I pace the floors, praying for Lilith to return my calls. I'm too scared to call Blair. What would I say? *"Uh, hi, I know you could go into labor any second, but I think your husband is brainwashing and sex trafficking women and may have something to do with the deaths in my home."* Yeah, that would go over well. I'm way too scared of Amara, and I doubt Luna would even take my call after the way we left things.

I go back outside. I'm sick of waiting in that house. Lilith's car is in her driveway. Instantly relieved, I jog over and go around to the side door to knock. *Finally, someone sane to talk to.* The door swings open. I freeze. Air escapes me. My voice retracts into its shell.

A man stands in the doorway. He has a round face and button nose. Ink flashes from his open shirt and flexed arms. He cocks his shaved head. Red eyes squint at me with suspicion. A sickle grazes his cheek. The words *'El Diablo'* are scrolled neatly beneath his collarbone.

Holy shit!

I scrape together my vocal cords. "Is Lilith home?" I croak.

"Naw, sorry, she's out all day. Some doctor's appointment."
He smiles and extends a hand. "I'm Angel, her husband."

"Uh...hi...I'm Cass."

He wraps an inked paw around my hand and crushes it. My whole body winces.

"Cass...yeah...nice to finally meet you. Lilith wouldn't stop talking about our new 'cool as shit' neighbor. I'll tell her you stopped by." He gives me a goofy smile, releasing the door. It slams in my face.

Holy fuck! Jessa wasn't lying. I need more than Lilith. I need backup. I need armed services. I practically run back home, dialing the local police from my phone.

"OCPD. What can I do you for?"

His monotonous voice takes the wind from my sails. "Hi, um, no emergency. I don't think. I don't know. My name's Cass, Cass Maccabee, and I just moved into the Gardens of Orchid Hill at 111 Lycaste Lane, the murder house. You probably know that already; anyway, I, um, wanted to speak with someone regarding Jessa...Harvey's case."

"What did you say your name was again?"

"Cass. Cassandra Maccabee."

"How do you spell that?"

"M-A-C-C-A-B-E-E. I go by Cass."

"Hello, Ms. Maccabee. How can I help you?"

I pace the living room, chewing my nails to death. His lack-adaisical attitude infuriates me. "I'd like to speak with someone regarding the deaths that took place last year in my home. The deaths of Jessa Harvey and her family."

"About what?"

My cuticle starts bleeding. I groan inwardly. My patience evaporates into something less productive. "Regarding the circumstances. Is there anyone I can speak to about the case?"

"Not at the moment. You can find any public information online. We don't just open our case files to every civilian that has a whimsy."

"I have reason to believe other women are in danger." That should get his attention.

"Are you in danger, ma'am?" He sighs. I picture him balding and forty pounds overweight.

"Well, no, not at this precise moment...but maybe."

"Are you or aren't you?"

Wow, the compassion in this guy! "Listen, sir, I have reason to believe the women of Orchid Hill are being brainwashed and—"

"Lemme stop you right there."

"I know how it must sound, but I have proof."

"Proof? What kind of proof?"

"A notebook—a diary—of the woman who used to live here, Jessa Harvey. It details years of abuse."

"Ma'am, that case closed not too long ago."

"She mentions Dr. Novak doing horrific things she didn't consent to. Please, if someone could take a look."

"Novak? Dr. Daniel Novak?"

I stop picking my cuticle in relief. "Yes! That's the one!" Finally, we're getting somewhere.

"Ma'am...you have yourself a good night."

CLICK.

Chapter 31

AMARA

Amara Sullivan paces the corridor off her kitchen, studying the red door. The door that leads to safety and survival. The door that hides so many secrets. She's passed this door countless times without issue, but today, it's giving her pause, and she doesn't know why. This is the door that leads them to protection and preservation. This is the door that leads to Dr. Novak's office, where all of the women of Orchid Hill go to feel better. Why would she fear it? Suddenly, she finds herself dreading the walk down this hall. Her hair follicles stand at attention. It's a feeling similar to déjà vu. She hasn't felt this edgy since she served.

Another door worries her even more. The side door off the garage. Levi will be arriving any second, and tonight, she'll finally tell him the truth, well, as much of it as she can muster. Now that she's with child, maybe he won't punish her so harshly.

Amara sulks in the silent, laminated kitchen and pours herself a glass of water, mentally rehearsing. As she tilts the glass to her lips, a wave of crippling nausea swamps her. She sprints toward the powder room, shattering the glass on the polished floor. With crumbling limbs, she slides to the toilet, barely getting the lid up before she retches.

The side door slams.

Levi's home.

The keys to his favorite Jaguar jingle as he hangs them by the garage door. His Oxfords *tick-tick-tick* closer, a time bomb halting menacingly close behind her. Levi stares down at his sick wife. His cherubic face folds into a scowl, the one reserved for her.

The rest of the world gets his dimples, and I get his scorn.

"What's the matter? You look like shit." He sneers at his rumpled, mucky wife cowering on the bathroom floor.

She flusters in front of him. Curling her insanely long legs beneath her, she tries to smooth her wrinkled blouse, ensuring there isn't any leftover spew. She tugs on her sleeves, hiding as much of herself as possible. Amara looks up, eyes wincing. "Su-sur-prize!" The stuttering exclamation sounds like a deflating balloon.

"Get off the floor. You look like a dog begging to be pet." Levi grabs a sharp elbow and yanks her up in one easy swoop.

She wobbles as blood rushes back in place. "I was waiting to tell you to make sure everything was going to...to stick. I didn't lie. I promise."

"What are you rambling on about?" Levi releases his grip and stands before her, puffing up like a rooster. He slowly rolls the pink sleeves of his designer shirt to his elbows, displaying a fat gold watch and thick, hairy arms. His skin flaunts a natural tan. He removes his Panama hat, tossing it on the coffee table, and walks to the couch. Pinching the fabric of his white pants, he bends to sit on the leather statement sofa. His large, manicured hand pats the empty seat beside him.

Amara obeys.

Levi waits for her to settle next to him. "So, what's this all a—"

"I'm pregnant."

Levi doesn't respond. For a moment, one that stretches into eons for Amara, he doesn't move a muscle. He's frozen, as if he's suffering an acute stress response. A vein throbs from his thick neck as he stares straight ahead into the future.

Amara looks away. First, she hears his knuckles crack, a sound she recognizes. Kaleidoscopic emotions shift to fear. She wraps herself in her grey leisurewear, repeatedly folding herself like origami, unable to get small enough. She can feel the heat radiating off Levi, his hate palpable. She repeatedly compacts herself, by half and half again, trying to disappear, preparing for the blow.

Just when her anticipation grows unbearable, Levi tips back his head, jaw gaping, and starts to laugh. Big heavy guffaws echo around their massive, empty home. His maniacal outburst lasts several minutes. As his breathing returns to normal, Levi pulls out a monogrammed handkerchief and wipes away tears.

Tears of joy?

Amara softens and starts to unfold, little by little, a hedgehog unfurling. "So...you're happy?" The timid notes of her voice curl upwards in hope. In desperation.

"That motherfucker!" Levi's hand curls into an angry fist. "He's gone too far."

"What? Who?" Amara's militant eyes record everything: The reddening neck of her husband; the laughter disappearing from his voice; the anger slowly, dangerously seeping in; the number of inches separating her from his fists; the number of steps from her to the nearest door; the cells multiplying inside her belly.

He knows about the affair!

Amara tries to play dumb. A technique that's gotten her out of trouble in the past. "What are you talk—"

Before she can finish the word, Levi's left hand shoots out, gripping her by the neck, choking her into submission. She struggles to breathe, making wet, gurgling sounds as she squirms on the couch beside him. "You thought I didn't know? You really think I'm that stupid?" Levi seethes beside her, twisting her neck and face inches from his. His eyes are bloodshot with rage. Spittle flies through clenched teeth. "I know everything. All about you and the good doc. We had a deal. You were nothing but a transaction. A down payment for top service."

Bewildered, Amara continues with wincing eyes. He's too angry. If she admits everything now, who knows what Levi will do, to her, to the baby. She tries to remain calm as he squeezes the life out of her. "Doc...tor?" she gurgles. "The fert...ility doctor?"

Levi drops her, immediately wiping his hand with his handkerchief, like she's nothing more than a dirty, used-up rag.

Amara gasps. Squeezing air through her bruised vocal cords, she inches away to the opposite side of the couch.

"Ha! Those fertility treatments were supposed to keep you busy. Keep you out of trouble. Then you had to go and do this!" A frantic fist flies out and motions in her direction.

Amara flinches and places one hand over her belly as the other braces her neck. "I thought you wanted me pregnant. That's all you ever talk about since we married."

Levi groans. "No, dear, I wanted you to *want* to get pregnant, not actually get pregnant. There's a difference."

Amara reaches the end of the couch. "I don't understand. I thought you wanted a family." She plants her feet firmly on the ridiculously expensive rug and stands.

"Honey, if I wanted kids, I would've never had that vasectomy back in med school." Levi stomps over to her. "Now, shut the fuck up so we can clean up this mess you made." With that last word, he reaches into his breast pocket and pulls out a taser.

The pain is worse than anything Amara has ever felt. As she falls to the floor unconscious, her temple smacks the coffee table.

Crimson drips off the polished wood. A gold puddle forms on the antique carpet beneath her.

When Amara wakes, she's hanging from the ceiling in the little black room. Judging by the light through the window, she must have been unconscious for a while. Levi's never been this out of control. She can't see her body, but she can feel the bruises. The back of her head feels sticky. She smells foul.

My baby!

Instinctively, she yearns to reach down and grab her belly. Her hands are bound at an awkward angle behind her. Any slight movement could dislocate a shoulder—a lesson she learned the hard way in the past.

"Well, well, well. Look who came to in time for the party." Levi taunts her as he circles her. He no longer has on his tie, and his shirt is unbuttoned to his belly button. He stinks of bourbon.

Amara chokes on a makeshift gag: Levi's tie. She can't scream. Not that anyone in this neighborhood would hear her with the houses built like fortresses and sitting acres apart, nor would they dare get involved.

Mind your P's and Q's!

"Who are you thinking of screaming for?"

Amara stares at the floor. She mustn't taunt him. She must de-escalate the situation, like that time in Afghanistan during her mandatory military service after West Point. The distant memory, once shrouded in darkness, flickers to light. Amara commanded a team of soldiers who accomplished their objective with tremendous force. The praise she amassed from her superiors and the big promotion did not go unnoticed by her masculine team. They celebrated their unit's success with a makeshift party. It was the first time Amara had let her Barbie hair down, and it had been a while since the men had been home. Innocent jokes turned inappropriate and could've escalated physically if Amara hadn't kept her cool. She downplayed the dangerous situation, using her wits and sharp tongue to disarm them. She left unscathed, leaving them in fits of laughter while they mocked each other with insults. Later, when one of her men falsely accused her of misconduct, the others backed him up. Her accuser was rewarded with her promotion.

This is just like that. You trained for this.

"You think he cares about you, don't you?" Levi observes his wife's face and smiles. "You do! You actually think he likes you. Hell, you probably even think he *loves* you." He opens the carved wooden cabinet and brings out a mechanical silver device. He places it on the table below Amara, who's unadorned and dripping with blood.

The machine looks like an oversized toaster with two little arms attached with spiral cords. At the end of each limb is a small paddle.

Levi finds the electric cable and plugs it into the wall. The machine zings to life.

Amara can feel the hairs on her body prick. It's as if her body remembers things her mind cannot. She grunts and writhes in Levi's web. The strain on her bent elbows and shoulders reminds her to remain still. *Stay calm.* She attempts slow, deep breaths. She envisions a beach, an open ocean, a safe place far, far away. She's almost there when his voice cuts in—

"Do you know what this is? You probably don't remember, considering the side effects. So, the other day, I thought to myself, *Hey, I'm a doctor. I can order one of these myself. Why let Novak have all the fun?*" He picks up one of the wands and presses it to Amara's thigh.

A current of pain wracks her body. She bites down on her gag, trying to still her tortured nerves.

"Did you like that? Not as bad as that taser, huh? I just want to make you feel good, my darling wife." He places the wand on her buttocks.

Waves of agony flood her. Acrid fumes of burnt flesh reach her nostrils. She tries to move as little as possible, swallowing the sensation.

"You know what else I got? Misoprostol. Fun fact! Misoprostol causes uterine cramping, bleeding, and even—drum roll please—miscarriage. Don't worry. I always keep some on hand—just in case. I dosed you while you were out. Oh yeah, and I got both holes, if you know what I mean. I figured better safe than sorry."

All Amara can do is stare at this man she called her husband. Galaxies of hate and disgust funnel towards him. Amara flexes and clenches her pelvis, a feeble attempt to dispel the betrayal. A sore rawness unfurls inside her.

"Look at that ass. What kind of husband would I be if I let another man tap that and stood back and did nothing? Huh? What kind of man?" The rage in Levi's voice intensifies. "It's going to be a long night, honey. I have big plans. Let's try the nipples next."

THE NEXT TIME AMARA regains consciousness, she finds herself in a room strapped to a chair similar to the phlebotomy chair she gets her blood drawn in. The windowless room smells sterile. Bright lights glint off stainless steel. Digital screens cover the entire wall before her. Her name and vital signs blink across a monitor with a 3D image of a brain. Her brain? There's a beeping sound coming from the corner. She tries to twist her head to see, but her head is restrained by thick straps. Amara struggles to move her body. The straps won't budge. Her eyes dart around like fish. Tears forge. Is she in the hospital? The last thing she remembers is Levi leaving her suspended in the black room after tormenting her with his new toy. Luckily, she passed out before he made it past her nipples. She didn't want to know where he went next.

"Shhh. There, there." A familiar voice attempts to soothe her from behind.

Amara feels a hand pet the top of her head. "Daniel? Oh my god!" She sobs. "Get me out of here. Levi's gone crazy. He knows about us. About the baby—oh God, the baby! Daniel, you have to help me. Levi forced— Daniel? *Daniel*! What're you doing? Why aren't you untying me!" Amara's voice shrills.

"Hush now," Dr. Novak says soothingly, stroking Amara's head like a lab rabbit. "It'll all be over soon." He stops fondling her blonde hair and reaches to fiddle with something. He remains behind Amara as if to shield himself from her terror.

"What're you talking about? Daniel? Why can't I see you?" She struggles in her straps. "Daniel, please," she whimpers. "Please, tell me...what's happening?" His silence is abhorrent. "Why are you doing this?"

"Oh, my dear, dear Amara." He sighs with what sounds like remorse. "It was never supposed to be this way. You'll feel so much better. There will be no more suffering. I promise. I have finally reached perfection." Amara hears squeaking and the hiss of gas. Dr. Novak places a rubber mask over her mouth and nose. "There, there, just breathe. It'll all be over soon."

Chapter 32

KIT

On Thursday, Kit wakes up to a text: three purple devil face emojis and a message:

`Do or die Kitty. U have until midnight tomorrow.`

Kit pleads with her mother to stay home, feigning sickness.

Blair stands in the kitchen squinting at a thermometer. Kit can tell she's trying hard not to be annoyed. Her mother's bare legs swell under her robe, one hand on her hip. A gesture that signals to Kit she is deep in thought and swarming with underlying frustration.

Kit wonders if her mother secretly longs for a day of drinking to quiet her mind. Once this baby arrives, life will return to normal, just like after she had Buster. But, for now, her mother drinks. Kit secretly prays her father is finished expanding his legacy. Normalcy is a luxury these days.

Blair reaches out to feel Kit's forehead with the back of her hand. "Well, you don't have a fever." She peers at her daughter's bloodshot eyes and dark circles. "Okay then. Back to bed."

Kit spends most of the day unable to sleep, feverish, regardless of what her mother says. When she shivers, the walls shiver with her. She pulls her duvet over her head and invokes sleep. At half past noon, Blair brings up soup. Kit doesn't touch it.

"How about we watch that movie, *V for Victory*? I could set up the screening room, bring some blankets."

"It's *V for Vendetta*." Kit shrinks under the covers, shaking her head. Greasy strands of strawberry hair stick to her pillow.

"I could make vanilla milkshakes. Your favorite." Blair uses that singsong voice people use when trying to persuade someone to do something they don't want to do.

"Fine," Kit's tiny voice says from under the duvet.

Blair makes milkshakes, but she insists Kit finish both while she sips from her tumbler. They share popcorn seasoned with rosemary and parmesan cheese. Everything appears ordinary again, as if last week never happened.

Kit chews her bottom lip as she eyes her mom. This is the largest Kit's ever seen her. Her mother seems delicate in her inflated condition, stretched taut like a giant egg or an overinflated water balloon. What would happen if her parents divorced? Would she have to live in two homes like Amber?

"Mom?"

"Yeah, honey?" Blair's eyes remain fixed on the screen.

"What does Dad do exactly?"

"He's a doctor. He helps people."

"I know, but what does he actually do?"

"What?" Blair sips from her tumbler, eyes fixed on the screen.

"Downstairs in his office..." Kit persists. "What does he do down there all day and night?"

"I don't know, honey. He counsels people." Blair picks up the remote to rewind back the last five minutes.

"Mom?"

"Yes, Kit. What is it?" Blair holds the remote like a handgun, ready to fire, as soon as her daughter finishes Twenty Questions.

"What would you do if Dad was having an affair?"

Blair rotates her head so fast, for a second, Kit thinks it will spin all the way off. "Jesus, Kit, what's gotten into you? You know better than to speak of your father that way." She shovels handfuls of popcorn into her mouth and returns to Natalie Portman's shaved head.

"But what if he did? What would you do?"

"What's with you today?" Bits of chewed popcorn escape Blair's mouth. "Can't you just settle and watch the movie? I thought we were having a fun time together. Just you and me." Kit's mother slurps from her tumbler. "Don't worry," she says, her voice an octave higher. "Your father and I are fine. Our marriage is fine. Everything's fine." More sips. "There's nothing for you to worry about, okay Kit-Kat?" More sips.

It's pointless.

Kit snorts and slouches into the plush theater cushions to watch fireworks blow up Parliament. As Tchaikovsky's 1812 Overture blasts, her mind wanders to the texts. Kit realizes what she needs to do. There's no other way around it. She'll have to break into Amber's room, log onto her computer, and delete the original video from her cloud account.

As the movie Kit's already seen a dozen times reels before them, a warm, happy feeling blooms in her belly, a speck of relief from the week of agony. A glimmer of hope.

On Fridays, Amber goes to her mom's house after school.

THE FULL MOON CASTS a cool hue on the Gardens of Orchid Hill. Kit hides in her backyard, waiting for the Peaty house to sleep. She watches each light flicker off as she sips the last of the flat pink punch. She pulls out the joint from the pocket of her hoodie. It's fat in the middle and twisted closed on one side while the other remains open. She lights the twisted end. Her lips hesitate for a moment before she inhales. It's sweeter than expected. Her chest burns, reminding her she's alive. She's still here.

The metal top of the old Zippo snaps shut with a satisfying click. Kit runs her fingers over the insignia carved into the lighter. Supposedly, her father bought it off some guy who stole it from a Nazi he killed in WWII.

Gross.

She slips the lighter into the back pocket of her black jeans. Her dark hoodie hides her strawberry-blonde ponytail. Incognito. Her palms sweat. She wipes them on her thighs. It's hot, even at midnight. Twenty-four hours until her life implodes. She unzips, exposing a black tank top underneath. Finally, her armpits can breathe.

They say you don't get high the first time you smoke pot. Well, Kit definitely feels something. It's like that time she smoked a real cigarette, but way better. She feels fizzy, swimming in her mother's punch. Waves of bumblebees zipline over her, weaving a blanket of tangible energy around her. She can feel the Earth, hot and pulsating. Rotating. Very. Very. Slowly.

Without warning, her head topples over. It's too heavy for her neck. She has to prop it up with one hand. She sits cross-legged on the little bench behind the gardening shed. From this spot, no one can see her. But they may see the smoke. She giggles, watching the garden gnomes and drawing stories in her mind: The shed puffing chimney smoke. "Honey, the elves are back again," they'd say. Kit giggles at her cartoonish thoughts. Elves living in her shed, wearing little hats and little pointy shoes with bells on the ends. Her laughter catches fire. Before she can stop herself, wild snorts carry her off and into the night.

After her third hit, Kit floats back to reality, surfing waves of energy, watching the final lights go out next door.

She stubs out the joint and looks for a dry spot to save the rest for later. She picks up a garden gnome, preparing to leave the contraband inside the hollow opening. But when she turns it over, she's surprised to find a stash of notebook paper folded neatly inside a ziplocked bag.

What the hell?

You don't have time for this.

Without a second thought, Kit stuffs the baggie of papers inside her hoodie pocket and readies herself.

It's Go Time.

With a full moon lighting the way, Kit sneaks over to the Peatys and through their garage. She's relieved but not surprised the door leading from the garage into the house is left unlocked. No one in this neighborhood locks their doors. Not even after the tragedy down the street.

Why would they? We've been told it's all safe.

The Peaty house is silent. Out of all the homes in Orchid Hill, it's the most modern and technically advanced. Luckily for Kit, the home's security system is programmed to recognize her as a non-threat. As soon as she passes the threshold, the wall panels light up in a welcoming hue, a relic from her years of friendship with Amber. Kit tiptoes across the warm floorboards, past the parents' wing and the corridor that leads to the babies' rooms, and upstairs to Amber's suite.

Almost there.

In minutes, she'll be hacking Amber's computer, deleting that video for good. Giddiness bubbles within her. She fantasizes relief. Just as Kit is about to place her hand on the door to Amber's suite, it swings ajar without warning. The hallway glows deep fuchsia. Kit recoils. "Oh, fuck!" Blood pools in her feet.

Amber. Is. Home.

"What the hell are you doing here?" Amber's pigtails quiver in disbelief.

"You're not supposed to be here," Kit whispers, more to herself than to her nemesis.

"Like you know anything." Amber rolls her eyes and flips one bouncing curl over her shoulder. "My dad's making me go to that stupid block party tomorrow."

Kit doesn't know what to do next. She flattens herself against the wall, trying to be absorbed.

"Yo, Kit! What's wrong with you?"

Kit doesn't speak. Instead, she stares at Amber's breasts poking out from her camisole. She's wearing the pink fuzzy slippers Kit bought her for Christmas two years back.

"What're you trying to do anyway?" Amber crosses her arms self-consciously. Her eyes drink in Kit's black ensemble, motorcycle boots, red puffy eyes. "Holy shit! You were trying to delete the video of you sucking off Ethan, weren't you?"

Kit's eyes plummet. Blood rushes back to her cheeks.

"You're a pathetic loser who sucks at giving head! I bet he couldn't get it up 'cause you're a *lezz-bo*." Amber's tongue flickers like a snake as she exaggerates the word that crushes her enemy. She tips her pretty head back and roars with laughter—right in Kit's face.

Game over.

The delicate, frayed elastics of Kit's psyche finally snap. The thin veneer of her reality evaporates. She can't take any more. She won't take it. All the conditioned sweetness leaks out of her. Her egg has finally cracked. "Fuck...you!" Kit roars.

Amber takes a frightened step back. She tries to close the door to her room, but Kit moves faster, jamming her boot in the door jamb before Amber has a chance.

"At least I don't have to blackmail anyone to get a date to a prom at a high school I don't even attend yet. I asked *both* my brothers, and they *both* said they wouldn't touch you with a ten-foot pole. Believe me, I tried. Begged. I even offered to pay. And they *still* said no!"

Enraged, Amber whips out her ever-present phone. "Oh yeah, let's see what the world thinks of perfect Grace-Katherine after *this.*" Kit watches helplessly as Amber attacks with angry thumbs. "There. Done. Posted. Good luck with your life now, *bitch*!" Amber retreats with a vicious smile, triumphant.

Unbeknownst to her, as if controlled by dark forces, Kit's arm flies out. Her closed fist whacks Amber across the jawline. For a stunning moment, Amber's jade eyes flicker. She glares at Kit. Then, she smiles when her tongue finds blood in the corner of her mouth. Kit turns to flee. Everything spins. The house becomes a maze. Dizzy with defeat, she gropes the walls, making her way downstairs. An ocean of light follows her.

On her way to the garage, she slides along the walls, using memory to guide her. Right before she passes the red door, it swings open, blocking her exit. Just as swiftly, it closes with a familiar *swoosh*. Standing before Kit is a ruffled, sweaty Jeff Peaty. His breathing sounds labored, like he ran around the block.

As if he ever ran.

Red-faced and glistening, he smiles when he sees her. "Well, hello, young lady. Wow! You're growing up fast. I remember when you were this big." Jeff extends his hand past his knee and steps closer. "Heard about the dead girl?" His words slur. "Our nanny went missing too. Better ask your father about that one. Just another notch on his belt, I bet. You should also ask him where your last housekeeper disappeared to."

Kit stands frozen, obedient, waiting for dismissal.

He fingers her spaghetti strap under her unzipped hoodie. "Since your father likes to share so much, maybe he won't mind if I take a little taste." Jeff's breath reeks of propane.

Kit takes a step back and knocks over an expensive vase. Sparks fill her head. She feels like shattering too. She spins, running down the hallway into the garage. Fleeing through the cars, she smacks her knee against a five-gallon canister full of gasoline.

As she runs home, limping and defeated, Kit tucks her hands inside her hoodie pocket and retrieves the mysterious ziplocked bag of folded notebook paper.

CHAPTER 33

JESSA

MONDAY, APRIL 2, 2018

I'm not sure where to start. I went about this completely wrong. I could've died! The only good thing is that Michael has finally come around to see things from my perspective. But we're in trouble, treading dangerous waters. He knows it too. We must find a way out of this hell before Dr. Novak gets rid of us first.

My plan didn't go as easily as I'd expected. After I settled in his office for one of our weekly sessions, I calmly informed Dr. N. that I knew everything—the drugging, the mind control, the sex ring—all of it.

He didn't flinch. Didn't even bat an eyelash. Instead, he laughed loudly and rudely right in my face. He called me crazy. Called me a liar. Blamed my delusions on feminazis in the fashion industry brainwashing me. Dismissed me like I was a child. He even pointed at my purse and told me I could stop recording.

But I wouldn't give up. I pushed back. I told him I knew the tattooed man was real. I lied about details. Said I'd go to the police. That's when his nostrils flared. His eyebrows creased. His handsome face twisted into a malicious sneer.

"I don't care what you think you know. I'll make sure the police understand what a demented lunatic you are. I'll have you committed. You'll never see your husband or your children ever again."

Before I could respond, he lunged. A pinch in my neck. As I faded into darkness, my eyes caught his strange lamp. Instantly, I realized what the moldy paper really was. Skin. Human skin. Complete with a six-digit serial number tattoo.

When I came to, my whole body felt air-fried. I was in the guest room of our house. Again. Michael hovered in the corner, curled into himself with tears in his eyes. The girls were nowhere to be seen. In the other room, safe from worry, I hoped. Bianca was on one side of the bed, looking concerned as ever, and there was another woman. One I've never formally met before. She had the face of someone who possessed beauty in youth but had seen the test of time. Short salt-and-pepper hair framed a permanent frown. A stethoscope hung from her ears as she checked my blood pressure with a cuff. I assumed she was a nurse, but she wasn't in uniform. A paramedic?

"She's awake," I heard someone say.

"Thank God!" Michael sounded like he'd shatter any moment.

The nurse identified herself. "Jessa, my name is Susan. I'm your neighbor. You're safe at home. Your husband's here. Can you tell us what happened?"

I suddenly remembered Susan—the lone woman segregated from the rest of us at the Welcome Party. I told them my plan, how I confronted Dr. Novak. Bianca's lips remained glued. Her golf ball eyes said it all. I thought they'd pop right out and roll across the floor. Michael sobbed in the corner, apologizing on repeat. I could barely look at him.

Susan remained calm, her mouth a somber line. "Your vitals are normal. It'll be a few days before you'll start to feel better. You had an extreme reaction to your Rebirth session earlier. It caused you to become unconscious and incontinent. Dr. Novak called me in to assist. Your husband returned home as we were putting you to bed."

I looked between Michael and Bianca with shame and confusion. Incontinent? Rebirth? Was that the experimental treatment they were pushing so hard for?

"Don't worry," whispered Bianca, "we cleaned you up before he got home."

After Susan and Bianca left, I confronted Michael. Dr. Novak's Rebirth Protocol is essentially Electroconvulsive Therapy. ECT. It's all part of a new experiment ELITE has been working on—Project PSS. He said I had eventually agreed to it. Even signed a waiver. He showed me a copy from his office. It was my signature, but I have no recollection of signing it. Of course, with all the months I've lost, who knows anymore.

All I know is that it's not safe here for me, for the girls, for our family. It's time to pack up and leave the Gardens of Orchid Hill for good before something more sinister happens.

Thursday, April 12, 2018

Michael has not stopped apologizing. He's been consumed by fear since he saw the state I was in the other night. He said he's never been so wrong. I was right all along. He promised to get us somewhere safe, so we can focus on being a family again.

It's everything I ever wanted to hear.

He seems genuinely terrified. He's been avoiding Dr. Novak at all costs. Same with me. I've canceled the last few sessions, claiming the flu, a migraine, cramps, anything. There's no way I'm going back there. I keep picturing that skin lamp. I told Michael we should go to the police, but he advised against it. Says Novak's influence runs deep.

Our best bet is to leave California altogether. Michael has already lined up interviews and looked into quietly putting the house on the market. It's only a matter of time until ELITE is alerted. He's concerned how his boss will react. It makes me think back to that night he was drunk and spilling his guts. I can't help but wonder if Project PSS is connected? How deep is my husband's involvement? Is whatever's happening in this neighborhood happening to other women? This isn't the only ELITE neighborhood in the area. There are others. My head spins. I can't wrap my mind around it. I can't save the whole world. I must focus on my girls.

The plan is to lay low the next few weeks as we prepare our midnight departure. There's another Welcome Party for the newest neighbors. I really, really don't want to go. Michael said it'll look suspicious if we don't.

I can't wait to be rid of this hell hole.

I'll miss Luna the most.

SUNDAY, MAY 6, 2018

I saw him! El Diablo! The demon! He was at the party surrounded by laughing, smiling faces. Those liars! He's the one who's been terrorizing me at night. I froze when I saw him. I couldn't move. Couldn't speak. Michael asked what was wrong. I couldn't form the words. I grabbed champagne off a passing tray, choked it down, and started coughing uncontrollably. The coughs turned to laughs. The laughs turned to screams. Michael stood back, horrified, as I berated the gawking crowd. I called them sheep. All of them. Because that's what they are. Even Luna.

At some point, the husbands tackled me. They got grass stains on my new dress. I miss my old clothes. My old friends. My old life. I was escorted home by a group of grabby, half-drunk, patronizing men. I'm basically under house arrest until they figure out what to do with me.

Michael is trying to play it off as stress, buying time before his new job starts and we can move. I just have to keep it together for a few more days.

Those men acted as if I was armed and dangerous.

If only I had been.

Which gets me thinking—

Time to unpack Daddy's gun.

MONDAY, MAY 7, 2018

This morning, Bianca gave her two-week notice. She's leaving us to go work for the Novaks. Dr. N. requested her specifically.

My body breaks out in gooseflesh just writing this.

As she hugged me goodbye, she whispered a warning, "You need to leave. It's not safe for you here." She begged with the whites of her oversized eyes.

I didn't know how to tell her...I'd just sound crazy, but she's the one in need of warning.

FRIDAY, MAY 11, 2018

There's something not right. In my head. In this neighborhood. I can't seem to put my finger on it. Like trying to tie a word to my tongue.

My tongue.

My tongue feels thick and numb. Blood tastes metallic and cold. I feel sluggish. Shiny. Everything sparkles, but clouds. A dream made from mist.

I don't want to be here. They won't let me leave.

The other day, I let go of one of the girls in the deep end of the pool. I was teaching Janey to doggy paddle. She just slipped off my arms. I watched as her tiny body floated down, down, down to the mosaic floor. I counted each bubble as they floated up.

That's when I realized I can make this all stop. If I don't end them now, it will just keep going, spreading like a virus—an invisible pandemic circling the globe, and I can end it. Right here. Right now.

Then Michael came out to the backyard. I can still hear his screams. Shrill and fearful. He promised to make me better. Fix me. That's why we came here. To button me back up. Lacquer the cracks. Make me shiny and new.

Better. Perfect. I just want to be a good mom. A good wife.

I will be a good wife.

I love my husband.

I love my life.

I am a good mother.

I will obey.

CHAPTER 34

KIT

THE SUN CLAWS THROUGH the curtains in Kit's yellow-striped room. She was up all night with Jessa's last words. Kit remembers Jessa fondly. She babysat for her girls on occasion. That's why this is all so shocking and disgusting. It's worse than any horror novel she's ever read, which is a welcome distraction to current events. Kit devours the diary pages repeatedly, trying to forget her personal plight. The diary is genuine. The horror undeniable. So, what does that make her father? *A modern-day Dr. Frankenstein.*

She checks her phone for the millionth time. Dark circles ring pale blue eyes. She can't quite remember the last time she slept. It feels like days. The last time she checked her phone, the video had seventeen views and one share.

She keeps telling herself it could be worse. It's just a video—of herself, holding a flaccid penis like a microphone, on her knees like a nymph, attempting, *unsuccessfully*, to suck off one of the biggest nerds in her grade—right before she enters high school.

A fail video, if anything. A How-Not-To. She'll be a YouTube laughingstock by noon. Every parent's nightmare. A Girl-Gone-Wild story mothers will warn their daughters about. The fact her parents haven't seen it yet hangs over Kit like a guillotine.

Twenty-one views and six shares. *Fuck.* It's only seven o'clock on Saturday morning. So far, it's only been seen by other students. Mostly.

Only a matter of time.

Kit watches her life implode in slow motion. It's like her body has turned inside out, so all the raw, painful parts are on the outside, hurting and on display. She wants to die and be reborn into something new, something different, like a butterfly. Hell, she'd settle for a slug at this point. Her life has sunk to the lowest low. Her parents' marriage is a sham. Her father is a mad scientist, or worse—a serial killer. Her ex-best-friend ruined her life and possibly broke her heart.

My future is over before it even starts.

Kit takes small sips of wine from a tumbler. *Cheers, Mom!* She scrolls through her phone. Forty-eight views and sixteen shares. The comments are the worst part:

```
A fall from Grace-Katherine
I'd like to sit on that face!
```

```
What a dis-Grace lol
Where are the parents?
For a good time, call Kit Novak!
Goodbye Kit. Hello, Lolita!
Dude! That kids so lucky
GO ETHAN!!!! Ur the man!
```

Her DMs are even worse. Not only is she getting messages from kids at school, mostly Amber's crew and some of her brothers' friends, but also men older than her father.

```
I'll give you something to suck on!
OMG, Kit! Is that you?
Hey @kitkatnovak, need a date for the
prom? LOL
Hey pretty baby!
Go take a dirt nap SLUTTTTTTTTT!!!!
I can't wait for u to get to hs
My fantasy bae. Mmmm...
```

They go on and on and on. Kit throws her phone across her room. It hits the wall with a thump and slides to the floor. A walk will do some good. A hazy plan forms to get out of the house, finish off that joint, and numb herself into oblivion. After pocketing the Nazi Zippo, she sneaks into her mom's stash to top off the tumbler with wine. She slips out the back without anyone seeing her. She's getting surprisingly good at hiding herself.

Pretty soon, I'll be invisible.

She unearths the unfinished joint from under the gnome. The hike up the bluff behind their neighborhood is steep, but the view is worth it. You can see all the way to the ocean from here, where the air is fresh and salty. Below, the whole neighborhood rises early. Everyone is getting ready for the block party.

Catering vans line the street as vendors set up their stations. Two teenagers struggle to tack a giant inflatable jungle gym to the ground in the park's center. Mr. Huang argues with the young man setting up the DJ station. *Probably insisting on handling all the music himself, like usual.*

Kit watches Luna meditating in her Zen garden. A loud revving sound comes from the Peaty's garage right before Amber and Jeff speed off for a ride on his super-cycle. Amber has a new sparkling pink helmet to protect her perfect hair.

Kit rolls her eyes, taking another hit. Sweet smoke fills her lungs. She holds it in as long as she can, like in the movies, and releases with minimal coughing. She smiles, happy she isn't one of those dorks who hack up a lung with every puff.

Her head expands after each exhale, a blimp detached from the universe. She melts onto the rocks, limbs growing slack. Her head rolls back. She swallows the sky. Or maybe the sky could swallow her? Before shit really hits the fan. Before she watches her parents' faces crumple with disappointment. Before her future gets cremated. She wills the sun to incinerate her on the spot, for a solar flash to obliviate her. If only she could turn to dust and blow away. She wants to be nothing. The absence of anything.

Ashes to ashes. Dust to dust.

There is nothing left to do. No more plans to hatch. No way out. She's left with only one choice. Survive or not. Live or die. Excruciating shame or palpable peace.

Kit lets her mind drift like a View-Master. A carousel of sensory images attacks her. Amber's soft tongue. Mr. Peaty's hungry fingers. Amara's tearful confession. Her mother's secret drinking. Bianca's dead body. Jessa's revelations. *And my father, doing God knows what, in his mad laboratory.*

On the walk home, she passes the Peaty house, the garage door still open. Kit's knee throbs in painful memory. A blue-greenish bruise has formed along with a new plan.

The gasoline!

Without hesitation, Kit descends the hill, slips down Amber's driveway, and ducks into the garage. She lifts the plastic red container with two hands and lugs it carefully back home, invisible.

CHAPTER 35

BLAIR

AT DAWN, BLAIR NOVAK stands alone in her bathroom, willing herself to perk up before the Maccabee's Welcoming Party. Without the Botox, worry lines would ravage her face. There's something up with her daughter. Blair doesn't know what to do. This morning, she found an empty mason jar in Kit's closet that smelled suspiciously of party punch. The one Blair dosed with LSD per Daniel's request. If she went to him now, he'd be furious—at her for not being a better mother. But how is Blair supposed to watch them every second of every day? There just isn't enough Mommy to spread around. It's impossible. She's overwhelmed by the expectation to produce a race of perfect specimens born from a blend of love and laboratory precision—the pinnacle of Daniel's achievement.

And Blair, the sacrificial lamb or willing accomplice?

Soon, it'll be her daughter's turn. That poor child. What will she be subjected to? When will she get the needle that'll alter her, control her, turn her into an avatar to be modified and molded as the player sees fit? Now that she thinks of it, Kit's been off lately. All those questions the other night. Maybe she's already chipped? Perhaps she saw something, knows something.

Perhaps he silenced her like the others.

There were so many others. So many friends. Lost. So many women.

What have I done?

Blair will rot in hell for what she did. She's the worst kind of mother. The kind that knowingly puts her children in danger and does nothing about it. The kind that puts herself first. No, worse, the kind that puts her husband above all else. She has allowed him to control and manipulate her, rather than fighting for her true identity as a mother, a creator, a survivor.

But what is she doing about it now? Nothing. Drinking like a sorority girl at Rush. Drinking to unfeel things. It's better when she's not pregnant. She doesn't have weird thoughts or nightmares. Her mind wants to call them memories, but she knows that mustn't be true. It just can't. She's a nice girl with good morals and manners, a southern belle who makes the best darn macarons anyone this side of Georgia has ever tasted.

Not a woman who stands by as her husband...

She shudders at the thought. Countless guinea pigs. They keep getting younger. For too long, Blair has turned a blind eye and enjoyed her auspicious lifestyle. For too long, denial and alcohol were the keys to her success.

The toxicology report came back on Bianca. Police came last night to personally deliver the news to her husband. Bianca had massive amounts of LSD in her system. The coroner found scratches and lacerations covering almost every inch of her body. It also appeared she may have been sexually assaulted. The men called it "rough sex." When Buster's bath had finished, Blair made coffee and eavesdropped from the kitchen. She heard Daniel inform the police about how he treated Bianca for addiction and depression, detailing a history of self-harm.

Now, standing in her bathroom, Blair remembers the timid, bug-eyed girl and swallows the truth.

Jessa.

Her name is like a whisper in the night, a haunting plea from an old friend.

Blair stares at her inflated self in the bathroom mirror. If she takes all her pills right now, it'll all be over. She looks at her global belly, double chin, and flabby arms. No, not like this. She will get herself together. For her children. For herself. For her daughter.

Grace-Katherine.

Kit.

Kit-Kat.

Her daughter's name rings out like a hammer striking iron.

Who did I really marry?

A monster.

A monster is after my daughter.

Blair grasps the gravity of her situation. Divorce, while a seemingly viable option, is off the table. With Daniel's extensive connections, he could prolong the legal battle in court for months, possibly years. And there's an even more daunting possibility: the children might choose to stay with him. Bound by an ironclad prenuptial agreement, Blair faces the stark reality of being left with nothing.

Fleeing presents its own set of challenges. Daniel's resources and determination mean he'd eventually track them down. Convincing her children to abandon their current lives for a fugitive existence is not only unfair to them but also financially untenable.

Murder flits through her mind as a dark alternative, yet it carries an immense moral and legal cost.

In this intricate web of constraints, Blair realizes there's only one viable course of action left: expose ELITE for what it is and the men along with it.

CHAPTER 36

LUNA

IN THE DIM LIGHT of the early morning, Luna Peaty stands sentinel in her white lacquered kitchen, her eyes flicking cautiously towards her erratic neighbor. Blair's knock at the front door came just after the sun rose, and now, her words spill out in a frenzy of madness. The methodic clicking of Luna's acrylic nails reverberates against the shiny, sterilized surfaces and decorative panels hiding the appliances. Everything looks pristine and spotless, just how Jeff likes it.

"Blair, you know I can't help you. That would go against my core values. A woman must never disobey her husband. You're being unreasonable. This is silly." Luna stops clicking her nails. Her dramatic eyebrows shift as far as Botox will allow.

"No, Luna." Blair sits at the kitchen counter with her hands folded tight. "You don't understand what you're saying. You're not...you."

"What are you talking about? That is ridiculous. You are over-tired. Exhausted from this disgusting pregnancy. Here, have some water." Luna leans to fill a glass from the carafe on the counter.

"I don't need any fucking water, Luna. I need your help!"

Luna's eyebrows struggle to rise as she watches Blair's anger bubble over.

Blair clasps and unclasps her hands before placing her palms down on the cool countertop, her fingers spread wide as if in silent prayer. "I want you to help me take down ELITE. We need to stop them. They're brainwashing us and forcing us to live lives we didn't choose. They're going to do it to Kit, and they'll do it to your girls too. None of us are safe here."

"Blair." Luna purses her exaggerated lips. "What are you talking about? This is the safest neighborhood in California. We have the best life. Look around, honey. It doesn't get much better than this. What more could a woman want?" She waves her arms dramatically. They finally settle on the hips of her fitted jeans.

"Luna!" Blair pleads. She taps an angry finger against her temple. "You don't even know what you're saying. There's a chip in your head controlling your thoughts."

Luna's eyes narrow as she tries to understand her friend. Blair seems a little...frazzled. Her usually perfect hair is in disarray, not to mention the weight she allowed herself to gain. *How does her husband put up with it?* Luna would be out on the street faster than—She banishes the thought. "Oh, my dear, you are talking gibberish. I'm calling the doctor. You sound *luda*. We will fix you right up."

"No, please, don't call Daniel!" Blair's eyes fill with desperation.

Luna looks away, her throat bobbling. She ignores dark thoughts. "Okay, fine," she says, "but only if you stop talking this crazy talk." Luna strides over to the freezer disguised as a shiny white panel and pulls out a bottle of *rakija*. "Here, this is an emergency." She grabs two tiny glasses and fills them with clear liquid.

Blair stares at her wide-eyed and straightens up.

"What?" Luna snaps. "You don't think I've noticed your drinking? *Au bre!* What kind of friend do you think I am?" Luna pretends to be offended while she sips the chilled liquor.

Blair looks over both shoulders as if expecting Daniel to jump out from behind the counter. "Oh, what the hell." She sighs. Shoulders slump. She picks up her tiny glass and tips her head back until it's empty. She inhales, feeling the soothing sting in her lungs. She makes a final plea. "Luna, please? There will be nothing to find if they have nothing to hide."

A long silence follows. Each woman challenging the other, begging the other to break first.

"Think of Jessa," a defeated Blair whispers.

Luna doesn't bat an eyelash at the low blow. She simply refills her friend's cup. "So, what will you wear at the Maccabee Welcoming Party this afternoon?"

CHAPTER 37

DANIEL

DR. DANIEL NOVAK IS in his element. Holding court in the Gardens of Orchid Hill community park, the nucleus of the Maccabee Welcoming Party is taking a break. He's on the brink of changing the world, surrounded by family and friends, and reveling in their praise.

The good doctor does God's work. After all, he's God's Gift, a mantra his father's parents ingrained in him. *A genius since birth*, they'd said. He's sharp as a tack. Doesn't miss a thing. Daniel is always aware of everything that is happening at all times.

Like Dr. Sullivan, who's obviously drunk and irritated. You can practically see the steam radiating from his collar, on the edge of ruining Daniel's perfect Saturday. And what a day it is. The hot California sun has dried up any evidence of rain. The park bursts with green festivity. The birds are chirping. The children are laughing. And Levi is fuming.

Daniel surveys the scene, watching as his colleague fidgets and mumbles to himself in a deserted corner by the swings. He strides over to diffuse the situation. No need for another recurrence of last year's spectacle.

"How's everything, my friend?" Daniel slaps Levi on the back. "Amara finally settled now with the new upgrade? I'm calling it Eternal Echo. What do you think?

"Yeah. Sure. Whatever." Levi nips bourbon from a gold flask. "Probably would've gone down easier if you hadn't knocked her up, you son-of-a-bitch!"

"Whoa, whoa." Daniel places his hand on Levi's shoulder.

Levi jerks away. "Get off me!" He spins and stumbles backward.

"Hey, old friend." Daniel grabs his arm to steady him. "Let me help you."

"You've helped enough, Doc," Levi blubbers with wet eyes.

Daniel's blue eyes grow wide before narrowing. He tightens his grip on Levi and leads him to a shaded area away from everyone.

Fat tears mar Levi's unshaven face. "What've I done? She'll leave me like all the others. She can't. She can't leave me, Doc." Dr. Sully sobs. His usual dimpled face puffs red.

Daniel grits his teeth. "Get ahold of yourself, Sullivan. Yes, the situation is...less than ideal. I would've appreciated you coming to me first before you...did what you did; furthermore—"

"I know. I know. I'm sorry, Doc." Levi cries. "I was just so...so...angry. And ashamed. Ashamed she wouldn't want me after she found out I can't...reproduce."

"Furthermore," Daniel continues, calm and collected, "I can see the situation was...emotional for you. I'm prepared to put the past behind us if you are. What do you say, old friend? Another round on me?" He slaps Levi on the shoulder and grabs the back of his neck in comradery. Levi clears his throat, shakes the tears from his face, and accompanies Daniel back to the party.

Jeff Peaty's voice booms from the group of men standing together at the far side of the park. "So, I keep telling her, 'Luna, baby, just because you want to stay home with the kids doesn't mean I have to.' I might swap her out for a new one. Ya know what I mean?" Jeff tips his head back, forming thick fat rolls behind his fading hairline. With a hand-rolled cigar jammed between his yellow teeth, he half-coughs, half-laughs. "My daughter's friends are coming of age nicely. Eh? Eh?" He elbows the men beside him, all cloaked in casual slacks and comfortable shoes.

The semicircle sniggers. The baleful gleam of their weekend watches glint in the sunlight.

Chapter 38

CASS

"Wow, you can see them all sparkling from over here," I say to Sean as we walk to the party being thrown in our honor. I wipe my hands on the back of my dress for the umpteenth time and steady myself in Luna's hand-me-downs.

"Nervous?" Sean asks as he takes my sweaty hand.

I've barely seen him since we moved in, a blessing in disguise, really. I've been on pins and needles since that policeman hung up on me. This morning, I tried my best to play along, be the dutiful wife. I got ready all on my own, like Luna showed me, cat eyes and all. This past week took a toll, but I must admit, the red bandage dress looks even better now than it did a week ago. When Sean saw me this morning, he couldn't resist. I tried to play it off like I was tired, had a headache, just finished doing my hair, my makeup, but he wouldn't take no for an answer. For a moment, my old Sean was back. Now, I feel...disgusted? Comforted? Confused.

"No, not nervous...well, maybe." I adjust my straps. I can barely move, let alone breathe. "How did your dad hear about this place again?"

"We lived in an ELITE neighborhood in Connecticut. My father was referred through work, I think."

"Is that why he suggested this place over one of those new townhouses by the beach?"

"Huh?"

"You know, the ones we fell in love with before we toured this place." My hands look for something to do. I should've brought a purse so I'd have something to hold, but I never mastered juggling a clutch and a drink at one of these things. I ache for my overalls with the pockets.

"I don't recall." Sean's neck reddens. He pulls me along, a tugboat of determination. "Besides, there's no better investment than ELITE real estate."

"Oh, okay." I fiddle with my wedding ring, a simple gold band, elegant and tasteful.

"Just like you," Sean had said when we picked them out. "My very own Jackie with the accent and everything."

He squeezes my hand to keep me from fidgeting. "My father said a neighborhood like this can make a person."

My spine snaps. It's as if my zipper has frozen. "What the crap does that mean?" I turn to meet Sean's gaze, my smooth, flat ironed hair a veil in my wake.

"You'll see." He opens the cast iron garden gate in an exaggerated display of chivalry. A precise performance for our neighbors. "Oh, and try not to impose any of your conspiracy theories on anyone. I'm running for office soon. Remember that," Sean mutters as we walk onto the field.

I can't peel myself away fast enough. As soon as I spot Blair by the erected bar, I make a beeline before my husband can bark more orders. I'm unnerved. Upside down. In desperate need of a drink and a confidante. Lilith never returned my calls, so Blair's my last hope. I clamber over the grass to my pregnant neighbor, trying not to sink in Luna's stilettos.

Blair glows in a blue gingham dress, teetering in ankle-braking espadrilles.

"Ma'am, I don't think I can legally serve you," a pimpled-pocked teenager in a catering uniform croaks. His face twists in discomfort.

"I beg your pardon?" Blair places a French manicured hand above her cleavage as if physically assaulted by his insult.

"Uh," the red-faced student stutters, "you're pregnant?" He hesitates, making it more of a question.

"I know I'm pregnant, you..."

I catch the last of the awkward quarrel as I hurry over. "Blair, hi! I came to help...uh...with the refreshments." I lean in to accept Blair's half-hug. "But it looks like you've already hired help."

"Wow, Cass, you look ah-MAY-zing!" Kiss. Kiss. She laughs. "Ah, the old 'help with drinks' trick. It's what we say to the newbies to make sure you show up. Can you believe some people think they have a choice?" She play-slaps my bare shoulder, laughing at her own joke. The nervous bartender stares. Finally, Blair turns to the bizarre young man. "May I have two Cosmopolitans, please?"

"Ma'am?" His voice breaks. He pulls at his collar, gulping air. *This probably isn't the easy buck he was imagining.*

"They aren't for me, obviously." She makes a hand gesture, referencing her global belly. "They're for this young woman here and my friend over there." She waves to a woman with sleek jet-black hair and a hot pink frock surrounded by the rest of the Orchid Hill wives.

Covered in familiar tattoos.

"Wow! Is that...Lilith?"

"Yes! Doesn't she look lovely?"

"Uh, yeah, it's just...I barely recognize her. Did Luna give her a makeover too?"

Blair snatches the drinks from the ungainly server, hands one to me, and leads us to the group. "Uh-huh." I pretend I don't notice her sneak a sip. My eyes are locked on Lilith. "She resisted at first, but Luna finally wrangled her. Worse than breaking a Mustang, that one." We reach the adult seating nook under the arbor. Blair hands a pink Cosmopolitan to the new sparkling Lilith. "Here you go, my dear. Oh look, it matches your outfit!"

"Ooh, thank you, Blair," coos Lilith. She sips dramatically before looking up.

I take in the heavy mink eyelashes and sharp contoured face. There's something else, like a nose job or chin implant. *Strategically placed Botox and fillers*, I decide.

Lilith eyeballs me as she carefully sips with newly plumped lips. "Ohmygod Cass, you look, ah-MAY-zing! Doesn't she look ah-MAY-zing?" Lilith turns to Sonja and the others, wide-eyed and smiling.

They nod and twitter in agreement.

"Yes!"

"She does."

"Perfect!"

"About time."

"I would die for that hair!"

"And that ass!"

"Don't you just want to peel off her skin and wear it?"

"Oh, uh, thanks. It's all Luna." A feeling of foreboding fills me as I smile and drink. I shift awkwardly in Luna's heels as I try to pinpoint the source of my discomfort. "Lilith, I was looking for you the other day. I met Susan on a walk and—"

Lilith cuts me off. "Ew, gross! That nut job?"

As if on cue, all the women cease conversation. Their eyeballs probe me.

"Well, she told me some...things...about Jessa."

"Who?" Lilith asks.

Panic surges like bile up my throat. "Uh, Jessa. The woman who lived in my house. Your old neighbor." I look to the other wives for support. They stare blankly. Breathing becomes difficult. I can feel heat from their glaring eyes, gathering to prey on me. Beaks ready to crow. Talons waiting to tear me apart. Just like my haunting dream. "Wow! You all put this together so fast." I flail my arms, but I can't fly away. "How did you manage to get all the vendors here in such a short time?"

The women snap back to life in unison.

"Oh, it's no trouble."

"We do it all the time."

"We have the guys on call." Wink. Wink.

"Just one big happy community..."

"...here at the Gardens!"

"We just love any excuse..."

"...for a good old-fashioned..."

"...block party." Wink. Wink.

I smile and nod, unsure what to say or do next. I scan the park. It's the first time I've seen it in full swing. It's precisely how Jessa described it. Games and caterers divide the grassy field with a bar on each end. Music ranging from Beethoven to Gaga pulsates from the DJ booth erected in one corner. The other side hosts a giant inflatable obstacle course. In addition, the children have a choice of wholesome (perhaps a tad old-fashioned) games. There's sack racing, cornhole, and a piñata. The grills at the far end overflow with a cornucopia of vegetables and the best meats and seafood California offers. In a shaded corner, a pirate ship sculpted from ice drips with freshly shucked oysters and the craziest crab legs I've ever seen.

"Hey, babe!" Sean waves a hotdog at me, dripping mustard as he talk-chews. "They have the same hotdog stand I used to go to with my pops back in the city. Can you believe it?" A glob of yellow plops on his new polo shirt. "Shit." He drops his head, lowering his wiener to look for a napkin. A server swoops in for the rescue.

I wince, feeling a tug in my chest. My eyes water. I look to Blair, who grabs a travel tumbler and wanders toward the community toilet. Just when I turn to follow, I walk smack into Luna, a beacon of elegance in black and white, and wearing the most ridiculous hat.

Luna poses under her oversized headpiece, making a show of looking me up and down. "Well, look what the cat dragged in." Her thick accent dangles unapologetically between us.

"Hey, Luna." I step back from the dramatic brim and away from the chatty women. My eyes search Luna's face for hostility. I haven't seen her since she stormed off with her *rakija* and rolling suitcase.

"Oh, to be so young and tight again." Luna stares off at the teenager with dark ringlets flirting with the DJ. "That's my step-daughter, Amber. Jeff's first marriage. Pretty little thing. Got all of Jeff's good genes." She crosses her arms and leans back on one hip. "You look good too. I must take all the credit, but you did good."

"Thanks, again, for the clothes, the makeover, everything really." I shift my weight in Luna's heels, pulling the hem of her bandage dress lower. "Uh, Luna, may I speak to you for a moment? I want to apologize about the other night."

"No need." The former pop star uncrosses her arms to fold me into a quick hug under her awning. "All is forgiven. Now, I must go check on the kids. *Au bre!* They keep removing their bonnets. I keep telling the nannies we must not scare the other children!" And with that, she laughs off to a group of eager, young nannies guarding a line of strollers and designer diaper bags.

As the music thumps along, I listen to conversations swirling around me.

"Nothing like a break from laundry and lunches."

"Cheers to that!"

"Did you ladies hear about that woman they found in the water tower?"

"I heard it was Bianca."

"I heard it was drugs."

"Oh, that's terrible."

"Yes, indeed."

"I heard Seth talking to Doc about it. Suicide...by overdose."

On the other side, the men are discussing the same.

"Police determined no foul play. Case closed."

"Terrible waste of a good ass."

"Tell me about it. I never even got to try her out on the OV."

"Easy now, guy. You've had everyone else on the Obsidian Veil."

"Yeah, in record time too!"

"Don't be jelly. It's all PSS, baby!"

"Cheers to that!"

I spy Susan sitting alone in a row of Adirondack chairs tucked under the trees. Her crisp white shirt is rolled to her elbows. She has a drink in hand—in a fancy copper mug she must've brought from home. She tips her gardening hat towards me when our eyes meet. Before I can greet her, Sean's voice beckons me from across the field. I smile briskly at Susan before I suck in my stomach and tiptoe across the lawn to Sean and the other husbands.

The men stand in a wide semicircle with drinks in hand, some with cigars, all looking shiny and expensive in the most casual, relaxed way. Sean stands in the center with Dr. Novak. His Ken doll hair and Camelot smile fit right in.

"Ahh, there she is." Sean takes my hand and gives me a little twirl, catching me off guard. "Cassandra, I'd like you to meet Dr. Daniel Novak."

I stumble awkwardly, leering at my husband, but I play along. "It's nice to meet you."

"The pleasure is all mine," Dr. Novak purrs. He's alarmingly handsome, charming even, and tall. Taller than I expected. And fit. His unbuttoned pinstripe shirt reveals a toned, hairless torso. He smells of oranges. I swoon a little when he caresses my hand. "I hear you struggle with addiction. Marijuana, is it? I'm happy to help. Your husband set an appointment for us next week."

My face blazes, eyes snap to Sean. He smiles serenely, but he doesn't rush to my defense. The men frown. I can sense their disapproval, their judgment. Displeasure radiates off them, enveloping me like an airborne infection. I'm suffocating. The air thick like mud in my lungs. My breath quickens, heart chugging. It's as if the earth is swallowing me whole. *When's the last time I ate?*

A black bubble of fear overtakes me.

Dr. Novak reaches out with steady arms. With soft shushing noises, he folds my cold hand over in his and begins massaging the muscle between my thumb and pointer finger. "There, there," he soothes. "A mild panic attack. It's over now."

"Babe, are you okay?" Sean hands off his drink to Mr. Huang, pulling me into him.

"Yeah, I'm fine. Sorry. This dress..." I tug at the elastic. "I can barely breathe." I try to laugh it off. My eyes catch those of the other men.

"Well, darling, it sure looks perfect from where I stand." Jeff raises his glass.

"Here! Here!" The others chime in, nodding approval.

"I'm going to get some water. Excuse me." I untangle myself from Sean and walk toward the water fountains.

"Leaving so soon?"

I jump, skin prickling. "Shit, Susan, you scared me." I claim the empty Adirondack chair beside her, eager to rest my feet. It's only been less than an hour, and I want to slip back into my trusty Birkenstocks.

"How are you? You, okay? You look pale." She passes me her copper mug. "Here, sip this. It'll put hair on your chest."

"Thank you." I sniff the minty cocktail before taking a sip. "This is delicious. Did you make this?"

"Sure did. Got the mint from my garden." She takes the cup back, wiping away condensation.

"Yeah, well, I was going to head home. This is all..." My hands flail.

"A little too much? I'm sorry about the other day. That was a lot to put on you."

"Just a little."

"You probably shouldn't let them see you talking to me. It might make things difficult."

"Yeah, well, too late." I push myself up from the wooden chair and smooth down the front of Luna's dress.

Out of nowhere, Amara stalks up, regal as a swan in a turtle-neck chiffon gown. *In this heat?* "Cassandra, what are you doing?" Amara sings in a bubbly voice and exaggerated makeup. Oversized sunglasses shield her eyes. "You should know better."

"I should?" I look from Amara to Susan, who simply shrugs and sips.

"If you associate with crazy people, one will assume you're just like them. Go! Enjoy this good old-fashioned party with your hubs. Oh look! Here comes Blair. Isn't she the most gorgeous expectant mother you've ever seen?"

As Amara gushes on, Blair trudges up and flumps into the empty seat on the other side of Susan. "Oomph! Bless this heat," she groans to no one in particular, kicking out her swollen feet. "My dogs are barking!" Eventually, Blair turns and notices Susan for the first time. She startles when their eyes meet. "Oh, hey, Susan."

"Hello, Blair."

"Long time no see." Her voice sounds casual, not entirely friendly.

"Humph." Susan takes another sip.

I suck in air and hold it like a hit off a bong, anticipating their interaction.

Amara crosses her arms, eyeballs like lasers. "What the fuck, Blair?"

Susan spits out her drink and coughs.

"Pardon me?" Blair returns with unmasked irritation.

"Why are you speaking with the enemy?" Amara half-whispers, half-sings in an eerie chipper tone.

"Damn it, Amara!" Blair pulls a handkerchief from her cleavage and swipes her face. "I don't have time for this."

"For what? What don't you have time for, Blair?" Amara continues unabashed. Susan and I ping-pong silently between them. "You don't have time to practice what you preach?"

"Amara, stop. Please, I'm asking as a friend."

"Stop what? For years, you've warned us to stay away from Susan—The COL—and now you're all buddy-buddy with her?"

"Amara, there are things you don't understand."

"Like what, Blair? Why don't you enlighten me, please? Inform us all." Amara spreads her arms like Vanna White and waits on her high horse for Blair to explain.

"Is this about Jessa's journal?" I jump in. "It's full of accusations. Blair, I've been meaning to talk to you…"

"And here we go." Susan slumps into her seat as she slurps, pulling her gardening hat lower for protection.

"Dear Lord. I knew it! It's gone too far." Blair pants.

"Um, this might not be the best place…" Susan whispers, looking at the groups of neighbors chattering in the distance.

"Who the hell is Jessa?" Amara cuts in.

"Oh, dear Lord!" Blair cries.

"I know! Lilith said the same thing!" I shriek.

"No, my water broke!"

CHAPTER 39

SUSAN

"Oh fuck." Cass's hands fly to her mouth, eyes like spoons.

Susan springs from her chair. "All right now. Let's get her to the hospital. Who has a car?"

"My van's still in the shop."

"Don't be ridiculous," snaps Amara. "Daniel should drive you!"

"It doesn't matter," cries Blair. "She's coming now." She spins her head towards Amara. "You mustn't tell Daniel! Whatever you do!"

"Hush now," soothes Susan as she strokes her neighbor's hand. "You can have this baby at my house. It's right over there. And the last place they'll look."

"What the fuck, Blair? I don't understand." Amara's voice amplifies with authority. "I'm getting Daniel. Now!"

"No! Amara, I beg you. Please. As my friend, do this for me."

Amara crosses her arms and huffs in response.

"We'll need a distraction." Susan looks at the nosy neighbors grouped on the other side of the park. So far, no one has noticed the commotion in the shaded corner.

"I'll go. I can do it." All eyebrows jump. Cass looks surprised herself. "I'll keep them...entertained, so you can...do what you need to do." Cass locks eyes with each woman in oath.

Susan pulls out the flask of bourbon she hid in her bosom. "Here, you'll need this."

Cass takes a hefty swig. "Thanks. A joint may have been better." She wipes her mouth with the back of her hand, teetertottering towards the husbands, taking slow deep breaths.

"All right, Amara, help me with Blair."

They each secure an arm to hoist her up, leaving puddles on the white wood and earth below. With some effort, they sneak out the side entrance and over to Susan's, managing the weight of Blair down the sidewalk, behind the blossoming home, past the fertile garden, to Susan's back porch.

"I don't think anyone saw us." Susan pushes open her sliding door. They help Blair through the cluttered kitchen and into a guest bedroom. "Here, lay her down on the bed."

Blair examines the tidy, flower-patterned room. "But the bedding, it'll be ruined."

"Hush now." Susan helps her onto the floral duvet. She gently feels Blair's wrist, monitoring her pulse. "What else is a bed for if not to bring children into this world. Okay, now, Amara, fetch me some towels, boiled water, my nursing bag. It's in the hall closet. You can't miss it."

Blair's moans muffle under the base of the DJ. Having been in Blair's position numerous times before, Susan can empathize. Unlike Blair, Susan's contractions were medically induced, and her outcome always ended in unspeakable loss. *Then came the visions.* As the contractions wash over Blair, memories rush in like the tide. Susan recognizes it in Blair's panicked eyes.

"Don't let them near my baby! Promise me! Make sure none of them come in here." Blair cries out, panicked.

"Don't worry, dear, you're safe. We won't let them near you. I promise." Susan tucks pillows under Blair, propping up her legs.

Amara returns juggling towels, water bottles, a large leather bag, and a bowl of wet rags. "There's a pot of water on the stove. Here's your satchel."

"Thank you, dear."

"Guard the door!" Blair screams. "I don't want to die like Jane Seymour."

Amara's eyes flash with concern. "Is she delirious? What's she talking about?"

Susan wrings a cloth and mops Blair's forehead. "I think she's referring to Henry the Eighth's third wife. She died not long after childbirth."

"What happened?"

"Men happened. It was the first time the king allowed them in the birthing chamber. He was maniacal for a son. The labor proved to be difficult. Recommendations were pushed by both sexes. In the end, the men's arrogance outweighed the experienced midwives. Poor Jane died shortly after delivering the king's first male heir."

"How awful. Why would they do that?"

"Who knows why men do anything." Susan wrings out the face cloth.

Blair bellows.

"The contractions are coming fast." Susan checks her watch.

"Something's wrong. There's something wrong with my baby!" Beads of sweat drip down Blair's white face faster than Susan can wipe them away. "It's all my fault. I did this. I overate. I drank. I didn't want this pregnancy. Another leash. A noose!" Blair weeps. "I resented her since day one, and now I'll lose her. Oh, God, please help me!"

"Hush now. It'll be all right. You're safe here." Susan moves between Blair's legs and lifts the hem of her dress. "I'm going to check and see how dilated you are. Amara, let's get her comfortable. You take off those shoes. I'll get the undergarments."

Amara turns pale. It seems as though watching Blair in labor has stirred something. Once buried deep, it now buoys to the surface.

"Amara!"

Amara snaps back to life and unties Blair's espadrilles.

"So, you're a midwife, then? Or a doula?" Blair asks between gritted teeth.

"No, dear, I'm a retired registered nurse." She places Blair's wet underclothes neatly on the floor. "Don't you worry. I've delivered plenty of babies in my day." She finds latex gloves inside her nursing bag and slips them on.

"Really?" Blair appears amazed. "I didn't think any of the wives had a real job."

"It's wonderful. You should try it sometime."

"After this, maybe I will." Another primal growl escapes Blair's throat.

"This baby's coming fast. You're almost fully dilated. Hopefully, since this isn't your first rodeo, it should be easy sailing." Susan gets into position.

"Like muscle memory," Amara offers, eyes filled with worry. She perches on the bed near Blair, clutching her hand. "You can do this. We've got you."

"Yes, dear, you're among friends," Susan says, "surrounded by love and the very bond females have shared since Eve birthed her first daughter."

Blair gasps through another contraction. "Why...why are you being...so nice? I thought you were...You hate me. I've been...awful to you."

Susan feels Blair's gaze intensely, a profound connection forming as Blair delves into the depths of her familiar blue eyes. These are the eyes Blair has seen in her dreams. The same ones in Lilith's paintings. It's a moment of raw connection for Susan, sensing Blair's search for something beyond the surface, as if Blair is trying to reconcile the woman she has known with the images that have lingered in her subconscious.

Susan softens. "I don't hate anyone. Especially women. The men—no, I wouldn't say I hate them, but if I saw them drowning, I probably wouldn't go searching for a lifesaver—if you know what I mean."

"I...I don't blame you. After everything...they put us through." Blair looks at them, tucks her chin, and wails, "I'm so ashamed!"

"So, you knew," Susan whispers. Her question hangs in the air.

"I...I figured it out...eventually." Blair manages, her words broken by labored breathing.

"Why did you stay?"

"At first..." Blair gulps for air, struggling to form each word, "I honestly...didn't mind. If...if Daniel...wanted a...a proper housewife, so be it...I needed...change...My life...wasn't that great...starting out."

"So," Susan probes gently, mindful of Blair's condition, "you're saying you *chose* this life?"

"Actually...he chose me...Plucked me...from the club...I thought...I thought he...was rescuing me...But...But I'm...remembering...Bits and pieces. Arghhh!" Blair cries out as another contraction guts her, the pain palpable in her contorted expression.

"Oh, Blair!" Amara can't hold back the tears. She wraps herself around her neighbor in an awkward hug, her head resting on Blair's sweaty forehead.

Blair's voice huffs. "It wasn't...until I got...pregnant. The women started...disappearing. So many girls...too young. Then Jessa. Now Bianca...she didn't deserve...what they did. She was too...fragile. It could've been...Kit. Oh God!" Blair sobs. "I didn't choose it, but I...I never tried...to stop it. I'm so...so sorry! I helped...ruin...all your lives!"

"Blair, I have a confession too." Amara whimpers. "I've been having an affair with Daniel. I got pregnant, but Levi forced me..." She breaks into sobs. "...he forced me..."

"Oh, dear God!" Susan mutters.

"I'm so sorry. I don't know what got into me. You've been nothing but a true friend, and I did the worst thing a woman could ever do to another woman. I understand if you never want to speak to me again."

"Oh, Amara." Blair squeezes her hand, panting through the pain. "It's not...your fault. It's none...of your fault." She shoots Susan a knowing look. "It's...Daniel's."

"And ELITE's," Susan adds, breaking from Blair's gaze with remorseful longing.

Blair continues to stare into those blue eyes. "He's been...manipulating you...and every other woman...in a ten-block...radius," she grunts, each word punctuated by a struggle for breath.

Turning her face toward Amara with effort, she continues, "I should...be apologizing...to you...I want...to make it right...I have a plan...to fix everything. We'll finally...expose...this neighborhood...for what it is. Arghhh!" Her voice breaks as another contraction hits, the intensity of her pain mirrored in the urgency of her words.

"Here comes the big one." Susan coaches with grace. "I want you to push, Blair. Push!"

"Push, Blair! You can do this! We got you. I'm right here." Amara grips her friend. Under her long flowing dress, Susan suspects she's wearing a pad collecting the remnants of her unborn child. Despite her battered, raw state, Amara endures the pain for Blair. Susan longs for their bond, one that strengthens with each contraction.

One child enters this world while another departs prematurely.

"Don't forget to breathe," Susan says with her head between Blair's legs. "The head is out!"

"Blair, did you hear that? She's almost here," Amara gushes into Blair's ear.

"One more big push now!"

"I can't! I can't!"

"Yes, you can, Blair! You can do this! You've done it before. Come on, now!"

"Arghhh!"

"Good girl!"

"You did it! You did it, Blair!"

Blair collapses on the pillows. "Is she okay? Is she breathing?" Her breath labors.

Susan cleans the tiny human with a fresh cloth. The child wails. "You have a daughter."

Amara peers over, taking her first look at the newest resident of Orchid Hill. She inhales sharply. She locks eyes with Susan. "Um...I'll fetch the water. It...should be boiling by now."

"What? What is it? Is she okay? Let me see her."

"Hold on. I've got to cut the cord." Susan wraps the infant in a clean towel and hands her to her mother.

The beautiful, tiny girl, with her round face, button nose, and shock of silky black hair, bears little resemblance to her pale, angular siblings. It's undeniable. This child shares no genes with Daniel.

Depleted, Blair cradles her tiny child in her arms. She parts the towel to reveal her daughter's face. "Oh my." Blair startles at the deep brown eyes. She was expecting Novak blue. "She's...she's..." she looks at Susan, bewildered, "...absolutely gorgeous. Don't you think?"

"Yes, yes she is," Susan says, tears in her eyes.

"I'll name you...Hope," Blair mumbles.

"That's a beautiful name."

"Oh, I don't feel so good." Blair slumps. Her arms grow slack. "Something's not right." Her head lilts onto the pillow, eyelids fluttering before they droop.

Susan snaps up Hope, securing her between pillows. She lifts Blair's bloody dress. A pool of crimson flowers beneath her.

"Get me more towels. Go!" Susan snaps at Amara, who's wide-eyed and frozen. "Stay with us, Blair. Stay with Hope." She frantically rummages through her battered medical bag for something, anything to turn the situation around. Blair is slipping away. Inside Susan's bag is medication that can save her. Susan pauses to stare at the baby wailing on the bed. She makes a choice. "Amara, go!" With the flick of her wrist, she gives Blair an injection—her tried and true remedy. A glimmer of a future with Hope.

CHAPTER 40

DANIEL

DR. DANIEL NOVAK WANTS you to like him. And you do. His charm and handsome appearance disarm you. He makes you feel safe. When he speaks, you lean in, as if he's inviting you into his personal space, like you're the only person in the room. He's confident. Magnificent. Polished. Impeccable. The seeds of his success were planted by his paternal grandparents when he was a young boy.

Tall, pale, and angular with blonde hair lightened with age, he's a real handsome fella. His signature blue eyes—the ones he's bestowed upon all his children—sit slightly too close together on his aquiline nose, but that only adds to his allure. He's hypnotizing. Supernatural. Superb. He can jump remarkably high and click his heels together like a leprechaun. Children think he's magical.

There's a rumor he's borderline inhuman. Whispers of feline reflexes and hawk-like vision. He once caught Buster as he fell off the monkey bars with one hand behind his back. Daniel wasn't even looking. He never even broke conversation.

Nothing gets past Daniel. He notices everything—like his wife leaving with Susan and Amara. A burning urge to gallop over there and take the reins ignites him, but before he can seize control, Mrs. Maccabee half-stumbles, half-charges up to him. Clearly on some sort of mission and reeking of liquor. It's irritating and inconvenient. Daniel abhors intoxicated women. They remind him of his mother.

His face flinches at the smell of bourbon, yet he maintains his serene smile. "Cassandra, you're back. How lovely."

Cass lets him caress her hand. She shudders at the sound of her full name. Daniel activates her pressure point with his thumb. He feels her heartbeat slow and her breath steady.

"And to what do we owe this pleasure? Has something happened to my dear wife? I've noticed she has left the party she is hosting."

"Oh, Blair? She's fine." Cass flails her free hand, dismissing his comment. "She has a headache, so they took her home to lie down. No worries." She smiles and bats her eyelashes as if channeling Luna. "Actually, I came over here to see you."

"Oh, really?" Daniel straightens, smoothing his shirt. *This should be good.*

"Yeah, word on the street is..." She looks around, scrambling for ideas. The men ogle her, entertained by this clumsy creature in a tight dress. "Smoking is...really, really bad." She makes a pathetic face, obviously angling for sympathy.

"Yes, Cassandra, we've established that." Sean steps forward, grabbing her elbow. She shrugs him off. He scoffs at this slight in front of his new friends, but clears his throat, resuming his presidential persona.

"I heard you're the best," she purrs to Daniel, trying to sound as sultry as the infamous singer. "That you can cure anyone of anything in just one sitting." Her little white lies are her armor. "Tell me." She places a newly manicured hand on his bare arm. "What's your secret?"

Daniel clears his throat and grins. "My secret?" He smiles. He's finally got her where he wants her.

"Yes, Doctor, what's your...process? I'm fascinated to hear *all* about it." She adjusts her hips, stands tall, shoulders back. Her breasts now have the men's full attention.

"Well, I can tell you..." Daniel looks around at the grinning men.

"Or he can show you." Jeff sniggers.

The air becomes sludge. Cass glances at Sean, only to catch him exchanging knowing looks.

"What? Here?"

The men laugh collectively, a baying of hounds.

"No, not here, my dear." Daniel takes Cass's clammy hand and leads her towards the park gate. "My office. Come, there's a short-cut."

CHAPTER 41

CASS

BEFORE I CAN CHANGE my mind, Dr. Daniel Novak leads me out of the park and away from the party. Sean follows. Panic surges like an iced enema. My brain races to catch up. *Jessa. The journal. Susan's conspiracy theories. Blair giving birth. The wives of Orchid Hill and the ones yet to come.* I march on.

"Where are we going?" My voice wobbles with my legs.

"You'll see," says Daniel.

"Isn't this the Huang's residence?" Sean asks.

"Yes," Daniel replies. "They have the closest entrance to the tunnels leading to my home office. My access code works in every residence."

"Tunnels?" I swallow a lump. "You mean the red doors?"

"Yes. Please, follow me." Daniel leads us to the Huangs' side entrance, which accesses their black and white tiled kitchen. We go through the dining area and down a hallway to a crimson door. He uses one hand to block the keypad as he punches the keypad by the entrance. I count the beeps. One. Two. Three. Four. It opens with a *swoosh*. A stale industrial smell engulfs us. Daniel steps past the threshold and proceeds down the stairs. "This way, please. Watch your step."

With Sean flanking me, I follow Dr. Novak into the darkness, down an entire story to a dimly lit hallway curving left and right. An odorous, musty carpet, which may, in fact, be the same one from Roosevelt's presidency, covers the concrete. Modern lighting sconces guide our way. The windowless walls are bare except for pipes and the occasional gap for stairs.

"What's with all the pipes and staircases?" I ask, desperate to fill the void.

"These pipes transport gas from our neighborhood's recycled waste. The staircases provide access to our homes. For example, those stairs lead to the Peatys' house. Each house is connected to this underground shelter, designed for catastrophes. In case of an emergency, you simply exit through the red door, go down the stairs, and follow this hallway to the shelter. Please, follow me and watch your step."

We continue down the bending hallway. I get the feeling that if we follow it, we'll eventually make a complete loop. Our footsteps echo over the hum from the halogen bulbs. My breath quickens with a sinking thought: *If I were to scream, no one would hear me.*

"This one belongs to me." Dr. Novak points as we pass the staircase leading to his home. Further down the hallway, two doors appear on either side. The one on the left is double-wide chrome made of ten-gauge steel. The digital lock and five-pronged handle resemble a vault. "That leads to the bunker," Dr. Novak informs us. The door on the right is smaller and painted black with gold-leaf lettering. *Dr. Daniel Novak, Ph. D.* It has the same fancy lock and handle but with gold accents to match the lettering. "And this is my office." Daniel punches the four-digit code into the keypad and opens the door to the right.

Once we're through, the atmosphere changes. The room feels brighter somehow, even without windows. I inhale pleasant-smelling air before stopping short.

The room appears exactly as Jessa described it. Rich woods and creamy leather adorn the sophisticated office. Paneled walls hold multiple pictures, mainly of the doctor posing with various global leaders. There's a display of World War II relics, specifically a collection of German paraphernalia. A few family photos dot in between.

And there's the desk big enough to host the last supper, complete with a compendium of books organized between two brass bookends: Jung's *The Red Book* and the *Psychology of the Unconscious*, *The Collected Papers of Milton H. Erickson on Hypnosis*, *The Anunnaki Chronicles*, *Toward a Science of Consciousness* volumes

I, II, and III, and *The Fountain of Youth: Cultural, Scientific, and Ethical Perspectives of a Biomedical Goal.*

There's a door in the back with matching gold lettering: *LABORATORY.* I shudder.

Daniel motions for me to sit on the couch. He takes his place on a chair facing me.

Sean mimics Novak, taking the chair beside him.

I fidget alone on the sofa.

Daniel begins right away using his soothing psychiatrist's voice. "All right, Cassandra, I want you to relax. Find a comfortable spot. It may be easier if you lie down."

I look from the doctor to my husband and back again, my mind churning with my stomach. "I'm okay like this. If that's all right."

"Fine." Daniel's jaw flexes. In a gentle voice, he continues, "I want you to take a few deep breaths and concentrate on my voice."

I comply and tip my head back on the headrest.

"Close your eyes and breathe deeply. Good. Now...relax each muscle...starting from your toes...to your ankles...up to your legs...your torso...and through your entire body...stretching into your head. Good. Keep breathing. Perfect. You are now in a deep state of relaxation. Excellent. Now, I want you to imagine your toes getting warmer. Can you feel the heat?"

"Yes."

"Excellent. Imagine that heat traveling up your legs, each leg getting increasingly warmer. Feel that heat spread through your body. Your belly and rib cage are warm. Can you feel it?"

"Yes."

"Now, your arms and your neck are warm...Follow that heat as it spreads to your face and head. Can you feel the heat penetrating your whole body now?"

"Yes," I say, my breath calm and even as I fall deeper and deeper into an altered awareness.

"Good," says Dr. Novak. "Very good."

CHAPTER 42

DANIEL

DANIEL TURNS AND BECKONS silently for Sean to step into the next room. Sean follows him to the far end of the office and into the laboratory. "She's now in a deep state of submission."

"That was fast. Can't she hear us?"

"Her brain thinks she is sleeping. Don't worry. My methods are tried and true. Are you sure you want to proceed with Eternal Echo? As you know, other services may be more suitable, but require more time."

"Look, I appreciate your concern, doctor, but I have an expedited campaign to get through, and all parties agree this is the easiest and most practical way to proceed. I love her, Doc, don't get me wrong, but Cassandra's becoming more of a...free spirit. I thought we'd nipped it in the bud. Things were manageable initially, but recently, she's been harder to control. And I can't let anything get in my way. This'll be good. For both of us. My parents are a perfect example."

"If you insist." Daniel turns to a digital machine and adjusts the settings. "We'll need to move her here."

When they return to the other room, they find Cass sprawled on the couch with Jeff Peaty on top of her. Cass's dress rides up to her hips. Jeff fumbles with her elastic undergarments. "Jesus Christ, do they have to make these things like fucking chastity belts!"

"What the hell's going on?" Sean jumps towards him. "How the hell did you get in here?"

Jeff staggers back. "Calm down. I have an access code. Just wanted a little taste. As the company's main shareholder, I'm entitled." He smirks at Sean. "You had mine last week, remember?"

Sean stalks towards Jeff, fists tight balls, jaw clenched. "That was different. I used the Obsidian Veil like every other gentleman in this neighborhood. What do you have to say for yourself?"

Jeff rolls his thick shoulders back. Standing at full height, his eyes meet Sean's nose. "Listen, son, as your biggest campaign contributor, I don't have to say anything, and I especially don't have to answer to your leveraged ass. Do you hear me?"

"No, you listen, man." Sean jams his finger in Jeff's pocked face. "This is the future First Lady and my *wife*, and I've said you've had enough."

"Gentlemen. Gentlemen!" Daniel steps between them. This is the last thing he needs. "Let's not tarnish a symbiotic relationship over such silly trifles."

"Fine," Sean spits at Jeff, fists on his hips, forehead sweating. "But show some respect, and clean her up when you're done."

"Come now, Sean. We need to talk specifics, anyway." Daniel leads Sean back to the procedure room and shuts the door. "Have you finalized all the behavioral calibrations for Cassandra?"

CHAPTER 43

CASS

IT'S AS IF I'M in a dream...but not dreaming. I feel weightless but not entirely mindless. Motionless, but not quite dead. Peaceful, really. Nothing feels unpleasant at all. Until my limp arm slides against the lamp perched on Novak's desk. The dehydrated shade scratches against my moisturized hand, snapping me out of my reverie and into a nightmare. The lamp topples over with a sickening crack. *The same lamp Jessa wrote about!* I hear a gasp. Was it me?

Sean and Dr. Novak are carrying me to another room. Sean has my underarms. Novak, my legs.

My legs.

My legs feel wet and sticky. Luna's dress is ruined. She'll never forgive me. Jeff stands in the corner, buckling his pants. Pain pulsates from my core. They put me on a chair.

Am I at the dentist?

"What's going on?" I'm unable to focus. Do I have a cleaning? Too many lights beeping, blinking. A familiar face zooms to the front of the stage. "Sean? What's happening?"

Silence.

I search my husband's handsome face for comfort, reassurance, but find a mournful expression instead.

"It'll all be over soon." Sean pats my arm before gently sliding on a wrist restraint. It's padded. For my comfort.

Wait! What?

I'm tethered. Panic surges through me—Jessa, journal, Susan, chip, Blair, baby. I buck wildly. "Oh my gahd! Stop! What are you doing?"

Dr. Novak hastens to fasten my other wrist. "A little help over here!" he snaps at Jeff.

Jeff Peaty holds my legs. The stench of his cologne sets the room spinning. I can't help but lean over and vomit.

"Not my fucking shoes!" Jeff booms.

"Why is she awake?" Desperation fills Sean's voice. "You said she wouldn't remember any of this? You said you wouldn't fucking hurt her."

Dr. Novak shrugs. "Something must have called her out of the trance. Or maybe she's becoming tolerant to hypnotic suggestion." He fiddles with something behind me. "Anyway, it doesn't matter. We're here now. We can only move forward."

I spit on the floor, unable to clean the sick from my face. Tears wash away the rest. The straps on my legs tighten. Soon, I won't be able to feel my feet. Bound in Luna's clothes, I don't recognize my own body. A black hole of panic swallows me. *Susan was right!* I struggle to ride it out, try controlling my breathing. Physically, I'm no match. I can't believe I left my home, my van, everything I knew just to die here, in this dungeon, by the person who promised to love me for better or worse. My body goes slack. I stifle a sob. "Why? Why are you doing this?" I glare at Sean. He slinks to the corner, looking wide-eyed and childish. Twisting to scowl at Dr. Novak, I ignore Jeff's repulsive face.

"Actually, you should be thanking me, dear," Dr. Novak says with a smooth, even tone. "This will afford you the greatest advantage in life. I want nothing but the best for you, and humanity as a whole."

I untangle my clouded, semi-cognitive mind from the void and tug it back to the present. "How's this bettering humanity?"

"Allow me to share a secret about women. You all aspire to be like men, yet that's an ambition you can never fully achieve. Would you like to know why?" He waits a beat before continuing. "Because we won't allow it! And that leaves you feeling less, feeling defeated, insecure, depressed...Need I go on?"

"Yes, please!" I beg for more time. "Tell me everything. I need to know." *It's the least you could do, you psychotic prick.*

"I'm trying to help you. Don't you see? All women want, want, want, but none of you know how to take it. This will make you become everything you've ever aspired to be. The perfect specimen. A paradigm of womanhood." He holds up a cartoon syringe. "This will relieve you of all your suffering."

I squirm in the suffocating dress. "And what is that, exactly? I'm guessing it's not Botox."

"This, my dear, is my greatest creation. My contribution to society. What I will be remembered for."

"Damn straight, Doc." Jeff chimes in from his corner. "And don't forget about your partner over here. Give credit where it's due."

"Yes, Jeff." Dr. Novak sighs. "None of this would have happened without your amassed fortune and your talents for technology and marketing. Thank you, again, for your contribution."

"So, what's in the needle?" I persevere, willing to drag out each antagonizing millisecond. Maybe it would be easier if they just end my misery.

"This is one of our most popular services. I call it Eternal Echo—a bio-neural processing unit designed by yours truly, distributed by ELITE, and calibrated with your husband's specific preferences."

My eyes find Sean. *How could you?*

He refuses to meet my gaze.

"So, I won't be...*me* anymore?" My voice sounds ear-piercingly high. "So, what, you want me to become like Blair or Amara, or some kind of lobotomized housewife, slaving away cooking and cleaning? And bearing your fucking presidential children? Is this what you need me to be?"

"Cassandra, my dear girl." The doctor attempts to lull me with his soothing voice. "You're going to become what every woman worldwide dreams of being—a loving wife and mother. And who knows, maybe even the next First Lady." He winks at Sean. "I promise, you won't be displeased. I've never had a disappointed customer." His tinny, shallow laugh grates my nerves.

"You think by controlling women, you can make the world a better place?"

Dr. Novak looks from Jeff to Sean and then at me. "As a matter of fact, I do."

"You're insane."

"I'm ahead of the curve," he coolly says as he prepares the syringe.

My neck strains. "You belong locked up. All of you! You're all nuts!"

"Some may think so, but more importantly—prominent men of our society do not, and that's who counts." He flicks the needle, turning to me. "Please, hold still."

"Sean, please. You don't have to do this. I'll give up the pot, whatever you want. I beg you!"

"It's for your own good, Cassandra," mumbles my pathetic excuse for a husband from the corner behind me. "It has to be this way."

Coward! Sean hides from my sight while I'm forced into his control.

I frantically think, refusing to give up. Remembering my promise to Blair and the others, I try a different tactic. "You really think Blair is happy? You know your wife's a drunk, right?" All three men gape like I'm the asshole who exposed the emperor's nakedness.

Dr. Novak pauses before replying. Sean and Jeff remain silent, anticipating his response. But, to my surprise, Novak doesn't flinch. "Yes, as a matter of fact, I do. You see, there's something off with the chip during pregnancy, and I'm always in need of practice."

"So, you admit to experimenting on your own wife and unborn child? You're disgusting."

"Disgusting? My dear, Blair is my *willing* participant, not that it's any of your concern. We made a deal, she and I, a long time ago. She knows everything. If it weren't for me, she'd still be baring her breasts in some seedy club in a back ally. I knew the second I saw her—she was the one. When I made her almost perfect, I kept her for myself. Married my muse. I know...such a cliché. But you see, Blair's the lucky one. And so are you. You've been chosen for this wonderful gift."

"Do you wash that self-righteousness off before you kiss your family goodnight? Or maybe you don't notice your own stench anymore. You don't. Do you? You're rotting in deceit. But one day, your sons will know. And your daughter will know. They'll see you for the monster you truly are."

"Are you quite finished?" Novak shakes the excess fluid from the tip of the needle.

I submit. Pathetic. Powerless. "What are you going to do with me?" My muscles exhaust into the sterile chair. I succumb to padded shackles.

"Whatever we want. Get the gas," Novak says impatiently. "She's obviously resistant to hypnosis. I thought the EST we tried last week would have done some good."

"Please, somebody help me!" I scream until I'm hoarse. My wrists burn as I struggle, but it's no use. *God, please, this can't be happening.*

Jeff hands him the rubber mask. It hisses as the doctor wrangles it onto my face.

I won't make it easy for them.

"Now hold still, my dear girl." Dr. Novak whispers out of the darkness. "This won't hurt a bit."

CHAPTER 44

KIT

KIT IS FUCKED UP. Definitely drunk and possibly hallucinating. She doesn't know for sure, but it may be the weed. Or maybe it's the wine. It seems more potent than the punch she finished.

The world is a wobbly place.

She hiccups inside the treehouse as she watches Amber flirt with the DJ—so obvious it makes Kit's teeth hurt.

Kit didn't even want to come to this stupid thing, but with all the chaos buzzing inside her, staying home wasn't an option. So, super early this morning, she snuck out the house before her mother could get a look at the mess she was in.

She swigs from her tumbler, her glazed eyes sweeping the scene below. From here, Kit can see everything. Like her mom, leaving with that weird lady through the back exit, wearing those ridiculously high-heeled espadrilles. *If having cankles isn't enough to deter*

a person from wearing stilts, being one-hundred months preg-
nant and unable to see your own feet should—not my mother.

Meanwhile, her father departs in the opposite direction, es-
corting the guests of honor towards the Huang residence. Kit's
attention shifts to Mr. Peaty as he sneaks off to follow them. A
sudden, intense cramp seizes her stomach—a pain so hot and
so white, for a moment, she wishes she would die.

DING! DING!

Kit almost leaps out of her skin. Her phone has been chiming
non-stop since this morning. Intestines coil around her spine
as she thumbs through messages.

`OMG Kit is this u? *LINK TO VIDEO`

`Girl u gonna b grounded 4life!`

`Shit Kit didnt no how hot u r. Gotta`
`date 4 prom?`

`I'll give you something to suck on.`

Kit is sick. Sick of thinking. Sick of living. If she could,
she would crack open her own head and rip out her brains.
Thinking only leads to imagining the worst about the people
she knows the best. Her life has catapulted out of control and
into a different dimension. She watches adults smile and lie,
pretending everything's perfect. That Bianca isn't dead. That
her father isn't an adulterer. Or worse. That her neighbor isn't
pregnant with her half-sibling. She'll never be able to walk the
school halls again.

Kit watches Mr. Huang stroll over and interrupt the DJ and Amber's flirting. Amber whips her hair, nostrils flare. Kit smiles as Mr. Huang ignores her frenemy, leaving her stewing. Amber wastes no time. She tugs her phone from a multicolored belly bag and swipes at her screen.

Checking her LIKES, no doubt.

The last time Kit checked, there were over one hundred comments. She's surprised it hasn't made it to the parents yet, but with all of them here and intoxicated...

Amber spots Kit in the treehouse and smirks. Her obscene baby doll dress and pigtails make her look younger. Innocent, even. Kit looks down at her own outfit. She's still wearing her black burglar ensemble. She unzips her hoodie. She's sweating worse than her brothers after hockey practice. Kit feels Amber's taunts from across the park. Her knee bounces uncontrollably. Amber turns away from the uninterested DJ and stomps towards Kit and the treehouse.

Holy shit!

Kit hears those familiar violins before she can make sense of the unfolding events. They ascend with the sun, solemn and seductive, summoning her. Each note an emotion. Each chord a tear. Slow, soothing strings cry out to her with their sorrow. Fearful flutes, timid in their tones, fight and forfeit to powerful strings. It's her funeral hymn, her elegy. A profound tribute to all who've been wronged. Horns, light and lifting, envelop her. Their soundwaves wrap around the Gardens of Orchid Hill. For a fleeting moment, she's enraptured by bliss.

Could this be heaven?

Suddenly, the tumultuous tempo of musical instruments combat. It's a battle of good versus evil. Violent cymbals clang her out of reverie. It's as if the sky cracked open and reached out its hand—a life preserver in a sea of anguish.

It turns out, Mr. Huang's favorite song happens to be Tchaikovsky: Symphony No. 5 Overture 1812, played by the Berlin Philharmonic. Kit couldn't have planned it better. She *loves* this song. It's the best part of the story. The triumphant redemption. The Big Fuck You. It's too perfect. Sometimes life works out that way. Just like in the movies. Just like magic. She knows exactly what she needs to do. The drums and trumpets command the army within her.

Everything Kit thought she knew is a lie. Her dad isn't a hero. Her mom's a joke. Their unyielding determination to raise her as a proper young lady...

Fucking. Pointless.

As the violins climb with trepidation, Kit's psyche unfurls a scream. Like the untamed trumpets, she can't contain it. The wild wail becomes her constant companion. It shrieks while she descends the treehouse and shoulder-butts Amber. It wails while she runs out of the park, past the plastic houses, all the way home. It squeals as she steps through her front door, ascends the stairs, and delves into the boys' closet. It shrills as she struggles to carry the loaded box to the garage. It howls when she grabs the gasoline and Hitler's Zippo. It cries as she places the box at the end of the cul-de-sac. It caterwauls as she pours a gasoline wick leading to the explosive cache. It doesn't ebb until she flicks open the metal lid, pushes her thumb against the rough flint wheel. The heat in her hand is instant. She holds the flame against the puddle of gas at her feet. All is finally quiet.

WHOOSH!

Kit's breath stops. She jumps back to watch the flames climb the box of illegal fireworks her brothers painstakingly collected. She thinks of all the mighty men getting away with murder as she gets slaughtered online for trying (unsuccessfully—she might add!) to give a blow job. The injustice of it all is insufferable.

The eruption of fireworks times perfectly with Tchaikovsky's cannons. In quick succession, a rainbow of fireworks bursts forth. *Pop! Pop! Pop!* Three Roman candles zip off in disorganized directions. Reds, greens, blues, yellows. One crashes off the Huangs' front window and into some shrubs. Another one flies off towards the Peaty home and into their open garage. A herd of ground spinners barrel down the road and up various driveways. A bucketful of Black Cats burst into flames. Smells of sulfur and benzene assault the air. A cacophony of whistles and sparks, *zings* and *zangs*, compete with the clanging cymbals blaring from the deafening neighborhood sound system. Novelty fireworks whiz in all directions in tandem with Tchaikovsky's synchronized cannons. Pyrotechnics screech. Trumpets rejoice. Bells explode.

It takes minutes for the people at the party to comprehend. This is not part of the song. The smoke is blinding. Yards are on fire. The residents of the Gardens of Orchid Hill careen recklessly.

Chaos!

Kit smiles, triumphant. But she's not finished yet. She has one more stop before taking her final bow. She grabs the half-full gasoline canister and stumbles back inside her home.

"The time has come for me to meet my maker and to repay him in kind for all that he's done."

Kit's read every book. She knows a villain when she meets one. Her father is Dr. Frankenstein, another Adam Sutler, and needs to be stopped. It'll be her life's greatest achievement. Her parting gift to the world. Maybe she'll be reborn into a new life with a new family. Or perhaps she'll hang out in heaven with Uncle Buster and Bianca and the rest of them. So many lives lost for the pleasures of men. For Kit, it's abundantly clear the wants and needs of men will always remain top priority in this world. Things never change. Equality is a joke. Time's up for who exactly? It doesn't seem fair. Why should she even try when it's like swimming against the tide? She doesn't have the fight in her. She thirsts to float away quietly into the night.

But first...

Kit lugs the plastic container to the red door. She finally has everything she needs: password, gasoline, lighter, courage. She reminds herself *this'll all be over soon* and punches in the four-digit code. As she struggles down the sterile stairway and down the curved hall, she hears shouting.

Kit follows the familiar voices to her father's office. She almost drops the canister of gasoline as she bursts through the door. "Daddy!" she cries, wild-eyed. His office appears empty, but voices float from the lab in the back. That's when she sees the skin-lamp lying broken on the floor. Instantly, all her worst fears are confirmed. Rushing past her father's desk, she pushes the laboratory door open, the canister of gas spills onto the carpet. She sees her father holding a needle poised near Cass's ear.

Daniel hesitates, appearing quite alarmed.

"Daddy, stop!" Kit watches her father plunge the needle into Cass's neck. "What're you doing to her? Let her go!"

Novak's tone sweetens. "It's not what you think, Kit-Kat. Daddy is helping the nice lady."

"No, Dad, stop!" Kit's voice rises with authority.

"This is beyond your level of comprehension, Kit. You're hysterical. Now go back up to the party like daddy's little girl." Novak sniffs the air then spies the tipped canister behind his daughter. Kit notices his complete understanding of the situation as his pupils dilate and nostrils flare.

"No, you stop. All of this!" She looks around the room, noticing the other men for the first time. Mr. Peaty's pudgy red face greases. His armpits are soaked. Kit can smell the booze all the way across the room. Mr. Maccabee averts his gaze. *In shame, or is it fear of being caught?* "What did you do to her?"

Novak's face goes crimson. "Grace-Katherine, I am your father, and you will do as I say. Get out. Right now!"

"No!" Kit plants her feet firmly on the ground.

The three men exchange looks of annoyance and humor, as though silently communicating they would never take orders from a little girl.

Jeff takes a step toward Kit, offering one of his perverse smiles. She whips out the Zippo and lights it in a single, practiced motion. He freezes, eyes betraying fear.

"One step closer, and I'll burn this whole place to the ground, with all of us in it," Kit says, her voice deep and steady. "Now, father…" She challenges her patriarch, eye to eye, "…tell me what you're doing to these women."

"Me?" Novak laughs. "I'm a doctor, Kit, as you are well aware. I help people."

"You're lying. I know things. I hacked your system."

Three sets of eyes inflate with machismo disbelief.

Silence.

"Yeah, I know all about your secret project and the *services*." Kit threatens with the flame as she continues. The brass case sizzles, apathetic in her hand. "I know you hurt Bianca, and Jessa too."

Novak swallows, obviously unprepared for this particular scenario. He appears at a loss on how to handle his unexpectedly defiant daughter.

"So, what're you doing to them? Human sex dolls?" Kit says to her father.

Jeff Peaty clears his throat. "It's nothing like that, hon. It's mostly immersive simulations. You know, like virtual reality." He shuffles awkwardly, mumbling, "I should've stayed at the frigging party instead of getting my dick wet."

"Oh, really?" scoffs Sean.

"Hey, Mr. Peaty." Kit taunts him with a fiery wave. "I know you like the younger ones. You know, the kind you guys refer to as *jailbait*. What did you say to me the other night? Something about how my father should share?"

"Dear Lord, man!" Sean spits from his corner.

Jeff returns the icy stare coming from Novak. "It's not what you think."

Kit rolls her eyes. "More weak lies." She brandishes the white-hot Zippo. Her steadfast fingers don't feel a thing. "Now, tell me exactly what is going on, or we all burn."

CHAPTER 45

AMARA

"GET ME MORE TOWELS. GO!"

Amara snaps into action and returns with an armful of towels and blankets. "I grabbed anything I could find." Her voice sounds solid and steady, but her insides dissolve. *This can't be happening. Why is this happening?* Her militant-trained eyes watch Susan's futile attempts to quell Blair's hemorrhaging.

There's too much blood.

"More towels!" The cries of Susan combine with the screams of newborn Hope.

A deadly calm overcomes Amara. She looks at her dear friend. Blair's eyes are open and dilated. She hasn't blinked once since Amara came back into the room. Amara leans over, pressing two fingers on Blair's neck. "She's gone," she whispers, but Susan doesn't hear. Instead, she's methodically replacing towels. "She's gone, Susan." Amara places a soft hand on Susan's shoulder. "Blair's dead."

Susan stops working and sits up, her button-down shirt stained with blood. She gropes Blair's wrist, her neck.

The two women look at each other and then at the baby.

A blast sounds off in the distance.

"Was that..."

"What in God's name?"

"Fireworks?"

Then comes another whistling discharge followed by another.

Susan wipes her hands on the blood-soaked duvet and peeks her head out the window. "There's smoke coming from the cul-de-sac. It looks like a garbage fire."

Amara stands there doing nothing. She can't take her eyes off her deceased friend. *Is she really dead?* So much has happened so fast. Amara doesn't recognize her own life. Her own self.

Another whistling discharge, this one closer. Susan barks orders. "I know you're struggling with that chip in your head, but I need you to pull yourself together."

Amara stares at her, blinking like a lighthouse.

"Amara, honey, I know you can do it." Susan coaxes Amara as she cleans herself off and attends to the screaming infant. "Something about pregnancy always glitches those things. Come on! We got to get this infant out of here."

Amara shakes her head. "Susan, what are you talking about?" She peels her eyes off her dead friend and stares at her weird neighbor as if she grew orchids out of her eyeballs.

"Here." Susan hands the swaddled baby to Amara and leads them through the cramped house and into her bathroom. Buckets of flowers fill the room. Susan moves a few off the sink counter to allow more workspace.

Amara gently bounces the baby in her arms, soothing the infant with soft *shushes*.

Susan closes the toilet lid so Amara can sit. She opens the medicine cabinet and retrieves everything she needs: cotton balls, iodine, gauze, medical tape, a band-aid, tweezers, and a scalpel sealed in a sterilized autoclave bag.

"What the hell is that for?" Amara whispers. She cradles the infant to her chest.

"It's okay. I know what I'm doing."

"What *are* you doing?" Amara watches wide-eyed. "What the fuck is going on, Susan?" Hope starts to cry again. Amara rocks methodically. Who she's trying to soothe at this point is anyone's guess.

"Hush now." Susan lays out the instruments in order. "And language, please. This poor thing has been in the world for barely half an hour and has already been exposed to more than enough."

Amara relaxes her posture and looks Susan dead in the eye. "No spite. No games. Just answers. Please, Susan, explain what's going on."

"Okay. But I need you to hold perfectly still. You have a device embedded behind your ear. I'd like to remove it for you. Would that be okay?"

"What?"

"Dr. Novak is working on a program with Mr. Peaty and ELITE. Together, they've designed a bio-neural processing unit to control the population. They've been experimenting on women for a long time. Almost every woman in this neighborhood has been chipped at one point or another, including myself, along with a quarter of America and probably the world."

"What?! Yes, take it out. Take it out!" Amara shakes her head manically to dislodge it herself.

"No need to get hysterical. You'll get the little one to fuss again. It's quick and relatively painless."

"Really?"

"Well, it may hurt a bit." Susan feels around Amara's ears and neck. She gently pulls down the damp collar of Amara's chiffon turtleneck and gasps.

Amara doesn't flinch, avoiding Susan's eyes.

"Are you tender here?"

Amara nods.

"My poor dear. You must have been sweating worse than a working girl in church." Susan steels herself and continues with featherlike hands, avoiding the bruises. "They usually put it on the left to coincide with the Vagus nerve on that side. Yup, here it is. Tilt your head to the other side for me." Using iodine and a cotton ball, she sterilizes a one-inch diameter behind Amara's ear. Once completed, she picks up the scalpel. "You may feel a little pinch. Hold still, and whatever you do, do *not* drop that baby."

With Hope in her arms, Amara closes her eyes. She sniffs the fuzzy top of the newborn's head while Susan gets to work.

"I knew this day would come. I just knew it," Susan mumbles to herself. "I've been cleaning up after those men for decades. I kept telling them they were going too far, but would they listen to me—a woman—not if they were on fire and I was the last bucket of water! They'd rather burn in Hell. I told them they were crossing the line. I did. Especially that Angel. He's the nicest man until he drinks. Too sloppy. 'Accidental overdoses' *my ass*. After what happened with Jessa—may she rest in peace—I thought they'd end it."

"End what?" Amara squeezes her eyes shut, nose buried in Hope's soft spot.

"Taking turns with the women, dear. Hold on. You may feel some pressure."

"Ow, fu...fudge!" Amara opens her eyes and observes the tiny child with delicate brown eyes and round features in her arms. There's no mistake. This is *not* Daniel's child.

Susan holds a pair of bloody tweezers, sandwiching a tiny foreign object between the prongs. "It doesn't look like it's been there long. They must've swapped out the old one with the latest prototype."

"May I have that?"

Susan wraps the miniature processing unit in tissue paper and hands it to Amara.

As Amara stares at the tiny device, she recalls her last fight with her husband and the last time she saw Daniel. She boils with rage. "How long?" She looks at Susan. "How long have I been...chipped?" Amara's eyes search for some semblance of understanding, answers for all the years stolen from her.

Susan's face twists into an apology. "Probably started the day you moved in. Or before, when you first met your husband. It's hard to say. Each protocol is different. They usually start with hypnotherapy and medication. They have to prepare the psyche before they can manipulate it. Otherwise, the patient may go haywire."

"Like Jessa?"

Susan laments. "That poor, poor girl. She didn't do what they said she did. They messed up bad, had to cover their tracks. The husband wasn't as compliant as they thought. Novak and Peaty didn't think they had any choice. They murdered those two precious girls!"

"And you helped cover it up?" Amara's mind chugs to life.

"Amara, please understand. I did what I had to do. They were never going to stop. They knew I wanted to be a mother more than anything. And I couldn't get approved for adoption at my age. Especially as a widow. Not legally, anyway. They said they'd use their connections—promised me a baby—if I helped them out occasionally. They even paid for my nursing degree. How could I say no? They already took everything else they could from me. All those miscarriages..." Susan cries. "The chip becomes faulty with pregnancy. Communication between mother and fetus disrupts the program. When that communication is cut off, the baby can't survive. I think they figured it out after my fifth loss." Susan slumps to the floor and puts her head in her hands. "The joke's on me, as I'm yet to embrace motherhood."

"Oh, Susan!" Amara reaches for the pariah's hand. She thinks of her own loss and of Levi sneering at her while she hung and bled. "We can't elevate ourselves in their favor by turning on each other. Women need to band together." She looks down at the wriggling baby. "Maybe if they didn't oppress us so much, we wouldn't feel the need to." She pauses, lightly kissing the top of Hope's tiny head. "Well, this little lady is going to need someone." Amara hands the cherubic face swathed in towels over to Susan, who sits crumpled against the floral tiles, entombed by orchids. "Maybe you could be her person?"

Susan looks from Amara to Hope and smiles like it's the first genuine smile in years. "What're you going to do?"

Rage fills Amara as she thinks of Levi and his cocky dimples. "Something I should've done a long time ago."

CHAPTER 46

LUNA

LUNA TOSSED OUT HER pills immediately after Blair left this morning. She's hardly had a moment to think, haunted by Blair's desperate voice rattling inside her head.

You don't understand what you're saying. You're not...you.

They're brainwashing us and forcing us to live lives we didn't choose.

There's a chip in your head controlling your thoughts.

Sure enough, when Luna had gone digging around her perfectly smooth skin, she found a tiny lump. So unremarkable, she would've never noticed it if she didn't have reason to look. Going against all beauty advice and ignoring her disciplined inner voice, she retrieved the cuticle scissors and tweezers. She used *rakija* to disinfect, then took a shot to steel her nerves. What she found shook her to her core.

Once she had removed the tiny device, a flood of memories assaulted her.

Her recollection of meeting her husband washed over her like a cold shower. The desperation of her dire situation eclipsed the hope of love. He had said all the right things. Knew all the right people. He wanted to help. Luna remembers checking into a posh hotel and not being allowed to leave. Endless rounds of "treatments" to make her "better." So many pills. And injections. That's when she started with the Botox and fillers. Sometimes they injected her in areas she wasn't self-conscious about, like her shoulder, upper arm, or neck.

It's hard to remember every detail during that dark time. The fog of her memory is dense with emotion that overshadows everything.

One thing does stand out in her mosaic mind—her reward when it was all over. Once she reemerged, newly healed, and rebranded as the wife of a tech billionaire, Luna had the entire set of Louis Vuitton luggage waiting for her in the honeymoon suite. They became her most prized possessions. She'd never worked so hard for something in her life.

Another memory nags her: A dark room with chairs facing in an outward circle; the gentle pads at her temples, navel, and wrists; the soothing voice of Dr. Novak guiding her into a meditative state; and the thick fog of pleasure that enraptured her soon after. The experience left her body contented and soaked in sweat, but the fuzzy flashbacks make her want to vomit. Want to scream. Want to run.

Externally, she looks the same, practically perfect in every way. But internally, something has snapped open. It's as if the last remaining elastic holding her favorite bra together has finally given up. The last rubbery thread abolished, leaving her vulnerable. She's not sure what it all means. The only thing she is sure of is the fear spreading from her gut. Deep black roots claw their way inside her, through her, grasping at any and every cell, screaming.

Get out! Go home! Be with family!

Now, when Luna hears detonations from her position in the park, she's instantly transported through time to when she was a frightened child crouching in the community bomb shelter in Novi Sad. During the prolonged conflict in Serbia, food became scarce. For months at a time, over seven years, they subsisted on lard and bread—the only sustenance available, purchased from street vendors. Reliable access to water and electricity was a constant uncertainty. Subterranean shelters were established for each community to provide protection. By day, they were innocent hills for children to play on. By nightfall, when the bombs were most likely to drop, they were damp, cramped spaces shaking with each nearing detonation.

Calmness spreads throughout her, abolishing black roots of fear. For the first time in a long time, Luna knows what's truly important. Family. Her children. Love. True love. Not the transactional affections between wealth and beauty. Luna's old enough to know (but would never admit it) that life throws curve balls, fills the roads with speed spikes. Beauty and wealth are fleeting. Yes, it's true—if you have enough of one, you can hold onto the other, at least for a little while, but in the end, neither will give you what you truly need.

She thinks of Jessa with a heavy heart.

Another booming whistle fills the air.

Au bre! That one was close.

Luna jolts back to the present. She stands in the park, hidden under her ginormous hat, surrounded by vendors and screaming neighbors.

Tchaikovsky accompanies the chaos.

People scatter. Panic infuses the air. She looks for her husband, but Jeff is nowhere to be found. She snaps her fingers at the nanny. *What's her name again?* The two women lock eyes, in sync with their thoughts. They need to get these babies to safety, like yesterday.

Luna frantically searches for her children amidst the commotion. She grabs her son's stroller while her nanny retrieves the twins' doublewide pram. Together, they scramble across the dehydrated lawn, struggling over the trampled grass with stubborn rubber wheels.

Fireworks careen in every direction, sending sparks throughout the neighborhood. A brush fire here. A palm tree ablaze there. The bushes lining the Huangs' walkway burn around a Roman candle. Smoke billows from Luna's garage as they approach. There's no place safe. Not even the fortress of her own home. They're forced to use the front entrance.

"We need to leave. Now!" Luna screams over the anarchy. They rush around the cold mansion, gathering essential items for the children.

"Where's Mr. Peaty?" asks the nanny. She tightens the straps on the children's car seats.

"Hell, if I know." Luna pulls out her luggage. "Start packing. Just the expensive stuff."

Why can't I remember her name?

Because deep down, you know how it'll eventually end, and you don't want to get attached.

Like with Jessa.

Luna stops, realizing this will be her last time in this house. She takes a moment to mentally say goodbye to the home she painstakingly furnished piece by piece.

We had the most magnificent mansion on the block.

You mean the prettiest prison.

A whizzing firecracker smashes against the front windows. The children cry. It's time to go.

Emma (*that's her name!*) tries to console them as she flinches with each bang.

"Time to go, Emma! Get the kids in my car, and I'll meet you there!"

"But the garage is on fire. There's no way to get the cars out."

Luna looks longingly at her Louis Vuitton luggage, once a symbol of her wealth and status, now a reminder of pain and loss. *And shame.* The memories of what she survived claw at her. She doesn't need any reminders. "Fuck it. Leave it all here. I'll call for a car."

"What about Mr. Peaty."

"He's not our concern anymore."

Luna runs to the safe to collect everything she'll need—passports, jewelry, enough cash to restart—again. The bank account she established for her small business will finally prove useful. She races back to the front foyer to meet Emma, who, so far, has exceeded all job expectations. The petrified girl should've taken off by now.

That's what I would've done at her age.

They drag the children down the cul-de-sac and past the gilded gate. Luna offers Emma ten thousand dollars cash to assist her for the rest of the weekend. All expenses included. It takes ten minutes for their car to arrive. They go directly to John Wayne Airport, where Luna buys five first-class one-way tickets to Belgrade with her hard-earned money.

CHAPTER 47

KIT

KIT COMMANDS THE ROOM with the threat of fire and an authority that surprises her. "And remove that gasmask." She gestures towards Cass with the Zippo, its flame flickering ominously.

As Mrs. Maccabee lies unconscious and vulnerable on the chair, her husband, looking bewildered and defeated, moves to obey. It strikes Kit as absurd, this grown man taking orders from someone barely in her teens. He seems lost, torn between disbelief and despair, his gaze fixed on Cass's tear-stained face. *I bet he's questioning his life choices right now.*

Kit's father observes the room. There are no other exits. They're deep underground. The only way out is through Kit. She can almost hear his thoughts. If he's lucky, he can make it to an outside exit. If not, he'll have to lock himself in the bomb shelter and wait for the fire to pass.

She faces her father. "Tell me what you're up to, or so help me..." Kit waives the Zippo wildly above her head. Her eyes burn with determination. Her courage feeds off their fear, especially the terror in her father's eyes.

He's staring at me like I'm a freak of nature rather than his daughter.

Kit sees her father clearly now. The way he looks at her as if she's a puzzle, a project to be fixed before she spirals further out of his control. His determination to 'help' is like a scientific experiment. His concern for women clinical. In his mind, he's doing a service, a twisted form of charity driven by a savior complex and the allure of compensation. But beneath the surface, Kit knows a part of him genuinely believes he's doing the right thing. It's a messed-up situation, especially for a fourteen-year-old.

The truth shall set them free.

"Doc, get your kid under control," says Peaty from the corner.

"Hey, let's all calm down for a second." The politician kicks into high gear. "We can all work together to get to the bottom of this. Does that sound okay? Who's Bianca?" Sean inches towards Kit, hands up, palms out, like he's surrendering to a SWAT team.

"Don't come any closer!"

Sean freezes.

"Next time someone says something that isn't true, kaboom!" Kit holds out her free hand to show them she's serious. From her clenched fist, she flashes five angry fingers. The childish gesture looks more like a mic drop than a firebomb. Her wild, red-rimmed eyes flash to each man in the room. One. Two. Three. If they don't speak soon, she'll incinerate them anyway.

"I have no fear anymore. I am completely free."

Her father speaks first, slow and steady, as if talking her off a ledge. "Bianca was my patient. She significantly contributed to the advancement of my research. I introduced a novel prototype into her system, albeit with certain imperfections. Her reaction diverged from my anticipated outcomes, and regrettably, it resulted in her demise. There. Are you satisfied?" He clears his throat and waits.

"How did she end up in the water tower?" Kit chews her bottom lip, hopping from one leg to another. She has the sudden urge to pee. She thinks of releasing herself right then and there. That would really freak them out. She needs the whole truth but isn't sure she can trust her father.

Novak stands between his daughter and Cass, flanked by Sean on one side and Jeff in the corner behind him. "That evening, she exhibited considerable agitation. I employed all standard interventions, including administering a sedative, which has proven effective for numerous patients. Unfortunately, she experienced an adverse reaction, manifesting as hallucinations. Distressed, she fled. I've had no contact with her since. I surmised she returned to Sweden, perhaps seeking solace in familiar surroundings."

"Really?" Kit tilts her head. "She got out of *this* place?" She motions to the underground compound with her arms, flames still licking out of the lighter in one hand. The metal case hot enough to erase fingerprints. "You think I'm stupid, don't you? This place is harder to get out of than detention if you don't have the passcode." She smirks.

A pained groan comes from behind her father.

"Cassan—Cass, my darling girl." Sean leaps to his wife's side. "Are you alright?"

"What...what happened? Why can't I move?"

Sean clears his throat before answering. "You asked Dr. Novak to hypnotize you, to help you quit smoking. Don't you remember?"

"Don't listen to him. He's lying! My father..."

At this precise moment, a silent-until-now Jeff Peaty bulldozes his overfed, underworked body towards the door. "Fuck this shit!"

Dr. Novak lunges for Kit's torch-bearing arm. For a moment, they lock eyes, their biological similarities never more apparent. After all, she is her father's daughter. Kit smirks at him. His face reflects hers, dark, ominous. Her claw-like hand unfurls like a clam. Flames erupt onto the gasoline-drenched carpet. Kit smiles as her father shrinks. Flames lick across the rug.

"You little bitch!" Jeff screams, steamrolling his way toward Kit. She spins and flees from the room. Novak leaps after her.

CHAPTER 48

AMARA

ANOTHER FIRECRACKER BLASTS OFF near Susan's home. The two women exchange looks. Amara's makeup starts to wear off. Light blues and purples peek out from behind her foundation.

Susan stands with Hope bundled in her arms. She cups Amara's face gently with one hand, careful not to inflict more pain. "Go. Go!" She pushes Amara towards the bathroom door.

"What're you going to do?" Amara's eyes flicker. She hesitates.

"I'm going to save as many as I can. Starting with this little one." Susan tucks the towel around Hope's face. "If you see any of the others, send them my way."

"Will do." Amara grasps Susan's shoulder, kisses Hope's soft spot, then turns to leave. Her blond hair splays like a cape behind her.

"And give the bastard hell!"

Amara leaves them in Susan's bathroom. She silently prays for her new friends as she goes to say goodbye to Blair. She finds her way through the flowering home and returns to the guest bedroom.

Blair's limp, swollen body lies bloody, spreadeagled across the floral guest bed. The room reeks of mortality.

Amara moves silently, oblivious to the mess she's making of her chiffon dress. She removes the sopping towels and after-birth, placing them in the kitchen sink. She wets a cloth under warm water and cleans her friend as best she can, removing dark maroon smudges from visible skin. She gently tucks Blair's legs together, smoothing the sticky skirt of Blair's blue gingham dress to conceal the worst. She finds the discarded espadrilles under the bed and ties each one on. Choking back sobs, she stares at Blair's pink-painted toes, swollen and squished, and hanging off the ends of her impossibly high shoes.

Amara collects her purse, which is tossed in the corner of the room. She takes out her color correction palette, ignoring tears as she touches up Blair's face, beautiful even in death. When finished, Amara kisses Blair's forehead, the skin still warm against her lips. She leaves her hair alone, a halo of red curls. A champion friend, even if Amara didn't quite reciprocate. She should've been warmer, more genuine. Especially after Jessa.

Such a waste.

A fiery fury engulfs her. Amara has one thing on her mind, one thing only.

Levi.

Feeling like a puma uncaged for the first time, she unties her gladiator heels, grabs them in hand, and races home. It doesn't take long with Amara's record-breaking legs. Her house is three doors down towards the cul-de-sac and the exploding firework display. Barefoot, she maneuvers down the street with soldier reflexes, avoiding fires and hazardous smoke. Her newly computing mind doesn't have time to comprehend the situation. Not yet, anyway. She's laser-focused, a tactical machine bursting with hyper illumination.

Levi!

She vaults over the stone steps to her house and finds the front door unlocked. She glides past the dark, laminated kitchen into the living room. He's ready, waiting for her. He wobbles, holding a thick glass of bourbon, which sloshes onto the replaced carpet.

"Where've you been?" he slurs, eyes red and puffy.

"Levi!" Amara roars. She aims her stilettos like missiles at his head and lets them fly.

"What the—" He ducks too late, catching a heal across his brow. The blood is instant.

Amara doesn't waste a second. She bombards him, towering over him in bare feet. Majestic. Her cream chiffon gown glistening with blood. Her long hair dancing behind her. Gray eyes sparking.

She locates his arrogant face and attacks. Before Levi can finish his sentence, Amara's right fist connects with his left dimple. There's a sickening crack of bone on bone. Levi falls backward, sitting awkwardly on the ugly statement piece sofa, clenching his empty glass.

Amara stands tall with her legs firmly planted, ready to pounce. "I'm leaving you, Levi."

"Over my dead body!" He rocks his jaw and tries to stand, but she knocks him back down with a sharp knee to the ribs.

"So be it!" She forces him up only to clock him again. This time, her knuckles connect with his bulbous nose. *That stupid nose!*

There's blood. A lot of blood. She pictures Blair lying dead in Susan's flower-infested home.

Amara's unborn child dies inside of her.

Her muscles maneuver robotically, stagnant at first from years of unuse. She shakes out her fist, engaging in a combative stance. Amara smiles. Like muscle memory.

All those years!

She hits him again and again and again. Each strike potent and precise. Years of stagnant training and pent-up aggression release, like the long-anticipated orgasm at the end of tantric sex.

Levi drops his glass, covering his head. His stout frame's no match for his military-trained wife.

"A cadet will not lie, cheat, steal, or tolerate those who do."

Amara pummels him until she's panting, then wrestles him to the ground. Levi doesn't stand a chance. He curls into a pathetic ball on their living room floor, begging for his wife to stop, promising her anything and everything. Before long, he passes out.

Ignoring the whistling blasts and retching smoke, Amara takes a moment to gather herself. The room stinks of soot and sweat. And more blood. Her dress is ruined. Her heart is pounding. She has a raging headache, and some of her fingers may be broken, but she feels...

Invigorated?

Rejuvenated?

Alive!

For the first time in what feels like forever.

She climbs the marble staircase. Bare feet slap against the tiles. The wall to her right displays staged snapshots of her counterfeit life.

Their engagement photo in Central Park, taken three months after they met, was exhibited in the New York Times. Levi's arms imprison her while he beams for the camera, showing off his prize. A bright white smile is plastered to Amara's face.

There's a picture of the couple in black tie for the Met Gala, posing with the soon-to-be forty-fifth president. Both men sandwich Amara, who's wearing a delicate Christian Dior gown and dripping in diamonds.

Then come the wedding pictures, which were auctioned off to the highest-bidding fashion magazine. A photo of the ceremony is taken of their backs as they face the altar inside a Gothic church, Amara's ten-foot train of hand-sewn lace arranged artfully. There's another posed picture on ocean cliffs, with Amara's veil blowing dramatically in the wind. Lots of smiling. Bright red lips. In all the photographs, Levi lovingly gazes up at his wife. He looks more like a ring bearer than a bridegroom.

Was I even there?

As Amara's tired, battered body moves on, her swollen hand swipes the gallery wall. Each photo falls and shatters, leaving a wake of broken glass behind her.

She intuitively turns towards their bedroom at the top of the stairs, past the four-post bed, and into her bathroom. Her oversized tub looks seductive. She'd give anything to sink into a lavender-scented bath and soak. Knowing she'll never enjoy her tub again, she decides to never give it another thought. Instead, she turns her focus to the mirror. With excruciating effort, she unbuttons the delicate turtleneck dress, letting it slip to the floor.

She carefully removes her undergarments to examine herself. Her eyes start with her toes. Her feet are sore from surviving a shoeless sprint. Not to mention combat. She smiles. She's still got it. She can still surprise herself. Her feet held up better than Levi's face. Her eyes catch the fine purple lines starting at her ankles and lacing up her legs. The rope burns are not as intricate or symmetrical as they used to be. *Levi's getting sloppy.* The burn pattern traces up her torso and wraps around her arms, framing more bruises and cuts. Some older, sprouting yellow and green with deeper violets. Some are so new they haven't made it to the surface yet. She can feel their presence. Bright red welts mark their path. Levi's fingerprints fence her neck. She captures images of her body with her cellphone, for insurance purposes, in addition to the microchip she received from Susan.

For a while, Amara's eyes dance around their own reflection. It's been too long since she had a proper look at herself. She removes her makeup with silent and methodical precision, taking her time to expose the truth. After a few deep breaths, Amara finally surrenders to the eyes in the mirror. Overwhelmed, she comforts the woman she sees. Radiating compassion, she wraps her arms around her body. She prays for strength, for her future. She prays for her aborted child. She hopes everything has a reason, and she prays this, too, will be revealed in time.

She throws the bloody chiffon in the trash. Inside her walk-in closet, she changes into her most comfortable jeans, an old army tee, and running shoes. She hasn't felt this satisfied in years. She skips makeup. The marks on her body, badges of honor. For the first time in her life, Amara will not hide behind beauty.

When she returns to the upended living room, she can't find Levi. Instant disappointment floods her. Their little playdate is over too soon. She spies him crumpled behind the coffee table.

A salacious grin blooms across her face. Amara saved the best for last. She acts fast. The fires are closing in. Smoke leaks inside. Any second and the Smart alarm system will go off and alert authorities, if they haven't been alerted already.

She picks up her unconscious asshole of a husband and carries him over the glass shards, up the stairs, and into their special place. The room with the black walls. This time, Amara's in control. She is powerful, more potent than her pathetic excuse for a husband. She drops him on the table and strips his clothes. The pleasure she gets is nonsexual. She's full of venom and dying for blood.

How does the saying go?

An eye for an eye.

Staring at Levi's limp, naked body, she hardly recognizes him. His face is swollen, the jaw misaligned. His ordinarily bushy eyebrows look Neanderthal. Odd-angled lumps misshape his forehead, and his nose bends awkwardly. A mixture of blood and snot leak from his nostrils, congealing under thick, purple cuts from her wedding rings.

As the top plastic surgeon in Orange County, Levi, let's just say you're not looking your best.

She removes her rings and puts them to one side. She turns to the antique cupboard and traces her fingers over the carvings, smiling at the series of panels. In the final one, the innocent doe escapes the rabid hounds. Amara opens the cabinet door and pulls out the purple parachute chord she has come to know intimately.

With maximum gratification, she expertly coils her unconscious husband and hoists him to the ceiling. She makes it look easy.

Duty, Honor, Country.

As soon as Amara has her husband where she wants him, she picks up the portable EST machine from its place in the cabinet and waits for it to power up. When it's fully singing, she presses the paddles to Levi's scrotum. His elevated body jerks violently. Urine drips onto the table below. He roars awake.

She zaps him again. "How do you like it now, Levi? Feeling...aroused?" She zaps him again.

Levi struggles in the ropes, spewing rage.

She grabs his tighty-whities from the floor and stuffs them in his mouth. "What's the matter, Levi? Cat got your tongue?"

He moans through the gag.

"Wait, what's that? You want more?" Amara dials up the power.

Levi bucks in the air, eyes swollen shut. Fear betrays his smothered voice.

Amara zaps him. "That's for lying since the day we met!" She zaps him again. "And that's for tricking me into marrying you!" Another zap. "And that's for putting a chip in my head!" *Zap.* "And *that* is for killing my baby!" She holds the paddles against his shaved balls as long as she can.

Eventually, Levi stops writhing.

Amara slumps against the wall, a decade of tears yearning for release. She doesn't have the luxury of crying on the floor. Smoke fills the little black room. The Smart home system activates. Fire alarms blare. Amara snaps to attention. *Time to go.* Her eyes catch something glinting on the massage table. In one smooth motion, Amara pops up, grabs her platinum wedding ring set, and thrusts ten carats of diamonds up Levi's ass.

"Eye for an eye, you sick fuck."

He stirs briefly but doesn't regain consciousness.

Satisfied, she leaves him hanging. *He's a big boy. He can fend for himself.*

Amara doesn't pack a bag. She doesn't need to. She doesn't want any reminders. Well, maybe just one. She snags the set of keys dangling by the garage door and leaves her old life behind in Levi's favorite car.

CHAPTER 49

KIT

Kɪᴛ's ʜᴇᴀʀᴛ ᴘᴏᴜɴᴅs ᴀs she spins to flee. She runs out of the lab, past the giant desk, and through the office door. She doesn't hesitate to punch the four-digit code to open the steel door across the hall. One. Nine. Nine. Five. It beeps unlocked. She turns the five-pronged handle with all her strength and pushes her way into the underground bunker.

Before she can lock the vaulted door behind her, Novak slips in. The door clinks shut behind him. They're in the common area. Dim LED lights blink on, recognizing their presence. A faint hum buzzes off the slab floor. The air smells stale and rubbery, as if the room has been sealed in plastic.

Kit looks around the bunker, a place she's become familiar with since she started skipping school. Utilitarian furniture adorns the common area, designed to take up minimal floor space and convert for multipurpose use. Dining tables and benches made of retractable wood, fold or extend to seat two to twenty. A transitional sofa with interchangeable sections flanks one side. On the opposite wall, mounted desks hang with stools ready to add instant workstations. Overhead, an intricate network of pipes and wires zigzags across the ceiling.

"Grace-Katherine Novak, I command you to stop!"

Kit spins to face her father. Same pinched nose and pointy chin. Same stubborn, steely eyes sneering back at her.

"Command me? You're a joke!" She erupts with giggles.

"Are you...drunk?"

Kit stumbles two steps backward. "What do you care?"

"Just like your mother. Nothing but a dim-witted tramp when I found her." He takes a step forward. Inside the bunker, the sounds of the outside world are nonexistent.

"Oh yeah, is that why you married her?" Kit puts her hands on her hips and pouts her lips. "Do you have a thing for younger girls, Daddy? Is that why you're screwing Amara?"

"That's enough!" He leaps forward and vice-grips her bicep.

"Am I making you uncomfortable, Daddy? What're you going to do, beat me into submission?"

"Kit." Novak releases his daughter, stepping to one side. His voice softens. "Stop this madness at once."

"Why stop now? Did you know I gave a blow job to a boy from school? There's a video to prove it. Here, let me show you." She whips out her phone from her back pocket.

"*Enough!*" His voice booms around them.

Kit halts. She glares at her father. "No, *father*, enough from you. You think I don't know what you're doing? You think I don't know what you are?"

She watches him study her delicate features. *Like looking in a mirror from his past.*

"You know, we're a lot alike, you and I." He crosses over to a sofa and sits.

Kit walks backward to the furthest spot on the opposite side of the room. She pulls a stool off the wall. "I'm *nothing* like you. You're sick."

"Am I?" Dr. Novak folds his hands over his crossed knees. "And what is it you think I'm doing? Please, enlighten me."

"You know what you're doing." Kit fidgets with her phone. "You hurt people. You hurt women."

"You mean, I help women."

"Is that what you call it? Tell me the truth about Jessa. I know you did something to her. She wrote about it in her diary."

"Jessa didn't respond well to treatment. Her husband threatened to compromise my operation."

"So, you murdered them all. A whole family."

"I did what I had to do." Novak's words seethe through clenched teeth.

"Do you hear yourself? You killed kids! You're a villain, a mass murderer, just like Hitler!"

Tinny sounds bubble, growing louder, until her father's manic laugh consumes the room. "My dear daughter," Daniel says in between fits of laughter, "what a wonderful insight you have." He wipes tears from his eyes. "You see, Hitler was the most misunderstood genius of his time."

"Hitler was a psycho, just like you."

"Macabre, yes. Psychotic, I'm not so sure. I admire his feeble attempts at advancing civilization. Were there better ways to achieve what he was trying to do? Of course. But he was not looking at the bigger picture. He thought too small. You see, Hitler failed because he was more concerned about vanity, superficial traits like hair and eye color, skin tone. He was only concentrating on a small bit of the population. The human race as a whole will never be corrected if we don't treat the root cause of humanity—the women who birth us. He had the right intention with the Lebensborn Project, but not quite. He *was* a racist."

"You really think you're helping people? You think, what, that you're, like, saving the world?"

"There's always some backlash when technology is new."

Kit rolls her eyes. "Give me a break."

"I'll have you know, I've helped hundreds—thousands—of women."

"Yeah, right. By ruining our lives?"

"You think *you* have it bad? Let me tell you a story. When I was a young boy, much younger than you, I lived in a crummy, roach-infested apartment with my mother and younger brother."

"Uncle Buster?"

"Yes, Buster. It was just us three. My father succumbed to a stress-related heart condition. Most likely brought on by my mother's endless...issues."

"You never knew your father?"

"I did not."

The muffled sounds of the Smart alarm system echo around them.

"Shouldn't we leave?"

"This is the safest place. This bunker was built to be impenetrable. As long as we remain here, the fire can't reach us. As I was saying, I wasn't as lucky as you and your brothers, living in a grand house filled with designer clothes and endless toys. We barely had food in the fridge.

"My mother—if you can call her that—was a self-obsessed alcoholic. She didn't give a damn about Buster or me. All she cared about was getting drunk and getting screwed. She was never home, constantly out on the town with the latest man of the month. She would pop in to shower and change. Sometimes, she'd be gone for days at a time."

"If only we could be so lucky," Kit mutters.

"One morning, Buster woke up ill. I was only eight. He was barely six. I remember his skin boiling as we lay on the bare mattress. He cried incessantly. I didn't know what to do. I didn't dare leave him. I stayed close and waited. Finally, I fell asleep beside him, holding his hand. Eventually, he stopped crying.

"The next day, I awoke to my mother's screams. She sat wailing on the floor, rocking Buster. When I asked her what was wrong, she attacked. She blamed me! I was raw and bloody by the time authorities intervened. They sent me to live with my father's parents."

"What happened to your mother?"

"My mother, well, she was deemed unfit. Hysterical. Not in the right state of mind. She was put in an institution. I never saw her again."

"That's so sad." Kit's eyes soften.

"Sad? Moving in with my father's parents was a pivotal moment, dear daughter. Your great-grandmother exemplified maternal perfection. Each Friday, without fail, she would prepare my favorite confection. Her influence was profound. She instilled in me the confidence to pursue a career in medicine. Taught me the true essence of being a gentleman. From a tender age, I understood that if all women could emulate her exemplary demeanor, needless tragedies like Buster's could be averted. I pledged to dedicate myself to any endeavor that might prevent such unfortunate occurrences. So, there you have it. See, all of my work has been to *help* women, some with addictions. Like your mother. I'm not the villain you think I am."

Kit tilts her head to one side. Low LED lighting spins around the common area of the bunker. Everything twinkles. Her father's face corkscrews across the room. How could they look so alike but be so different? Didn't he understand anything? "So, you were going to what...turn me into an android...so I could be more like great-grandma? What's it called again? Project PSS."

Dr. Novak uncrosses his legs. "I'm curious, daughter of mine, where exactly are you getting this information? It seems you know a lot more than you're letting on."

Kit beams. Her eyes twinkle in the dim lighting. "Oh, *father*, I told you already. I hacked your system."

"Yes, you mentioned that." Dr. Novak coughs, voice filled with irritation. "Please enlighten me on how my teenage daughter is able to hack into the world's most influential tech company."

Angry tears ignite a fire in Kit's belly. "Why is it so hard for you to understand? Is it that difficult for you to accept that I'm smart? I thought you wanted to dial down my intelligence. *Pending program?*"

"For someone who holds themselves in such high esteem, you're missing the bigger picture," her father says with a smug smile.

"Oh yeah, what's that? Please *enlighten me* on how your menu of mind control gimmicks is going to enhance the well-being of mankind."

Daniel sits up straight, chest puffed out. "Mind control and implants are old news. It's been done since the early fifties. The latest in biotechnology is consciousness." His fingers trace the ends of the armchair as he seems lost in thought. "It's so hard to get the programming perfect on you girls. It can take several years before I get the formula just right. That's why I've been working nonstop to discover a solution. Think of all the time and money saved if we could recycle those perfectly crafted minds. I'm working on something special. Something that will change everything, including life as we know it." Novak looks up, steepling his fingers before him. "My dear, your father is on the cusp of something revolutionary. Award-winning. History-making!"

"Oh, yeah? What's that?"

"*I* have discovered a way to transfer one's consciousness."

"What? How? Where do the original minds go?"

"Ah, great question! I relocate them to the Obsidian Veil program."

"You mean your 'immersive virtual reality simulation' that 'blurs the line between fantasy and reality'? In other words, your psychedelic sex dolls. That's what the Round Room's for, isn't it? Ew, Dad! What are you doing with those suits?"

"Round Room? Oh, you mean the Obsidian Center. The boys call it The Game Room. We have quite a lot of fun in there. Those suits are simply for entertainment. But you're missing the point. I nearly perfected a process to replicate and transfer the quantum states within brain cell microtubules from one subject to another, transmitting consciousness and cognitive coherence from a donor to a host. Once the host mind is transferred, there's room for another perfectly molded mind to enter."

Kit's face blanches. "You're sick. You need help."

"I possess a remarkable intellect. Do you not comprehend the implications of this discovery? Your father, your progenitor, has unraveled the cosmos's most intricate dilemma: mortality. Every sentient being on this planet harbors an innate dread of death. It is this very fear that hones our reflexes and instills the sensation of pain within us, all as mechanisms to forestall the inexorable approach of our demise. Now, envision the paradigm shift when I reveal to the world that death is no longer an obligatory conclusion."

"So, your master plan is to hawk immortality like some snake oil salesman? Jesus, Dad, don't you have enough money?"

Dr. Novak scoffs. "It's not about the money. It was never about money. This is about my legacy. *Our* legacy. This family."

"So that's why you've been living underground like an ogre? Working on your legacy?"

"Immortality, my dear. The Novak name will go down in history. Imagine a world where you never have to die. When the body reaches its fated limit, the mind can now be transferred to a new vessel. I'm calling it Psycho-Nexus, working title."

"Ohmigod! Can you hear yourself? *You're* the psycho!"

Before Daniel can respond, a shockwave rocks the foundation. Alarms infiltrate the bunker.

Kit jumps off her stool and casts weary eyes at her father. "What was that?"

"It sounded like an explosion. Most likely from the fire you started in my laboratory. The nitrous oxide tank, perhaps? There goes decades of research. You're lucky everything is uploaded to the cloud, or I'd have you to thank for destroying my life's work."

Kit crosses her arms and makes the disgruntled face typical of a defiant teenager. "Ugh, it stinks in here." She flares her nostrils, mirroring her father. Toxic fumes pollute the air. "Dad, what's that smell?"

Novak pinches the top of his nose and remains silent. A penetrating fog assaults them.

"Daddy!" Kits screams at her father. "What is that?"

"It's smoke, Kit." He stands up and peers around the room at the vents. Acrid smoke pours into the bunker. "See those pipes?" He points to the ceiling. "They pump gas made from decomposed garbage. It powers this bunker along with the entire neighborhood. The explosion must have disrupted those pipes, causing a gaseous emission breach. We need to head towards the opposite exit before the rising toxicity levels render this area untenantable."

Kit follows her father down a hall, past the cafeteria, and to another wing with residential units. They stop at a door identical to the one they entered.

"The air on this side is easier to breathe." Kit sighs. Panic ebbs.

Novak looks at the vents leaking above them. "It won't be for long." He punches in the four-digit code. *BEEP. BEEP. BEEP. BEEP.* Nothing. He punches it in again. *BEEP. BEEP. BEEP. BEEP.* Again, nothing. "Dammit!"

"What is it? What's going on?"

"The door is malfunctioning." Novak turns to face his daughter, blue eyes fierce. "The safety lock mechanism has activated, preventing us from entering the inferno outside."

Kit's veins frost. "What do you mean? We can't open the door?" Her wide eyes meet her father's concern. "So, you're saying we're stuck in here?" She backs against the wall and slides to the floor. This isn't how she planned it exactly, but it'll have to do. "Great. Just great. I'm going to die in here with my asshole of a father."

"Not necessarily." Her father ignores the adolescent dig, studying the monitor beside the door. He turns to her. "Think you can hack this thing?"

Kit rests on the polished concrete floor, arms slack on bent knees. Her idle hands dangle in front of her. "Hah! Now you want my help? I thought you didn't think I was smart enough. Not that you'd ever know since you spend all your free time with the boys. Or murdering women and children." She chokes on thick, hot air, trying to laugh at her own joke.

Her father's gaze rests heavily on her, taking in her disheveled state. Kit is acutely aware of how she looks. Her fingernails are bitten down to nubs. Her clothes are wrinkled. Heavy bags droop under her eyes. Strawberry blonde hair is slick with grease. She smells ripe. She hasn't slept or showered for days.

"My darling girl. I've misjudged you. I should have never assumed. I've done you a great disservice. I'm aware now. I'm sincerely sorry for all the pain I've caused. I never meant to make you feel...inferior. Honestly, I thought I was helping you evolve. I see I've made a grave error." He pauses, looking at his daughter, stunned by her serenity. "I think, maybe, I'm somewhat of an...asshole, and I am sorry for that. Can you ever forgive me, Kit-Kat?"

"Why now, after all this time?" She eyeballs her father. "You're only saying this because we're going to die. This is all just," she circles a pointed hand towards him, "self-preservation. Even if I could override the system, which I probably can't, I wouldn't."

"Grace-Katherine!" Novak's tone takes a nasty turn. "Open the goddammed doors at once! I am your father, and you *will* obey me!"

Her voice rings calm and clear. "No, father. It's over. *This* is how we save humanity." The revulsion of being related to someone so evil makes her choice easy.

"You're nothing but an ignorant child, clueless and insignificant. Your opinions are worthless. Nobody cares about your thoughts. You've barely reached puberty."

"'Alone, a symbol is meaningless, but with enough people, blowing up a building can change the world,'" Kit says calmly. "Don't worry, father. This'll all make sense soon."

"You're speaking gibberish! This is nonsense!" He reaches down and pinches her arm, jerking her to her feet. "This is not a game. This is the real world. This is my *life*! You're naive to think you can actually make a difference. I've busted my ass for years—decades. You will *not* destroy my life's work. I will *not* be undone by some intoxicated, oversexed teenager! Is this how you repay your father for taking care of you all these years? You're nothing but a spoiled brat!"

Kit jerks her arm away from his violent grip. "Some *fucking* life. You think I should thank you for putting a roof over my head or food in my belly? Well, fuck you!" Spittle flies towards her father's face. Oily strands of hair plaster her cheeks. She sucks in noxious gas, takes a bold step forward, her face inches from his. "Fuck you for never being there for me. And fuck you for ignoring me when you were there. And fuck you for never truly loving me. Fuck you. Fuck you! *Fuck! You!*"

CHAPTER 50

CASS

FLAMES NIP AT MY toes trapped in someone else's shoes. Melting carpet and burning plastic char my nostrils. I twist and contort my body in desperation. My legs buck, yet my wrists remain firmly locked in restraints.

"What's happening? Why am I tied up?"

"Shhh, it's okay. It's going to be okay," I hear Sean say.

We've been abandoned. Dr. Novak took one look at us and the fire and bolted out the door, chasing Jeff and the girl. My husband remains by my side. Fingers trembling, he unties my right wrist.

"Hurry, Sean!" Every inch of my body throbs, prickled with pain, from my toes, down my legs, between my thighs. I have the most hideous migraine. "Sean, please!"

"I'm trying. Hold on a sec."

A pungent fog darkens the room. Sprinklers release. Water rains from the ceiling, drumming a tipped canister of gasoline that causes the fuel-fed fire to spread. I strain to find my husband's face. His eyes panic. "Sean." I cough on bitter fumes. "Get out of here...Go...Save yourself." Tears streak my sooted face. Maybe the crying is a reaction caused by the smoke.

"Fire. Fire," a calm, robotic voice repeats between the horns. "Fire. Fire."

"One down!" He ignores me and works the other wrist.

One of my unfamiliar shoes starts melting.

"You have to get out of here." I start to wheeze, weak and dizzy. If Sean doesn't leave this room soon, he may never...

"Got it!" My heroic husband flings my arm around his neck and helps me stand. The heels don't help, but we don't have time to fix it.

"Fire. Fire."

Sean drapes his jacket around me as we leap through the flames and into the sitting room of Novak's office. I bat my hair, extinguishing my locks. My feet are toast, but I don't care. All that matters is getting out of here alive. Together.

We follow the lit EXIT signs out the office door, down the hall to the right, looking for an exit.

KABOOM!

An explosion rattles from the direction we just left. A rush of hot sulfuric air envelopes us. We push forward.

"What the hell was that?"

"The nitrous oxide tank in Novak's lab," Sean mumbles, half dragging, half carrying me.

"Sean, what's going on? I'm scared."

He doesn't answer, grunting as he tugs me along. We pass staircase after staircase. He stops after what seems like miles (or was it mere feet?). "I think this is the one."

We follow the flashing lights up the stairs, each step more painful than the last. I can barely stand. Finally, we reach the top. Sean turns the handle and shoulders a red door. It doesn't budge.

It's locked.

Cold fear grips my lungs. My chest and feet throb. "What are we going to do?" I cling to Sean. We can't end like this. I'm suffocating. Or maybe it's a heart attack? I collapse on the top step, unable to breathe or think or move...

This is it.

"Hold on just a little longer." Sean's voice echoes in the background. He sounds eons away, tucked under layers of noise.

BEEP-BEEP-BEEP-BEEP—BUZZZZZZZZ.

The red door swings open.

"Just needed the passcode." Sean pulls me into his arms.

Out of the cauterized darkness, I can finally breathe. "Good thing you remembered." I cough.

"Nonsense," he says tenderly, tucking away a curl of my mangled hair. "I could never forget the day I found you."

CHAPTER 51

AMBER

AMBER PEATY HATES SLEEPING at her mother's. She despises the revolving door of losers, the lack of boundaries, the passive-aggressive parenting. All she truly wants is a real relationship with her father, to be protected and loved by the one man in the universe who's supposed to protect and love her. But her father doesn't make her feel like that. In fact, he does the opposite. He makes her feel unloved, insecure. Unprotected.

He's only happy when she brings over friends for him to ogle. Amber hates that. She feels used and dirty and ashamed. Once, she caught him staring at her in her cheerleading uniform. It's gross. But he is her dad. She feels ashamed for feeling that way. Like it's her fault. Maybe it would be different if she didn't look so much like her mother.

Amber only gets her parents' full attention when she's in trouble. That's why she flirts with everyone. She loves the attention. She loves how the boys lust after her. How they fight each other to be near her, tripping over their sagging skinny jeans just to touch her hair. She pretends she's annoyed, giving them a look under her thick eyelashes, so they know she's slightly amused underneath her I'm-too-cool-to-care attitude. Every day—it seems to Amber at violently increasing rates—the boys try to one-up each other just to get her to smile. They orbit her.

Like it's hard to be popular. None of the other girls even know how to give head.

And I have the video to prove it!

Amber especially loves how other girls despise her. Even though in school, they eclipse her like hungry moths. Deep down, she knows they're all jealous. After all, she gets everything she wants. *Well, almost everything.* It's hard to believe Kit's brothers would deny her. Didn't they care what happened to their precious sister? In today's day and age, data is everything. Knowledge is power.

That's why Amber followed her father when he snuck out of the block party. She needed to find out what he was up to.

And from her hiding spot behind Dr. Novak's gargantuan desk, Amber had a clear view of the sofa and the door to the laboratory, allowing her to see and hear—*puke!*—exactly what kind of pervert her father is. Her face blazed with jealousy when her father grunted over that unconscious nobody. Didn't he know *she* was somebody? Why couldn't he just love *her*?

So, Amber did what she does best. Impulsively, she whipped out her phone from its colorful pouch and started recording. She knows firsthand how easy it is to cancel someone, especially if that person is already *Page Six* fodder. *Like my father.*

Her plan was simple enough. She finally had proof. Her father was shameful. The video would be her golden ticket—especially since she also recorded Mr. Maccabee and Dr. Novak discussing their disgusting plan. If Amber can't get her father to love her, she'll get him to pay. But when Kit showed up and started waving that lighter around, Amber got ready to run. When Kit opened that hand, Amber slipped out the office and took a left.

Now, Amber runs along the underground hall, presumably ahead of everyone else. But she doesn't know where to go. Confused, she stops and runs back into the smoke from where she came, looking for somebody, anybody. But there's no one to be found. Smoke darkens the corridor. She's losing visibility. At last, she sees her father lumbering before her, rasping and red-faced.

"Daddy!" Amber plows into him for a frantic embrace, unable to connect her tiny arms around his thick body.

He flings her off, coughing wildly. "What the hell are you doing down here?"

"I came to find you." Her voice is small, childlike.

"Why the fu—" He hacks uncontrollably. "Oh...shit."

"Daddy!"

He claws at his chest and falls to the ground, gurgling.

"Daddy, what's wrong?" Amber falls to her knees, using her tiny hands to shake his leaded arm. "Daddy, get up."

"Amber," he wheezes. Pain expands his chest. "Get...out of...here."

"No, I won't leave you." She tugs at her father, an unmovable boulder.

An explosion shakes the corridor, rattling the pipes across the ceiling. They flinch in unison. Dark smoke thunders towards them. The smell, the heat, unbearable, yet Amber remains by her father's side.

"Do it, girl...now." He coughs again. Thick spit dribbles down his cheek.

"No, Daddy." Her voice shrills with hysteria. She grips his heavy hand. If she lets go, she'll never see him again. "Please, Daddy, get up. I beg you!"

She looks to him, sobbing, waiting for what she needs him to say. Her wild eyes hold him hostage. Her bottom lip quivers like when she was a toddler, crying for him to hold her.

His eyes surge with tears. It's like he's finally longing to give her what she's always wanted, always needed.

With bated breath inches from his face, she wills him to say the words.

Jeff Peaty looks deep into his daughter's eyes. "Amber, get...the fuck...out of here! I can't...look...at your stupid face. Go!"

The words rip through her like a chainsaw. Horrified, she unlocks her father's fat fingers from hers. She scrambles backward, her beautiful face contorted in pain. All her deepest, darkest fears spring forth. On unsteady footing, she flees her bestial father—The Great Jeff Peaty—and leaves him collapsed on the ground, gurgling and clutching his chest, trying to contain his shattered heart.

CHAPTER 52

CASS

AS THE RED DOOR opens, light replaces despair. I recognize our kitchen.

"Fire. Fire."

We emerge from the bunker and into our home. Clouds of soot chase us. The Smart alarm system blares around us, flashing lights and ear-splitting sirens.

"Fire. Fire."

"Sean, what's happening?" I rack my brain. It's empty.

"Fire. Fire."

I wrap Sean's wet jacket around my soaked, shivering body, but he tosses the filthy thing aside.

"C'mon, we have to go." He grabs our favorite fuzzy bathrobe, tucks me inside, and leads us to the back door.

"What am I wearing? Why are my clothes all ripped?"

He won't look me in the eye. Instead, he looks at my feet and the melted stilettos I can't remember purchasing. "Can you walk?"

I look down too, charred feet and warped shoes. "Yeah, I think so." I spy my Taz slippers under the breakfast table and scoop them up. "I'll put these on in the car."

He grabs my hand and pulls me out the side door into the garage. He folds me into his two-seater and shuts me in. He pauses a moment with one hand on his hip, the other pinching his nose, sucking deep breaths before joining me on the other side.

We emerge from the garage and into the light. Teams of fire-fighters, ambulances, and police vehicles swarm the neighborhood. I see Lilith, swathed in garish pink, clutching her husband's arm, huddling with the Huangs. I strain my neck, looking for Susan, Amara, and Blair, but I can't find them anywhere. There's a horrible nagging in my belly like I've forgotten something.

As we drive past the scene, we're flagged down by police. Sean and I are assessed by paramedics and deemed fit to proceed to the station to give our statements once they bandage me up. I was lucky, they say. Only second-degree burns.

Sean insists on driving, waving away the police escort. He grips my dressed hand the entire drive, his words on a loop. "Everything will be okay. We'll get through this, together."

My mind blanks.

At the police station, Sean does most of the talking. My head throbs in tandem with my heart, inflating and deflating with every pulse. The harsh fluorescent lights of the icy interrogation room are pure agony. I sit slumped in the corner with my head in my pillowed hands, warding off a migraine and my feet throbbing in bandages stuffed inside slippers.

I stay that position for most of the interview until I hear an officer say, "Well, there's isn't much we can do since most of the evidence is probably incinerated, not to mention the powerful enemies you'll be making if you pursue this."

The officer sounds oddly familiar.

"Oh yeah? How about this for evidence?" Sean reaches for his lucky pocketknife then grabs my neck.

"Ow, Sean, what're you doing?" I struggle against his grip as he makes an incision behind my ear.

He pulls out a tiny, bloodied pellet. The detectives and I stare wide-eyed.

The vise on my brain releases instantly. Glimpses of the last twenty-four hours unreel.

"Listen," Sean says to the police, "you need to look into ELITE and their mission to implant mind control devices in women around the globe. I know, it sounds crazy. I first learned about it from my father but never understood how it worked. I honestly thought it was like counseling. Just a little therapy and maybe some pills. I had no idea it was so...invasive." He looks me in the eye for the first time since we left home.

I struggle to compute what he's saying.

Police bag the evidence. Sean answers endless questions. Finally, we're released to go but discouraged to return home.

As soon as we leave the station, I turn to this fraud I've known as my husband. "We need to talk."

"I know." He hangs his head.

As we sit in the back of a local pub, layer upon layer of untangled dark memories bubble and pop around me. I pummel Sean with questions as I'm confronted with images.

Cradling my glass of bourbon in my hand, I finally ask, "So, Dr. Novak really put a chip in my head?"

Sean hesitates before answering, "Yes."

"And you were all for it?"

"Not exactly."

"What does that mean?"

"It's complicated."

I take a sip to steel myself as I wait for him to continue.

"I was pressured...by my campaign team. The biggest mistake of my life."

I don't know what to say, so I change the subject. "Have you seen Blair? Or her baby?"

"Blair had the baby?"

"And what about Jeff Peaty? Was he...involved somehow? I have this feeling..." Disturbing images haunt my mind, images that surely arise from a nightmare, as the alternative is too dreadful to even consider.

"Let's not worry about all that right now, babe." Sean grabs my fidgeting bandaged hand from across the sticky table. "The most important thing is you're all right. We'll get through this...together."

I jerk my charred fingers away. "You can't be serious, Sean."

He looks at me offended—with those luscious eyelashes—and leans in closer. "You think I would purposely hurt you? After all I've done for you? Given you? I did this for us. For you! Don't you know how much I love you?"

"I need some time...to get my thoughts in order. This is all...too much right now. If you really love me—like you say you do—you'll give me some space."

"Fine. Of course." Sean sits back in the booth. The dimly lit bar hides his face, but I can hear the desperation in his voice. "Listen, Cass, I just want you to be happy. I'll always love you, no matter what happens between us.

I INDULGE IN A room with an ocean view, finding solace in the waves that serve as my therapy—and I desperately need it. My days oscillate between tears and fruitless attempts to locate the other women. Sean's daily calls and texts, pleading for my return, are constant reminders of his guilt.

Initially—though it's difficult to acknowledge—a part of me yearned to return to him and that Kennedy smile. Given all that transpired, I found myself coveting the warmth of family and the soothing embrace of the familiar.

But then the memories flooded in. At first, my mind rebelled against what my brain and body were trying to communicate. It wasn't until my blood test results from a Planned Parenthood health center confirmed I had chlamydia that I genuinely faced myself in the mirror. Bruises, after all, don't lie.

WEEKS PASS, AND I'VE not heard from any of my former neighbors. The police are withholding all information until their investigation concludes, not that they've offered any assistance to begin with.

When I finally muster the courage to report my rape to the authorities and inquire about the case against ELITE, I'm met with the disheartening news that they've 'misplaced' the evidence. Without it, their hands are tied, and the underlying suggestion is clear: I should leave town before I'm forced out. With no evidence, there's no case, prompting me to delay filing my report. Jeff Peaty and the others will walk away unscathed.

I'll have to confront this matter alone.

Frustrated and angry, I send Sean a text: `I miss you. Can we talk?`

Sean responds immediately: `Meet me at the same pub as last time.`

CHAPTER 53

CASS

THE PUB SITS DARK and empty on a weekday afternoon. I spot Sean hunched at the bar, drink already in hand, looking disheveled and annoyingly charming. He starts talking before I even have a chance to sit. "Cass, thanks so much for coming. You don't know how much this means to me. First off, may I say, you look beautiful."

I look down at the dress I bought at the hotel shop for this occasion. It's light blue and hugs my curves. Luna taught me well. "Thank you, Sean. That's really sweet." Sincerity butters my voice.

"So, you said in your text that you miss me." He grins like he just argued his most significant case and won.

I work hard to suppress my repulsion. "I did. The bed feels cold without you." I flutter my eyelashes, coated in mascara and accentuated by a flawless cat eye.

He pulls out the bar stool close to him.

"Maybe we should move to a booth," I say. "It'll be more private." I place my hand on his arm and give my husband a warm smile.

"Sure. Anything you want."

Once seated in the corner, we face each other for the first time in weeks. I place my handbag on the table next to me.

The server appears dressed in black. A smile involuntarily spreads across my face at the sight of her shirt: *The Patriarchy Kills My Vibe.*

"By any chance, do you have *rakija*?"

Her violet eyes narrow with confusion behind black-rimmed glasses.

"Bourbon and hot tea, in a mug if you have one, please." I smile. She shoots me a what-the-fuck look, then leaves.

When she disappears, Sean grabs my hand, "Cassandra—Cass—my love, my wife, I've been so afraid of losing you. Ever since I found you on the side of the road, I knew you were meant for me. I envisioned our whole future in that instant. Our faces splashed across the country. Our tour across America. You're my Jackie! That's why I had to do it. You probably think I'm a monster. A thief! That I stole something from you, but you have to understand. What I gave you was so much more. Can't you see?"

I pull my hand away. "I want to understand. I really do, Sean. I want to make this work."

The server brings me my mug and stomps away.

My head clouds. I take a sip, following the burning sensation into my belly. It engulfs me, igniting my anger. "But in order for this marriage to work—this partnership—we have to be completely honest with each other. Do you think you can do that? Be completely honest with me?" I look into his dark, brooding eyes and hold his gaze.

He sits, shoulders slumping, taking sips of whiskey neat. After a long pause, he sighs and begins. "I guess I should've told you all this the last time we were here. I owed you that, at least, but I was scared if I did, I'd lose you forever."

"What are you talking about, Sean? You could never lose me." I force another smile, struggling to keep my voice light and even.

"Please, Cass, let me finish what I have to say, then you can decide what you want to do. Okay?"

"Of course." I sip my hot toddy, and I wait.

Sean looks around to ensure no one can hear us and begins. "This may be difficult for you to hear. Your name isn't Cass..."

"What?" I choke on my drink and cough.

Sean holds up a hand. "Please."

I sit back in the booth, absorbing his words, mind whirling.

"Your name is not Cass. That's the name you gave me, but that's not your real name. You never told it to me. You ran away from your family and never looked back. All you shared was that you needed an escape and wanted to start fresh, reinvent yourself, so you came up with the name Cass—not Cassandra—as you're so fond of saying. So, I let you be Cass. I didn't care what your name was. Honestly, all I cared about was how you made me feel when I was with you. But you were so sad, so haunted by something or someone in your past. Something you never shared. It tormented you, tortured you every night with nightmares.

"I called my father out of concern, and that's when he pointed me to Dr. Novak and The Gardens of Orchid Hill. Turns out, Novak's clinic needed another patient for his trial. And when a residential opening finally became available, it felt like destiny. Using Dr. Novak's Void Protocol, we were able to erase your memories. Your mind could start from scratch. Just like you wanted."

My heart ricochets inside my ribcage. "That's so...so...kind of you, Sean. That you would do that for me." I want to vomit across the table, but I keep him talking. "So, when did this...Void...happen?"

"Not that long after we met." He reaches for my hand again. "I did it for you. For us! Don't you see that? You can't deny how happy we were up until now."

I squeeze off a smile. "I do. I do see, Sean. Thank you for being so honest with me. This'll make our marriage stronger. You'll see." My hand squeezes his. He returns a smile. "Just one more question, and please, I need to know the truth. I promise I won't be mad."

"Anything. What would you like to know?" His eyes twinkle just like old times.

"Jeff Peaty." I let the name hang in the air like a noose.

Sean drops my hand and sits back. His jaw shifts side to side as if he's contemplating whether to tell me or not. The silence stretches into despair. "Not my finest hour," he says eventually.

"It's okay," I say. "You can tell me. We're in this together."

"There were tradeoffs. Jeff became a significant donor to my cause and demanded more and more in return. What he wanted most of all was you. I tried to deny him as long as I could. But all the other husbands were trading their wives like baseball cards. He took advantage of you when I had my back turned. When I challenged him, he threatened to remove my funding."

"So, you let him rape me."

He hesitates. "Yes, I guess, technically, but *rape* is such a strong word."

"But I was unconscious."

"Yes, but..."

"But nothing!" My mounting rage erupts. I spring from the booth, clutching my purse, and loom over Sean, pointing my finger in his shocked face. "You're pathetic. Disgusting! I can't believe I ever loved you. You're deluded. Not fit to be a lawyer, let alone president!"

"There've been way worse presidents than me, and all of them are doing just fine."

"If you think I'm going to sit back and let you live out your little fantasy, you have another thing coming!"

"What? What are you going to do?" He taunts me with narrowed, charcoal eyes.

I pull my phone from my bag, revealing the active audio recording with its ticking timer. I can almost see the panic set in as he scrambles to devise a speech to talk himself out of this one. For the first time, fear visibly mars his face.

Without warning, Sean violently lunges at me, desperation fueling his attempt to seize my phone.

I scream as one hand savagely claws at mine while the other tightens around my neck. I fight for air. Darkness engulfs my vision.

"Get the fuck off her!"

I hear glass breaking. Light returns.

"Are you okay?" Wide, lavender eyes blink at me with concern.

I see the server, clutching a broken beer pitcher, with Sean lying unconscious on the bar room floor.

My hands find my aching throat. "Yeah, I think so."

"You dropped this." She hands me my phone.

It's still recording.

SO-CAL NEWS

TRAGEDY STRIKES AGAIN: THE DARK UNDERBELLY OF ORCHID HILL UNEARTHED

Six months after an appalling blaze ravaged the prestigious Gardens of Orchid Hill, claiming the lives of five residents, including an innocent child, authorities have concluded the fire was intentionally set by a minor. A chilling sequence captured by surveillance cameras within the neighborhood reveals Grace-Katherine "Kit" Novak positioned at the center of the cul-de-sac, pouring gasoline onto a box of fireworks before igniting the deadly inferno.

Following an extensive investigation resulting in dead ends, law enforcement officials have finally made a discovery, albeit disturbing. A video has emerged featuring Kit and another student engaged in an intimate act. It has come to light this video went viral on the morning of the tragedy. This revelation has become a focal point in the case, intensifying the scrutiny surrounding the circumstances leading up to the catastrophic event.

In a shocking revelation, Orchid Hill's minor resident and the daughter of late tycoon legend Jeff Peaty, owner of ELITE Technology, has been charged as an adult for creating and distributing explicit videos. Amber Peaty, who allegedly created and uploaded the controversial video, now faces severe legal consequences. The body of her father, Jeff Peaty, was discovered in the neighborhood bunker. Preliminary autopsy reports confirm the business magnate succumbed to a heart attack triggered by smoke inhalation.

His widow, Luna Peaty, a pop icon of yesteryears, departed from the country that same night with their three children. The bereaved family remained under the radar until Luna re-emerged on the internet with a stirring #MeToo statement and a chart-topping new single. In her explosive public address, Mrs. Peaty lambasted certain influential individuals and media outlets for ruthlessly exploiting young talent. Her fanbase was taken aback as she unveiled a series of appalling revelations. Among the most shocking was her claim of being kept captive in a hotel room, subjected to drug-fueled abuse, and—in a sensational turn of events—reportedly implanted with mind-controlling software via a microchip. This has led Irvine Police to a new investigation into ELITE.

Adding to the complex narrative, video footage provided by Amber Peaty, Luna Peaty's stepdaughter, corroborates the accusation made by the grieving widow. Released as part of Amber Peaty's plea deal, the cell phone footage—captured on the same afternoon as the tragic fire—presents damning evidence of sexual assault. Moreover, it includes a full confession related to the ELITE Corporation's alleged plans to subjugate women through their controversial Project Psycho-Sanctum Services.

While law enforcement officials have refrained from disclosing the name of the victim in the footage, they confirm the existence of advanced technology evidence, including a virtual reality sex ring discreetly named Obsidian Veil. Investigators hope this will substantiate the unsettling allegations associated with ELITE's covert operations.

Assistant District Attorney Sean Maccabee finds himself embroiled in controversy, facing questioning over allegations that now include kidnapping and trafficking. In a startling development, it has emerged that his purported wife, Cassandra Maccabee, has been on the missing persons list since the summer of 1999. Her real identity came to light when her parents, William and Cynthia Trevore—members of one of Cape Cod's most esteemed families—recognized her on the news and immediately alerted the authorities. "We thought she ran away when she was fifteen but never gave up hope," they told news reporters. They assert they have never encountered the man who claims to be their daughter's husband.

What happened between the time she disappeared and encountered Sean Maccabee is still a mystery. According to official records, Sean Maccabee was reported to be 20 years old at the time of her disappearance. Still, he denies meeting her until the summer of 2017. Authorities are closely examining Maccabee's whereabouts and activities during that period as part of the ongoing investigation into the mysterious case. This detail adds another layer to the complex puzzle that law enforcement is diligently working to solve as they seek to understand the connections and circumstances surrounding the events of that time.

Amidst this scandal, the once-promising political future of Maccabee, a potential presidential candidate, teeters on the brink. Further complicating matters are unverified reports that Maccabee's spouse, actually named Abigail Trevore, has initiated divorce proceedings and obtained a restraining order against him. Ms. Trevore has recently criticized the local police department, alleging that her prior complaints about these issues were dismissed, with officers advising her to leave town. "Had they heeded my initial report, many victims would now be safely at home, enjoying dinner with their families," she lamented.

Throughout this chaos, Ms. Trevore's first book, "The Garden of Wives," which chronicles her ordeal over the past year, has soared to the top of the bestseller lists, capturing the public's attention.

In another unnerving development, the body of Dr. Levi Sullivan, also known as "Dr. Sully," was discovered under highly suspicious circumstances. Found bound, devoid of clothing, and hanging from the ceiling of his own home, police are scrambling to discern whether this disturbing scene is the result of a sexual game gone awry or a more nefarious instance of foul play. Authorities are actively searching for Sullivan's wife, Amara Sullivan, as she has mysteriously vanished since the night of the peculiar incident and seemingly wiped all traces of her existence on social media platforms.

Further disquieting news from Orchid Hill emerged as Blair Novak, wife of Dr. Daniel Novak and mother to Kit Novak, was found lifeless in neighbor Susan Franco's residence that same tragic evening. Preliminary investigations suggest Mrs. Novak succumbed to complications following childbirth. Mrs. Franco, a long-time resident of The Gardens of Orchid Hill, is currently unaccounted for, and the infant believed to be under her care is also missing. Mrs. Franco is sought for questioning, as her property has become the focus of a chilling discovery—her otherwise serene orchid garden appears to have been used as a makeshift burial ground. Officials have matched DNA found at the site with several women reported missing over the decades. Authorities are appealing to the public for any information related to these victims.

In the aftermath of these shocking events, the remaining Novak children are now under the guardianship of the eldest son, Maxwell Novak, who was away at university during the incident.

Adding to the grim tableau, the bodies of Dr. Daniel Novak and his daughter Kit Novak were discovered together in a residential unit within the bunker, evidently attempting to flee the deadly fumes. Further investigation reveals Dr. Novak had been collaborating with Jeff Peaty, using ELITE Corporation to fund his Project PSS, the purported program that has now become the epicenter of the scandal.

The cause of death for both Dr. Novak and his daughter was determined to be smoke inhalation. Their final moments were marked by a poignant scene—their bodies were found in a heartbreaking embrace, with Dr. Novak appearing to have attempted to shield his daughter from the engulfing flames.

Epilogue

MEANWHILE, SOMEWHERE IN THE South Pacific...

"Well, I'll be damned!" declares a woman in a crisp white shirt rolled to her elbows. She folds a newspaper and places it on an elegant table overlooking the ethereal ocean. A wide-brimmed hat shields her salt and pepper bob from the midafternoon sun. A contented infant with oversized brown eyes and sun-kissed skin sits patiently in a brand-new pram facing her.

The melodies of seabirds serenade them, a soothing symphony reminiscent of Tchaikovsky. A barefoot waiter wearing a billowy gauze shirt gracefully carries a tray adorned with a solitary cocktail. He sets it before her with a respectful nod, then departs.

She removes the garnish and smiles.

Bright purple dendrobium.

Placing the flower delicately on her pristine napkin, she reaches for the Mai Tai. "I have news." A smile graces her lips. "It seems, my darling girl, according to the Irvine Police, you're officially an orphan. It's just you and me against the world."

The infant blinks unabashed.

"With Novak gone, we no longer have to look over our shoulders. Project PSS will fade from existence. Some may even end up in jail." With one finger, she stops to catch a tear of condensation on the edge of her glass. "It was an abomination. Experimenting on women without consent. Not that *that's* never been done before, mind you. It's disgusting how some people will go to the ends of the Earth in search of the Fountain of Youth. Novak thought he found the key to immortality. Did you know he was planning to swap out your mother's body for a younger model? He already had a girl picked out—Bianca. He wanted to ensure her consciousness was pliable. Attempted a trial run with Jessa. But there was a misfire, a missed calculation. I mean, what did he expect, playing God like that?" She listens to the ice clink as she rotates the glass by the stem. "Anxiety, my dear girl, will fester. Like rot in the roots. Untreated, it destroys delicate flowers. Both women deteriorated quickly after the procedure. I was forced to put them down. Same with Blair. I gave them all peace in the end."

The child cries out in protest. Her agitated arms and legs wriggle like an upturned insect.

"Don't worry, dear. Your mother didn't feel a thing. Just a gentle prick while Amara stepped away for more towels. Morphine. A peaceful release from her suffering. All that pent-up guilt. It's no wonder she ended up the way she did, drowning you in alcohol and diabetes."

The infant's face scrunches into a tiny pout.

The woman fiddles with the straw in her drink. "Don't look at me like that. We deserve happiness too. Haven't we been through enough? I was the one they always called to clean up their mess. All those women. And that garden! Just the thought of it makes my back spasm. I didn't put Bianca in the dirt as I was instructed. She was still alive when I left her in Bommer Canyon. At least I gave her a fighting chance."

The child settles as the woman continues.

"Jessa spelled it all out in her journal. After her death, I found it in her backyard, poking out of the stone wall. I hid the worst parts in your mother's garden, hoping she'd read it and take notice. It won't make up for all the deaths, but I did what I could." She leans over to caress the infant's face. "Yes," she bows her head solemnly, "sacrifices had to be made."

Raising her glass, she proposes a toast, the amber liquid shimmering in the sunlight. "To your sister Kit, whose self-immolation will forever remain etched in our memory." She takes a measured, contemplative sip. "And to you, the child I've been praying for, and our family of two, may we live happily ever after."

As Susan Franco looks into Hope's innocent eyes, a mix of determination and uncertainty fills her. Life has taken a dark turn, and the path ahead is uncertain. Yet, she senses a glimmer of the future, a chance for a new beginning, and the possibility of a different kind of happiness—one she believes every woman deserves.

Author's Note

Dear Reader,

If you've made it this far, you already know: Orchid Hill isn't a place so much as a mirror. Every woman who steps through its gates carries something she's trying to bury—or bloom.

When I first began *The Garden of Wives*, I wanted to write about control disguised as care, love disguised as duty, and the quiet ways women adapt to survive. What surprised me most was how easily the lines blurred between nurture and manipulation, safety and imprisonment, beauty and decay.

Thank you for walking through this world with me—for listening to the women who whisper between its pages. I hope their voices linger, long after you've closed the book.

Warmly,

Danielle LaCarak

Blair Novak's Signature Party Punch

"A hostess should always have something chilled, sparkling, and just dangerous enough to forget the night before."
— *Blair Novak, Orchid Hill's reigning queen of cocktails*

Ingredients

    1 ½ cups pomegranate juice

    1 cup pear nectar

    ¼ cup orange-flavored liqueur (such as Grand Marnier)

    1 bottle (750 ml) Champagne

Directions

In a large pitcher, combine pomegranate juice, pear nectar, and orange-flavored liqueur.

Slowly add the Champagne just before serving.

Pour over ice — and don't forget the matching lipstick stain on the glass.

(Adapted from a recipe originally featured by Martha Stewart Living.)

For entertaining...or surviving.

Book Club Discussion Guide

1. **The illusion of perfection**

   Orchid Hill prides itself on appearances. How do beauty, order, and control function as both protection and weapon throughout the story?

2. **Cass Maccabee's awakening**

   At what point do you think Cass begins to see her world differently? Was it a single moment, or a slow unraveling?

3. **Masks and mirrors**

   Many characters hide behind carefully curated versions of themselves. Which mask felt most familiar—or unsettling—to you?

4. Love vs. loyalty

The Garden of Wives often asks what love costs. How do the characters justify their sacrifices, and where do you see echoes of this in real life?

5. The quiet conspiracies of womanhood

How do the women of Orchid Hill protect one another—or betray each other—in the name of survival?

6. Faith, fear, and façade

Several scenes blur the line between devotion and delusion. What role does belief (in God, in love, in status) play in sustaining the lie?

7. Domestic horror

The story never relies on overt violence, yet dread builds steadily. What everyday details made the atmosphere feel most dangerous?

8. The question of guilt

When truth surfaces, no one is entirely innocent. Who do you think carries the most responsibility for what happens—and why?

9. Cycles and inheritance

How do the events of Orchid Hill suggest that certain patterns—of secrecy, silence, or control—are passed down through generations?

10. **The final image**

Without spoilers, what do you think the ending says about freedom? About what it takes to leave?

Behind the Garden Gates

Every story plants a seed.

My next novel, *Nothing Good Grows Here*, takes root a few hundred miles away—but the soil is familiar. Different decade, different secrets, same question: what happens when something meant to protect begins to rot from the inside?

Because every garden has its ghosts...

NOTHING GOOD GROWS HERE
SNEAK PREVIEW

*The following is an early excerpt from Danielle LaCarak's upcoming novel, **Nothing Good Grows Here**.*
Some details may change before publication.

PROLOGUE

Cape Cod, 1999

It wasn't supposed to be like this.

They're standing in the woods, where the trees grow too close together and the air smells like rain-soaked pine needles and rot. A single body-length shadow stretches across the ground, fractured by the moonlight slipping through the branches.

One girl steps forward. Her breath comes fast, hot and shallow in the thick summer air. The other is still, smiling faintly, like she's waiting for something. Like she already knows how this ends.

"It was supposed to be a game," the first girl whispers.

The second leans closer, almost gentle. "It still is. You just forgot who's winning." She's always had that tone—light, amused, like nothing matters. Like nothing ever could.

The first girl hates it now. Hates how small it makes her feel. How powerless. "I thought I could fix you," she says, more to herself. "I thought I could—"

"Control me?" The second girl steps closer, feet silent on the forest floor. "You tried."

And it's true. She did. She'd pulled the string so carefully, convinced herself she was the one behind every move. But the whole time, the other girl was just letting her think that. Watching. Waiting.

She sees it clearly now. She's not the puppeteer. She's the final act.

The second girl's hands are steady. Fingers close around the gun, hot metal and heavy promise. "I'm sorry." She smiles.

The first girl smiles wider, "No, you're not."

For a heartbeat, it feels as if the world itself fired. The blast rings in their ears.

The echo fades. The night exhales. One of them doesn't.

CHAPTER 1 Abi

The morning light spills across my room in neat, expensive stripes, over the coffered ceiling, the glossy white trim, the chandelier my mother swears looks "Cape Cod chic." Outside, the Atlantic Ocean glitters like it's doing it on purpose. Everything pristine. Curated.

I lie still, letting the moment hover. If I don't move, I can almost believe I'm the girl this room belongs to.

Then the dampness seeps through.

My stomach drops before my body does. I lift the sheets with the same precision I use for everything that needs to stay hidden. The stain is pale against the white linen, already cooling.

I gather the bedding quickly, silently. No panic. No mess. Just routine.

In this house, the worst things are the ones nobody talks about.

The house is still asleep as I creep downstairs to the laundry room. I load the washer, add detergent, start the cycle before anyone wakes.

I like things clean. Orderly. Predictable. Mom says it's a good habit. She thinks good girls are born that way.

They're not.

Back in my room, I open the doors to my balcony. Fresh, salt air assuages my childish guilt as I take in the backyard and the view of Buzzards Bay.

Spring has sewn new grass into our lawn. The hedges are edged with light green sprouts. The ocean sparkles beyond the pool, each wave rising and falling like a sleeping body. This is the kind of morning people dream about when they think of the Cape. The kind of morning that pretends everything's fine.

The alarm clock radio shrieks to life with Hole's "Celebrity Skin." Courtney Love snarls about being the girl with the most cake.

I guess that's me. Perfectly iced.

I shut it off with a thud.

Down the hall, I hear my mother's heels clicking across the white oak floor, the same rhythm every morning. The kitchen will smell like espresso and something citrusy. There will be a stack of pancakes arranged on fine china, waiting to be ignored. Mother likes things that photograph well. A picture perfect family. Especially for my father, William Nathaniel Trevore IX, or Bill, as my mother calls him.

School used to be my escape, my salvation. That changed last year, when I walked into Baybridge High as a freshman, my dad my principal.

Lucky me.

My closet doors slide open with a whisper, revealing rows of pre-approved outfits: pleated skirts, pastel sweaters, blouses with Peter Pan collars. Let's not forget the stacks of penny loafers still in their boxes. Mother's vision of what a well-bred girl should look like. I grab a navy cardigan, a pale-yellow skirt, and my Doc Martins.

I don't care. No one really sees me anyway. They see my family.

The Trevores (pronounced Tre-VORE, not Trevor-AYE, as so many idiots mispronounce) have been on the Cape longer than the street names. Our ancestors came over on the Mayflower. First settlers. First landowners. First everything. Around here, that kind of legacy doesn't fade. It calcifies. It puts your last name in gold letters on plaques and library wings. People don't question a Trevore. They admire us. They protect us. They obey us.

Downstairs, the kitchen gleams under recessed lighting. Marble counters spotless. Oversized bay windows dressed in gauzy curtains frame the ocean. Even though I hate it here, I'll never get sick of that view.

My mother stands at the sink in a cream silk blouse and pearl studs, the picture of effortless wealth. Her chestnut hair falls in glossy waves, soft like Andie MacDowell, but her mouth is set with Annette Bening's brittle ambition. Always in control of her looks, always aware of who's watching. Even here, alone in the kitchen, she performs. She flips through *Good Housekeeping* like it matters, lips painted a perfect mauve that never smudge her coffee cup. Part of me hates it—the act, the gloss, the way she makes perfection look easy. Another part knows I'll never escape it, because she's proof that control is power. "Good morning, Abigail, sweetheart," she says without looking up. "Pancakes are fresh and your blazer's hanging in the laundry room."

I offer a half-smile and perch on the edge of a stool.

Across the island, my brother Nate hunches over a bowl of soggy cereal, chain-doodling skulls in the margins of a composition notebook. His shoulders are tense, muscles strung like wires ready to snap. His fingers tap the pen against the page with a restlessness that sets my teeth on edge. Light brown hair falls into his eyes, shadowing the sharp planes of his face, making him look older, darker. There's a dangerous beauty about him, part brute force, part razor-sharp instinct for where to cut deepest.

"Didn't think princesses got out of bed before noon," he mumbles, avoiding eye contact.

"Nathaniel," our mother chides, voice flat. "Not today."

"Not any day," Nate mutters, louder this time. He gets up and grabs his backpack, knocking his milky spoon to the floor on purpose.

Our father steps in from the garage just as the back door slams behind Nate. He's freshly shaven, smiling, radiant in a crisp button-down and navy tie. His short-cropped brown hair shows only the faintest trace of a receding hairline, his kind face sharpened by ice-blue eyes that miss nothing.

"Rough crowd this morning," he says cheerfully.

Hairy dad arms poke from rolled sleeves as he sets his brief-case on the counter, the simple gold band on his finger catching the light. He crosses the kitchen, rests a heavy hand on my shoulder, and kisses the top of my head. The weight of him is warm, steady, impossible to shrug off. I smile up at him like always, because I love him. Daddy's little girl.

"You ready to make me proud, kiddo?"

I nod. That's what I do. That's what's expected.

He turns to mom. "Everything under control, Cynthia?"

"Of course," she says, already wiping down a counter that doesn't need it.

It's a picture-perfect moment. A polished kitchen. A proud father. A quiet, beautiful daughter.

Cicero, a fat, gray Persian with yellow eyes and a scowling face, jumps onto the countertop and meows loudly to be fed. It's barely been a year and already the absence of the cat's favorite human is more than anyone can bear.

And yet no one says my sister's name. Not over breakfast. Not at school. Not ever. The upstairs bathroom door still creaks when it opens. The room that used to be Kelly's has been scrubbed clean. Fresh paint, white linens, throw pillows arranged just so. As if she was never here.

I managed to swipe a few things before Mother dropped everything off at Goodwill and tossed the rest. Like she was spring cleaning. Like Kelly was just another mess to be tidied. I saved what I could: my sister's favorite overalls, a sweater that still smells like her, a journal with a silver lock I haven't had the nerve to break. I keep it hidden behind a row of books in my room. A secret shrine to the only person who ever really saw me.

I miss her every day.

I stand, grab my backpack and kiss my mother on the cheek. Her skin smells like expensive lotion, but her breath holds just a trace of white wine from the night before.

Outside, the air is cool, salted. The waves roll in like clockwork. We live on Mashnee Island. Technically it's a peninsula now, connected to the mainland by a milelong causeway built in the thirties. The area is known as Gray Gables. President Grover Cleaver had a home here. We have the best view of the bay.

I walk to the front of the house, out of sight from any window, and light a cigarette while I wait for Nate to drive us to school.

From the street, our house looks perfect. A magazine spread. A dream home. But even the ocean can't wash everything away.

At the corner, a telephone pole is plastered with another flyer. Another girl gone. Her smile is wide, her teeth crooked. She can't be more than sixteen. I look away quickly, but the face follows me. People vanish here all the time, swallowed by the tide, erased by the sand. Sometimes I wonder if anyone would notice if I did too.

CHAPTER 2 Sandra

I wake to the stench of stale wine and burnt-out joints. It takes me a few seconds to recognize where I am. The New House. For a while, I don't move, just stare at the ceiling and trace the cracks that spiderweb across the plaster. I've been watching them spread for a week now, the way they stretch a little wider every time this house shifts and groans under its own weight. An omen.

The TV is still on in the next room, flickering blue light down the hallway crammed with unpacked boxes. A news anchor's voice hums low, serious:

"...bringing the total to three reported cases in just under eight months. Authorities say the latest disappearance took place late Sunday evening. The girl, fifteen-year-old Rachel Marsh of Mashpee, was last seen leaving a friend's house just after dusk. She has not been seen since."

The couch creaks. Mom must still be there—half-conscious or fully passed out—buried under that old throw blanket that reeks of sweat and cigarette smoke.

I swing my legs over the side of the bed, feet meeting cold wood. The same unwashed jeans wait on the floor, stiff from days of wear. I slip them on and thread my way through the wreckage: clothes strewn like casualties, an ashtray kicked over, empty wine bottles catching the light. Cheap trophies from a one-woman party gone on too long. One skitters under my toe, rolling until it kisses my mother's dead hand where it dangles off the couch.

No reaction.

The TV continues.

"...police are urging residents to remain cautious and report any suspicious activity. This marks the third missing girl in the Cape Cod area since September..."

I grab a wrist to find a pulse. Layers of poor dietary habits and bad decisions make it impossible.

I feel nothing.

My heart quickens. Not fear. Excitement. Has my mother finally accomplished the inevitable? Have my wishes been answered?

I lean down and listen for her breath.

I hear it, the faint rasp of someone who's been smoking too long.

My shoulders slump in defeat. I pluck a half-smoked joint from the ashtray, rolling it between my fingers. The filter is stained Clinique Black Honey, her favorite shade, always smudged by noon. I wrap the joint in cellophane from an empty cigarette pack and slip it into my fifth pocket. Then I pull my oversized flannel tighter around me and head for the kitchen.

The fridge hums when I open it. The light inside buzzes weakly over half a can of flat Diet Coke, an open pack of processed cheese slices, and a crusted tub of butter. I close it. Breakfast hasn't been part of the routine since I was old enough to pour my own cereal. Except we never have cereal.

I've been getting myself to school since first grade.

A year ago, Dad would've been up by now, muttering about my grades, the bills, Mom's "uselessness." I'd be bracing for the stomp of his boots across the floor, for the sharp clink of a bottle hitting the table. But now the house is quiet. Now I don't have to hear his voice at all.

I grab my backpack, shrug into my jacket, and slide into my trusty Chucks before heading for the door. I don't look back.

Outside, slivers of sunlight spread across cracked pavement. The air tastes like the ocean, close enough to touch even though it's half a mile away.

Today is my first day at Baybridge High.

Back at my old school, I was supposed to finish the year, but that unraveled fast. "Transfer" was the official word. Unofficially, it doesn't matter. People are easy. Feed them a story and they'll swallow it whole, choking all the way down.

New school. New faces. New chances to be whoever I decide to be.

Here, I'm Sandra Tate.

If they ask about my father, I'll smile.

The truth doesn't hurt. It's hollow. That's what people never understand.

Evil doesn't arrive with warning. It grows where no one's looking, and by the time they notice, it's too late. It's already part of them.

CHAPTER 3 Abi

The hallway reeks of floor wax and burnt coffee, undercut with the sour edge of teenage sweat. Lockers bang open and shut in a clumsy rhythm, metal on metal, while voices pile over one another until they blur into a single restless hum. Overhead, fluorescents stutter, buzzing. The first bell hasn't rung yet, but the whole place feels impatient, vibrating on the edge of release.

Crooked posters sag against the walls, congratulating the Class of '99. Their curled edges look tired, like even the paper can't be bothered anymore. Like the seniors drifting through their final weeks.

I move through it all like I'm above it. Because I am. People part for me without realizing they're doing it. Not in a dramatic, movie-scene way, but enough that I notice. I don't have to say much to be heard. Trevores carry weight here. My brother Nate made sure of that. My sister Kelly did too, in her own way.

Today, I'm watching.

They're all whispering about the new girl. Sandra Tate.

"She got kicked out of Falmouth High, right?"

"I heard she punched a teacher."

"No, it was an abortion."

"Someone told me she tried to kill herself in the locker room."

"I bet she's, like, actually dangerous."

"Dude, what if she's the Cape Cod Killer?"

Rumors are a kind of power. The trick isn't knowing what's true, it's knowing who *needs* it to be.

And there she is—Sandra Tate—leaning against a row of lockers like the world can wait. Dark hair, unbrushed. Oversized flannel over ripped jeans. Endless bracelets clink when she moves. A strand of gum stretches between her teeth, slow and lazy, that kind of calm arrogance that says she couldn't care less who's watching. She's not pretty in the way most girls try to be. Wavy dark brown hair and dark eyes. She's something sharper. Hungrier.

I slow just enough to study her from the corner of my eye. She doesn't flinch. Doesn't even glance my way. The bell rings. Students slam lockers, grab books, and shuffle off like cattle. I fall into step with the crowd, but my eyes stay on her. She drifts toward my homeroom. I follow a few paces behind as she chooses her seat.

Back corner. Of course. Furthest from the teacher, closest to the window. Easiest escape.

I walk straight over, stop at her desk, and let my voice come out calm, almost bored. "You're sitting in my seat."

She glances up at me. "And?"

I raise an eyebrow. Most people would already be halfway out of the chair apologizing. Not her. She just leans back, tilts her head a little, like she's daring me to make this a thing.

"They say you got kicked out of your last school," I say, low enough so no one else hears.

Her eyes sharpen, locking on mine. "They say a lot of things, don't they?"

I can't help it. My mouth curves. Slippery answer. Deflective. Smart. And the way she's looking at me—steady, unapologetic—it's like she's holding a lit match to my fuse just to see what I'll do.

She pops her gum and grins. "You gonna move me, or you just like standing there looking pretty?"

I let the silence stretch, then give her a slow, deliberate smile.

Yeah. This might be fun.

Acknowledgements

To every reader who stepped through the gates of Orchid Hill and stayed long enough to hear the whispers beneath its perfect lawns — thank you. This story found its heartbeat because of you.

To the reviewers who took the time to share their thoughts, highlight their favorite lines, and tell others about *The Garden of Wives*: your words carried this book farther than I ever could have on my own.

To the bloggers, bookstagrammers, and the incredible BookTok community — thank you for your creativity, your enthusiasm, your aesthetic flatlays, your emotional videos, your DMs, and your fierce support for dark, complicated women on the page. You made this world feel alive. You gave it a second life.

To the book clubs who gathered over wine, dessert, and spirited conversations about Orchid Hill's secrets — I am honored to sit with you in those moments, even from a distance. Your discussions, questions, and debates reminded me why I wrote this book in the first place: to explore the hidden corners of womanhood, the beautiful ones and the dangerous ones.

To everyone who has recommended this book to a friend, gifted it, taught it, or brought it to the beach — I see you, and I'm endlessly grateful. Word of mouth is the true magic of publishing, and you've given this story far more than I ever expected.

And finally, to those who reached out to say this book meant something to them — whether it unsettled you, inspired you, comforted you, or simply stayed with you a little too long — thank you. That is every writer's dream.

Thank you for believing in my work, for championing my debut, and for welcoming me into your shelves and your conversations. I can't wait to share what's growing next.

With gratitude and a full heart,

Danielle LaCarak

About the author

Danielle LaCarak is a fresh voice in psychological thrillers, drawing readers in with her emotionally gripping stories. With a Bachelor of Fine Arts from Roger Williams University, she skillfully blends light and dark themes, creating tales that stick with you long after you've turned the last page. Originally from Cape Cod, Danielle now enjoys the vibrant life of the West Coast. Her passion for crafting dark thrillers is matched by her love for creating intricate plots that dive deep into the human mind. When she's not writing, Danielle enjoys spending time with her spouse, snacking, playing video games, and devouring books of all kinds.

If you'd like to stay connected, share your book club thoughts, or glimpse what's blooming next, visit **@daniellelacarak** or **dan iellelacarak.com**.